LEISURE BOOKS NEW YORK CITY

To Dad,
who told me to keep trying.

And in memory of Mom,
who knew I wanted to.

A LEISURE BOOK®

August 1998

Published by

Dorchester Publishing Co., Inc.
276 Fifth Avenue
New York, NY 10001

ISBN 0-8439-4416-1

Printed in the United States of America.

"Two are better than one,
because they have a good reward for their labor.
For if they fall,
one will lift up his companion.
But woe to him who is alone when he falls,
for he has no one to help him up.
Again, if two lie down together,
they will keep warm;
But how can one be warm alone?
Though one may be overpowered by another,
Two can withstand him . . . ."

—Ecclesiastes 4: 9-12

The MASK

Chapter One

England—July 1201

His journey had ended, but the wanderer felt neither joy nor relief. Futility hung upon him like a cloak of lead.

Far had he traveled and for many years.

But all he had achieved was to return to where he began.

Uneasiness slithered down his spine as he came upon the village. Eleven years had passed, but Thornbury appeared little changed, as if it were a spellbound hamlet awaiting its enchanted lord's return.

Tethering his horse, Galen Tarrant, Lord of Rosethorn, gave a bitter smile. Thornbury might well have been spellbound, but he was far from enchanted.

Cursed, some called him.

Galen eluded the moonlight's silvery grasp as it crept across the lane. Nary a sound did he make. Not even the air stirred about him as he blended into the shadows of the sleeping village. Only a cat, curled upon a gatepost, marked his presence with eyes that glimmered an eerie green.

Galen scratched under the animal's chin, and with a mew of feline approval, the cat resettled upon the more comfortable perch of his proffered arm. Stroking its mottled pelt of black and gray, Galen felt a strange kinship with the creature. Like the cat, he prowled only at night.

With his new companion ensconced in the crook of his arm, Galen wandered further into the village. A second look revealed changes which at first he had missed. Few were heartening. The thatch of some cottage roofs sagged. Shutters hung askew on others. On most, the wattle-and-daub walls showed long neglect. A few of the cottages even looked deserted. And the livestock—Galen scowled. Where was the livestock? Most villagers kept a pig or perhaps a goat. There should be oxen dozing in the broken-down stable, sheep bedded in their pens. He found a few ragged beasts, but they were but a shadow of what had once existed.

What evils had Thornbury suffered?

Galen turned his gaze north, beyond the village. Dark and desolate against the star-pocked sky, the towers of Rosethorn Castle rose above the trees, mocking him.

He knew the answers, could see it all—the dead lord within his crypt, outlaws terrorizing the defenseless village, and the son who never returned.

I am a man. Let me prove myself.

His own words from long ago haunted Galen. And what sort of man had he proven himself to be?

"Look in the mirror, fool."

The cat redoubled its purring at Galen's muttered words and kneaded his arm with its paws. Galen tore his gaze from the castle and rubbed the animal's ears.

Well, the son had returned, after all. Galen snorted as he trod on. Though how many would hail his return with joy, he dared not speculate. And when the villagers beheld what had become of him? A chill crept down his spine.

He would cross that bridge when he came to it.

A light, glowing from around a bend in the lane, brought Galen to a halt. The cottage there seemed unusual, standing so apart from the rest, and so close to the wood.

Most folk in Thornbury thought of the forest as a necessary evil, and their tales urged caution. Elves and fairies and the other folk said to dwell within made it a perilous place.

Galen shook his head. Elves, indeed. Then he frowned. Though the moon had not yet risen to mark the midnight hour, it was still late for these folk who rose with the dawn. Who could be about?

Considering that eleven years had passed since he was last in the village, Galen was not surprised when he could think of no answer. Curious, he took a path through the trees so as to peer unobtrusively into the yard.

A wood elf. Lowering a branch blocking his view of the cottage, Galen was immediately reminded of dainty, golden-haired sprites.

A girl sat upon a bench near the door, one leg curled under her. The bare foot of her other leg tapped in time to the tune she hummed. Galen watched her draw a comb through her hair. In the firelight from within the cottage, the silky mass that tumbled over her shoulder to her lap shimmered like gold.

She was not beautiful—not exactly. She was just a girl, like countless girls he had seen over the years, but something about her held Galen entranced all the same.

Wood elf. He smiled. The name suited her.

Her humming faltered, and with beetled brows, she turned toward the cottage door. After a moment, her frown cleared and she turned back, resuming her task.

The drab gown she wore shrouded any hint of her form, but as she lifted her arms to bind her hair with a thong, the gown tightened. Only for an instant, but it was long enough to lock Galen's breath within his throat. His knuckles whitened upon the branch.

Merciful saints, she was near perfection, with curves that fanned the embers smoldering low in his belly into full flame. Heat flooded his loins, and his flesh reacted as instantly as it did uncomfortably.

God above! Galen scowled. What sort of beast was he, ogling a maid from the shadows?

Too late, Galen realized his hold upon the branch had weakened. It slipped from his grasp, and the cat hissed at the crackle of leaves and twigs.

* * *

Anne of Thornbury turned toward the cottage door, her attention caught by a stirring within. Dire warnings tickled her tongue. If those two scamps were still— She heard the sound again and turned away with a smile. Just a log crumbling into the hearth.

Thank heaven, her father would return on the morrow. Perhaps then she could get some work done. Anne rolled her eyes. Precious little had she accomplished today, save chasing her brother and sister from one end of Thornbury to the other. And begging pardon at every stop on the way. Bad enough for them to upend a pail of water on the miller's son—not that the little brute did not deserve it—but did they have to drop the mouse into old Dame Margaret's lap?

Anne fought a grin. She would die before admitting it to those little sinners, but *that* had been funny.

At least Derek and Lyssa were finally abed, and she could relax her guard. Her favorite hour, this was. With the cool breeze whispering to her, and the scent of summer blossoms in the air, she could forget her cares and dream the dreams any maid of seventeen might have.

Not that her dreams were so grand. A carpenter's daughter must have simple wishes, if she expected them to come true. But sometimes, it was nice to let her thoughts ramble far into—

The sudden rustling of leaves did not alarm her. Night was the time for woodland creatures to roam. But no fox or hare uttered the muffled curse that followed. Her heart pounding within her breast, Anne gazed into the woods, but not a shadow out of place did she see. Another crackle, like a footfall in the bracken, made frost finger into her belly.

"Wh-who goes there?"

Silence reigned for a heartbeat; then, from within the darkness, she heard, "No one who wishes you harm."

"Come out, whoever you are." Gripping her comb like a dagger, Anne staggered to her feet. "Out where I can see you."

The cottage door felt reassuring under her hand. Anne clung to the security it offered. Her gaze locked beyond a branch that slowly rose. A figure stooped under it.

The man who straightened in the shadows at the edge of the trees was tall and lean, clad in black from the cowl over his head to the boots upon his feet. Broad shoulders filled his short surcoat. A leather belt encircled his trim waist. Anne squinted into the gloom. No weapon. She frowned. Not even a dagger. Now, what sort of man wandered the night unarmed?

And with a cat?

He held the creature in the crook of his arm, his hand cradling its head, his fingers stroking its chin. Even from where she stood, Anne could hear its purring.

"Who are you?" she demanded.

"One who found that his road led here."

His voice, low and a bit rough, sent a shiver down her spine. Not quite from fear, Anne decided, but caution kept her hand firm upon the door.

"We see few travelers in these parts." And even fewer who braved the roads at night. "Where are you bound?"

"I have been a wanderer, bound wherever the wind may blow me."

Anne knew something of wanderers, and her heart chilled anew. Since the old lord's death three years before, the only wanderers who came to Thornbury were outlaws. Perhaps if Lord Geoffery's son returned to take his rightful place— But he had not returned and, so said the village elders, likely never would. With no lord keeping watch from Rosethorn Castle, the keep was deserted. Thornbury went in dread of marauding packs. Often what the outlaws did not steal, they destroyed. Crops, livestock. Sometimes even people. Aye, Anne knew something of wanderers. With a gasp, she sidled further into the doorway.

"I mean no harm," the man said, and lifted his hand to prove his honesty. "Not to you or any who mean no harm to me."

Strange, but Anne believed him. Or did she just want to? "You have traveled far?"

"Very far."

"You have no home?"

"Not yet."

Anne wished she understood why his answer unsettled her so. "Have you a name?"

"I have." But he did not speak it. Instead, his hooded head tilted. "Have you?"

"I have," she replied tartly. Two could play at his game.

The silence stretched. Then Anne heard his low chuckle, and her own lips curved. She fancied even the cat seemed amused, nuzzling the man's hand with a deep purr.

"You are in Thornbury, a holding of Rosethorn," she told him.

"I passed through the village. What happened here?"

Anne nipped her lower lip. A clever outlaw seeking a weakness to pounce upon, after all? She wished she could be certain. Because she could not, she allowed only, "Hard times come to all places. God, in His wisdom, sends them."

"Aye," he agreed, and Anne watched entranced as he stroked the cat. A hand so large, with such evident strength, should not be gentle, but his seemed so. "But perhaps 'tis more the work of man's folly than God's wisdom."

"Perhaps."

"I pray fortune smiles again upon Thornbury one day soon." He gave her a shallow bow. "I leave you in peace."

As he turned, Anne saw his shoulders slump, as if they bore an immense burden, and her heart clenched within her breast. If hard times had befallen her village, at least she had a village to call home. And at least she had more than a cat as companion, more than a long road leading to no welcome.

"Wait," she called softly. The man hesitated, turned back. "Wait, please? Just a moment?"

Anne darted into the cottage. Holding a cloth by the corners to make a small sack, she opened the larder and filled it. Relief warmed her belly when she found the man still lingering at the edge of the wood, though the sensation puzzled her. She shook it off and started toward him.

"Come no closer."

His command cracked like a whip, and he backed away, like a wild creature fearful of human nearness. Anne stumbled to a halt, her heart skipping a beat.

"You can take this after I am within. You've my word

I'll not spy upon you.'' Never taking her gaze from him, Anne laid the bundle on the ground and, backing away, gave him a tentative smile. ''Godspeed to you. May your wanderings lead you home.''

True to her word, the girl closed the cottage door, and no sliver of light betrayed a shutter being cracked open.

Galen stared at the small bundle on the ground for a long moment. His legs felt stiff as he stepped forward and crouched before it. The cat flowed from his arm and nudged the sack with its nose. Why his fingers shook as he plucked at the knot, Galen could not say.

Half a round loaf of bread. A generous hunk of yellow cheese. And a small flagon of what smelled like ale.

A mere pittance. And yet, it was a feast.

May your wanderings lead you home.

Galen corked the flagon again and swallowed the lump lodged in his throat. He slipped a dagger from its sheath strapped at the small of his back and sliced off a sliver of cheese. Mellow, with just a tang to give it life, the cheese melted on his tongue. He sliced off another bit and offered it to his feline friend. Gathering the gifts, he stood and gazed at the darkened cottage, and the lithe form of a wood elf and her gentle smile lingered in his mind.

Humbled, and yet lighter of heart than he had been in years, Galen turned and blended into the shadows once more.

This did not bode well.

Anne skidded to a halt in the middle of the lane, and despite the hot August sun, a chill prickled the skin of her arms. The trio of stern-faced riders leaving the blacksmith's yard did not bode well at all. Two of them she did not know, but the center man—Bryan, the new seneschal of Rosethorn castle—had become a familiar face in recent weeks, if not an altogether welcome one.

From his stony expression, Anne feared Rosethorn's new seneschal had gone and done the last thing he should have done. Dismay flattened her lips. Anselm the blacksmith held considerable sway in Thornbury. Folk listened to him, heeded his example. Heaven help Bryan if he had offended the man!

As the riders trotted past her, Anne stepped aside and curtsied, as befitted a village girl before men of rank. The seneschal acknowledged her with a nod, but he neither slowed his pace nor relaxed his rigid back.

Gazing after him, Anne shook her head. Bryan of Rosethorn seemed not such a bad sort. Rather handsome, he was, with his chestnut hair ruffled by the breeze and his manly form garbed in a fine tunic and leggings. But if the man hoped to rally the villagers to his cause, he needed to learn to bend a little. And a smile every so often would not come amiss, either.

Still shaking her head, Anne strode to the smith's gate. "Good day to you, Master Anselm."

A burly fellow, well past youth, the blacksmith scowled into the sun's glare. Then his face broke into a smile as he came forward and ushered her through the gate.

"Why, Mistress Anne, what brings you here on this morn?"

"Your good wife bade me come to help with some sewing." Her basket swinging on her arm, Anne cast a wry glance over her shoulder. "I see you've had other visitors, too."

"Aye, seneschal of yon keep," Anselm muttered darkly. "Ordered fire irons, he did."

" 'Tis good of Lord Galen to use a village craftsman, rather than take his trade elsewhere."

"Oh, aye." Anselm fell alongside her as she walked toward the cottage adjoining his smithy. "But I tell you, lass, I've a queer feeling in my bones about events of late. 'Tis powerful strange, Lord Galen returning so sudden. Not a soul even knew he yet lived until this seneschal of his showed up and announced his lordship is back in residence."

Not for the first time over the past several weeks, the memory of a black-cowled wanderer sprang into Anne's mind, and a queer feeling spread through her own bones. The Lord of Rosethorn skulking in the shadows at the edge of the wood? The idea was absurd. And yet, try as she might, Anne could not rid herself of it.

I have been a wanderer, bound wherever the wind may blow me.

You have no home?

Not yet.

"Perhaps," she said slowly, "he wished his return to pass quietly."

"Not bloody likely," Anselm snorted. "And you'd think, after all them years away, his lordship would make more effort in rebuilding this village."

What happened here?

Hard times come to all places.

"He ordered repairs started on the cottages." Anne scowled, indignant and unsettled by her memories. "And eased our rents after the poor harvests. I hear he even gave allowance to those who could not—"

"Aye, so he did," Anselm grunted. Then his eyes narrowed. "But have you even glimpsed the man since his return?"

Come no closer.

Anne shook her head.

"Nor has anyone else." The smith turned to gaze at the craggy heights of Rosethorn. "What has he to hide, I wonder?"

"Hide?"

"No man keeps himself so apart without hiding something, lass. Gone to the East for years, he was, and they say them infidels know ways of poisoning a man's heart."

"Oh, Anselm." Anne laughed shakily.

"Scoff if you please," he countered, "but more than one crusader returned a different man, and yon lord was odd enough even before. Not like his father, Lord bless him. You'd not remember, being so small when he left, but the lad had a dark streak. The priest used to say he feared for the lad's soul. Not even his father could fathom him. Oh, I tell you, those two struck sparks fit to start hell's own fire between them."

Anne's laugh steadied. "Anselm, you should be ashamed, spreading such tales."

The smith peered down his nose at her. "Far be it from

me to cast doubt upon another man's soul, being a sinner myself, but no telling how them years marked Lord Galen."

Anne skipped from stone to stone across the brook. After all, why bother with the bridge a few paces away, when the water laughed its merry challenge? At the other side, she settled her basket on her arm and started down the lane once more.

It was a tame adventure, fording the brook, but one Anne contented herself with. She grinned. Thanks to her mischievous brother and sister, she found more than her share of adventure, anyway.

Apart from wondering what deviltry Derek and Lyssa had conjured in her absence, Anne spared little thought for mischief. Deciding what design to embroider on the gown and bliaut Anselm's wife had requested was more important. It felt like an eon since she had gotten so promising an order, and if she did good work, others might follow. Even her father, the village carpenter, had started getting more work. Peace was returning to Thornbury. Anne prayed prosperity was not far behind.

She left the lane for the shortcut home through the wood. Anne relished the crunch of leaves strewn along the narrow path. With a laugh, she kicked them into a swirl. Her laughter faded, though, and her step sobered as she caught sight of the castle.

May your wanderings lead you home.

But had his heart come home as well?

The towers of Rosethorn stood high above the trees, stark and forbidding. Not that the castle crumbled from neglect any longer. Indeed, as soon as the Lord of Rosethorn returned, scaffolds had sprouted along the walls. Yet, even with men hard at repairs, the castle still looked as empty as ever.

The Lord of Rosethorn.

Anne furrowed her brow. Should she have kept her secret?

At first, she kept silent about the dark wanderer because she knew the scolding she would get. Anne knew she had run a great risk by not slamming the door on him, but at the time, after her initial fear had eased, it had not felt like such a risk.

I mean no harm. Not to you.

She had believed him then, and she believed him now.

Since, word had spread. The Lord of Rosethorn had returned, and Anne found fresh cause to hold her tongue. Could the lord and the wanderer be one and the same?

Unlike Anselm, she remembered very little of Lord Galen before he left all those years ago; she had only a vague image of a tall figure astride a powerful steed. She had been quite young, and he could not have been far into manhood himself.

Why had the lordling taken up the cross? Religious zeal? Anselm had hinted at a rift between father and son. Had that driven him away? Or had he, like so many, followed King Richard's crusade in search of adventure? Perhaps, like the late king, he found more than he bargained for to keep him away so long. So many questions and so few answers.

But lack of facts, Anne conceded, did not prevent folk from speculating, and their tales grew wilder as suspicion of their reclusive lord deepened.

Maimed by infidels, some said of him. Rendered simple by battle wounds, others claimed. And darker whispers had spread as well. A sorcerer, one tale alleged that he had become, taught his demonic rites by heathen priests in faraway lands.

Anne shivered, then laughed at herself. Change often proved unsettling, even change for the better. She could not deny that simply having so many strangers about provoked talk as well, for Bryan of Rosethorn was not the only new face. The castle staff and Lord Galen's men-at-arms had all come from elsewhere. And they all kept as aloof as their master. Aye, misgivings ran deep among the villagers, and no doubt their gossip was infecting her. Whatever his reasons, if Lord Galen preferred solitude, why should anyone care? A fair-minded lord who saw justice done, even from afar, was more than Thornbury had before.

A rustle from the tangled undergrowth snapped Anne's eyes back to the path, and the skin of her arms prickled. Outlaws were rare in Thornbury these days. Lord Galen's men had seen to that. But no one could yet claim them extinct.

A sleek, brown rabbit leaped into the path, and Anne let out the breath caught in her throat.

"So, Sir Rabbit, you think to accost me, do you?"

The rabbit froze at her voice, but as she spoke quietly and made no move, he eased.

"You'd find yourself sorely rewarded, I fear. I carry only cloth and thread. Not a cabbage leaf in the lot." The rabbit sniffed at her, and Anne shook the hem of her gown at him. "Off with you, now. You know better than to sit in the open for any hunter to find. Go on, shoo."

The rabbit shooed, diving into the tangle of vines. But Anne discovered it was not her warning he heeded. It was the scent of predators. Two-legged predators.

"Well, well, what have we here?"

Anne whirled. So stealthily had they crept, she had not heard them, but now she saw four unkempt men encircling her like wolves.

"Sweet little thing," one drawled, and Anne recoiled from the grasp of his grubby hand. "Ever seen such hair, Bertram?"

Bertram bared his yellow teeth in a grin. "Pure gold, I wager. And look at them eyes."

Her heart pounding, Anne scrambled away from the pair only to come against the third man. He snatched at her arm. "This wretched village is looking better. Come on, girl, be nice and we'll not keep you long."

"Or hurt you bad." A fourth man closed off the circle.

"Let me go," Anne commanded as steadily as she could manage.

"Been a while since I had anything sweet as you beneath me." The third man tightened his grip on her arm. His chuckle sent a gust of sour breath into Anne's face, and she grimaced. "Aye, sweet and soft you are."

Enough! Anne swung her basket and clouted him in the head. Twisting, she sank her teeth into the surprised man's forearm and broke free.

"You bitch!" he snarled. "You filthy little—"

Crunch! went her basket again, square in his face. The blow staggered him. A low-hanging branch did the rest, catching him at the back of his head. Anne leaped over his sprawled body, but not fast enough. Bertram snagged her braid. Pain brought tears stinging into her eyes. Rage kindled the spirit of battle in her heart. She raked her nails down his face and, not satisfied with his yowl, brought her knee up hard. He sank to the ground, hands clutching his groin and beard-roughened cheeks a faint shade of green.

Two down. Two more to escape.

Clawing fingers scraped the side of her neck and caught her gown. Worn though it was, the garment conceded only a rent at the shoulder. Anne shrieked more in fury than terror. She whirled, all scratching nails, flying basket, and bared teeth, to the attack.

"Little whore." He tore the basket from her hand. "I'll teach you, I will."

Anne heard the blow more than felt it, a sickening thunk of his fist against her jaw. Bright lights danced before her eyes, and she dropped to her knees. The tang of blood strong upon her tongue, she dug her fingers into the leaves and dirt. He bent over her, and she sent the whole mess flying into his face. Howling, he backed off. Her head spinning, Anne staggered to her feet and ran.

"After her, you dolts!" one of them shouted. "If she gets away, the master will have our hides to wipe his boots with!"

Bile seared the back of her throat, but Anne forced it down. She ran as hard as she could toward a shimmer through the trees. The rush of water roared in her ears. Or was that the hammering of her heart?

She fell more than ran down the steep bank and splashed into the brook. Anne looked back and saw two of the men pause at the top of the bank. Then one leaped after her. A shrill cry burst from her lips, and she scrambled for the other side.

Soaked in the knee-deep water, her gown feeling as heavy as lead, Anne kept going. If she beat them to the other side, she could climb that low-branched tree at the edge. Once in its boughs, she would raise such a ruckus that the whole shire would come running. If not— She would make it. She had to.

The bank offered no foothold, but an outcropping of rock jutted from it. Anne clawed at the stone to pull herself up. An arm caught her about the waist from behind. Her scream tore through the air. She tumbled into the brook and, coughing and sputtering, gained her footing once more.

"Rut on you or kill you, girl," the outlaw spat, and drew a dagger from his belt. "Makes no difference to me."

Sunlight dappled through the trees, glinted off the blade. Anne opened her mouth to scream again, but fear and rage knotted her throat. She stumbled back, run to ground but still unable to admit defeat.

"Do not move!"

Anne heard the cry but could not obey. Pebbles rolled beneath her feet. She felt herself falling, as though detached from herself, just as she saw the dagger lift. Her last thought, before the world burst in a blinding light, was that her rescuer would be too late.

Chapter Two

So, he was not the only hunter on the prowl.

Galen sent his horse pounding into the brook, bow still gripped in his fist. Reining his mount to a halt, he slipped from the saddle.

His longbow was useless at close quarters, so he drew his dagger as he neared the body sprawled in the water. The arrow had lodged deep between the man's shoulder blades. Still, Galen kept the dagger poised as he nudged the man with his booted foot. Not even a tremor passed through the carcass. What little he had seen before firing justified his grim smile.

Passing his head and arm through the bow to hang it upon his back, Galen slipped the dagger back into its sheath. He turned, then, and waded toward the girl.

Little fool, braving the forest alone. Galen ground his teeth. Devil take her! He could hardly leave her, though every instinct demanded he send men after the other bastard. But at the rate the outlaw had fled, Galen figured the man would be in the next shire before pursuit could be mounted. Well, at least it was unlikely the bastard or any comrade would venture back soon. Word of what befell outlaws on these lands would spread quickly.

Galen knelt beside the girl, started to reach for her, then drew back. Despite the warm afternoon, he flipped the cowl of his surcoat over his head. If she woke, the sight of his face would hardly reassure her.

She lay curled on her side like an ill-used doll, the thick braid of her hair obscuring her face. Her pulse skipped unsteadily below her jaw, but it was there. Blessedly, she had fallen with her head clear of the water. She would have a fine lump where her temple had struck the rocks, but at least she had been spared from drowning.

Galen ran his hands along her limbs and muttered in astonishment. She was so slight. Then astonishment sizzled into rage. God's blood, what monster hunted down a mere child to slake his lust? Turning her gently, Galen's breath shuddered to a halt before his chest heaved to life again.

"Wood elf." He mouthed the words.

There could be no mistake. Galen smoothed the wet tendrils of golden hair from her face with trembling fingers. No other possessed those same lips, now parted slightly with her shallow breathing. No other owned the same delicate jaw and lean curve of cheek. And no other had such soft skin—

Galen's gaze wandered from her face.

Soaked through, the gray of her gown deepened to near black and outlined every bit of her, from the taper of her slim waist to the gentle flare of her hips. The worn cloth was torn at the shoulder, and beneath Galen's large palm, the laced bodice gaped to bare a silken valley. He found her flesh cool and smooth when he brushed the back of his fingers over the curve of a half-revealed breast.

Galen snatched his hand away. Hell and damnation, had the girl escaped the clutches of two beasts only to fall into the grasp of another?

"Ohhh . . ."

On a low moan, she shifted. He held her shoulders to still her, marveling anew at her slenderness, but breathed a sigh of relief. If she could move so easily, he doubted any serious injury had been done within. There was no danger in lifting her.

Except that he had to touch her to do it.

Her eyelids fluttered, stilled, and then fluttered open. With her fair coloring, Galen had known her eyes would be blue. But he had not known they would be the bluest blue he had ever seen. She parted her ashen lips.

"N-not dead?"

The hoarse sound rumbling from his throat shocked Galen. Not a laugh, surely. He had not laughed since—since he had sparred with a wood elf over who would reveal their name first. Within the shadow of his hood, his brows lowered.

"Nay, girl," he assured her gruffly, "you are not dead, though you'll wish you were soon enough."

He meant only that her ill-used muscles and battered head would throb mercilessly when the languor left her, but she blinked and heaved a resigned sigh.

"Strike fast."

Her eyes closed, and her head lolled in his palm.

Galen stared in bemusement. No fear. No pleading. Just resignation that her fate lay in his hands.

He gathered her into his arms, and his belly gave a queer roll at how well she fit there. Her head tucked under his chin so naturally, and her shoulders nestled into the cradle of his arm as if she had been made for his embrace. Galen's quickening breath had nothing to do with the effort of lifting her.

He gave a whistle, and his stallion ambled over. When he had the girl settled in the saddle before him, her head and shoulders against his chest, Galen paused.

He had not thought her beautiful before, but now he reconsidered. A lovely little creature she was, even if the scrape at her temple was the only color in her chalk-white face. His fingertip traced her jaw before his palm cupped her cheek. His mouth tightened at the bruised split on her lower lip. She had given as good as she got, though. The dead outlaw had his share of scratches, too. Galen's brow furrowed. Still, if he had not been there—

"I've been remiss, little wood elf, in repaying your kindness," he murmured, "but never did I dream anything like this."

Holding his wood elf secure in his arms, Galen nudged the horse up the bank and out of the brook.

Hot. She felt so hot. And thirsty. Her head throbbed. Her whole body ached. Anne could not escape the pain, no matter how she tried to twist away.

"Shhh . . . Quiet, wood elf."

That voice. Anne knew that voice, low and deep, like night settling within the forest.

" 'Tis all right, sweet."

"H-hurts," she whimpered.

"I know." Gentle fingers stroked her cheek, her hair. "I know you hurt, wood elf. 'Twill not last."

She wanted to see him, her dark wanderer. Anne struggled to open her eyes, but the effort proved too much.

"Be still, and I'll help ease the pain."

"Please . . . Make it go away."

"I will." Anne felt herself lifted, supported by a strong arm. A cup pressed to her lips. "Drink, wood elf."

Liquid trickled over her tongue, and Anne swallowed. The brew tasted strange, faintly sweet, but not unpleasant. She growled weakly when the cup went away.

"More."

"Nay, no more," the voice refused mildly. " 'Twill make you ill if you take too much."

The strong arm, the gentle hands, lowered her again into a soft nest behind her. Then there was silence. Such a deep silence, stretching on and on, that Anne jerked from drowsiness and reached out in fright. A warm grasp caught her hand.

"Do not leave me alone." She gripped the roughened fingers entwined with her own. "Please, do not let them take me."

"Hush, sweet. You are safe." A cloth, wet and cool, bathed her face and throat. "I'll not leave you, and no one will take you from me."

Tears stung her eyes. "Want to go home."

"Soon." The cloth stroked between her breasts. The voice faltered and grew hoarse. "You can go home soon."

She frowned, her eyes still closed. "Who will cook supper?"

"I will," the voice assured her. Could a voice smile? Something that felt very like a kiss brushed over her brow. "Sleep now."

The words sounded over and over, always in the same deep murmur, always joined by the same tender touch. "Sleep now." Anne sighed and did what the voice commanded her.

Galen clenched his jaw until it ached as he tugged the bedclothes over the girl, concealing her nakedness from his gaze. But not from his mind.

It was too late for that. His memory knew every inch of her, every smooth curve and silky hollow. He knew how full her breasts were, the dusky rose of their crests. He knew that the curls framed by her hips were only a shade darker than the honey-gold hair tumbled across the pillows. When he thought he could do it without moaning, he released the breath caught in his chest.

Beautiful? Aye, she was beautiful in her elfin way, but he had known other beautiful women. None had captivated him like this one. None had paused and spoken to him when others would have fled. None had brought him a gift of kindness, and then wished him his heart's desire as though she truly understood.

May your wanderings lead you home.

Every night since, he had longed to return to her cottage. Not to speak to her. Not even to let her know he was there. Galen knew the folly of that. He just wanted to see her, treat himself to the sight of her sitting outside her cottage enjoying the night. But he had not. If he had gone to her, Galen knew he would have spoken to her, might even have dared reach out and touch her. She tempted him that much.

In the evenings as he had wandered the shire alone, before his men had joined him at the castle, the temptation had been all but unbearable. Never had he been so glad to see Bryan in all the years they had been comrades.

Once his seneschal caught up with him, with the men-at-arms and the staff gathered from his other holdings, Galen had found little time to indulge in temptation. His lips quirked. Or rather he had made little time for it. If the urge to wander to the cottage close to the wood grew too strong, he just found more to do. If questions about the girl burned upon his tongue, Galen bit them back.

But it seemed all his effort had been for naught.

Galen shook his head ruefully. He, of all people, should know how fate had a way of taking charge of a man's life. He looked at her.

She slept with her brow furrowed. Galen smoothed it with his fingertips, then threaded them into the silk of her hair. The elixir would ease her pain and help her to sleep. He pulled the covers closer about her shoulders. She was so small, so slender. She could so easily take chill. There was little else he could do but keep her warm and let her rest.

And assure her that she was not alone.

Do not leave me alone.

Too well he understood that pain was best endured with company: a touch, a few words. It mattered little what the touch did, bathe a fevered brow or hold a hand, or what words were spoken. The comfort was all that counted.

But why did he torment himself by nursing her?

Sitting beside her, Galen brooded as he watched her sleep. Others could care for her. He had only to give the word, and he could be free of her; servants would leap to attend their master's ward. And yet, she trusted him to abide by his word and not leave her. Just as she had once trusted the word of a wanderer that he meant her no harm.

Whatever it cost him, he would not yield her care to another. He would sit by her. He would give her the gift of his touch and words as she had given him the gift of her trust. He would stay until she regained her senses and could leave whole and well.

No one will take you from me. . . .

Galen shuddered and ran a hand over his face. Good God.

Had he gone mad? He did not even know her name.

And already he dreaded the thought of her leaving him.

"Fools! Idiots!"

Bertram cowered with his two mates in a corner of the broken-down cottage and weighed his chances. Three against one were odds Bertram preferred when plying his trade on the open road, but what good were odds against a demon?

Satan, so it seemed, was not the hideous serpent in the tales told by priests. Nay, he took the form of an angel, golden-haired and comely, to better tempt souls to his service. Beholding this handsome creature, his blue eyes glittering with rage, Bertram believed in evil.

He lifted a trembling hand. "Master . . . master, please—"

"Silence!"

The lash his master held uncoiled like a black snake and slashed his hand. Bertram howled, more at the sight of his own blood trickling between his fingers than at the stinging pain. He huddled on his knees.

Behind him, his mates edged away. The dogs! Fleeing like mongrels and leaving him to face their master's wrath alone! But not fast enough. The lash snapped and laid open the cheek of one. It snapped again and raised a livid welt on the neck of the other. Yowling, the two men scurried back to safety, out of the lash's reach.

"How could you have been so stupid?"

"Master, we tried—"

" 'Twas so simple. Just take a look around, I said. Keep your heads low and your eyes and ears open. And what do you do instead?" The lash slapped at the master's boot. Bertram flinched at each flick of that wicked tip. "You fall for the first twitching skirt that crosses your path. And then you lack even the wit to silence the little whore."

Bertram opened his mouth, ready to refute the charge, but closed it again. One village slut routing four burly men? If his own groin did not still ache from her blow, he would never have believed it himself. And God above only knew what his master would do if presented with such a tale.

"B-but we did." When those eyes, bright with fury, bored into his, Bertram nearly retracted his lie. Nearly. "Aye. Aye, master, we made sure she could not spread tales. That she—"

He squealed as his master snatched a fistful of his hair and yanked his head up. Bertram looked into that handsome face and trembled for his soul.

"She is dead?"

"Aye, master." Bertram tried to bob his head and winced. Risking the wrath of God for lying seemed nothing compared to risking his master's wrath with the truth. "She is dead. Ewald . . . He saw to it. A dagger. He struck her down."

"And poor Ewald was struck down himself?"

"Aye."

"By a hunter."

Bertram worked his head into something like a nod.

"A hunter who saw him? Saw you?"

"Nay, we fled."

"And you are sure the girl is dead."

Bertram drew a tiny breath of relief when those fingers released him. He nodded. "Aye, master."

"Liar!"

His master gripped him by the hair again, jerked him to his feet, and flung him across the cottage. Bertram's shriek ended on a grunt when he slammed into the wall. A dagger blade quickly scraped at his unshaven throat.

"You are lying to me," his master hissed. Bertram waggled his head in frantic denial. "Aye, you are. How are you so sure she is dead if you fled? Do you know what price I demand for lying? For failure?"

Bertram's lips moved, but only a gurgling gasp emerged.

Perfect. Philip de Coltrane watched the dagger slice into his hireling's flesh. Such a perfect slit, right across the throat, thin and clean. And the blood—

Coltrane did not relish the sight of blood itself. That would have been barbaric. He savored the more subtle nuances—the horror in Bertram's eyes, the helpless working of his lips, his disbelief and how his fingers pressed to his throat. These were far more satisfying than mere blood. Coltrane stepped back, breathing deeply, to better view his handiwork.

Others would see a man clutching at a mortal wound. He saw a man realizing the true power of his master.

Bertram staggered, then went to his knees. Delight seared Coltrane's veins. Even with his lifeblood spurting between his fingers, Bertram begged. He lifted glassy eyes to plead, tried to speak, and uttered only a strangled gurgle. A smile, thin as the slit he had laid open, curved Coltrane's lips. Finally, Bertram's eyes rolled back in his head. He fell onto his face and moved no more.

Cheated! Coltrane's smile twisted into a snarl. Like a man teased into rigid arousal and then denied his climax, he had been cheated of fulfillment again. His hunger growled and gnawed at him in revenge. The hunger. Always there. Always demanding, throbbing within him. Never sated.

But soon—very soon—he would satisfy it.

"Now," Coltrane murmured, his voice quavering ever so slightly, "I want the truth."

Now on their knees, his remaining hirelings stared at the body before them, sprawled in a thickening pool of its own blood. Slowly their eyes lifted to his, and they trembled. The story spilled forth in mumbles and disjointed bits.

"So, the girl is alive," he said when the tale stumbled to an end, "as well as the hunter who felled poor Ewald. How foolish of you. How stupid."

"Master—"

"Silence." The word hissed between his teeth. He lifted the dagger, admiring the gleam of silver against scarlet. "Ah, well, 'tis done. We all have our moments of weakness. We all make mistakes. You must learn from yours."

"W-we will, master. We'll not fail you again."

Coltrane slid them a narrowed glare. "See that you do not. You will be handsomely rewarded for your services, all the more without your comrades claiming their share, but only if I am pleased with your work. Is that understood?"

Both men nodded eagerly.

"Now, tell me what you managed to learn before your unfortunate mishap." He wiped the dagger with a cloth, meticulously cleaning every trace of blood from the blade. A master must take care with the tools of his craft. "The Lord of Rosethorn has truly returned?"

"Aye, master, so 'tis said."

"You did not see him yourselves, then." Small wonder. Coltrane smiled. He doubted Galen Tarrant permitted many to see him. Now. "You missed a rare spectacle. He is quite hideous, you know. Or at least part of him is."

"H-hideous? You have seen him?"

"Oh, aye, I have seen him."

Within the polished surface of the blade he held before his eyes, Coltrane caught a glimpse of the past—an arid wilderness and a prison cell, chains and a dagger. *This very dagger.* And if he listened very carefully, he could almost hear the screams.

"Tarrant dared to defy me, years ago. And I taught him a lesson for it." He shook his head slowly. "But not well enough. He dares to defy me again, dares to think the past is forgotten. He must be taught. Once and for all."

He lowered the dagger. The past would live again, and the hunger would be sated at long last. But first, there was much to prepare.

"You spoke to our friend in Thornbury?"

Both men gazed at the floor, at Bertram's body. "Nay, master, we had no time."

"Between accosting so many village whores and escaping so many hunters, 'tis no wonder." He heaved a sigh. "Since I obviously cannot trust you to control yourselves, I will have to do it myself. And you had best pray I do not find Tarrant sniffing along your trail, or there will be hell to pay."

"Surely, master, one village girl is not worth—"

"True enough, but Tarrant has a strange sense of duty. Especially where young girls are concerned." Coltrane chuckled. "You'd think he would have learned his lesson about that, too."

Anne lay still, but her eyes worked ceaselessly. What was this place? She remembered the chill of the brook, the glint of a plunging dagger. And then, nothing. How had she come to this splendid chamber? Was this heaven?

Anne shifted against the pillows at her back and moaned, then fingered her tender lip. If she was in heaven, Thornbury's priest spoke falsely about the bliss one found there. She doubted heavenly bliss would leave her feeling she had been on the wrong side of a war. And naked. Her eyes rounded as awareness sank in. She twitched the covers up, only to clasp them tightly to her throat. Sweet Mother Mary, she was as naked as a babe under the bedclothes!

Groaning, she propped herself up on one elbow, covers bunched under her chin. The chamber was huge, as big as her father's entire cottage. Why, she and all her family could lie in this bed and still have room left over.

Certainly, home had no tapestries to rival the one draped over the frame supported by posts above the bed. It flowed down to enclose her on three sides. Anne stroked her fingertip over the exquisite stitches worked in shades spanning the rainbow. A strange design, it was, one curve after another for the entire length of the fabric. Nor did her home have such fine linens and excellently woven brychans. And a feather mattress! Mischief, battered but not beaten, brought a smile to her lips, and she bounced to test the mattress.

Anne instantly regretted doing both. The smile pulled painfully at her lip, and a throbbing ache sang through the rest of her. She drew several deep breaths and lay back against the pillows, determined not to whimper.

With the tapestry drawn back on one side, she could admire the large rug laid upon the smooth, timbered floor. Rich in jeweled colors, it bore another unusual pattern of squares and spirals that spoke of faraway lands. A fire licked lazily at logs within the great hearth, banishing the slight chill held by the room's stone walls. She could not see the window, but beams of sunlight danced across the floor.

A lovely chamber, indeed, she decided. But she still did not know where she was or how she had gotten there.

The door banged open, and a woman strode in. Finding Anne wide-eyed and alert brought the woman to a halt. Her mouth flattened into a tight line.

"So." She spat out the word as though it tasted foul. "Awake, are you? About time, girl."

"I—" Anne cleared her rusty throat and tried again. "I have been asleep?"

"Asleep?" The woman rolled her eyes. "Asleep, says she. You've been clean out of your senses for days, girl."

"Days?" Anne's mind went blank with dismay. "How many?"

"Do I look like a timekeeper to you? Long enough to make a bother of yourself."

Anne scrunched down into the pillows. She tried a smile to warm the woman's chill.

"What is your name?"

"I am called Mayde." The woman appeared in her middle years perhaps, but her stern expression made her look older. The pale gray bliaut and dark blue gown, over a form entirely composed of angles and planes, was neat and of good quality. Her gray-streaked dark hair was pulled back into a merciless knot. She set her jaw. "Up with you. Out of that bed."

"But—"

"You're to have a bath," Mayde went on, crisscrossing the chamber, stoking the fire and flinging back the bed's drapery. "Though why I should bother is beyond me. Told him, I did. Little village cat like you probably would not know a bathtub if you fell into it and drowned. You're awake and in your right senses. He should pack you back to where you belong."

He? What he? Anne had never felt so bewildered in her life. Out of her senses for days? How many days? Oh, her father would be frantic!

"Please, Mayde—"

The woman drew herself up to her full height, not impressive in itself, but those narrowed eyes and the sour curve of her lips daunted Anne. "Do not go getting above yourself, girl. Address me as mistress, for so I am to the likes of you."

Anne gritted her teeth. Sour old dragon.

"Mistress, I am Anne, daughter of Daniel, the carpenter

in Thornbury. Do you know if anyone has carried word to my family? Do they know I am safe?''

Mayde sniffed. ''How should I know? No one came crying for you here, so I doubt you were much missed.'' She grasped the bedclothes that were Anne's only covering and whipped them away. ''Out of that bed, girl. I'll not tell you again. I've wasted enough time playing nursemaid to you already. I do not propose to waste more.''

Anne bolted upright, ignoring the howl of her abused body, and grabbed to retrieve her covering. Mayde's bony fingers proved too strong. After a brief tug of war, she yanked the covers beyond reach and tossed Anne a brychan.

''Here. You can cover yourself with that, if you must.'' Mayde tugged at the linens, stripping them off the bed and bundling them into a lump she tossed on the floor. ''Those must be scrubbed before they are fit again. I am off to see about that bath, and I want you on your feet and ready for it by the time I return. There will be no more nonsense. Understood?''

''A-aye.'' Anne's fingers fumbled as she wound the brychan about herself. ''Mistress, wait.'' Mayde halted at the door, impatience ill-concealed. ''Where am I? How did I come here?''

''Fool girl.'' Mayde clucked her tongue. ''You are in the lord's chamber at Rosethorn. His lordship himself, Lord Galen Tarrant, brought you here.''

Chapter Three

‘‘What a very pleasant woman,’’ Anne wryly informed her feet after Mayde swept from the room.

‘‘Aye.’’ Anne’s gaze flew to the doorway and found a different woman offering a rueful smile. ‘‘Mayde often has that effect.’’

‘‘I beg pardon, mistress. I did not mean—’’

‘‘Why argue with truth?’’ the woman demanded merrily. ‘‘Mayde has all the charm of overdone porridge.’’

In spite of her chagrin, Anne chuckled. The woman entered with the light step of youth, though her braided hair, gleaming like silver-streaked copper, betrayed her middle age. Her well-fleshed form garbed in a gown of gray and a white bliaut, she stood a head taller than Anne. The woman set the cloth-covered tray she carried on the bedside table, then took a bundle from under her arm.

‘‘I dare say we two are not of like size, but better clothing too large than none at all.’’ She shook out a simple gown of sunny yellow and laid it upon the bed. ‘‘Your own, I fear, was quite ruined.’’

Anne fingered the gown with wonder. It was fashioned of the finest wool she had ever beheld, and such stitching!

"Thank you. I shall take great care of it until I can return it."

"Oh, you need not fret over that, child. 'Tis old, and I have plenty. If you do not wish to keep the gown, perhaps some needy soul about the village would be the better for it. 'Twould be repayment enough, if you'd see it into such hands."

Anne blinked. This woman's castoff made her own best garment look like naught but rags. Feeling that she had waded into waters deeper than she could swim, Anne called up a wobbly smile.

"I will, indeed, mistress."

The woman beamed at her. "I am called Freya, and you are called Anne?"

Anne nodded, disquiet prompting her to grasp Freya's hand. "Tell me, please. Has anyone sent word of me to my family?"

"Have no fear, child." Freya patted Anne's hand. "His lordship's seneschal sent criers to the village soon as Lord Galen had you safe within the walls. I know not what came of it, but if you've kith or kin in Thornbury, they'll be found."

Relief soared within Anne, and she laughed contritely. "I seem to have caused no end of trouble—kept Mistress Mayde from her duties and surely frightened my father witless."

"Well, I am sure your father is quite concerned," Freya allowed, uncovering the tray. Anne's belly rumbled at the selection of bread, meat, and stewed fruit. Such a feast! And all for her? "But I doubt you proved a bother to Mayde. She made it her affair to be about other tasks."

"But she said—"

"Lord Galen himself tended to you."

"He did?" Anne squeaked, and the slice of bread she held tumbled from her fingers. She clutched the brychan tighter to her throat, keenly aware of her nakedness beneath.

I mean no harm. Not to you.

Anne squeezed her eyes shut. She believed him. She did. But never had she felt quite so . . . exposed.

"Aye." Freya poured wine into a goblet. "He would let no one else come near you, not even me when I offered so he could rest. He stayed by you, night and day, since he brought you here four days ago."

"Four days?" Anne pressed her hand to her brow.

"Why, child, you've paled. Naught but broth or water have you taken, so you'd best eat. And then, after your bath, you should rest."

"But Mayde said—"

"Bah!" Freya waved the worry aside. "Never you mind what Mayde said. His lordship has taken you under his protection. 'Tis he, and no other, who has say whether you go or stay."

"She should go, and now."

"Oh, Mayde," Freya countered soothingly, "the child has only awakened this morning. She is yet weak and needs rest."

The two women were squared off on either side of a large table in the kitchen. Mayde slapped a ball of dough on a floured board and kneaded it mercilessly, while Freya sat shelling beans with nimble flicks of her fingers.

Mayde was the housekeeper of Rosethorn. It was a position she guarded, lording over her realm as haughtily as any queen ruled her kingdom.

Freya's place was less defined, not quite housekeeper but not a common maid either. She assisted Mayde in the many tasks necessary to run a keep. Had she been of another sort, she might have roused the housekeeper's suspicions, but Freya knew her place and gave no sign but that she was content.

It could not be truly said that Freya liked Mayde, or that Mayde felt any fondness for Freya, but they rubbed along together with few sparks between them.

"She can rest well enough in her own home," Mayde declared.

"But she is here. We've beds enough to spare, surely."

"Then let her be moved to one more suited to her kind. The girl could make herself useful and repay her lodging by lending a hand to these addlepated twits.'' A few scullery maids scurried about, doing their best to avoid their mistress's glare. ''A village girl has no place in the lord's chamber.''

''And yet,'' Freya said smoothly, '' 'tis his own chamber where Lord Galen carried her.''

''And for his own purposes, I've no doubt.''

''Mayde!''

''Oh, do not look so shocked, woman.'' The housekeeper finally took pity on the hapless bread dough and shaped it into a loaf. ''We both know he kept the little creature naked as the day she was born. And whose word have we but his that she was dazed the whole time?''

''Are you suggesting—''

''Though, I grant you, I can and do believe she was senseless. Even a village girl could not look upon that face and not suffer for it.''

Freya could only stare, speechless.

''And I grant, too, she might grow reconciled to what she may have seen.'' Mayde floured the board for another ball of dough. ''Promise of enough coin can cushion shock quite well, and a girl can always close her eyes.''

Freya stood and banged the bowl of beans onto the table. ''I'll hear no more of this, and I'll take myself off before my tongue speaks what is best not said.''

''Mark my words,'' Mayde predicted dourly before Freya could quit the room. ''Much as I doubt she ever was, if that little village cat leaves this keep a virgin, 'twill be a miracle.''

Freya had counseled rest, but Anne decided she had rested quite enough.

The tolling bell of the village church floated through the unshuttered window of the chamber, announcing the divine office of Sext and, with it, the noon hour. Few of Thornbury's faithful would attend; in high summer, there was little time to spare. Anne pictured the village men coming and going from the fields, others working their crafts in workshops open to the summer breeze. Women would be cleaning away dinner, preparing for supper, tending to the host of other tasks that made up their day—washing and mending, weeding the family garden, looking after the fowl.

Even within the walls of Rosethorn, the hustle she saw below her window did not pause. The stablemaster and his boys groomed the horses. The clang of metal from somewhere out of sight told Anne the lord's men-at-arms were training. Voices floated to her from where the washerwomen worked through the mounds of linens and clothing.

Everyone had a job to do. Everyone, that was, except her.

The longer Anne sat, the more her thoughts turned homeward. Were Derek and Lyssa behaving themselves? Did her father know where everything was to prepare their meals? Would someone remember to feed the chickens? Were they worried about her? Anne nibbled the tip of one finger. For even with Bryan of Rosethorn sending word, her father must still be worried sick.

Much as she hated to admit it, Anne knew that sour old dragon, Mayde, had the right of it. She was awake and, though still aching and stiff, otherwise none the worse for wear. She needed to go home.

His lordship has taken you under his protection. 'Tis he, and no other, who has say whether you go or stay.

Anne had not pondered those words when Freya said them, but she did now. And the implication unsettled her. She sat on the edge of the massive bed and pressed her hands into her lap. She was being foolish. Freya had only sought to reassure her.

Lord Galen himself tended to you.

Snatches of what she had thought a fever-dream haunted Anne, even more because now she could not be sure they *were* a dream. A voice had murmured to her, gentle hands touched her. A cool cloth had stroked her face and throat, between her—Anne squirmed. Her cheeks warmed at the odd heaviness within her breasts and how their crests rose beneath the fabric of her borrowed gown. It had been no dream. She had lain before Lord Galen, bared to his gaze. And bared by his own hands! Her belly gave a queer little flip.

I mean no harm. Not to you.

She clung to that, but how much faith could she put into words uttered weeks ago by a man she knew nothing of? Anne pulled a face. Strange to say, it was easier to believe him when she thought him a wanderer. Now she knew he was a lord. Her lord. A man who held incredible power over her. And she had heard tales of lords who took maids and—

Anne shook herself. This would drive her mad. She could not just sit here. Too many gruesome fancies crowded upon her when she sat idle.

The bell for Nones wafted through the paneless window, telling Anne she had wasted three hours with her quibbling. Well, no more of it! If no one would come to her, Anne decided she would go to them.

Besides, she was honest enough to admit curiosity prodded her. She had only heard tales of Rosethorn. Now she had a chance to see it.

Anne giggled when she stood and looked down at the gown hanging upon her. True enough, she and Freya were not much of like size. Rolling the sleeves to her wrists, she conceded she could do little about the length until she happened upon needle and thread, but the gown covered her decently enough.

Braiding her hair proved more of an ordeal than she anticipated. Her sore arms tired easily, so Anne contented herself with combing her hair to fall loose down her back. No shoes or slippers were to be found. Like her gown, her shoes must have been ruined. Anne frowned, disgruntled at the loss she could ill afford. Then a smile dimpled her cheek. Heaven knew the gown was long enough to hide her bare feet.

Stepping over the threshold daunted her. No one had commanded her to stay in the chamber. Certainly, the door stood open, all but begging her to explore. But Anne could not forget she was a guest. One, she reminded herself, thinking of Mayde, with an uncertain welcome. Should she, or should she not?

Anne set her chin. Whether she should or not, she would.

The corridor proved to be more like a landing on the staircase spiraling through the keep tower. Two other chamber doors faced her. The stairs wound upward, and Anne could see another level above, no doubt with other chambers. The stairs also wound down, and her feet padded softly on the stone steps as she descended.

Even in late afternoon, the stairwell was dim and rather eerie. The chamber doors on the two levels she found were closed, and while her curiosity itched to look within, Anne heeded good sense and let them be. Exploring was one thing. Deliberately prying where she did not belong was quite another.

At the foot, a wide archway opened. Anne had never seen a lord's hall, and anticipation tingled down her spine. Reality, however, made her falter over the last step.

It was so . . . stark.

Anne felt as if she had stepped into some great cavern. Iron-gray stone formed the walls and stretched across the floor. Not even a tapestry brightened the gloom, broken only by weak sunlight from a few high windows. A pair of great doors led, Anne supposed, to the bailey.

Such a lonely place. She skimmed her fingers down the huge trestle table that looked naked without so much as a cloth to cover it. Flowers, or some such other decoration, were obviously out of the question. Anne could well understand why the hall was vacant. No one would willingly linger here. Only the pair of massive chairs, and the unlit hearth they stood before, escaped the austerity, but Anne could not claim they livened things up much.

The dragon's head carved into the stone mantel was very impressive, but the creature's menacing snarl sent a shiver down her spine. Thick, ruby-red cushions on the chairs lent the hall its only color. Anne admired the dark gloss rubbed into the wood, but the same uncanny beastie glared down from atop the tall back of each one.

Come no closer.

The words seemed to echo through the hall. Anne suddenly felt very small, keenly aware of her ill-fitting gown and bare feet. It was as if the hall were glowering at her for violating its solitude and shunned her very presence.

A mew and the silky slide of a warm body about her legs

made a shriek swell within her throat. Anne caught it just shy of her lips and turned it into a shaky laugh as she looked down. Kneeling, she brushed her fingertips against the cheek of the sleek, black-and-gray cat that had emerged to make her acquaintance. The animal slitted its green eyes and rumbled in bliss. Anne narrowed her own eyes.

"I know you. You came to visit me once. And you brought a friend, do you remember?"

The cat rubbed against her fingers, and Anne chuckled. She tickled the furry chin. Her chuckle deepened into a laugh as the animal batted playfully at her fingers.

"Where is your friend now?" she asked softly, more to herself than to the cat.

But the creature blinked at her and trotted to the foot of the stairs. Turning, it meowed.

Anne straightened and rubbed her arms. Nonsense. The cat could not have truly understood her. But she could not deny that the way the animal paused, looked back at her and mewed once more, was very eerie indeed. With an odd tingle in the pit of her belly, Anne followed.

"And if we rotate men on the east rampart, I think we can complete repairs inside a month." Bryan of Rosethorn narrowed his eyes at the drawing spread upon the large table. "That leaves only the southwest tower—" He broke off and looked at the man seated across from him. "Galen?"

It was not until his seneschal had called his name at least thrice that Galen realized his mind had wandered. Again. He bit back an oath and shook his head.

"You need to rest," Bryan declared. "You've not slept decently for days, ever since that—"

"I am fine." Galen leaned forward to peer at the drawing of Rosethorn. "You were saying?"

"I was saying you need to sleep."

Galen angled him a look. "Before that."

Bryan straightened and crossed his arms over his chest. "I was saying you should send that girl home before you lose what few wits you have left."

"You were not."

"Nay, but I should have."

Galen snorted. Much as he valued Bryan's frankness, it proved vexing at times. Especially when he knew his friend was right. The girl, this Anne of Thornbury, should be returned to her home and her life. It was just that simple. And just that correct, Galen admitted.

But admitting it made it no easier to face.

He had seen awareness stirring within his wood elf before dawn. He had known that he must leave her side for both their sakes, but Galen had detested the prospect of closeting himself within his study. It was not what he wanted.

He wanted to see her, hear her speak. He wanted to watch her wander about Rosethorn, discovering every nook and cranny of the old castle. He wanted to see her here, in his study, amid the old volumes he himself treasured. Perhaps she would draw one from its shelf and thumb through the antique pages. Could she read? He could teach her. He could teach her the mystery of words, share his home, share his—

Galen jerked himself up short. Foolish fancies, all of them. He closeted himself here for a reason. He could not forget that. He dared not forget it.

" 'Tis more than sleeplessness that plagues you, Galen."

"Am I that obvious?"

"As obvious as a bolt of lightning." His friend leaned forward, palms braced upon the table between them. "What is it about this girl? I have never known you to be so preoccupied."

Galen looked away. "Nothing. She is just a girl."

Bryan lifted a brow. "You can lie to me if you wish, but do not lie to yourself."

Galen said nothing, but he did not meet Bryan's gaze.

"She is a hard-working lass, they say," Bryan offered. "Looks after her father, a brother and sister."

Galen took the bait. "There is no mother?"

"She passed away some seven years ago, from what I gather."

Anne would have been just a child. He had been a child when his own mother died, so young Galen could remember little of her. What memories did his wood elf have of her mother?

"They say, too, she is quick-witted," Bryan added, then his lips quirked wryly, "though I question the wit of a girl who wanders through the wood alone."

Galen snorted. "Time was, a walk in the wood was as safe as strolling through Rosethorn's bailey."

"Aye, well, many years have passed since then." Bryan grimaced at his overly frank words. "I did not mean—"

"I know. But the fact remains I have been remiss. Rosethorn has stood empty since my father's death."

Even now, part of Galen could not quite believe the old man was gone. The castle—this very chamber—still echoed with his father's presence, his booming voice.

God as my witness, boy, I'll not tolerate a challenge from my own son. Get out, damn you! Go prove your bloody manhood to your heart's content, but get out of my sight.

Father, I did not—

And when you return, when you find out what sort of man you are, you come to me on your knees. On your knees, you hear!

It seemed so improbable that his father, obstinate soul that he was, should have let death take him without having the last word over the son he had all but cast off.

"Your father is remembered fondly in the village," Bryan murmured, drawing Galen from his reverie.

"I can imagine." Galen bit off a humorless laugh. "Good Lord Geoffery. How sad his son proves not his equal."

"Not his equal?" Bryan snorted. "God's blood, you've done more for these people in the past weeks than he did in all the years since you left. If they've any sense at all, they will not fail to see that."

"You think not?" Galen's lips curved. "They will see what they wish to see, Bryan. You'll soon hear whispers that the folk of Thornbury did not think highly of me before I took up the cross. And now? Well, no longer am I the fresh-faced lad of twenty they remember." His fingertips brushed his cheek, and his voice lowered. "I am no longer even what I remember."

"There is already talk in the village."

Galen shrugged. That came as no surprise.

"About the girl."

But that made Galen scowl. "What talk?"

Bryan met his friend's gaze without flinching. " 'Tis whispered by some that the Lord of Rosethorn has already found a mistress."

Fury blazed within Galen's veins—at fate, at village fools and their wagging tongues, but most of all at himself. He should have expected it. He could just imagine what Bryan left unsaid, the sour speculations and sly questions. Yes, they would ask her. After all, a mistress would have to have looked upon her keeper, would she not?

"*Has* he found a mistress?" Bryan prodded silkily.

Galen clenched his jaw until it ached and said nothing.

"Peasant or princess, who you choose to warm your bed is none of my affair, but consider what you are doing."

"You've the right of it," Galen growled. " 'Tis none of your affair."

"Galen—"

His lord hissed, "Enough."

"You know nothing about this Anne girl." Bryan leaned close again. "And she knows nothing of you."

Galen balled one hand into a fist. "I said, *enough*."

The two men measured each other in taut silence. Then, Bryan breathed a curse and straightened.

"I hope you know what you are doing."

Galen had to swallow before he replied. "So do I."

The cat led her back to the third level, then trotted past the door of the lord's chamber. When Anne hesitated, the animal looked back and meowed.

"I do not think I should—"

The creature lashed its tail, and its mew sounded almost irritated. Anne shook herself. Fanciful nonsense. All the same, she took a deep breath and followed the cat.

And ran smack into Bryan.

The sudden appearance of the tall, broad-shouldered man

nearly made Anne leap from her skin. She turned her gasp into a contrite laugh.

"My lord, I—"

Anne had no chance to utter another sound. He grasped her arm and all but dragged her back down the stairs. When they stood before the lord's chamber, he rounded upon her, his fingers a band of iron on her upper arm.

"What do you think you are doing, girl?"

"I—Nothing." Anne twisted in his grasp. "Please, you are hurting my arm."

He ignored her, his hazel-green eyes narrowing to slits. "Nothing? Wandering about the keep, prying where you do not belong is nothing?"

"I was not prying," Anne countered indignantly, and tugged harder. "Let me go."

"You are in no position to issue commands, girl. You are here on his lordship's sufferance, and I doubt he would suffer your snooping lightly."

Anne narrowed her own eyes. "I was not prying, snooping, or spying on anyone. And if you are so concerned, you should have locked me in the chamber rather than leave the door wide open."

His jaw worked, and a shiver of alarm worked down Anne's spine as he pushed her into the lord's chamber. What if he really did lock her in?

"My lord, please, I—"

"Listen to me, girl." Bryan gave her arm a yank. "I know not what your scheme is, but I give you warning. Bring any harm upon Lord Galen and I will personally see to it that you live to regret it. Do you understand?"

Anne's jaw dropped. Then fury melted any vestige of caution. "I have no scheme! And how dare you threaten me!"

"I'll not watch the likes of you tear him to shreds."

"The likes of—" Anne tilted her chin and met his gaze stonily. "Let me go."

He released her at the exact moment she pulled against his grasp the hardest, and Anne stumbled back. No doubt he had done it on purpose, the great oaf. Feeling a fool, she refused to avert her gaze, half-expecting him to toss her out of the keep. Instead, he transfixed her with a glare.

"So long as we understand each other, girl."

He pulled the chamber door closed.

Anne stood for a long time, not knowing whether to curse or laugh. She waited to hear the bolt of the lock slide home. But no such sound came.

I know not what your scheme is.

Give you warning . . . see that you live to regret it.

Watch the likes of you tear him to shreds.

Sleep had never proved so elusive. Anne lay in the great bed, incredulous, and counted the hours as the fire in the hearth burned low. Curled in the curve of her body, the cat rumbled a drowsy purr. Anne caressed its ears, stroked its sleek back, unsure of whom she sought to comfort, herself or the cat.

Live to regret it.

The likes of you.

Even Freya had sensed something amiss when she collected the tray she had brought with the evening meal.

"Do you not feel well, child?"

"I am quite well."

"But you've barely touched a morsel."

"I was not very hungry."

"You need to rest, child."

"Do you think I could meet with Lord Galen tomorrow? I am grateful for all he has done, but I need to go home."

"I do not know what his lordship's plans are."

Remembering how Freya had spoken, and how her eyes never quite looked up, sent a shiver down Anne's spine even now. Every shadow in the huge chamber, every thought that flickered through her mind, seemed tinged with menace. The Matins bell marked the midnight hour, and the night crept on. Dawn was still a mere promise when Anne knew she could bear no more.

Perhaps one day she would look back and laugh at her foolishness.

Live to regret it . . . The likes of you.

Then again, perhaps not.

Flipping back the covers, she rose. The cat's purr ceased as if sliced by a knife. It sat up and gave a questioning meow.

"Shhh, not a peep out of you," Anne whispered as she dressed, careful to remain as quiet as possible.

The chamber door made not a sound as she opened it, and Anne frowned. Why issue warnings but leave her free to wander? Strange. The whole matter was too strange for her comfort. The sooner she put distance between herself and Rosethorn the better she would feel.

Her bare feet flew silently down the stairs. Peeking into the hall, she found it vacant. Anne darted for the door. Castle life began with the Prime bell at dawn. She had only a short while before Rosethorn would stir. Anne flinched at the creaking hinges on the great portals leading outside.

In the shadow of the entrance, she sought the best route of escape. Nay, not escape. Anne shook her head. Village girl or no, she had a right to leave if she chose. She was simply choosing before anyone could say otherwise.

The drawbridge was down, but the gates blocked her way. Anne squinted into the gloom and saw a small door set in the gate, barred with a stout plank. She looked for the guard and found him slumped in a corner, his chin lolled upon his chest. Anne sniffed. Bryan of Rosethorn would do well to pay closer attention to his men-at-arms, rather than worry over imaginary schemes. Still, she seized the opportunity.

A quick darting here, a waiting in the shadows, another scurrying there, and she reached the gate. Anne tiptoed past the snoring guard. He snorted and muttered, and she froze, not even daring to breathe until he settled again. Quietly, she lifted the bar and slipped through the door. The missing plank bore witness to her passing, but she could do little about it. Anne closed the door and crossed her fingers that no one would notice it too soon.

She had succeeded in getting out of Rosethorn. Now what? Should she stay close to the walls until full light? Anne wrinkled her nose. She would be missed early and could not be anywhere close when the hue and cry went up. She had only an hour or two until dawn, and the lane led straight to the village. She could not lose her way in the woods.

Remembering the outlaws, Anne hesitated. Could they still be about? Good sense nagged her, chastised her for tempting fate. At least she had been safe within Rosethorn. Or had she? Gathering her overly long gown from about her feet, she set off.

She had gone perhaps half her journey before she heard the first rustling. Hoofbeats in the leaves? Anne took a deep breath and quickened her step. The rustling kept pace. She kept her eyes forward and tried to hurry. Memories of the outlaws' chase sent a chill prickling along her arms. A snapping stick brought her feet and her heart to a halt. Someone *was* there.

"What the devil are you doing here, girl?"

Anne shrieked and whirled. Her gown tangled about her feet and down she went in the middle of the lane.

He sat on a sleek horse, both rider and mount as dark as the night. By the moon's faint glow, she saw a hood drawn over his head, an eerie darkness where his face should have been. Anne tried to scramble to her feet but landed on the lane again.

"Wh-who are you?" she demanded.

The rider nudged the horse closer. "Answer my question first. What are you doing here?"

Something about him, the set of those broad shoulders perhaps, tickled Anne's memory even through her fear.

"Lord Galen?"

He dismounted silently. Moonlight glinted off a length of metal-studded leather at his waist. A length just right for a dagger's sheath. He drew closer, and Anne recoiled from his sinewy fingers, reaching out like clawing talons.

But only the warm grasp of a man caught her arms and hoisted her to her feet, then set her free.

"You *are* Lord Galen."

A hoarse sound, which might or might not have been a laugh, came from within the hood. "Of course, girl. And you can thank God for letting you tempt fate twice without disaster.'' His voice sharpened. ''Then you can thank me for not turning you over my knee for it.''

Anne narrowed her eyes. Indignation, relief and the lingering echoes of fear swirled into a brew that seethed within her. Before she realized what she was doing, Anne drew back her arm and swung.

Chapter Four

"You!"

Galen's breath whooshed out as the girl's fist plowed into his belly. He had taken harder blows, but the surprise of this one doubled him over. That put his jaw nicely in range, and her next swing cracked his teeth together.

"You knave!" Like a Fury, she flung herself upon him, and they tumbled to the ground. "Lout!"

Galen twisted from under her. Catching her fist with one hand when it narrowly missed his nose, he snatched at the cowl slipping from his head with the other. Even pinned on her back, the girl proved far from helpless. One knee jerked up between his legs. Galen decided close enough was too close.

"Enough!"

Battle-hardened warriors had been known to flee at his enraged bellow, but this girl snarled right back.

"You scared me witless! I thought you were going to slit my throat!"

Lower lip throbbing, Galen wondered why he wanted to laugh. "I might yet, so do not tempt me, girl."

Straddling her with his thighs, gripping her wrists in his

hands, he had her beaten. But if he had greater strength, she had weapons of her own. Clawing Fury she might be, but she was yet a woman. And he was a man. Every move she made, every twist of her hips under him reminded him of it. Galen breathed a curse at the heat gathering and thickening low in his belly.

"Let me go!"

"Only if you calm down."

She stilled, narrowed her eyes, and nodded. Galen released her and stood, honoring their truce by offering his hand to help her up. He caught the gleam of her smile too late. A muffled oath burst from his lips as her feet tangled with his, bringing him down with a thump.

Tumbling through the bracken with her, Galen found gaining the upper hand a challenge. She was quick and stronger than she looked, and no matter what hold he got on her, his hand nestled into a resilient curve that distracted him to no end. Just when he began to enjoy their tussle, Galen could not say, but his clenched teeth eased into a smile. Wood elves were fierce folk, after all. Not to mention unpredictable. At last, he rolled onto his back and let her pin him there.

"Thought I could not do it, eh?"

Hidden by shadows, Galen's lips twitched at her taunt. The moon's light illuminated her triumphant face. Her arms shook with exertion, and she panted breathlessly. So slight was she, that he knew he could toss her off with a flick of his wrist. But her look of triumph enchanted him.

"I admit it," he replied, breathless more from her enticing weight upon him than from effort. "You win."

A sound, more a growl of satisfaction than a laugh, bubbled from her throat, and she plopped down beside him. "I do not have a brother for nothing."

Without her draped across him, an odd chill quivered through Galen. He balled his hands into fists to keep from covering himself again with her warmth and softness. Instead, he unclenched his fists and contented himself with where he lay. The position gave his gaze free range of her in the moonlight, while he remained in darkness.

"Now that you've thoroughly pummeled your lord into

submission,'' he drawled, ''what will you do?''

Galen wanted to bite his tongue. She went utterly still at the reminder of his rank, and all the spirit drained from her face. ''I am sorry, my lord.''

''You are not,'' he replied, not displeased with the insight. ''I don't think you are sorry at all.''

She held her silence and drew her legs beneath herself like a doe readying for flight. Galen rose to one elbow, tensing to catch her if she sought escape. He had struggled against it, but if fate insisted upon bringing him and his wood elf together, he would be damned if she got away so quickly.

''What is your name?'' He knew, of course, but he wanted to hear it from her own lips.

''Anne.'' She gave it reluctantly, as though her name was a charm he could use to ensnare her for eternity.

''The carpenter's daughter?'' She nodded, watching him warily. Skittish little wood elf. ''Why did you flee Rosethorn?''

That brought spirit back into her face. ''I was not—''

''Aye, you were. Tell me.''

Her gaze dropped to examine a leaf, and her reply was guarded. ''I do not belong there.''

Galen regarded her narrowly. ''That is not a good reason.''

But her shrug said it was the only one she would give. Nor would she look at him. Sitting there amid the bracken, a halo of moonlight shimmering about her, she truly looked like a wood elf. A very forlorn wood elf. Within his cowl, Galen scowled. She looked as if he had captured her and, like hunters who caught elves in tales of yore, that he would now demand his due.

Hunted. Embers of anger glowed in his belly at the thought.

''Why do you flee Rosethorn?'' She shrugged again, and Galen sat up. Catching her chin in his fingertips, he tilted her face into the moonshine to read her expression. It was a look of wariness, and a bit belligerent. And afraid. Of him? ''Tell me, girl. Who drove you to brave the night alone?''

Even knowing the cowl of his surcoat hid his face well, Galen felt she could see straight into his soul with those eyes. Her chin trembled before she looked away.

"No one drove me." Galen had to admire her effort to keep her voice firm. "I simply wanted to go home."

White-hot anger shot through him. "You were no prisoner, girl. You had only to ask, and you would have been escorted in safety, rather than sent on your way like a barefoot beggar."

The glance she darted at him kindled Galen's anger into flames of fury. She did not believe him. Good God, what sort of man did she think he was?

You can lie to me if you wish, but do not lie to yourself.

Galen flinched at the thought he read in her eyes.

If she had asked, would he truly have let her go? Suddenly, Galen was not sure, and that brought guilt burning into his throat. The bitter taste only infuriated him more.

"Or was it more than homesickness that spurred you?" He lowered his voice to a hiss, perversely enjoying how she trembled. "Perhaps 'twas fear of Rosethorn's dark lord. They say I am a sorcerer, girl, with a soul as black as hell itself."

Her head came up. "I thought no such nonsense."

"Surely you knew your return, alone and before dawn, would cause just that sort of talk."

Her face blanched as pale as the moonlight. "Nay, I never meant to cause—"

"Then why did you leave me?" he demanded in a whisper.

She blinked. "Leave . . . you? Nay, I only wanted to return to where I belong, to keep others from—" She stumbled to a halt, and Galen's conscience smote him. She had been through so much, his little wood elf. Furious with himself, he had lashed out at her instead, and she did not deserve that. "I am sorry, my lord. I only—"

"Hush." His fingers pressed to her lips. When she tried to speak again, he shook his head. "Nay, 'tis I who must beg forgiveness from you. I spoke too harshly."

Enticed by the softness of her skin, he stroked the back

of his fingers across her cheek, smoothing back a tendril of her hair. Her wide eyes searched the shadows fruitlessly for his, her lips quivering, tempting him beyond endurance. Just once, Galen permitted himself to surrender to temptation.

Her eyelids fluttered closed as he brushed his lips over hers. A rough sound rumbled from his throat. How sweet. Dear God, she tasted sweet. Clean and fresh, with just a tang of mischief. His moan deepened.

Galen nibbled at her lips with his own, murmuring when she dared a tentative response in kind. His fingers trailed to her shoulder and drew her closer. Into his arms. Against his body. It had been so long since he held a woman, since he dared allow a woman this close. But this woman— If he was granted nothing else in his life, just to feel her warm and soft in his arms this once would be enough.

"Aye, sweet." His whisper throbbed in rhythm with the heavy pulse deep within his body. Arousal? Aye, she aroused him, made him yearn and need. But deeper than the need swelling his loins, another need ached within his soul. "Hold me. 'Tis so long since—Hold me, sweet elf."

He wove a spell around her. Never had Anne felt longing like this. Both his and her own desire swirled together until she no longer knew the difference. His mouth moved upon hers so gently, she forgot to be afraid. She forgot who she was, who he was. She forgot everything but his taste of moonlight and forest. The deep tones of his voice filled her ears. She heard his plea, the yearning that made her yearn with him.

She lifted her hand, and her fingertips brushed the warm roughness of his cheek.

He jerked back. In the gloom of waning night, Anne caught only a glimpse of a wild eye before the hood hid him once more. He held her at arm's length, fingers digging into her shoulders. All the fear she should have felt before chilled her now.

"Wh-what did I do?"

"Nothing." His denial rasped against her heart, and Anne flinched. "You did nothing."

She shifted within his grasp. "You are hurting me."

He released her instantly. Part of her wanted to cower from him, but another part wanted to fling herself back into his arms and not let him go until that forlorn need in his voice was sated. She could do neither. Bewildered, she watched him take an unsteady breath and rise to his feet. When he extended his hand, Anne felt that she teetered on the edge of the most important decision of her life. Would she trust him? After a moment's pause, she held out her hand and let him pull her to her feet.

He kept her hand firmly in his, as if he feared her escaping, and led her back to the lane. His broad-shouldered form was naught but a silhouette of darkness guiding her. His mount had not wandered and nickered at them as they approached. Without a word, Lord Galen lifted her into the saddle and then swung up behind her.

"Where—" Anne's breath locked in her chest at the feel of him, so large and male, at her back. "Where are you taking me?"

"Back to Rosethorn."

"But—"

"I'll not have the entire village saying you would rather face the road before dawn than remain within the castle."

Anne winced at his tone. She had wounded him. She had insulted his pride and honor with her foolishness. His arms came around her, framing her securely but careful not to touch. She dug her fingers into her palms to keep from caressing the large hands gripping the reins so tightly. "You will be taken home as soon as 'tis full light."

Turning the horse around, he headed back to the castle.

Three hours after dawn, the bell for Tierce tolled from the village church and floated to Rosethorn. Anne stood at the chamber window and blinked in the sunshine. Sounds in the bailey below drew her gaze, and her lips curved down.

Horses and men were gathering there.

True to his word, Lord Galen was sending her home.

Anne wondered why that made an ache swell in her throat. It was what she wanted, was it not? Or did she?

Turning from the window, her gaze fell upon the massive

bed. A strange warmth tingled through her veins.

This was the lord's bed. She had known that, but somehow, the full realization had not sunk in until now. Lord Galen slept here, laid his head on the same pillows she had. Anne smoothed her palm over the fine brychan that would warm his body, too. The tingle in her veins thickened and flowed like honey as she imagined him, a masculine form upon the bed. Firelight would dance upon his skin, flicker over the swell of muscle along his arms, across his chest to his flat belly. Down to his—Anne blinked to banish the image, and her cheeks flamed.

Four nights, she had lain in his bed. Where had Lord Galen rested during that time? Strange, how she had not wondered about that before. But then, he had not been so real before. Just a name whispered in village tales. Just a shadow on the edge of the wood.

But now, Lord Galen Tarrant was very real.

As real as his kiss. As real as his voice.

Hold me.

Lord Galen was all too real. She knew his warmth, the strength of his arms. She knew his scent of forest and night. She knew how gently his fingers could touch and how his lips whispered a longing that matched her own.

'Tis so long since—Hold me, sweet elf.

Anne drew a shaky breath. It was foolish, letting those words, that voice, affect her so. It had been dark, and darkness bound people together who would never—could never—be close in the light. That explained the hollow throb in her belly, the discontent gnawing at her heart. She had been fooled by a trick of the night.

He was a landed lord, a man of power and wealth.

She was a village girl, a daughter of a carpenter with no power or wealth at all.

To forget that would court certain heartbreak.

Why, then, did she keep forgetting it?

Remember Bryan of Rosethorn's accusation, she counseled herself. Indignation firmed her jaw. Anne welcomed the emotion, used it to rebuild the defenses around her fanciful heart.

I know not what your scheme is.

Give you warning . . . You will live to regret it.

Aye, he would not forget who she was, what she was. And remember Mayde? She had used the same words.

The likes of you.

But words breathed from other lips proved stronger in the battle within her. A tiny sob tore from Anne's throat, and she sank down on the edge of the bed. It was no use. She could no more banish Lord Galen's plea from her mind than she could stop the sun from rising.

Hold me, sweet elf.

If only she could. Anne pressed her fingers to her lips and squeezed her eyes closed. If only she dared.

"What in heaven's name are you doing, girl?"

Anne gasped, and her eyes flew open to find Mayde in the doorway, fists bunched at her narrow hips.

"Do you think folk have naught better to do than wait for you?" the woman snapped. "Get up from there this instant and march yourself to the bailey. Come on, step smartly, girl."

Anne came to her feet, color flaming back into her cheeks. Disagreeable old dragon, she fumed, but she sweetened her tongue until it fairly dripped with honey.

"I did not know anyone was ready for me yet."

Mayde snorted. "And no wonder, sitting there, mooning like a weak-willed ninny."

"Who, I am sure, you'll be glad to be rid of."

"Watch your tongue, girl. Remember your place."

Anne's step faltered as she neared the door, and she met the old dragon's gaze, proud that no quavering showed in her voice. "Oh, I promise you. I'll not forget my place."

Far above Rosethorn's bailey, within the shadows of his study window, Galen watched Anne of Thornbury prepare to leave. He saw her speak with Freya at the foot of the stairs leading into the hall and fling her arms around the woman in an embrace. She broke away, then, and started toward the waiting men, that atrocious gown she wore shining in the sun. Her step slowed as she neared Bryan. The seneschal acknowledged her with a nod and helped her into her saddle.

Galen balled his hand into a fist against the window frame.

She was leaving.

Anne was leaving.

Bitterness burned in the back of his throat. Envy? They had only a short ride, naught but three or four miles, but what would he have given to be in Bryan's place? Anything. God help him, he would give everything to be the one by her side.

He breathed deeply to ease the knot coiling through his belly. But if he were the man with her, would she let him touch her, even if only to lift her into the saddle? One corner of his mouth lifted without humor. Not bloody likely. Without darkness to conceal him, she would take one look and her face would cloud with horror. Or worse.

Bryan mounted and, with an escort of two others, rode with Anne toward the gates. Several about the bailey paused to mark their passing. Most looked on impassively, but one or two nodded. Freya waved, but her hand lowered when Mayde came to her side. Knowing Mayde as he did, Galen could well imagine what her opinion of their guest had been. He snorted. Like as not, the housekeeper had come to ensure that the girl left in short order.

Just then, Anne looked over her shoulder.

At first, he feared she had glimpsed him and he started to draw back, but then he realized that she was not looking toward his window. Indecision flickered across her face. A rough sound seeped from his lips when Anne beamed an overbright smile and waved. It was a show just for Mayde, and anyone with a grain of sense knew it. The sound from his own lips lingered in Galen's ears, smoothed and deepened until it became a laugh.

Then it hushed. She had passed the gates. Within moments, she would be out of sight.

Galen closed the shutters and turned away long before that. He could not watch her leave, could not watch those last moments before she vanished from his gaze. From his life? Denial shrieked through his mind, cramped his throat.

'Tis whispered the Lord of Rosethorn has found a mistress.

If only it was that simple. Galen shuddered. He could have been content with just a mistress were she any other woman. But not with his wood elf. With Anne, he wanted more. He wanted everything.

Standing by the table, Galen absently stroked a fingertip along the cheek of the cat sitting with its tail coiled about its legs. The animal purred and nuzzled his hand as if to offer solace. But Galen remembered only the feel of a wood elf's skin, smooth and warm, under his touch.

It was mad, what he considered doing, but he could not rid himself of the notion. The idea had taken root in his mind and heart and to tear it out would rip both to shreds. But to heed it would likely tear him to shreds, too.

What harm, then? Galen went to where a small drape hung solitary upon the wall. His fingers crumpled the corner of the dark cloth until his knuckles showed white, then he whipped it aside, doing something he did not often permit himself.

Lord Galen Tarrant looked at his reflection in the mirror.

Aye, what harm? He had nothing to lose.

Nothing, his reflection taunted, except Anne.

For reasons she took care not to examine closely, Anne refused to look back once she had passed Rosethorn's gates. It was over. Her moment of madness, of temptation, was finished. She had to look forward now.

Looking forward, though, brought its own set of problems. Thornbury was a quiet village. Seeing one of their own riding with none other than his lordship's seneschal as escort, not to mention two more men-at-arms just behind, would cause quite a sensation. And when word got around about the splendid mount she now rode—Galen's gift—well, Anne could already hear the talk.

For the mare she rode was quite wonderful, indeed. Dappled with gray so pale it gleamed like silver against her white hide, the mare made up for her lack of size with beauty and a lively gait. Such a creature could not help but draw comment.

And comment was exactly what Anne wanted most to avoid. The notion of causing more gossip to swirl about Lord Galen, no matter how innocuous, made her cringe. He had suffered enough without her adding to it.

"Is aught amiss?"

Anne cast a swift look at the man riding beside her and worried her lower lip between her teeth. Bryan of Rosethorn regarded her through narrowed eyes.

"Nay, I was just . . . thinking." She chose her words carefully. "I am grateful, my lord, but this escort is really not necessary. 'Tis no great distance. I can walk—"

"Lord Galen bade me see you home in safety, and so I will."

Chastised by his gruffness, Anne looked away.

"Besides," he went on, "no telling what sort of villain you might run into on the road alone. One might even want to slit your throat."

He knew! Anne felt her cheeks grow warm. Lord Galen had been careful that no one saw them return, but he must have confided her pre-dawn excursion to his seneschal. A quick glance at Bryan's profile showed no change in his austere expression. So why did she get the feeling he was amused? Anne narrowed her own eyes.

"Aye, 'tis true. But I am well able to defend myself."

Of all the amazing things, Bryan's lips twitched, and he angled her a look with twinkling eyes. "So I have been told."

Anne pressed her lips together to keep from laughing.

"Why would you prefer to return alone?"

His question, devoid of any lingering amusement, succeeded in banishing her own. Anne shifted restlessly in the saddle. The motion did not meet with her mare's approval, and the horse danced nervously. Anne tugged on the reins, but that only displeased the animal more. Her ears flattened in warning. There was no telling what would have happened if Bryan had not snagged the mare's bridle, calming her with soft murmurs.

He glared at Anne. "I thought you said you could ride."

"I can. 'Tis just I am not accustomed to—"

"This is a fine animal, not some sway-backed nag more suited to a plow. Handle her correctly."

"I am trying, but—"

"Sit still, dammit!"

His command came out on a hiss, and Anne narrowed her eyes. "Very well, my lord. As my riding skills do not meet with your approval, I'll absolve you of your responsibility and walk the rest of the way."

He barked a laugh. "And give the village gossips that to chew on? I think not, girl."

"They will find more meat to chew seeing me in your company," she fired back.

They measured each other in taut silence for a moment.

"Explain," he demanded.

Anne rolled her eyes. "A village girl escorted by the Lord of Rosethorn's seneschal on a mount as fine as this and with two other guards besides? Reason it out for yourself, my lord."

Bryan scowled, bemused by this girl. Others in her position would leap at the chance to make such a sensation. Why not her? But he could not deny she had the right of it. The village gossip mills had been grinding for days, and the scene she described would only add spice to the tales. Casting his gaze about, he nudged their mounts off the lane and onto a track through the wood just wide enough for the horses.

"What—"

"A compromise," he said shortly. " 'Twill take a bit longer, but the track bypasses the village. We can rejoin the lane just before your cottage."

Silence, broken only by the rustle of forest life, draped around them as they rode. Bryan stayed by her side, keeping careful watch on her handling of the mare and a speculative one on Anne of Thornbury herself.

He was an orderly man, and he preferred things and people to fit their expected pattern. But every time he thought he found a pattern for this girl, she refused to fit it. Why would a girl who sought to become her lord's mistress steal away in the night? Or bother herself with village gossip? Such women cared not a fig for such matters. It made no sense. She made no sense, and that irritated him no end.

"Why should you care what talk there is?"

She flashed him an incredulous stare, then shook her head with resignation. Being dismissed like a village idiot piqued Bryan's temper still more. His lips curved into a sharp smile.

"You obviously did not care much for gossip when you fled from Rosethorn last night," he taunted in a low voice.

Blue fire leaped within her eyes. "Why does everyone claim I fled. Cowards flee! *I* did not flee!"

"Quiet!" he hissed. "None but three know of last night." Then one corner of his mouth lifted. "Well, four. The guard you crept past will rue sleeping on duty for some time to come. Galen was furious."

"The man was not harmed, was he?" All color drained from her cheeks. "I could not bear it if he was whipped or—or harmed because of me."

As if Galen would whip a man! To strip away rank and privilege, even to imprison or cast off the man, that Galen could do. But to maim a man by flogging? No matter what the offense, Galen would not stomach that.

But this girl did not know Galen, Bryan reminded himself, or she would know how absurd her worry was.

At every turn, he found something about her that did not fit the pattern he expected. She did not even know the guard's name. Why should she care about his fate? Rather than irritate him, this time the question intrigued him. He had been so sure about her. After all, a lord's mistress was a position with great potential for wealth, even power. What woman would or could resist? Certainly, such an opportunity would be rare for a girl of Anne of Thornbury's station. His eyes narrowed. Either she was remarkably clever or—

Or he was wrong.

Even admitting the possibility forced him to consider other molds she might fit better.

"No harm befell the guard," he replied at last, and lifted a brow. "And you do your lord an injustice by thinking it.

Galen is a strict master, but not a brutal one.''

Anne's cheeks warmed, and she looked away. Injustice. To her sensitive ears, the word held a wealth of accusations. In heeding her own fancies and doubting his honor, she had done Lord Galen a grave injustice, indeed.

''I never truly supposed he was,'' she murmured. ''He seemed a fine man. 'Tis a shame that . . .''

He scowled when she said no more. ''What is a shame?''

Anne wanted to bite her tongue. ''Just that he does not give others in the village the chance to learn that for themselves.'' She dared an inquisitive glance at him. ''Why does Lord Galen keep so much to himself? Why does he not go among his people? I know others in the village would—''

''He has his reasons, girl.''

''But—''

''And those reasons are none of your affair; not yours or anyone else's.'' His fierce glare flashed like a whip across her heart, and Anne flinched. ''Leave him be, girl.''

The warning was unmistakable.

Remember your place.

And her place did not include Lord Galen Tarrant. Certainly not as her heart ached for it to.

Anne swallowed thickly. She had to remember that and forget the rest. All of it.

Chapter Five

In spite of her heavy heart, Anne could not resist a smile when her family's cottage appeared around the bend in the lane.

Humble though it was, with its wattle-and-daub walls and thatched roof, she took pride in it. The flowers she nurtured graced the tidy yard, and a trellis of blooming vines curved over the doorway. A large shed on one side served as her father's workshop, and it, too, was as neat as a pin.

The unkind were wont to remark that it was certainly uncluttered by its resident's trade. Those more generous allowed there was little call for carpentry in Thornbury of late. No one had coin to spare. Daniel of Thornbury's main income in recent years was a ghoulish one. But, said his defenders, Daniel crafted the finest coffins for three shires around.

Truth be told, Anne caught few unkind whispers about her family. She ran the household with a frugal hand, taking in sewing and the like for extra coin when she could. And if the little ones indulged in more than their share of deviltry at times, they were a sweet-hearted pair without a spark of malice between them.

Her father, though, puzzled the villagers. They allowed he was a fine man, much beloved by his children, but Anne knew they looked askance at him. This did not trouble her. She knew her father's faults and loved him in spite of them. Sometimes because of them. Daniel possessed the same distracted, sweetly scatter-brained nature at forty that he had as a lad. She knew, too, that he always would, until the day he left this world to join his beloved wife in the next. Even then, Anne suspected Saint Peter would have to call his name thrice to usher him within heaven's embrace.

But her father proved neither distracted nor dazed when the riders came within sight. The tall, slender man leaped from where he was planing a board and bounded across the yard, his dark hair flying. Two children erupted seemingly from nowhere and set up such a clamor that Anne's mount flattened her ears in protest. Bryan barely had time to grasp the mare's bridle before Daniel all but yanked his daughter from the saddle.

"Oh, child! Child!" He swung her around before clasping her close. "How we worried about you!"

"Anne! Anne, we missed you!" The little girl hopped from foot to foot before twirling on her toes. "Did you nearly get killed? They say you nearly got done to death!"

"Were they big outlaws, Anne?" the boy chimed in, his eyes round and sparkling as brightly blue as his hair shone gold in the sunlight. "Did they have *horrible* mean faces?"

Anne smacked a kiss on her father's cheek and lifted Lyssa for a hug. Dropping her sister back to her feet, Anne bared her teeth at Derek and assumed a threatening crowd.

"Aye, mean and horrible they were."

She snatched her brother close and tickled him until he collapsed in a fit of giggles. Her father caught her in his embrace again and held her tightly. She was home!

Everything, all the fear and uncertainty she had borne, was suddenly too much. In her father's arms, with the warmth of home rushing to greet her, Anne's heart ached and filled her throat. She buried her face in the hollow of her father's shoulder and wept as she had not done for many years. And Daniel, with the wisdom she loved him for, simply held her.

Both children froze.

"Anne is crying," the little girl whispered.

The boy rounded upon Bryan, eyes flashing.

"Did you hurt Anne?" Before Bryan could dodge, one kick cracked into his shin, followed by another. "How dare you hurt my sister!"

"Easy, boy!" Caught between a laugh and a curse, Bryan snared the lad in his arms and hoisted the squirming lad off his feet. "Settle down! Your sister is unharmed, I swear!"

The boy twisted to look into his eyes. "Cross your heart?"

Bryan nodded gravely. "And hope to die."

The lad pondered. "All right, I believe you."

Bryan set him down with a lifted brow. "Thank you."

"Why is Anne crying?"

A tug at his tunic drew Bryan's gaze down to a sweet young face framed with curls as black as a raven's wing. Eyes as blue as her sister's filled with tears, and Bryan felt a flutter of helplessness.

"Because, ah . . ." He stared at the small hand she tucked into his and blinked. This would never do. That quivering chin demanded an answer. "Because she is glad to be home."

"Oh." Lyssa frowned, puzzled, then turned to her sister. "Are you, Anne? Is that why you are crying?"

Relieved the child had directed her gaze elsewhere, Bryan blew out a breath. His duty was done. His only concern now was freeing his fingers from the little girl's grasp. God's truth, her grip clung like honey. An ill-concealed snicker from one of the Rosethorn men sharpened his unease. Let Galen run his own escort errands in future, by thunder!

Anne took pity and, dabbing her cheeks with the heel of her hand, gathered Lyssa close. "Aye, glad I am to be back."

She brushed a kiss upon Lyssa's soft cheek and made Derek blush by kissing him, too, before she rose to face Bryan. He looked overwhelmed, and she firmed her lips to hold back a laugh. If she read his half-wary, half-enchanted look correctly, Rosethorn's seneschal had little experience with children, especially little girls. She wondered if Rosethorn's lord shared the same lack. Had Lord Galen ever known the silvery laugh of a child, or felt young lips pressed against his cheek? Her heart clenched.

"Well." Bryan cleared his throat. "You are safely home."

"Aye," Daniel agreed, suspiciously hoarse. He encircled Anne's shoulders with his arm. " 'Tis grateful I am, to you and his lordship for seeing my girl home, safe and sound."

"Lord Galen had more to do with that than I," Bryan owned, "and I'll be glad to carry your thanks to him."

Her father lifted his chin. "Nay, my lord. I will do so myself by coming to Rosethorn and facing, as a man should, the one who has done us such a good turn."

Anne saw Bryan's face go blank, and his gaze lowered. She dared a small smile. "Surely Lord Galen would grant audience."

"Ah, I am sure he would," Bryan replied a shade too slowly, then added a shade too quickly, "if he were here. But he has business that calls him away." One corner of his mouth lifted uneasily. "Perhaps my service as messenger will do. This once."

He would not meet her gaze, and Anne lowered her own. Bryan did not fool her for a moment. He was an abominable liar. Though that counted in his favor, she could not understand why he would bother to lie. What harm could there be in Lord Galen accepting gratitude from one of his own people? Surely he could bend his preference for solitude that much. Unless there was some other reason.

Come no closer.

What had Anselm said?

No telling how them years marked Lord Galen.

A chill ran down her spine, and though she heard her father's voice, Anne paid little heed.

"Aye, I'd appreciate that, my lord. You'll stay for a cup of refreshment? 'Tis a hot day."

"Thank you," Bryan replied, "but I must return."

Caught in her thoughts, Anne came back to earth with a

thump when she realized that Bryan had already addressed her twice.

"My lord?" She made a pallid attempt at a smile.

"I wish you well," he repeated.

Anne dipped into a curtsy. "Thank you, my lord."

He seemed ready to speak again, but then he gave a brisk nod and turned to his mount. Anne watched, frowning, until he and his comrades had rounded the bend and wondered what Lord Galen was hiding that his seneschal had to forever act as a messenger.

After all the excitement, it took longer than usual to quiet Derek and Lyssa for the night. Even as she tucked them into their cots, they demanded that Anne tell her tale for the tenth time; each retelling had been more thorough and in bolder detail than the last.

"Lord Galen was the bravest ever?" Lyssa had wanted to know. Even at her age, Lyssa had a soft spot for romance, and what was a lord charging to a damsel's rescue if not romantic?

Anne had smiled and kissed her brow. "The bravest ever."

"And he was the handsomest?"

Anne had faltered. "I am sure he was."

Had she lied? Sitting in the breeze of the summer night, Anne discovered she could not say what Galen looked like. Not once had she seen his face. Nothing but a glimpse, and that only by moonlight. She might come face to face with him and not have an inkling of who he was.

Unless he spoke. That voice she would know in a heartbeat.

"You are not tired, Anne?"

She twisted to see her father in the cottage doorway and smiled. Patting the bench, she cuddled at his side when he joined her. A grown woman she was, but how nice it felt to snuggle beneath her father's arm.

"Not really," she murmured.

"Too full of thoughts?"

She nodded, soothed by his fingers stroking her hair.

"And what thoughts are you thinking?"

"Papa." Anne straightened. "Papa, do I seem a proper young woman to you?"

Daniel's brows rose, then lowered darkly. "And whose vile remark has made you wonder a thing like that?"

"No one's," she replied hastily. "I just . . . wondered."

If her evasion dissatisfied him, he said nothing of it. Instead, he pondered her question with a gravity that warmed her heart.

"There are ladies, and then there are ladies," he finally said. "Some ladies bear a title, and some do not. I have no title to bequeath you, so some might say you are no lady. But others might say nobility is not in the title one bears, but how one acts unto others. Your mother was such a person, may the Lord rest her soul. And you, my sprite?" He smiled. "You are the very image of your mother, and I would say you are such a lady, too."

Anne flushed, then leaned forward and kissed his cheek. "Thank you, Papa."

He liked her father.

Galen hung back in the shadows and watched the two of them on the bench outside the cottage door. He had heard her question, saw the uncertainty that pinched her features, and an ache pinched his soul. He listened to Daniel's answer and breathed relief at the man's wisdom.

Aye, he liked the carpenter very much.

She wondered if she was a lady, did she? Of all the great foolish questions, that had to be one of the greatest. Carpenter's daughter or not, his wood elf was more a lady than many queens. Lady Anne. His lips twitched.

Galen watched as Daniel stood and stroked Anne's cheek. He murmured something too low for Galen to hear, and Anne nodded. Her father went inside, while she settled against the wall once more. After a short time, the light was snuffed out within, and all was still.

How long he stood and watched her, Galen had no idea. Long enough for the moon to rise above the trees. Long enough for it to cast her in shades of silver. Long enough for the need to touch her to become all but unbearable.

"You can come out now." Her call floated softly to him. "If you wish."

Ice formed around his heart, but it thawed in the next instant. Bewilderment took its place, and Galen said the first thing that came to mind.

"How the devil did you know?"

A small smile curved her lips, and she slid a look toward the woodshed. "Some outlaw you are, my lord, to let your shadow mark your spot."

Galen looked down. Sure enough, the elongated shape of a man angled from beyond the building's shadow. He snorted. "Did your father see?"

Anne shook her head. "Nor did I, until a moment ago."

"It could have been an outlaw."

"Are you an outlaw? Outlaws move at night, and I seem to encounter you mostly in the dark."

"Perhaps that should tell you something."

"It tells me you must sleep during the day."

"Creatures other than outlaws prowl in the dark."

She did not seem impressed by his show of menace. "There is no full moon, so you cannot be a werewolf. 'Twas full day when you saved me at the brook, so you cannot be a vampire. And I do not believe in ghosts."

"Or goblins or ghoulies or other such things that go bump in the night?" he finished wryly.

Anne giggled. "Not a one."

"Then, lady, I must own it. I am a man."

"You truly can come out." She looked at her hands folded in her lap, then darted a shy smile in his direction. "I promise I'll not hit you again."

That tugged a laugh from him. His jaw still ached. And another part of him, somewhere deep inside, also ached at the temptation she dangled before him. His fears were crystallizing. He had come to her because he could not stay away. Already, he had broken one vow he'd made to himself. He had spoken to her. Galen could not afford to break the second. He must not touch her.

"Nay, I will remain where I stand."

"Very well, my lord," she agreed, and rose to her feet. "I will come to you."

"Nay!"

She froze at his hoarse command, but only for an instant. Step by step, she drew closer. Torn between reaching out for her and vanishing into the shadows, Galen clenched his fists.

"Stay there."

"Why?" she asked, and blatantly disobeyed.

"I—" *Dear God, stay away!* his mind screamed. *Come closer,* his soul pleaded. "I should not have come here. You should not be alone with me."

"Will you hurt me?"

She was almost within his grasp, and Galen dug his fingers into his palms. "And risk your brother kicking my shins?"

"Bryan told you." She smiled and took another step.

"For pity's sake," he rasped, "come no closer."

But she was already too close. He felt the feather-light touch of her hand upon his arm, braced against the shed. Galen whirled away, pulling his cowl forward. He heard her swallow and take a breath.

"Did I so anger you with my foolishness that you cannot even bear to look at me?"

His arm jerked under her hand. His throat tightened. "Nay."

"Then why do you turn away?"

"Please—" He could not seem to draw enough breath. "Please, go back."

"What is it?" Her fingers caressed his arm, and she laid the other at the center of his back. Such a gentle touch, yet it rocked Galen like a blow. "Tell me. I only—"

Galen twisted and caught her by the shoulders, so swift and sudden that she had no chance to elude him. He pulled her deeper into the shadows, where no gleam of moonlight could betray him. Both her wrists fit within one of his hands. The fingers of his other hand traced the curve of her jaw and tilted her chin as he pressed her against the wall.

Her mouth felt soft and pliant under his, and Galen drank the sounds she made like a man dying of thirst. After but a moment's protest, her lips moved in a tentative response, and her sounds were no longer frightened. Or, if they were, fright no longer took the fore.

He lingered over the kiss, savoring her taste and the moisture of her lips, before trailing his own mouth to her cheek. He whispered in her ear, then found the spot at her throat heaviest with her scent. A fragrance of blossoms and honey filled his senses, as though she had bathed in petals, and he nuzzled the skin below her jaw. When he flicked the tip of his tongue over the spot, Galen discovered she tasted of honey, too. She quivered as he strung a necklace of kisses on her throat, pressed another to her cheek, and returned to her lips. But not a sound did she make, not a cry or word, above a breathless murmur. Incredibly, he felt her smile tremble against his mouth.

Her smile came to life for only an instant, and then her gasp stole it away. Galen had brushed his hand over the swell of her breast by accident, but the sweet curve tempted him to linger. Rose pink were her crests. He knew it from the memories that taunted him, and he felt them bead against his fingertips when he caressed them through the fabric of her gown.

"Soft." He breathed the word more than spoke it. "Sweet Lord, you are so soft, wood elf."

The skin not covered by her gown was as smooth as silk and as warm as life itself. His blood heated and thickened within his veins. It rushed to his groin and pulsed there until his flesh throbbed. He needed. He needed to sheath himself within her, bathe in her spirit. His fingers traced her gown's opening but the laces thwarted him. Before he knew what he was doing, Galen had them loosened. And then he felt the heat of her flesh, measured the weight of her firm, round breast filling his palm. A low groan rumbled within his chest when his fingers found the delicate tip of her breast and teased it.

Anne jerked in his grasp and gave a thin cry. He was everywhere, surrounding her with his heat and his strength. His fingertips rasped tenderly against her nipple, and she felt it draw even tighter, ache even more fiercely. She shivered and arched her back, thrusting her breast into his hand, instinctively seeking more of his touch. He plucked upon the bud gently, each tug sending shards of delight through her. She tasted his desperation in the groan he breathed against her mouth. Or was the desperation her own? She no longer knew.

Hold me, sweet elf.

"Please." Anne twisted her wrists, locked in his grasp, and finally twisted hard enough against his thumb to weaken it. She freed one of her hands, but he was too quick for her other. No matter. One would be enough. "Please, let me—"

'Tis so long since—Hold me, sweet elf.

He shuddered when she wound her arm around his waist and pressed her body full against his. The hard ridge of male flesh nuzzling into her belly should have frightened her, but a cry of pleasure broke from her lips instead. She tasted tears at the corners of her mouth and burrowed her face into the smooth fabric of his tunic. He clasped her close, one hand splayed at the small of her back and the other holding her head to his shoulder. Anne took advantage of having both hands free and laid her palms upon his back, holding him close. She felt his cheek on top of her head, and the tremor quaking through him shook within her as well.

Then he kissed her hair.

"Forgive me," he whispered huskily.

Anne tightened her embrace, knowing he would pull away and dreading it. She shook her head when he grasped her shoulders and eased her from him. Anne clung to his tunic sleeves. He could not let her go. She would not let him.

"I want you. If I do not let you go now, I will surely—" He shook his head and firmed his grip upon her shoulders. " 'Tis not right."

"Of course, *my lord.*" Anne heard a terrible laugh and realized it was her own. She let her hands fall limp. Her cheeks felt both hot from her yearning and cool from her tears that now fell unchecked. "You must not dally with a village girl."

He clapped her head between his palms and snarled,

"Never, *never* let me hear those words again."

" 'Tis what I am."

"You are my lady," he whispered, kissing her brow. Anne felt his chest heave against hers and heard his breath catch in what sounded like a sob. "God help us both, you are mine."

He took her by her shoulders once more and turned her from him. One arm around her, he pulled her back to him. She felt his length still rigid against her and she quivered. His hands caressed her just below the swell of her breasts, and Anne heard his words whisper deep in her ear.

"Say my name. I want to hear it from your lips."

"Galen." She could barely form the word. "Lord Galen."

"Say your own name."

She frowned, baffled. "Anne."

"Nay." He kissed her ear, making her shiver with delight. "Your name is Lady Anne. Always remember."

He gave her a small nudge toward the cottage, and Anne was free. She waited a heartbeat, listened for another word, another sound. When she heard none, Anne turned and stepped back toward the shadows.

Galen had vanished.

Many creatures prowled the night, both predator and prey.

Coltrane hung back, cloaked within the shadows of the forest, and watched a small creature step into the path, one foot timidly before the other. Long ears rose and turned, straining to hear. No sound. Not even a rustle of leaves rubbing against each other. Still wary, the little creature emerged from cover.

Red-gold streaked from a tangle of vines. A snarl. A squeak. Thrashing. And then stillness once more.

Coltrane waited until the fox began to feed upon the rabbit before he stepped into the path himself. The fox snarled at the sight of man and fled. Satisfaction flowed warmly through Coltrane's veins as he looked down at the rabbit's carcass, its throat laid open by the fox's sharp teeth.

Aye, though the prey went in fear of the predator, the predator must go in fear, too.

Of the master.

He kicked the bloody lump of flesh and fur into the bracken and continued down the path.

He was the master. He ruled over all—wiser, quicker, stronger. None could challenge him. His eyes narrowed upon the craggy expanse of stone walls gleaming in the moonlight just beyond the wood. And any that dared must be punished.

Galen Tarrant had dared to defy him. Ten years had passed, but Coltrane had not forgotten. Or forgiven. For the sake of an infidel, Tarrant had challenged him. An infidel! For a Moslem bitch, Tarrant had called *him* a monster. Coltrane smiled, his hand creeping to the dagger sheathed at his belt.

He had proved then to Tarrant just who the real monster was, ensuring that Tarrant would remember every time he looked in a mirror.

But it seemed the lesson of obedience to the master's will had not gone deep enough. Tarrant had dared to defy him again, so the lesson must be carved deeper, all the way to the bone. All the way to the soul.

Perhaps, then, Coltrane's hunger would be sated at last.

Coltrane clenched his jaw. He would feed the hunger, let it gorge upon Tarrant's agony. Aye, and soon.

He chose a good spot just within the shelter of the trees, a place where he could see all that moved but where he remained hidden. He waited. The moon had risen high and lit the path for another, moving furtively closer. Remembering the fox and the rabbit, Coltrane smiled again.

"You are late," he murmured from the shadows.

The other gasped. "I came as soon as I could."

"Come closer. Here, within the trees. There are shadows enough to hide us."

Coltrane could smell the other's fear. Good. If he was feared, he would not be betrayed. Metal hissed against leather when his servant came within reach.

"No one saw you?"

"No one." The words came out oddly strangled, considering there was no hold upon the throat. No hold, save the dagger Coltrane held there. "I-I swear, my lord."

"And no one will hear of this night? Or anything said?"

"None, my lord." The voice broke. "Please, master . . . Why kill your humble servant? Your cause is my own."

Coltrane withdrew the dagger. "Serve me well, and you will be richly rewarded."

"My reward is seeing justice done. I desire no other."

"Aye, Tarrant has much to answer for. We'll see him on his knees, begging our forgiveness, before we are done." Coltrane smiled, already savoring the prospect. "Where is he?"

"I know not for sure. He keeps much to himself, but most likely, he has gone to the girl."

"Ah, the girl. Lovely creature, so I am told."

"You know of her?"

"I know many things." Coltrane pondered this development. "So, he fancies the little tart, does he?"

"Aye, and with good reason. You cannot have seen her yet, or you would know."

"How much does he fancy her, do you think?"

" 'Tis strange, for he rarely speaks of her, but I think she has hooked him deep. 'Tis disgusting."

"Why?"

"A creature like that? And such a lovely young lass? You know. You've seen him. 'Tis unnatural."

Aye, Coltrane had seen Tarrant. Or what remained of him. His servant was right. It would be unnatural. Coltrane smiled. Still, the unnatural had its own special pleasures. That Tarrant fancied the girl could prove useful.

"Has she seen him?"

His servant hesitated. "I think not."

The silence stretched. "Do you think he loves her?"

"Perhaps."

"Good. If he does, so be it. If not, he is fond of her. 'Twill serve just as well."

"You—She'll not be harmed?"

He looked sharply at the shadowy figure and then smiled almost gently. "Why should I harm an innocent? If innocent she proves to be. Like you, I seek only justice."

"But if she is no innocent? If he has—"

"Rest easy." Coltrane laid a hand upon his servant's shoulder. "Whatever she may be, she has done me no wrong. There is no reason, then, to harm her. In fact, we can avenge her lost virtue. For as you say, what young girl would willingly yield to the rutting of such a beast?"

His servant nodded. "Just so, my lord."

"You have done well, very well." He clapped his servant on the back. "But now, I must ponder upon all the paths open to us. We must not act rashly."

"You will do what must be done, my lord. Justice will be served at long last."

"Go now. Return to your post. Keep eyes and ears open."

"You'll send for me?"

"Never fear. I'll not deny your right to justice."

Coltrane watched his servant slink away into the night and chuckled. How curious fate was. When his bumbling hirelings returned, he had feared his plans were ruined before he could even set them in motion. Instead, he found he owed them thanks. They had, in their idiocy, handed him the perfect dagger to twist between Tarrant's ribs. Aye, it was truly curious how fate served both justice and revenge.

Justice, Coltrane cared little for. But revenge?

His revenge would be complete at last.

Chapter Six

Over the next few days, the carpenter's cottage proved an irresistible lure to the folk of Thornbury. Anne had expected it, but nothing like what had happened. At least, she consoled herself, her misadventure provided a windfall of trade for her father, for many seized upon the purchase of a new table or bench as an excuse to stop by.

"The old chest has worn so," an old woman was saying. "Daniel is a fine craftsman. His work will wear better, no doubt. And how are you faring, Anne?"

If Anne gritted her teeth more than smiled, old Dame Julia seemed not to notice. "Well enough."

" 'Tis a close call you had, child." The old woman patted Anne's hand, clenched into a fist upon the gatepost. Her beady eyes glittered with relish. "They say Lord Galen himself rode to your rescue."

"Aye, so he did." Anne tugged against the woman's surprisingly strong grip.

" 'Tis well he did his duty that much, at least." Dame Julia sniffed. "And here that seneschal of his had boasted how they'd cleaned the shire of such filth. Well, it just proves how pride goes before a fall."

Anne bit her tongue. If she had learned anything, she had learned to guard her words, but after a week of it, her patience was sorely strained.

"I hear no one knows who those outlaws were." Dame Julia leaned close and narrowed her eyes. " 'Twould not surprise me, lass, if they proved Lord Galen's own. Not a man of his comes from around here, and you cannot be too wary of strangers."

"I am sure they were just wanderers," Anne said cautiously.

"Well, I still say Lord Galen would do well to question what breed of men he employs."

"No doubt Lord Galen is very concerned about the safety of the village and is careful in choosing his men-at-arms."

"Humph." The old woman peered down her nose. "Not so concerned that he bothered himself with it before. He did not even have the decency to return when his father was laid to rest, and Lord Geoffery such a fine man, too."

Ire burned Anne's cheeks. "He had his reasons, no doubt."

"Reason enough, I should think." Dame Julia lowered her voice to a hiss. "He hated his father. Oh, the whole village knew it. Some even say Lord Geoffery banished the boy for his defiance. 'Tis certainly true Lord Galen waited until the old man no longer stood in his way before returning."

"There would have been documents, a will—"

"Bah! Wills can be burned, lass, and with his father no longer here, who would be the wiser?" The old woman darted a glance over her shoulder, then leaned close again. "In fact, I've often wondered about Lord Geoffery's death. A strong man, he was, despite his age. Lord Galen crept back stealthily enough. Who is to say he did not creep back before?"

"You—" Anne's throat cramped with outrage. "You are not seriously suggesting—"

"I suggest only that you guard yourself, child." Dame Julia's old eyes gleamed. " 'Twould not do to have your name coupled with such a man. Why, folk might start wondering."

Anne's jaw dropped.

"A handsome one, Lord Galen was. I'll say that for him. Aye, handsome as sin." The old woman smiled slyly. "He always had a way about him, even as a lad. A young girl like you might prove no match for such temptation. And you know how people are. 'Twould be a shame for talk to get around. Especially if it proved untrue."

"Please, I will fetch my father for you."

Anne twisted from Dame Julia's grasp and turned away in a horrified daze. Dear God. She knew the village was talking, but she never imagined—

Somehow, she kept herself from running to the woodshed and stumbled inside. In an instant, her father had her in his arms, his face lined with concern.

"Anne, what is it? What has you in such a state?"

"Oh, Papa." Anne laughed and cried at the same time. "I do not know what—"

"Hush, my dove," Daniel commanded gently. "Calm yourself."

Anne reached deep and found control from somewhere. "Dame Julia is here, about a new chest."

His smile held a wealth of understanding. "I see. I'll speak with her." He cupped her cheeks in his hands and kissed her brow. "And then I have an errand I must attend to."

"An errand?" Anne frowned, bemused.

"Oh, just a small matter I must see to, nothing to worry over. I should not be long."

The bell tolled for Matins, marking the midnight hour.

"I am here, as you asked."

The voice startled Daniel. He narrowed his eyes and peered into the shadows of the forest.

" 'Tis you who set the time and place, my lord," Daniel replied. "I would have had us meet face-to-face in the light of day, rather than in the dark of night."

"You fear the forest at night?"

Daniel snorted. "I have lived close to the wood all my life, my lord. It holds no fear for me. Rather I would have wished us to meet for the world to see. Not in secret."

Silence stretched, and then the voice said, "Your point is well taken."

"Can I not see you? 'Tis difficult, talking to a man hidden. I almost feel as if I am talking to a tree or a rock."

The other man chuckled. "Very well, but you will remain where you are. Make no move closer."

"As you wish, my lord."

Daniel saw a tall form emerge from shadows, garbed in black from the cowl pulled over his head to his boots. So, this was Galen Tarrant, Lord of Rosethorn. He had changed little over the years—a bit taller, perhaps, wider through the shoulders. His legs were long and appeared well-formed. A trim man. Nay, Daniel corrected. A hard one. Time had taken a sapling of a boy and made him an oak of a warrior. Daniel frowned.

"What is it?" his lord asked.

Daniel's frown cleared. "Nothing, my lord. 'Tis just, from all the talk, I suppose I expected some sort of deformity. But you appear quite normal."

His frankness shocked a laugh from Lord Galen.

Daniel smiled wryly. "You should hear the tales."

"I can imagine," Lord Galen agreed, amused. "As I said, I am here. What did you wish to speak of, that you could not say through my seneschal?"

"I think you know, my lord."

"Anne."

Lord Galen's voice caressed the name. The fact did not escape her father's notice, and a curious relief eased some of the tension in Daniel's shoulders. He heard fondness, and something else. Something Daniel heard in his own voice when he spoke of his own beloved, though parted from her for years.

But he said only, "Aye, I wish to speak of Anne."

The hooded head bowed, and a booted toe scuffed at the leaves. "She is well?"

"Nay."

The head shot up. "What is wrong? Has she taken fever again?" He clenched his hands into fists. "I knew I should not have let her leave so soon. She needed more rest. She—''

''My lord.'' Daniel tried the tone he used on his children, deep and commanding as only a father's could be. ''My lord!''

''Dammit, man, tell me! What is wrong with her?''

''Her body is well enough. 'Tis her spirit that ails.''

Daniel could all but see the perplexed frown. ''I do not understand.''

Daniel's heart went out to the man. To be so in love and be so blind to it. His heart went out to his daughter, too. A noble's love was fraught with peril for a village girl.

''She is a simple girl, my lord,'' he began slowly. ''Not foolish. Anne is quite wise, far beyond her years, but not of the world. I fear, however, she is learning quickly. And in the hardest possible way.''

''Explain.''

''You are a man experienced in the world, a man of power and wealth. You can choose to ignore what folk say, the talk they spread.'' Daniel shook his head. ''But my daughter has no such choice, my lord. When her name is slurred, when insults are flung at her, she has no shield against them. True or not, they strike at the very heart of her.''

''What insults?'' his lord growled. ''What slurs?''

''You may hide yourself within your castle, my lord, but you are not deaf. You know as well as I what the village says of her. They whisper that you kept her locked in a chamber until she yielded to you.'' The hooded head shook slowly, but Daniel went on mercilessly. ''They say you come to her at night. That she parts her thighs for you and lets you rut upon her.''

Galen shuddered as though Daniel has struck him a blow to the chest. He could only draw enough breath to whisper. ''Nay, 'tis not true. Any of it.''

''Do you deny that you spoke with my daughter the night of her return home?'' The carpenter's voice lashed like a whip. ''Do you deny that you came to our cottage, waited for her to be alone, and then lured her to you?''

Galen could not force the lie from his lips.

"Oh, aye, my lord." Daniel's smile mocked him. "I know what is said of me. That I would not see a tree if it were felled upon me. But this is *my* child I speak of, flesh of my own. Do you think I would allow anything—*anything*—to touch her life without paying heed?"

Galen swallowed thickly. "How did you know?"

"I heard your voices. I heard, and I rose to see her walking toward my shed. From how she spoke, I knew who was hidden in the shadows there."

Shame crept through Galen like a serpent. "What did—"

"What did I see and hear, then?" Galen nodded, and Daniel answered flatly, "Nothing. I returned to my bed."

Galen's mind went blank with confusion. "But—"

The carpenter's expression turned to amusement. "My lord, if I thought you would dishonor my daughter, do you seriously believe you would have survived that night? I may not be skilled in wielding a sword, but I was raised a village lad. Village lads learn tricks that lords do not. I knew Anne was safe with you."

Galen snorted. "You have more faith in me than I do."

"Aye, well, I am a bit older than you. I've more practice in judging folk."

"I've not come to your cottage since."

"I know." And it seemed to Galen he pointedly did not ask why. Instead, Daniel heaved a sigh. "But if I know this, so may others."

"What would you have me do?"

"What you do, my lord, is up to you. We both know I am in no position to make demands. You have the power—some might even say the right—to do as you please."

"You are her father." Daniel only nodded, and Galen growled with impatience. "Very well, then, if we were equals?"

"In that case, my lord, I would bless you both and wait for the grandchildren to arrive."

"Bless us? As what? Husband and wife?" Galen felt torn between laughter and anger. "You have no idea who I am, what I am. What sort of man your daughter would have to face.''

''I know enough, my lord.''

''You know nothing,'' Galen snarled. ''Sure of your judgment, are you? Well, let us put it to the test!''

There was a rustle of cloth, a scrape of leather against skin, and then Galen stepped from the shadows. He stopped only when a hand's width separated them. Moonlight slashed across his face. The carpenter flinched. Then he lowered his gaze.

''You've a heavy burden to bear,'' he said quietly.

''And knowing that,'' Galen replied in a rasp, ''do you think I could ask Anne to bear it with me?''

The carpenter said nothing.

Galen swept the cowl back into place. *Damn him.* He turned away and drew a shaky breath. Damn Daniel of Thornbury. Galen had never dared put his desire into words, not even within his own mind. And now, he knew why.

I would bless you both.

As what? Husband and wife?

Galen had known how foolish it was, how impossible. Hearing it said only made it seem more so. He could no more make Anne his wife than he could erase the past. Within his chest, where his heart should have been, a hollow ache throbbed.

''I can do little to stop the talk,'' Galen said huskily. ''I wish I could, for Anne's sake. 'Twill die in time, but I will do what I can to hasten its death.''

''And what of Anne, my lord?'' Daniel asked gently.

Galen flinched. ''I will come to her no more.''

''My lord, she is stronger than—''

''Go. Please.'' Galen heard the carpenter sigh, heard him turn away. ''Daniel?''

''Aye, my lord?''

''You are a good man, a fine father. I wish—'' Galen shook his head. What did it matter what he wished? It could not come true. None of it. ''Thank you for speaking honestly.''

Without permitting another word to pass between them, Galen returned to the shadows.

Anne breathed a sigh of relief as life finally returned to its usual rhythm. In the midst of harvest, Thornbury could not bother about the carpenter's daughter.

Her days were full. Between work and keeping abreast of her siblings' antics, Anne had little time to ponder. If night brought too much quiet for her comfort, she said nothing of it. If she looked too often into the shadows, paused too often thinking she heard a deep voice call her name, Anne took care no one noticed. Or so she thought.

The villagers saw her sitting before the cottage, her sewing forgotten in her lap as she gazed at something they could not see. They shook their heads and said the carpenter's daughter was growing too much like her father.

Daniel gazed at her, watched as her face grew drawn and her eyes glistened. His heart ached for her and for the man he knew she thought of.

Bryan met her occasionally on the road as they went about their different duties. He sighed and wondered how he could have been so wrong, wished he could offer her some word in comfort. But what could he say?

Another watched, hidden from sight, and thought how deliciously the trap would be baited.

The beginning of September saw Anne at the blacksmith's with the finished gown and bliaut. She had done good work and knew it, though she had not found her usual pleasure in making the garments. Truth be told, she did not take much pleasure in anything of late.

" 'Tis a fine fit, mistress," Anselm's wife announced, admiring the flow of the gown over her ample form. "Such lovely needlework, too. Where you come up with all these fancy stitches, I'll never know."

Anne's smile slipped. How could she say that this one came from her memories of intricate squares and spirals woven into a rug that adorned a lord's chamber? "I am glad you like it."

"Aye, 'twill make lovely garments for church." The

woman winked. "Though, to be sure, Father Elias would not approve of us thinking such earthly thoughts at the Lord's office."

"To be sure."

"Well, here is your fee. 'Tis well earned, and no mistake." The coins clinked when Anne tucked them into her basket. She lifted her gaze and found Anselm's wife regarding her critically. Her cheeks warmed with a blush. "You'll stay for a bite before you start home. You look like you've not been eating well, child."

"Thank you, but nay." Anne settled her basket under her arm and tried to keep her smile in place. "I must return to fix supper for Papa and the children."

"Well, see you eat more than a mere crumb yourself." The woman escorted her to the door. Anne caught her sidelong glance. "Strange, is it not, about Lord Galen?"

Frost fingered into Anne's belly. "What about him?"

"You've not heard?" The woman shrugged. "Well, I suppose not. Anselm only heard yesterday. Bryan of Rosethorn sent for him, to look at a horse what was ailing with foot-foul. While he was there, he chanced to ask after his lordship. And what do you think he was told?"

Anne shook her head, dread tightening her throat.

"Lord Galen is gone."

After a moment, Anne discovered that the earth remained beneath her feet, but she found it no easier to breathe. "Gone?"

"Aye, off like a thief in the night. Anselm heard it from a stablehand, who had it from one of the maids, that not even Bryan of Rosethorn knew until he found a message left for him."

"How long ago?"

Anselm's wife shrugged. "About a fortnight or so, Anselm says. They kept it quiet to avoid talk, I imagine. 'Twould not be hard, for Lord Galen never went about to be missed anyway. Anselm says the seneschal will remain at Rosethorn, to oversee the holding until Lord Galen returns." She snorted. "*If* he returns. Mind you, I wish the man no harm, but 'tis just as well if he never does."

"Why?" Anne snapped. "Rosethorn is his home."

The woman scowled. "You need not take that tone with me, child. I should think you'd be just as glad to see the back of him, after what he did to you."

"After what he—" Anne straightened until her spine could straighten no more. She stalked out the door, then whirled about. "Lord Galen did nothing to me. Do you hear? *Nothing!*"

She was beyond tears, beyond rage, as she flew from the yard and down the lane. Once out of sight, Anne stopped and a wrenching, dry sob tore from her throat.

He was gone.

Galen was gone.

And . . . and he had not even said good-bye.

Anne gave a terrible laugh that drifted off into the dusk. Foolish girl! Village girl! What should she have expected?

Well, by God, she was done with it. If he could forget so easily, so could she. Anne adjusted the shawl around her shoulders, gripping it so tightly that her knuckles showed white. Pushing one foot before the other, she continued down the lane. She had acted the fool long enough, eating her heart out over naught but a kiss and a whisper.

More than just a kiss, her memory taunted.

Sweet lord, you are so soft . . . I want you so much.

More than just a whisper.

Lady Anne . . . always remember.

Anne shook her head so briskly, her braid swung to lie over her shoulder. She would not relive it all again. As of this moment, it was finished. Over.

"We seem to have done this before, Lady Anne."

Anne stumbled to a halt. Her heart hammered so hard she thought it would burst from her chest. She did not dare turn around. If she did, she would look at him, and one look would shatter her. She started walking again. The thud of hooves on the lane echoed loudly in her ears.

"Forgotten your name so soon?"

Anne gritted her teeth and kept walking. "Go away."

"What? No kick at my horse? No stone thrown at the outlaw sneaking up behind you?"

The teasing words almost fooled her, but Anne heard the pain beneath the surface. Her heart felt close to breaking. "Leave me alone."

"Anne, please."

A command she could have ignored. A shout would have made her shrug. But that whispered plea she had no shield against. Anne stood, as still as stone, in the middle of the lane. Her basket dropped from her fingers, and she buried her face in her hands. As though from far away, she heard the creak of his saddle as he dismounted.

He was tall. She knew because she felt his breath brush the crown of her head. He had large hands and long, sinewy fingers. They swallowed her shoulders when he laid them there. He smelled of trees and fresh, clean air.

"Nay, wood elf," Galen whispered. "No tears."

"Why do you plague me so?" she demanded brokenly. "Just when I am ready to forget, you are there again, tormenting me."

"Is that what I bring you, Anne? Naught but torment?"

"You make me want." She swallowed her tears and clenched her fists. "You make me stop when I walk in the wood because I think I hear your step. I look twice at every shadow, thinking I see you there." She shrugged off his hands and strode down the lane. "For the love of God, leave me alone!"

"Anne!" She heard the creak of his saddle, then his horse snorted. "Anne, wait!"

Anne stumbled through the deepening dusk, her step quickening until she ran. She gave an enraged shriek when he all but fell atop her and dragged her to the ground. She did not go down tamely, twisting wildly for escape.

"Calm down!"

He had her beaten, holding her back against his chest, his arms looped over hers. Anne bucked against him, but it was no use. Galen was too strong.

"Calm down," he repeated, softer this time. "You'll hurt yourself."

"I'll hurt you, you craven worm!"

"I am sorry," he whispered, close to her ear.

All the fight went out of her, and a sob erupted from Anne's throat. "You hurt me. They said you left, and you did not even say good-bye."

"I never meant to hurt you. Never that. I only want you to be happy, and you cannot be with me. I would bring you only sorrow." Galen barked a travesty of a laugh. "But I could not stay away."

"Oh, Galen." Anne sagged in his arms, and the embrace, which had begun in confining her, turned comforting. She rested her head on his shoulder and felt his strength surround her. "Is whatever sorrow you could bring me worse than what I've known these past weeks?"

"Sweet elf." He kissed her cheek. "If you only knew."

"Then tell me." She tried to turn to him, but he held her still. "At least let me try to understand."

His lips moved against the skin just below her ear. Anne heard him start to speak, then suddenly, Galen went very still.

"Galen, what—"

"Silence!"

Anne flinched, but she obeyed. His arms trembled, not in fear, but in readiness for battle. She searched the trees but saw nothing. Her ears strained to listen above the thud of her heart, to hear whatever he heard. She heard nothing but the crackling sound of—

"Fire!" She breathed the word in horror.

"Come on!"

Galen lifted her, all but flung her into the saddle of his mount. Swinging up behind her, he set heels to the beast's flanks. The further they careened down the lane, the stronger the odor of smoke became. Anne saw others from the village racing through the trees, to where a roar grew louder and louder.

"The carpenter's cottage!" someone shouted. " 'Tis ablaze!"

A cry locked in Anne's throat as they rounded the last bend, and she saw the swirling black smoke. It was bad at first sight, but a second look drew a hysterical laugh of relief from her. Only the shed had gone up in flames. The cottage was still safe.

The horse balked at going closer, rolling its eyes with terror. Galen dismounted and pulled Anne from the saddle. The last thing he wanted was the beast to take fright and throw her.

"Stay here."

He tugged his cowl full forward and started to the cottage.

"Galen!" Bryan pounded toward him, followed by a troop of Rosethorn's men. "We saw the smoke and came running. But what are you—"

"I'll explain later," Galen snapped. "Start a water line. The brook is not far. Get as many as you can onto it." Bryan nodded and darted away. Galen whirled to where a knot of villagers hung back. "You! Start beating the blaze. Keep it from the cottage."

They stood, gaping at him.

"Now!" he roared, and every man of them leaped into action.

Galen turned full around, looking for Anne, and his heart stopped. Gone! Sweet Lord, she was gone!

In the milling mass of people, he despaired of finding her. Finally, he did. She darted toward the shed's door, but the heat drove her back. He was on her in a thrice.

"Nay, Galen, nay!" Anne pulled against his grasp. "My father, the children! I cannot find them!"

"Stay back, damn you. I'll find them."

They were both surging for the door, Galen scrambling to catch Anne, when a small figure staggered from within the smoke.

"Derek!" Anne cried as he fell into her arms.

" 'Twas bad men," he sobbed into her shoulder. "Bad men came. Papa told us to hide in the loft."

"Where is your father, boy?" Galen knelt by them and spoke as gently as he could. "Where are he and your sister?"

The little boy trembled. "Will you find my papa?"

"Aye." Galen stroked the lad's sooty brow. "I swear."

"Papa said to hide. Me and Lyssa . . . We hid under the

planks. Papa went down. The bad men called him names."

"Is he in the shed?"

Derek nodded and buried his face against Anne again. She huddled over her brother. "Find them, Galen, please."

Galen straightened and started to the shed just as Bryan came running.

"The line is going," he reported. "We should stop it from reaching the cottage, but God's truth, Galen, the shed is lost."

"Get a brychan. Soak it well. I am going inside."

Bryan's eyes rounded. "Are you mad?"

"Anne's father and sister are in that shed."

"Then they are lost as well."

"Dead or alive," Galen snarled, "she'll have more of them than charred husks."

Bryan cursed, then did as commanded. He returned with not one, but two soaked brychans. Flinging one at his lord, he wrapped the other around his own head and shoulders.

"Never think you are going in there."

"Try and stop me." Bryan flashed a grin. "You've dared greater for me."

Galen started to refuse, then returned the grin. He shrouded himself within the dripping folds. "Stay close. I'll not bother to drag your sorry carcass out, if you go down."

They dove within the shed.

Fire licked along the walls, spread across the roof. Sparks rained down, sizzling on the wet brychans. What breath the smoke did not steal from Galen, the searing heat did. He pressed a fold over his nose and mouth.

They found Daniel almost immediately.

Bryan shook his head, telling Galen all he needed to know.

He gestured for Bryan to drag the man clear. Bryan grabbed his arm, and Galen shook him off. They had yet to find the little girl. He paused only long enough to ensure that Bryan obeyed.

He almost stepped on her.

She lay crumpled at the foot of the ladder leading to shed's loft. How she had managed to get that far, Galen had no idea. He had been within mere minutes and was already close to collapse. And she was such a tiny thing.

At his touch, her body gave a jerk, and she rolled onto her back. Her high, keening wail nearly made him weep in relief. He lifted her in his arms.

Galen wrapped her in the brychan with him, cradling her close. God's blood, he could not see a damn thing. Ominous creaking from above told him time was short. Galen ducked his head and ran, praying he was headed in the right direction.

He ran until he no longer felt the flames licking at him and fell to his knees. The air outside was nearly as filthy as inside, but it felt fresh and clean in Galen's starved lungs.

Bryan whipped the scorched brychan from his head and shoulders. Galen heard the child retch and felt her little body wracked by coughing. He hugged her tightly and knew the worst was over when she began crying in earnest. Her throat would be raw, and it would be days before she regained her proper breath, but she was alive.

"Alive." His own chest convulsed with coughing. "Tell Anne . . . child is safe."

Bryan might have sobbed his thanks to God. Galen could not be sure. Certainly, thanks were due. His own prayer ended on a cough and a strangled laugh as he rocked the sobbing child in the curve of his body.

"Hush, little lass," he crooned. "Hush, now. 'Tis all over. You are safe and sound."

"Anne . . ." The child squirmed weakly.

"Aye, sweetling, Anne is coming."

She stiffened and pressed away from him. Her eyes, Galen saw, were as deep a blue as her sister's. Large and glazed, they searched his face, blinked and widened even more. Galen's heart thudded to a halt, then slammed back to life again. Those eyes devoured every detail. Her pale lips quivered and parted.

The child clawed at his chest and screamed.

Chapter Seven

"Monster . . . monster . . ."

Lyssa kept repeating the word, and though she no longer screamed, her broken whisper was somehow worse. Seated not far from the cottage clearing, Anne rocked her little sister in her arms and shivered. All Lyssa's terror seethed in that single word, and each time it seeped from her sister's pale lips, Anne's soul shrank a little more.

Dead. Her father was dead.

Anne squeezed her eyes closed. Bryan was mistaken. He had been too hasty. Papa was unconscious, dazed by smoke and heat. At any moment, he would wake up. A bit battered. A bit bruised. But not dead. Papa was not dead.

And yet, Anne knew that he was.

Resting her cheek upon her sister's hair, Anne clenched her jaw until it ached. Her sight wavered. Her chest burned. But she refused to blink, did not dare draw a breath. Nothing could loosen the knot coiled within her throat. Nothing could let the wail swelling behind it escape. She could not give way. She had to be strong. She simply had to be.

The moment passed. The horrible ache in her throat eased, and at last, she could swallow the grief and breathe again.

"Monster . . . monster . . ."

Anne cuddled Lyssa closer, assuring her sister that no monster could harm her. The chant finally ended, not because Lyssa was convinced, but because she had chanted herself to sleep.

"How is she?"

Anne's heart skipped at the voice, rough from smoke and shouting. Then her heart settled, for the voice did not belong to the man she wished for.

Bryan, his face haggard and smudged with soot, stood over her. By the eerie glow of the dying fire, he did look monstrous. And Galen had been inside the burning shed longer.

"Asleep now." Her eyes stung from the smoke, which made her blink so hard. "I think she'll be fine, once she rests."

Bryan crouched beside her and smoothed a dark curl of Lyssa's hair from her cheek. His fingers brushed the sleeve of the little girl's gown and lingered upon the scorches marring the fabric. Perhaps she imagined his hand trembled.

"Thank God Galen found her in time."

His heartfelt murmur raked at Anne. She swallowed hard. "Where is he? I've not seen him since—"

Since Bryan had led her to where her sister had screamed and clawed for freedom from Galen's embrace. Galen had released the child and, without so much as a word, disappeared into the shadows.

Monster . . . monster . . .

A chill crawled down Anne's spine, and she kissed Lyssa's brow. Later, she would let herself wonder. Later. Not now.

Bryan shifted and, so it seemed to Anne, pointedly did not answer her question. Instead, he cleared his throat. "About your father . . ."

"Please." Anne grasped his hand. "You did what you could. No one could ask for more. And you've shown us much kindness. I know the villagers only want to help, but I . . . I appreciate the solitude."

A trio of Rosethorn's men stood guard over them, sheltering her and her brother and sister from the prying eyes of well-meaning neighbors. Later, she would have to face the world, but until then, Bryan and his men kept everyone away.

He covered her hand with his own and squeezed. Then, as though realizing what he was doing, Bryan dropped her hand, and his expression hardened.

"I could do no other."

Anne hid her bewildered frown by lowering her brow to her sister's. A headache pinched behind her eyes, and Anne suddenly felt weary. Rubbing her brow with the heel of her hand, she waited for the tiredness to ebb. When it lingered, she shrugged it off. Later. She would surrender to it later. But now she had her family to look after. What remained of it.

It was easier to master the dull throb of grief this time, easier to soothe her stinging eyes with a few blinks. Aye, it would become easier. All she needed was time.

Her gaze settled upon her brother. Derek huddled beside her, his eyes as terrified as Lyssa's had been. He had not spoken since they had first found him. When she told him of their father's death, Derek had given only a wooden nod. Anne worried about that almost more than about her sister. She brushed her hand over his hair, but still he sat staring at nothing.

"Anne?"

She found Father Elias standing just beyond the men on guard. The town's little priest darted anxious glances from her to Bryan and back again before stepping forward.

"Your father—" He tucked fidgety hands into the sleeves of his habit. "He is ready for you to . . . prepare him. If you wish. I have laid him out in the chapel."

Anne closed her eyes. She must prepare her father, care for him this last time. Before she could respond, though, Bryan surged to his feet.

"For the love of God—"

"My lord, please." When Bryan met her gaze, Anne shook her head. " 'Tis my duty. I am his daughter, his eldest child. 'Tis fitting that I tend to him."

"But—"

"You could do me a small service, though," she hastened to forestall him. "The children. If you could find someone to watch them until I return? I would be most grateful."

He looked as though he meant to argue; then his mouth flattened into a line as tight as his voice. "Of course."

Fearing she had angered him with her request, Anne almost withdrew it, but what choice did she have? She could not take Derek and Lyssa with her, and strangely enough, Bryan was the only one present she trusted them with. Whatever ill he thought of her, Anne knew he would die himself before allowing any harm to befall her siblings.

She gathered Lyssa more securely in her arms to rise, then her breath caught in her chest as Bryan bent and lifted the child from her embrace. He held the little girl awkwardly, tucking her head into the crook of his shoulder. Lyssa stirred, then the child quieted with a sigh as Bryan rubbed her back. Dumbfounded, Anne stood and went to lift Derek.

"Take the boy, Marcus."

As the guard came forward, Anne's heart gave an odd thump at the voice she so longed to hear, and she twisted around. He seemed more shadow than man within the shroud of trees.

"Galen." She started to him, but something in his stance stopped her. It was as if he were braced for an attack. "Galen?"

"Go." His head nodded to the priest waiting for her and his voice softened. "Tend to your father. We'll see that the children are cared for."

Not until Father Elias touched her arm could Anne move, and as he led her away, she could not resist the urge to look back.

The men of the village lingered, staring at the burnt remains of the woodshed and muttering among themselves. But as Galen emerged from the forest, all fell into silence. Galen's step slowed, and he halted.

From habit, he started to lift his hand to ensure the cowl concealed his face, then stopped himself and curled his fingers into a fist at his side. The damn thing hid him well enough. No lantern, no torch could betray him.

Bryan and Marcus halted at his side, and he felt his seneschal's shoulder brush his own. "Galen?"

"Take the children inside."

Bryan hesitated, then obeyed. The small group parted for him and Marcus. Once they were within the cottage, though, the villagers closed ranks once more. Galen had faced battles with fewer qualms than he did the handful of somber men before him. His legs felt stiff as he stepped forward.

One man, a burly fellow with a fierce scowl upon his face, stepped forward as well. He gave a shallow nod of his head. "My lord."

Galen searched his memory, trying to match the face with a name. "Anselm, is it not? The blacksmith?"

"Aye, my lord."

Damn. The man was not making this easier. Galen swept his gaze past the others. None of them looked agreeable.

" 'Tis a shame, what happened here, my lord." Anselm narrowed his eyes, and Galen could all but feel that gaze search for his face. Again, he resisted the urge to tug at the cowl. "Aye, a damn shame."

So, Galen thought with an inward grimace, word had already spread. They were no fools. They knew. This fire and the carpenter's death were no accident. Galen knew that as surely as he knew his own name. The back of a man's skull would not be crushed, as Daniel's had been, but with purpose. The only questions were who and why.

"Did you, any of you, see or hear aught amiss before the hue and cry went up?" he asked, pitching his voice to carry.

Only the blacksmith replied. "Nay, my lord."

Galen matched the man's stony tone. "You are certain?"

"Aye, my lord." Anselm thrust out his chin. "The only thing of note to happen of late is that you took off for parts and reason unknown. It was today that you returned, was it?"

None but a fool could miss the insinuation. Galen was not a fool. "Aye."

The silence stretched taut before Anselm spoke again. "Reckon outlaws done this, do you?"

"Until I have proof otherwise."

"And you'll be looking for that proof?"

Galen nodded, and hidden within the cowl, he frowned. By rights, he could have this man flayed alive for daring to question him. Anselm no doubt knew that as well, and that made his boldness intriguing.

"And I expect everyone in the village to render whatever aid is required," Galen said silkily.

Anselm jerked his head in a nod. "Reckon we'll do what we can, my lord."

"Then, God willing, we'll bring those responsible for this outrage to justice."

"Aye," Anselm agreed in a rumble. "God willing."

"You've families to see to." Galen kept his tone even, but the command was clear. "There is no more that can be done here tonight."

Anselm thrust out his chin once more. "Mistress Anne—"

"Will be taken care of," Galen finished.

No one moved as the two men measured each other. Galen wondered how long they might have stood there, neither flinching from the other, had Bryan not broken in.

"You heard his lordship." The villagers turned at the seneschal's voice. Galen smiled. Bryan stood in the doorway, the little girl still asleep, cuddled in his arms, but his expression was far from warm. "Return to your homes."

They grumbled, but they obeyed. Anselm nodded gravely to Galen, who nodded in return, and followed the others. Only when they were gone did Galen allow himself to take a deep breath and unclench his fists. He approached Bryan.

"That went better than I expected." Galen sighed.

His friend shook his head in wonder. "They cannot believe you had naught to do with this."

Galen snorted. "Oh, they believe it."

"But why?"

"They are frightened, Bryan. One of their own has been struck down, and they are searching for a target to aim their fear at." He shrugged and this time did not stop himself from tugging at the cowl. "I happen to be the most fearsome person available."

Bryan only shook his head again and moved aside to let Galen enter the cottage. The soldier, Marcus, had sat the boy on the table and was now breathing life into the embers glowing in the hearth. As the flames flickered higher, light spread through the cottage.

By it, Galen saw a snug little home. Benches were tucked under the table, and a tangle of wildflowers peeped over the lip of an earthen jug in its center. He fingered one of the petals and thought of Anne.

An alcove held a narrow cot, and a set of rough-hewn steps led to a loft low enough for Galen to see two others. An opening in the wall close by, he discovered, led to a small room. He found another narrow bed and the trappings of a feminine presence—comb upon the small chest, a little basket of ribbons near it, and a mirror no larger than the palm of his hand. Simple treasures, and yet treasures all the same. Anne slept here, while the young ones no doubt bedded in the loft.

He met Bryan's gaze and gestured to the loft.

"Put the child in her bed," he murmured, and turned to Marcus. "I want you and the others to stand watch over the cottage tonight. Bryan will see that relief is sent in a few hours."

The guard nodded and went outside to stand watch.

"What of the boy?" Bryan asked. He ducked his head as he climbed the steps, to avoid banging it on the low ceiling.

Galen faced the child and prayed the light was dim enough. "I'll see to the boy."

The lad paid him no heed, and though part of Galen found relief in that, another part of him was worried. Derek just sat, his face blank. Galen had seen hardened warriors bear this same look of utter defeat, and he remembered all too well that some never lost it.

They were men, full-grown. This was just a child.

Lifting the boy, Galen stood him on the table and, with gentle hands, tugged tunic and leggings from the lad's slender body. The garments reeked of smoke, and Galen wrinkled his nose. Then he snorted softly. His own clothing was no better.

"We smell like a pair of burnt ropes, boy," he murmured, more to fill the silence than anything else.

Derek shuddered. Horrified, Galen caught the lad as he crumpled and held him as his small form heaved with sobs.

"Burned . . . Papa burned . . ."

"Nay, lad." Galen stroked the boy's back and felt him burrow his face into the folds of the cowl. "Nay."

"Anne said Papa is dead."

Tears. Galen tightened his embrace. The tears were healthy for the lad. " 'Tis so."

"Papa burned." Derek trembled, and his arms crept around Galen's neck. "Only the damned burn. Father Elias said so. He said the damned burn in hellfire."

"Nay, lad, your father did not burn." Galen thought of the man who had sired this child, of his honesty and deep love for all his children. He thought of the man's compassion and wisdom. "Not in this life, or any other."

Galen held the boy, murmuring to him until Derek gave a deep sigh and cuddled contentedly in his arms. When the child went limp, Galen dared a look and smiled. Derek slept, tears still wet upon his cheeks.

Bryan was tucking the covers around the little girl when Galen lowered the boy onto his own cot. Derek grumbled, flopped onto his belly, and stilled again as Galen covered him. The boy's golden hair felt as soft as silk under his hand, and he smoothed a tendril of it from Derek's brow.

"What of Anne, Galen?" Bryan asked softly. "She could be in danger."

Galen frowned. If this was a random attack by outlaws, it was unlikely they would return, especially now that the village was on guard. But was the attack random? Not all that long ago, Anne had been assaulted in the wood. On the surface, it seemed improbable the two incidents were connected.

Though he could not explain it, Galen could not rid himself of the nagging suspicion that they were.

That presented him with the same questions. Who and why?

"Galen?"

Galen shook himself. "I will see to Anne."

"What have you decided to do about her?"

The blunt question made Galen lift a brow. "Do about her?"

"Oh, I know why you left, and 'twas not the reason you gave in your message. Business at another holding, indeed," Bryan growled. "Give me some credit for intelligence. And your return tells me as much. Take the girl and have done with it! You want her. She wants you. A blind man could see it."

"Take her? Where? To Rosethorn? Make her my wife?" Galen laughed without humor. "And have her scream in my face on our wedding night? Nay, I'll not flay myself like that."

"Anne is nothing like—"

"Besides, I thought you were against the notion."

"I changed my mind." Bryan shifted uncomfortably, then he grinned. "You have to admit she has courage, if nothing else. She is the only person I know who dared punch you in the jaw and got away with it."

Galen chuckled. "True."

He sobered and gazed at the children sleeping so soundly. Their father was dead. All they had left was their elder sister, and all she had was herself. Or did she? He could offer her safety, security.

Aye, now that Anne was helpless, now that she had no one to turn to, he could offer himself. Galen sneered. Just how low was he to sink? To wait until a woman had no other alternative.

"I will see to Anne," he said again in a voice as hard as rock. He shot Bryan a look as he headed down the steps. "Stay here until I return."

"Galen—"

But Galen had already left.

* * *

It was an hour past Complin. Father Elias had forgotten the office. Anne wondered if she was the only one who noticed.

She knelt before the bier in the little chapel, her hands clasped as if in prayer. But she did not pray. She stared at the shrouded form of her father, laid upon the bier, and tried to feel something. Anything.

She had loved him, adored him.

She had turned to him for counsel, depended on his wisdom.

She was his child, his eldest child.

She should feel *something.*

But all she felt was a chill that reached to the depths of her soul. She felt empty. And alone. Never in all her life had she felt so utterly alone.

And then, she no longer was.

Anne did not need to hear the sounds—the rustle of cloth, the scrape of booted feet upon the earthen floor—to know it. She did not need the touch of his hands upon her shoulders to tell her he was there. She knew long before.

"I wish you could have known him," she said softly.

Galen said nothing.

"He would have liked you."

"He was a good man."

"Someone struck him, Galen," she said in a thin voice. "I saw the marks. His head—"

"I know." His fingers dug into her flesh.

"Why?" She breathed the word. "Who would kill him?"

His grasp eased, and he stroked her hair. "I wish I knew. But they will pay for it. I promise you that."

Anne drew a deep breath and nodded. "Father Elias will hold the service tomorrow. Papa would not want a delay."

"Then you must respect his wishes."

Anne chewed her lip and wondered how to ask. The words were out before she realized it. "Will you come?"

"Do you want me there?"

"Aye, please."

"Then I will come."

"Thank you for saving Lyssa. And me." She gave a small

laugh. "I never did thank you for that, did I?"

"She is a beautiful child," he murmured. "Very like her sister. I have a weakness for the lovely. Perhaps because I am so unlovely myself."

Anne's breath caught at the reference to the face he had never let her see. "She meant no offense when she—"

" 'Tis no matter."

Anne thought of challenging him, then and there, but let it go. She was so tired.

"Galen?"

He squeezed her shoulders. "I am here, wood elf."

"Why can I not feel anything?"

Anne felt him lift her to her feet. Then she no longer felt the floor under her and settled with a sigh into his arms, letting him tuck her head beneath his chin. She must have drifted into a doze because she remembered nothing of leaving the chapel. The next thing she knew she was home, and Galen was murmuring something to someone. She could not tell who. She felt him draw a breath, and a candle flame died.

He set her on her feet, and Anne realized that she stood in her own tiny room. Only when she felt the night air upon her bare skin did she realize that Galen had removed her gown. She gave a small sound and wrapped her arms about herself.

"Nay, wood elf." His whisper floated to her like a warm breeze. "There is no need for fear. The night hides you from my eyes, and my hands will only hold you. But Anne . . ." His voice roughened as he caught her wrists and pulled them gently from her breasts. "Anne, I do need to hold you."

Anne leaned into him and nodded. "Please."

He gathered her close, and his chest shuddered against hers. His lips moved in her hair, and his hands flattened at the small of her back. Anne quivered when his lips found hers and brushed over them, then floated to the hollow of her throat. Her sigh broke only when he kissed the shallow valley between her breasts, and then the skin of her belly.

Soft and undemanding, his kisses were a curious blend of the sensual and the comforting. And though an odd throb pulsed low within her, Anne felt safe and sheltered.

"Anne." He breathed her name over her flesh. "Sweet wood elf, I would spare you all pain, if I could."

She started to tell him that he need spare her nothing, that she was strong enough to bear what she must, but then his arms went around her. His right cheek pressed into her belly. His hair felt soft and thick, the strands curling faintly around her fingers. He shuddered when her fingertips grazed his left cheek. Anne thought to discover the shape and feel of the other, but held back. He offered her shelter and placed no price on that. She felt it only right to give him what comfort she could with no demand in return.

Galen rose and captured her hands, pressing a kiss into her palms before placing them on his chest. She felt his heart thud unsteadily, and his arms lifted her again.

He laid her on the bed and tucked the covers around her. When he pulled away, Anne cried out in protest and reached for him. He caught her hands.

"You left me," she whispered brokenly. "You left me, and you did not even say good-bye. Please, do not leave me again."

"Nay, wood elf. Never again."

He was a big man, and there was barely room for them both on her narrow bed when he stretched out beside her, lying atop the covers. Galen felt warm and very close, and Anne snuggled closer. His arms were a comforting weight around her.

"Go to sleep," he commanded softly. "Sleep, wood elf."

She smiled dreamily. "You called me Lady Anne before, in the wood."

"So you are."

"I am not a lady," she mumbled. "Not one with a title."

Her body went lax against his, and Galen knew she slept. When she murmured in her sleep and stirred with a whimper, he soothed her until she settled once more.

Not a lady with a title.

Galen stared into the night.

Nay, she was not. Not yet.

* * *

Coltrane stood, obscured by the trees, just at the edge of the wood. He smiled as the brace of men paced back and forth before the cottage. They were such fools. There they were, guarding their lord's precious new whore.

And their lord? Did they guard him as well?

He shivered with delight. Tarrant was no doubt lying atop his whore even now. He would have lied to her, offered comfort so she would permit his rutting. Coltrane breathed deeply. Or perhaps Tarrant need not lie. Perhaps she would part her thighs without the sweet words.

The father was dead, and while those brats had escaped, the blow had still struck deep. When Tarrant realized who had struck the blow, when he realized it was his own past that had made his precious slut the prey, his torment would be merciless.

Coltrane bit his lip to hold back a moan. He tasted blood as he ground his teeth into his lip.

Blood. He must strike again, while the blood poured fresh from Tarrant's wound. Over and over, he would strike, turning Tarrant's misery into agony. Already, Coltrane could imagine the pleading and the screams.

Just like before. Like Acre.

It would be as wonderful as Acre. Nay. He shook his head wildly. It would be better. Acre had not taught the lesson well enough. Tarrant had not learned.

But this time he would.

Coltrane panted and, as silent as a wraith, melted deeper into the forest until he finally stumbled to his knees. He groaned and cursed, whimpered and gritted his teeth. The hunger clawed at him, and he could not appease it. Not yet. His hands gripped his own flesh frantically.

If he could not yet satisfy the hunger, perhaps it would be content with what satisfaction he could offer.

Anne woke with morning filling her senses. She turned within her cocoon of brychans and heard the rustle of the straw mattress under her ear. Enjoying for a final moment the haven of slumber, she finally forced her eyes to open.

Galen was gone.

The spot where he had lain still felt warm from his body, so Anne knew he was not long from her side. Her palm caressed the spot and wished more than just warmth remained. But she understood better and better why he never let her see him by the light of day. As her suspicions crystallized into certainty, Anne also understood it was something they both must face, sooner or later. Still, though Galen was gone, his scent remained, fresh water and pine. And something else.

The fragrance that had filled her senses this morning was, in fact, the faint perfume of a rose. Where Galen's head had rested, she found a single rose. Each thorn had been meticulously trimmed of its barb. A statement?

He had given her an assurance. He could not do away with whatever perils and heartaches lay in store, but he would do all within his power to blunt their sharpness.

It was a late rose, rare in this season, even more so to still be little more than a bud barely opened.

He had given her a warning. Like the flower that must have grown in a secret place to escape discovery until so late, there would be places within himself he would not allow her to touch. She must be content with what he could give.

She accepted the gift with a kiss upon the rosebud. But would she heed the warning?

It was a difficult decision when she did not know exactly what she was deciding. For an instant of wild joy that set her heart a-tremble, Anne thought of his whisper in the night.

Do not leave me again.

Never again.

Lady Anne, he had called her. A sweet little name that held no meaning? Or a hint of his intention? Anne swallowed the emotion swelling in her throat. Foolish village girl! She was hardly the sort of woman a lord sought to make his lady.

But a lord's mistress?

He wanted her.

She did not need the signs explained. Control it ruthlessly he might, but Anne knew passion seethed within Galen. She knew because, when he touched her, when she heard his voice, she felt it seethe within herself.

Anne looked truth in the face. He wanted her. She wanted him. Still, even if there was no shame in their desire, for her to give herself to him was a different matter. To do so, would draw a line between herself and other women that could never be crossed again. The carpenter's daughter, the world would say, had become a whore.

Her chest ached as though she had been pierced by an arrow. Could she make such a sacrifice? Did she dare? Why must she? A tear trickled down her cheek and fell upon the rose. It was a terrible choice to make, but with all the promise and warning Galen's gift offered, Anne found the answers she needed.

She could. She would.

Because she loved him.

Chapter Eight

Anne was not sure which shook her more, the decision she had made or the reason she had made it.

She loved Galen.

She had known it, felt it deep inside, but putting words to the feeling made it somehow more real. Made it swell and coil into a sweet, aching knot in her belly. Anne smiled at how it wrapped around her heart like a warm cloak.

She stood and set the rose upon her clothes chest. Her gown was draped over the foot of the bed, all neat and precise. Her smile deepened as she took it up and donned it. Galen had put it there, of that she had no doubt. Her belongings must seem meager to him, hardly worth taking such pains over, and yet he had handled them with care and respect.

Perhaps—just perhaps—it would not be really so terrible to yield to such a man.

Anne heaved a deep sigh. She could not allow her decision to cast shame upon Derek and Lyssa. But how could she protect them? Take herself away? Send them away to some abbey or convent? Her heart recoiled. They would be cared for in such a place, shielded from the world's condemnation, but they were still so young, and she was all they had left.

All they had left . . .

Anne sank back down upon the bed, pain stabbing her heart. Her father. Dear God, what of her father? Would that gentle man, who had taught her of right and good with his every breath, have understood? Anne shuddered.

"Please . . . please, Papa, try to understand," she whispered.

Anne squared her shoulders. The decision was hers. Once made, she forfeited all right to forgiveness and understanding, in this world or the next.

She left her room. It took a moment for her to believe what she saw.

"Freya!"

The woman turned from stirring a pot hung over the hearth, and her face lit with a smile. "Awake already, child? Heavens, 'tis only just past dawn. The Prime bell has not even rung."

"What are you doing here?"

"Oh, his lordship bade me come. He did not wish you to be alone."

"But the children—"

"Are still asleep, bless their sweet hearts." Anne stood, dazed, as Freya came to her and took her in an embrace. " 'Tis sorry I am, child, more sorry than I can say, for your loss. 'Tis a hard thing, all the harder since you face it with those two little ones to care for. Alone. No kin to aid you."

Her words strangled off, and she dabbed at her eyes.

"Oh, Freya, thank you for your concern, but I'll do well enough. Lyssa, Derek, and I will make a little family all our own." Anne's smile wobbled. "As my papa would have wanted us to."

"Aye, child." Freya shook her finger at Anne's nose. "But never you think you are without friends. Nay, as long as I've breath in my body, you'll have at least one to lend support when you need it."

Anne smiled. "Thank you, Freya."

"And do not be too proud to ask. Oh, I see the signs about you. That chin belongs to no weak-willed woman, and those shoulders think they can bear the world. Perhaps they can, child, but just because you can do a thing does not mean it must be done. Nay, not while you have friends to help you.''

''Oh, Freya.'' Anne laughed and smacked a kiss on the woman's cheek. ''You are the very rose of Rosethorn.''

Freya flushed and waved her off. ''Enough of your wheedling ways. Sit you down and break your fast. His lordship would have my hide if I let you go one moment more without something hot and filling inside you.''

Anne sat at the table, her belly roiling at the mere thought of food, but she knew Freya was right. The last thing she needed was to faint from lack of nourishment. She eyed the daunting portion of porridge before her, but Freya's kindly gaze bore enough steel to squelch a protest. Anne spooned a bite, knowing if she did not, Freya would only do it for her. And make her swallow it, too, by fair means or foul.

''How is Mayde?'' she asked as she ate, remembering all too well the sour housekeeper of Rosethorn.

Freya straightened from her stirring and banged the spoon against the lip of the pot. ''She is Mayde.''

And that, Anne decided with a giggle, said it all.

It was a somber gathering at the cemetery surrounding the little church of Saint Joseph. Anne smiled sadly. Her father used to say he would never live in a village without a church so named. As everyone knew, he would say with a twinkle in his eye, Joseph was the patron saint of carpenters.

Most of Thornbury had turned out, but there were those who were absent. Elbert, the wool merchant, was off on his business. Dame Agnes was too old and infirm to leave her bed. The miller's wife had just delivered her latest child and not had her churching yet, but her husband and eight of their brood represented the family well enough. Anne saw a missing face here and there but knew a reason for each one.

Funerals were something of a social occasion in Thornbury, an opportunity to gather and pass news or gossip. Anne felt no rancor over that. If folk were quick to gather, they were just as quick to voice sorrow over the cause. And if their expressions this morning edged closer to speculation than grief, Anne sadly shrugged it off. After all, who could blame them?

It was not every day they laid to rest one murdered.

It was not every day the Lord of Rosethorn appeared among them.

"At the wish of the carpenter's daughter . . . Stayed at the cottage, he did . . . All night . . . And not a light to be seen . . . Did not leave until just before dawn . . . Aye, a strange man . . . Fearsome with that cowl drawn over his head . . ."

Anne had already heard some of the whispers and knew more would reach her ears before the day was out. Mourn her father they would, but they would wring every bit of information from the whispers, too. Told and retold, heaven only knew how the tales would grow. Her soul shuddered, but not a sign of it showed across her face.

They would remind themselves that not a month since, she had stayed at Rosethorn itself. In the lord's chamber, so it was said. For five days. While no one denied the outlaws had been real, no one took great pains to recall how long she had been ill. Whose word had they, after all? None but her own.

And Galen's.

Anne felt his presence at her back. He had arrived only after everyone was in place. He had not spoken to her or touched her. But she knew he was there. No other man's presence felt like Galen's. But more than anything, she longed to feel his arms around her.

Would he hold her? Here, before all the village?

The perfume of the rose wafted to her from where she had pinned it to her best gown. She knew he would, and she was comforted.

Father Elias spoke the final words, and Anne moved stiffly forward. She knelt by the mound of dirt and scooped up a handful. Derek and Lyssa stood somber-faced on either side of her. Anne poured a share of the soil into their small palms, and together, they bade their father farewell. The dirt cascaded from their hands down upon the coffin within the grave.

One by one, the villagers passed her, patting her hand or shoulder and murmuring their sorrow.

"A fine man . . . Good craftsman . . . Your father loved you all so . . . Gone to join his sweet wife . . . In God's arms . . . You'll tell us if you need aught . . . Bless you, child . . ."

It was over. Anne drew a deep breath. It was over.

She turned and found only Bryan standing behind her amid the milling villagers, his expression enigmatic. Her own must have betrayed her confusion as she darted a glance beyond him, for he stepped forward and spoke for her ears alone.

"He thought it best he not linger."

Anne frowned, and one corner of his mouth lifted.

"Do not worry. He'll not be far."

The other corner of his mouth joined its mate in a smile that was almost friendly. Then he turned and strode away.

Feeling she had somehow been accepted, and confused all the more because of it, Anne took the children by the hand and started for home. It was not quite over, actually. There would be a gathering at the cottage. Folk would drink and eat and remember the carpenter. They would stare at the burnt remains of the shed and demand justice. They would stare at her and whisper among themselves.

Anne knew who the villagers talked of as she moved from group to group. Conversation faltered. Heads nodded politely, but eyes were wary. Some even edged into coldness as they measured her. It was a foretaste of what would come.

Anne knew that, but knowing made it no easier to bear.

Finally, as the sun lowered past midday, and the Nones bell rang, Anne knew she must slip away. Just for a while. Just to clear her head and steady her nerve. She kissed her brother and sister, bade them to mind Freya, and took to the wood. There was always peace among the trees.

And there was Galen.

Seated upon a cushion of leaves, her chin perched on her raised knees, she heard his footsteps behind her.

"Do anything. Say anything," she entreated, then smiled tiredly. "But I swear, if you pat me and tell me what a good girl I am, I'll bite your hand off at the wrist."

Galen chuckled and settled close behind her. "I promise I'll not pat you, but you are a good girl."

Anne's own laugh ended on a sigh. "Would it be horrible to say I am glad 'tis over?"

"Nay, 'twould be human."

"I hope the children do not give Freya too much trouble." She shifted, then stilled when his hands kneaded her shoulders. "I feel guilty, leaving her with them, but I just—I had to get away for a while."

"Freya is a hardy soul. She'll manage."

Anne swallowed with difficulty. "He was my father, Galen. I loved him. Why can I not cry for him?" She did not quite realize her cheeks were wet, and her sight blurred. "Why?"

He pulled her back against his chest and wrapped his arms around her. Anne rested her head in the crook of his shoulder and closed her eyes. Her tears fell quietly, unchecked until they were no more. Still, Galen held her, murmured to her, stroked her hair. She wiped her cheeks with the heel of her hand and felt that terrible ache in her heart ease at last. She looked at where his hands lay over her own, his long fingers entwined with hers, and at his legs, clad in dark leggings and boots, braced on either side of her. Anne nestled in his embrace and let the protection of it seep into her soul.

"Better?" His voice rumbled close to her ear.

She nodded and smiled. "Aye."

He was silent for a long while, and when he spoke at last, he did so slowly. "Anne, we must talk. I wish I could be noble and wait until a more seemly time, but I cannot."

"What do you wish to talk about?" Somehow, though, she knew and braced herself.

"You and I are from different worlds." Her heart gave an odd throb. "Our lives have followed paths so different, they should never have crossed."

"True."

"I am wealthy man. I can offer you much." Everything a mistress could desire, she thought dully. "You would never go unprovided for or unprotected. The children are a matter I've not quite fully figured out, but—"

"They are young, Galen." She had no right to make demands, but on this, Anne would not budge. "I am all they have of what was once our family. I'll not set them aside."

He gave a small start. "Nay, of course not."

"I understand they must know a . . . a decent home." She had to swallow. " 'Twill be difficult, keeping them apart from—I'll find a way. You can trust me on that. I'll do what is right for them."

Galen scowled. "What on earth are you talking about? You think the home I offer would not be decent?"

"Of course not." She stroked her palms along his thighs as if soothing his ruffled pride. " 'Tis just that children are so swift to pick up on things not quite . . . well, you know. Derek and Lyssa would know things were not . . . proper between us."

"Proper!" Galen spat the word. "God above, woman, what do you think I am proposing? To make you my mistress?"

She went as stiff as a board. "Then what *are* you proposing?"

"To make you my wife!" His outrage knew no bounds. "I cannot believe you thought—"

"Your wife!"

Anne sat bolt upright and clouted his chin with the top of her head. Stars danced before his gaze, and Galen bit his tongue. She twisted like a wild thing in his arms.

"Sit still! Sit—" Galen grunted when her elbow jabbed his belly. Torn between laughter and cursing, he tightened his hold. "Sit still!"

"Nay, I'll not marry you! I cannot!"

"Oh, for the love of—" He broke off and took a deep breath, reaching deep to rescue his patience. "Why not?"

" 'Tis impossible!"

"Why?"

"You are a lord, titled and landed." She shrugged and uttered an almost hysterical laugh. "I am naught but a—"

"I swear before God, if you call yourself a village girl, I'll—" Do what? Galen clenched his jaw. He could not harm a hair on her lovely head, and he knew it. "I'll do something."

She stilled and declared furiously, "'Tis what I *am.*"

"You are a lady. You are my lady."

"But—"

"Nothing else matters to me," he said softly. "You were born a lady, whether in a palace or a carpenter's cottage." He tightened his embrace, hoping that if he held her close enough she would not—could not—refuse him. "You are mine, Lady Anne."

She heaved a deep, shaky sigh. "Oh, Galen, how can we wed? We know nothing of each other."

It was true. Dread crawled through his belly. She knew nothing of what manner of creature he was. "We will learn."

She laughed in despair. "I've never even seen your face."

That was the most fearsome thought of all. Galen's arms felt stiff and cramped when he released her. "Then turn around and see."

Anne thought her heart had stopped, and when her chest began to burn, she knew her breathing had. She felt him tense as though bracing for a blow. Finally, she turned.

He had once been handsome, incredibly handsome.

His eyes had once gleamed emerald green. His brows had once been dark and arched. His cheeks had been lean, creased a bit at the corners of his mouth. His lips used to be set in lines as masculine as they were sensual. He had a chin that was once the last word in chins, with a tiny dent right in the center, as though a fingertip had pressed a heartbeat too long when he was a babe. His jaw used to be strong, squared. All was once framed by thick, silky hair that curled just at the collar of his tunic and was as black as soot. Faint strands of silver streaked through it now, shimmered here and there.

Aye, Galen had once had a very handsome face.

He still possessed half of it, the left half.

Anne swallowed and remembered to breathe.

The right side of his face was hidden, from brow to jaw, by a mask. It was secured by bands over his head and covered from his right brow, down the side of his nose, cut away at his mouth to end at his chin. The concealment was complete. There was no slit for his eye. Made of leather, supple and black, it fit over his flesh like a second skin, impervious to expression.

She frowned and tilted her head, considering him.

"Well?" he asked in a hollow tone.

Anne touched his bare cheek and felt it twitch under her fingers. She traced his left brow and then stroked her fingertip along the line of his jaw until the mask thwarted her. The corner of his mouth did not move when she brushed her fingers over it. He was warm, his skin pleasantly rough with stubble. He was . . .

He was Galen.

"So," she murmured, "that is what you look like."

His left eyebrow rose. "No scream? No fit of vapors?"

She shook her head. "Sorry to disappoint you."

His shoulders jerked. Then, a sound rumbled from deep within his broad chest. Anne saw his throat work, as though he tried to swallow without success. His lips twitched, stilled, and then curved as he let the laugh escape.

"You have a dimple," she noted in charmed wonder.

Galen grabbed her close and fell back with her into the leaves, his laughter soaring up to the highest boughs of the trees. He rolled until he had her beneath him and silenced her startled shriek with his lips. She slid her arms around his neck, and he moaned when she pulled him even closer.

Her cheek pressed to his left one, and he breathed in her scent and nuzzled the silky spot just below her ear. Then, bracing upon his elbow, he looked down to find her scowling.

"You've crushed my rose," she informed him.

Galen chuckled, plucked the blossom from her gown and tossed it over his shoulder. "I'll find another."

She gazed up at him, sunlight dappling her golden hair, and tried very hard to look indignant. "Why is it that you always end up rolling me through the leaves?"

"I do not." He kissed her quickly. "Besides, you usually start it."

Her expression sobered, and she stroked her fingers over first his bare cheek, then the mask shielding the other. She started to speak, seemed to think better of it, then finally asked the question he knew would come.

"What happened, Galen?"

He was tempted to tell her, to lay before her everything that had blackened his heart. Not to hurt her. Not to drive her away. Dear God, never that! He was tempted because her expression was so open, she seemed so sure she could understand.

And because he was so tempted, Galen knew he could never tell her. He would take all she offered with shameless greed, but he could not repay her by casting that shadow upon her.

" 'Tis an old story," he said at last, voice roughened. When she started to speak again, he shook his head. "I'll not speak of it."

Galen's heart clenched at the gleam of hurt in her eyes. Then she cupped her palm over his right cheek and nodded. The hurt vanished so swiftly, he almost believed he had imagined it.

He pushed upright, bringing her with him, and settled her upon his lap, facing him. That simple act—looking at Anne looking at him—brought a smile back to his lips. He tugged on her thick braid and shook his head.

"I cannot believe you thought I wanted you as my mistress."

"What could I think? Lords do not wed village—"

"You are determined to push my temper right to the edge." He tipped her chin up and kissed her. "Say your name."

"Anne." He growled at her, and she laughed. "Lady Anne."

"Lady Anne." He brushed his thumb along her jaw. "Look me in the face and tell me you will marry me."

Her eyes shimmered with tears, and a smile glowed upon her face. "I will marry you, Lord Galen."

With her arms around him and her lips moving against his, Galen felt as though he had finally stepped from the shadows into the sun. *Aye,* he thought as her fingers threaded into his hair, *the darkness can never touch me again.*

He crept close, as close as he dared.

There they were. He smiled. How sweet they looked, lying together amid the leaves.

The arrow's shaft made a soft scraping noise as he pulled it from the quiver slung across his back. With quick fingers, he rolled the scrap of vellum around the wood and secured it with twine.

The bow felt right in his hand, perfectly balanced. He ran his finger down the taut string and drew a deep breath to still the flutter of excitement in his belly. The thrill of the hunt, he thought, and smiled again.

He tested the edge of the arrow's head with his thumb, then the point. Satisfied, he fitted the notched end onto the bow and looked again for his target.

The man had risen to his feet and, with her hands clasped in his, pulled the girl up with him. She spoke. Laughter floated through the wood, and he plucked leaves from her hair. Oh, she was a clever creature, spinning her web of soft words and kisses around her lord until he had no chance for escape.

Well, perhaps she would not be so eager to play the whore for him after this.

The archer readied his stance and pulled the bow taut. The shot had to be carefully timed, perfectly aimed. He had only this one chance.

Failure was unacceptable.

''Will you hold still?''

Anne chuckled and wrapped her arms around Galen's waist, pressing as close to him as she could. ''Is this still enough, my lord?''

His smile was slow and wicked. ''Aye, lady.''

His own arms went around her, and he kissed her slowly. Anne gasped as his hands slid down her back and over her hips, bringing them full against his. His hardness nestled into her softness, and their breath mingled into a shared moan. Instinctively, Anne arched in his embrace.

"Galen."

"I want you," he whispered against her lips. Anne felt the roughness of tree bark at her back. "Wood elf, I need you."

His hands traveled up her sides, and Anne could only utter a small sound as his palms cupped her breasts through the coarse fabric of her gown. She shuddered at the gentle tug of his fingers upon her crests and felt them tighten into aching knots. Pleasure seared her veins, coursed to a place deep inside her and melted her.

"Galen, I have never felt—"

"I know." She felt him smile, tasted it. "Neither have I. I've never wanted anyone as I want you. From the moment I first saw you, I longed for you."

"You did?"

"And every moment since."

It came suddenly, a high whine and gust of air that unsettled the wisps of hair that had strayed from her braid. Galen jerked her away from the tree just as Anne heard the hollow *thunk!* Her heart burst with terror, then slammed against her ribs. Her head turned, and she saw the long, slender shaft embedded mere inches from where she had been.

Not a rustle of leaf or snap of twig broke the silence.

Galen snarled an oath and whirled her behind him, both crouching low for cover. Lunging to the tree, he grasped the shaft and yanked it free with a vicious twist of his wrist. He held the thing in his fist so tightly that his knuckles showed white.

"Who would dare?" His question was all the more terrible for its very softness. The visible half of his face twisted with rage. *"Who would dare?"*

Anne blanched when he held up the arrow. Her lips went chill. Her eyes saw only shades of gray. She did not feel her knees buckle, but she felt Galen grasp her close.

"Nay . . ." She gasped and planted her feet firmly under herself. "I'll not faint."

"We must go. Now."

He was as pale as she felt, but his was the pallor of fury. He caught her about the waist and all but dragged her along, not quite running. Anne let him guide her, for her eyes were fastened upon the arrow he still clutched.

"Galen." She dug in her feet. "Galen, wait."

"Nay," he snarled, and pulled at her. "I'll not have you in their sights a moment longer."

"Wait!" Anne grabbed the arrow from him. "Look, here on the shaft. 'Tis a piece of vellum tied there."

With trembling fingers, she untied the string that bound the coil of vellum to the shaft. She unfurled the scrap, no bigger than the palm of her hand, and showed it to him.

"I know those marks." She offered him the message. "'Tis writing. Tell me, what does it say?"

Chapter Nine

Two words were inscribed on the scrap of vellum. Back at her cottage, Galen read them to her in a voice devoid of all emotion.

"Remember Acre."

"Who is Acre?"

Anne twisted and looked up at Galen. Hands braced upon the table on either side of her, he gazed at the message she held. In the muted light of evening through the cottage's open door, the visible half of his face looked as blank as the mask. Even his eyes narrowed to emerald slits, seemed empty. A shiver crept down her spine.

"Galen," she asked again, softly, "who is Acre?"

He straightened, spearing Freya with a look. "Where is Bryan?"

"He said he felt uneasy, my lord. I believe he went to take a look around."

"Uneasy, eh?" Galen slid his gaze to the arrow laid in the center of the table. "No doubt."

"Who is Acre?" Anne repeated, more insistent.

Galen ignored her. "Where are the children?"

"They asked to play with their friends by the castle fairgrounds.'' Freya wrung her hands. ''I saw no reason to say nay.''

''There was none, so far as you knew.'' He turned to the door. ''Marcus! Farrell!''

Footsteps scuffled, and two men looked in. ''My lord?''

''Go to the fairgrounds,'' Galen commanded flatly. ''Fetch the children. Mind you say nothing to alarm them. Tell them—'' He searched for a reason a child would accept. ''Tell them 'tis time to come home because I say so.''

''Aye, my lord!''

Anne huffed. ''Who is Acre?''

''Acre is not a person, child,'' Freya told her, kindly. ''Acre is a place.''

Anne flung up her hands. ''Very well. *Where* is Acre?''

''Galen!'' Bryan stumbled into the doorway. He leaned against it, panting for breath. ''Are you all right?''

''You spoke to Marcus?''

''Aye, but not before I found tracks—and this.''

Something bright flashed through the air. Galen caught the piece and held it up. An amulet, about the size of his fist, glittered with a golden starburst. Not a starburst. He turned it more fully into the light and saw figures engraved in the surface. It depicted rays from twin halos radiating around the Virgin and Christ Child.

''A medallion,'' he murmured. ''Where?''

''Nestled, light as you please, in a clump of brush.''

'' 'Tis Eastern.'' Galen examined the medallion again, turning it over. ''And here, see? The inscription is in Greek, not Latin. The clasp is worn through. It must have come free in the villain's flight. How far?''

''About a mile or so from here, toward Rosethorn. I found two sets of tracks, one full and with purpose, the other dug in at the toe and fleet.''

''Our archer stalked up, and then fled. But he took aim not yards from where Anne and I stood.'' He snatched the missive from Anne's fingers and thrust it at his seneschal. ''And he left us this. Read it.''

Bryan paled. ''Holy—''

''Exactly.''

Anne slapped her palms hard upon the table and bounded to her feet, glaring at them all.

"I swear, if I do not get an answer from someone, I will scream. I will scream very loud. *Where is Acre?*"

Galen stared at her long and hard.

"At the gateway to hell," he finally said quietly.

Brushing past Bryan, he strode out into the coming evening.

"Galen!"

Anne rounded the table and started after him. Bryan caught her arm as she passed. She struggled against his grasp.

"Let him go," he advised stonily.

"Nay!" Anne twisted and pulled, staring at where Galen had vanished. Her sight wavered, but her resolve stood firm. "I must go to him!"

"Trust me, lady." Bryan tugged her closer and slid his arm around her shoulders. "Let him go."

The bleakness in his hazel-green eyes stilled her struggles. He knew, as well as she, that Galen was in pain.

Anne let him guide her back to her place at the table. She sat and stared at the scrap of vellum.

"Tell me," she said at last in a subdued voice. "Please, Bryan, I want to understand."

Bryan said nothing for a long while, moved not a muscle as he gazed at her. Then, as though stepping over some threshold within himself, he nodded to Freya. The woman withdrew, a look of sorrow in her eyes when they darted to Anne.

"Acre lies in the Holy Land," he began as he sat across from her, "about a hundred miles north and east of Jerusalem."

" 'Tis said Galen went on crusade with King Richard."

Bryan nodded. "King Richard led the army that captured Acre. Galen was in the siege and battle."

Anne brushed her fingers over her cheek. " 'Tis where—"

"Nay." Bryan leaned forward, elbows braced upon the table. "Galen, as you know, was the son of a wealthy lord.

His father held not just Rosethorn, but many other holdings as well, as Galen does now."

This Anne knew. Galen's domain was widespread, though he, like his father, had made Rosethorn his home. Foreboding shivered down her spine. If Galen held all this, then she, as his soon-to-be lady, would hold it also. The enormity of what Bryan's statement laid before her made Anne cringe.

One thing at a time, she cautioned herself. She would deal with one thing at a time. She motioned for Bryan to go on.

"Because of that," he said, "and because Richard valued his skill as a warrior, Galen was given command of a regiment. I served under him. We were among the first within the city walls. Attacked from within and without, Acre fell."

He paused, clearly pondering what to say and what not to say. Anne drew a deep breath.

"Tell me all."

He looked at her sharply; then his eyes crinkled at the corners. "You sound like his lady already."

Anne's cheeks warmed, but she said nothing.

"When victory was complete, Richard demanded a ransom for those who had fought against us, but the Sultan, Saladin, could not raise such a sum in the time granted. So Richard commanded that the captives be executed. Over three thousand Moslems were put to the sword. Men, women, and children."

Anne flinched.

"Galen refused to take part or to order any of his men to participate in the"—he snorted—"the massacre. Indeed, he protested to the king, saying what a brutal waste it was. They all but came to blows over it, but Richard was determined to set an example for future foes. Then and there, Galen washed his hands of the whole bloody business and decided to return home. Many who served under him were as sickened as he and we made ready to return with him.

"I had taken the cross because . . . well, never mind why. I was hardly inspired by religious devotion, but I fully believed in the Holy Cause—the liberation of Jerusalem from the infidel. But the massacre at Acre made me wonder just who the infidel truly was. 'Twas such a waste, and it did naught but inflame Moslem hatred. They swore vengeance."

He fell silent, and Anne prompted him gently, "Go on."

"In the midst of all this, there was one of ours, a commander equal to Galen's rank. They disliked each other from the start. Galen discovered this man had looted the home of a wealthy merchant in Acre. That was bad enough, but then he learned the merchant's wife and daughter had been raped and murdered." Bryan rubbed a hand down over his face. Anne noticed that his fingers shook. "I was with him when he went to the house. We had been through hell's own battle, but what I saw there made me—"

He drew a deep breath and cleared his throat. "Galen was enraged. He denounced the man before the king. Looting Richard could have overlooked, and he viewed the execution of prisoners as part of warfare, but even Richard could not condone something as vile as what had been done to those women, an honest wife and an innocent maid." Sarcasm sharpened his smile. " 'Twas not something fitting for a Christian knight. Richard stripped the man of his rank, his titles, and his lands."

"And this man hated Galen for it," Anne murmured.

"As poisonously as ever a man could. The man knew of a band of Moslems who had escaped Acre's fall and took to the wilderness. He must have invented a tale, told them he could place in their hands the commander who led the massacre. For a price."

He swallowed thickly. "We had been only a day or so on the march from Acre. The attack came at night. Those who were not killed were taken into captivity. In prison, most of us were only beaten on occasion, though some faced worse. One man was given to our betrayer as the reward for his *assistance.*"

Anne trembled and whispered, "Galen."

"He was held in the cell next to mine." Bryan's fists clenched. His eyes stared, wide and lost to the past. "And I had to listen. To everything. 'Twas hell to listen to every sound, every scream, every—"

"Bryan, nay!"

Anne clasped her hands over his. After a long moment,

he shuddered and drew a deep breath. He stroked his thumbs over her knuckles.

"How he did it," Bryan went on, "I will never know, but somehow, Galen escaped. Even beaten as he was, he escaped. He managed to free the handful of us who survived, and we made our way out. And home, eventually."

Silence descended over them.

Remember Acre.

Anne understood the message now. It was a horrible taunt. A claim that this creature who despised Galen thought his due had not yet been paid in full.

"Who is he, Bryan?" Anne whispered coldly. "Name the man."

"Coltrane. Philip de Coltrane."

Galen stared into the night, but he saw only the past.

The pain. He could not breathe for the pain. His throat, raw from his own cries, cramped over another scream, dulling it to naught but a thin croak.

"You dare condemn me." The accusation cut through the mist of agony. "Well, by God, you'll carry the sign of your own black heart for all the world to see!"

A blade glinted. And then there was blood. So much blood. Pouring over his cheek. Onto his chest. And the pain—

Galen shuddered. Coltrane had been an excellent teacher. Kernels of grain were separated from the chaff by thrashing. Coltrane had taught him that a man's heart could reveal its truth by the same method. And then, Coltrane had carved his lesson deep, leaving the marks for all the world to see. Just as he claimed he would.

Ten years had passed since Acre—years of watching others shrink away from him, of knowing his very presence sent shivers of dread through any who looked upon him. He wore the mask to dull that ruthless truth, but Galen knew the truth hidden behind the shield he wore upon his face.

He was scarred. Twisted.

Or he had known it until he found Anne.

Anne made him wonder. She gazed at his face and trembled, but with warmth rather than fear. She smiled where others cringed. She reached out to touch that which others fled. Was she so foolish that she could not see the truth? Or were her eyes wiser than his?

For the first time in ten long years, Galen thought he had found a new teacher, one who could erase the bitter lessons of the past. Anne had taught him to laugh again, hope again. His Lady Anne offered him hope like a gift, and he had snatched at her gift with shameless greed.

But now, the first teacher had returned.

What would the lesson be this time?

Galen's shoulders slumped under the weight of what he had done. In his greed, he had let Anne get too close. He had hoped she could banish the darkness, fill the emptiness in his heart. Now, he knew his darkness would only swallow her whole. It had already destroyed her father and torn her family asunder.

Had he not learned from Coltrane well enough?

Dimly, Galen realized that he had wandered through the wood to the crossroads. One way led to Rosethorn Castle. Galen knew he should go that way. He knew he should turn away from Anne, protect her in the only way he could—by leaving her—but he turned and walked in the other direction. The path that led to the carpenter's cottage.

And Galen despised himself for it.

Anne woke between one breath and the next. Disoriented from her fitful doze, she stayed very still. Memory returned layer by layer.

She lay atop the covers of her narrow bed, still clad in her gown. She had not meant to sleep at all.

When Bryan had told her all there was to tell, or at least all he meant to tell, they had stared at each other for many moments. Marcus and Farrell had returned with Derek and Lyssa. Freya floated back at about the same time.

Anne knew what she must do.

Aye, Freya would take the children for the night most gladly. Guilt stabbed Anne's heart for foisting them onto another, but they did not seem to mind. Freya had already charmed Derek and Lyssa. To them, she seemed a curious blend of playmate and grandmother, and they went with her so blithely that Anne's conscience was at least partially soothed.

She had made ready, then, to wait with Bryan.

The Vespers bell rang. Anne had not asked the question foremost in her mind, knowing Bryan would have no answer. She knew they both waited for the same reason. Galen was out there, somewhere, facing the demons of his past. Though they had never spoken it, they both knew that if Galen sought human solace, he would return.

The minutes slid by and became an hour. The bell for Compline tolled. It was fully dark by then. Anne lit tallow candles and marked the time by watching them burn. Neither she nor Bryan spoke beyond a murmur every so often, as if reassuring themselves the other remained. There, in the flickering light, Anne felt a friendship form between them, forged in silence and tempered by respect. Even amid her worry for Galen, she felt gladness for that.

When the third hour crept to a close, Anne had begun to worry. The concern in Bryan's gaze said he did as well. She said something—she remembered not what—and went to her little room.

Now she was awake.

Some small noise had prodded her alert. Outside the cottage, she heard Bryan speak so low it sounded wordless to her ears, and her heart tripped in its beat. She heard a footstep, the sound of a door closing, and then all was silent once more. But Anne knew, as sure as she breathed, that she was not alone.

"I should not touch you. No part of me should ever touch any part of you."

His voice seemed part of the night itself. Anne said nothing and sat on the edge of the bed. He was in the room with her.

"You should have fled at the very sight of me."

She stood and heard him take a step toward her.

"I should leave you, here and now, before 'tis too late."

He was very close, within arm's reach, but Anne kept her hands at her sides. She heard his breath rasp.

"But may God have mercy upon me, I cannot."

A sob of relief caught in her throat as Galen's arms drew her close. His mouth laid claim to hers as though he meant to devour her. The fingers of his one hand cradled her head, holding her captive for his kiss, while his other splayed at the small of her back. He arched her over his arm, and his lips caressed her cheek. Anne felt them move to where her pulse throbbed just below her jaw.

"Tell me to go, Anne," he commanded hoarsely, almost pleading. "Tell me to leave you. 'Tis the only way I can."

"Never," she whispered, and her arms encircled him.

Galen shuddered and bit delicately at where her shoulder joined her neck, making her shudder in return. Anne ran her hands up his back, spanned the width of his shoulders, and threaded her fingers into the silk of his hair. She found the bands holding his mask in place, and a sound of protest seeped from her lips. She plucked at the knots securing the bands.

"Nay!" He rolled his head, trying to dislodge her fingers, and Anne's heart shivered at the desperation in his voice. "Nay, do not—"

"Nothing will be come between us this night," she murmured against his left cheek. "Nothing."

Galen's breath echoed harshly in the room as Anne drew off the mask and let it fall from her fingers. He buried his right cheek against the side of her neck and clutched her tightly to his body. Then his lips feasted upon hers again. Anne slid her hand to touch the flesh the mask had covered, to soothe and reassure. He had her by the wrist in a trice.

"You will never look," he warned, low and savage. "You will never touch. Never. Do you understand?"

"Galen—"

"*Never.*" Anne flinched at the snarled word. "Swear it."

"N-never. I swear it."

He stood, tense, his grip upon her wrist just short of cruel. Then the grip became a caress, his lips soothing the soft skin of her wrist. He turned it and kissed the sensitive pulse point, and Anne's breath caught. To prove her word, she kept her fingers lax when he pressed his lips to her palm.

"Hold me, wood elf." He guided her hand around his waist, and Anne stroked his back through his tunic. "Hold me close. Make me forget everything but you."

His large hands spanned her waist. She quivered and felt a knot form low in her belly. His sigh broke over her lips, and his fingers slid lower, bringing her hips full to his. The knot within her clenched tight. It heated her body, melted her in secret places, readied her for him. The ridge of his hardened flesh pressed intimately against her, and Galen's sigh deepened into a moan that mingled with her own.

"God help me." His mouth shaped the words against hers before sound came. "I need you. I need you now."

"Aye," seemed all Anne had the breath to utter.

He lifted her, and in one stride he laid her on the bed. Anne's hair formed her pillow as Galen pressed her into the mattress. He loomed above her, naught but a shadow in the dark, but Anne could feel the quivering of his arms under her hands. He kissed her lips, her cheeks, her throat. He controlled her, commanded her senses with an intensity that should have frightened her. Instead, Anne yielded with a cry of joy. Her gown thwarted his exploration, and they both growled in frustration. Galen caught the gown's opening in his hands and gave it a vicious jerk. Ripping cloth sounded like music to her ears.

The cool night air came as a shock to Anne's bare flesh. For the first time, she trembled with fear. But not of Galen. Never of Galen. She feared the threshold she stood before. Then his hands were upon her again.

"So soft," he murmured. His hands feathered over her breasts, and Anne gasped. "So incredibly soft and warm you are, firm and scented like blossoms. You fill my palms. And here. Here, you are like pearls cloaked in rose petals."

He plucked tenderly upon her crests, and Anne arched her back on a broken cry. He was relentless in driving her to the brink of pleasure and beyond. His fingers captured her little buds, tugging at them, teasing them, making them even more taut. Anne quaked beneath the wondrous torment he inflicted and whimpered at the heaviness within her breasts. Her hands covered his, seeking to end his touch, pleading for him to never stop.

"Galen . . . Please, Galen . . ."

"Please, touch you? Kiss you? Tell me, wood elf." His breathless taunt floated moist over her nipples, drawing a thin sob from her. "You have only to tell me what you want, and 'twill be yours."

"Aye . . . kiss me."

The heat of his mouth seared her, choking off what little breath she had as he drew one peak between his lips. Anne's arms fell limp to her sides, and she writhed. When he took his lips away, her breast felt chilled, but he warmed it with his palm while he savored its twin. His groan rumbled into her body as he suckled upon her.

And then he was gone.

"Galen!" Anne cried out and grasped for him.

Dual thumps sounded as his boots struck the floor. Anne heard the whisk of cloth drawn away and a muffled curse. Suddenly he was there again, warming her again, and she sobbed in relief. He caught one of her hands, and she let the other fall back to the bed. He kissed her fingers, entwining them with his own.

"Are you my lady?" he asked huskily.

"Always. I will always be yours."

The skin of his chest felt hot and damp. Crinkly curls over his breast teased the palm of her hand. Her fingers furled and unfurled as he guided them down the line of fine hair over his belly. His muscles quivered and jerked taut as he took her further, to where the line of hair thickened again. To where the heat of him throbbed the hottest. Anne gave a bemused cry and bit her lower lip, instinctively resisting him. But Galen's grip commanded her hand to obey.

"Anne . . . Lady Anne, touch me."

His arousal was fierce and strained against her fingertips. He wrapped her fingers around his length and taught her how to touch him, to explore him, to drive him mad. He showed her he could just as easily drive her mad as his fingertips gently probed her own hidden flesh. Anne gritted her teeth against what she feared would be a scream of pleasure when he found the most sensitive point of her. As he tortured her so sweetly, her hand grew bold upon him, and his flesh leaped within her grasp.

"Now. Now, wood elf." Galen was full upon her, his hips embraced in the cradle hers made for him. His chest heated hers, and Anne arched her back to increase the blissful weight of him on her breasts. He nudged her folds with his hardness. "I can wait no longer. Take me, now."

There was a great pressure at her threshold, a burning discomfort. Anne moaned as the discomfort sharpened, then cried out when it flowered into pain. Her legs shifted, seeking to ease the fullness within her, but she only took him deeper. Anne gasped and clutched at Galen's shoulders, trying to push him away, trying to pull him closer.

"I cannot . . . hold back." Galen gasped. " 'Tis so long since—Forgive me, wood elf, but I need you."

He took her wrists in his hands and held them on either side of her head. Then he surged within her, and his urgency kindled her own. He would not free her arms to hold him, so Anne embraced him with her legs, wringing a cry from them both as he thrust even deeper, faster. The kindling he ignited leaped into full flame within her. The flame spread, all-consuming.

Galen shuddered, moved inside her one last time, and shuddered again. The inferno consumed Anne, kept her arched, rigid under him, and their cries soared together into the night.

Dear God, what had he done?

Galen clutched Anne's limp body to his and moaned. She gave a little whimper and snuggled even closer, her hands curled between her breasts, trapped against his chest. He kissed her damp temple until she stilled once more.

He had taken her, used his sweet wood elf to ease the pain that had returned to haunt him. Galen could not breathe for a moment. He had used her. Anne shifted against him, the movement sliding his male flesh deeper within the silky clasp of her female body. He shivered and groaned as his body flamed into rigid arousal. It was impossible. He gritted his teeth. He had shattered her innocence, shed her virgin's blood, and God help him, he needed her again.

What kind of a monster was he?

"Galen?"

Her voice sounded dazed, sleepy. Galen tried to speak, but no sound could escape the knot choking his throat. Instead, he buried his lips in her hair, and with her hands still snared between them, he began to move inside her once more. Anne gasped and arched to meet his thrusts.

"Oh, Galen!"

Her body rippled around him, tugged at him and pulled him over the edge. She uttered a croon of pleasure, and Galen lost himself within her.

Still he could not speak. But his soul cried out. His soul begged her not to hate him for what he had done.

For what he would do to her yet.

Anne woke alone. She shivered, feeling the lack of warmth that had surrounded her all through the night, and rolled onto her back. Somehow, she had known Galen would be gone when she awoke, but knowing did not keep her heartbeat from quickening.

No part of me should ever touch any part of you.

Panic brought Anne to her feet. She grasped her gown, and the ruined garment only served to sharpen her fear. Galen had torn it from her, wild with his need for her. She had reveled in his wildness, then. Now, Anne could only remember his words.

I should leave you, here and now, before 'tis too late.

Anne pulled another gown from her chest and donned it quickly. Without even sweeping her hair from her face, she stumbled from her room.

Delight speared her heart. She skidded to a stop in the doorway. He was gone from her bed, but he had not left her.

Across the room, with his back to her, Galen crouched before the hearth, nursing the embers back to life with small bits of kindling. Anne hugged herself and shivered. Aye, the cottage was chilled in the pre-dawn gloom, but Galen would soon have a fire going. As he carefully laid wood over the infant flames, Anne gazed at him zealously.

He was clothed haphazardly. His dark hair was finger-combed. The silky strands made her fingers itch to touch them, and Anne curled them into her palms. He wore the mask, but its presence was expected and did not jar her suddenly ebullient spirit.

Still, something made her cross to him with careful tread. The muscles of his shoulder bunched taut under her fingers. He rose, but he did not turn. He did not take her into his arms and give her the kiss she craved. He just stood, looking down at the fire in silence.

"Galen?" Anne's light heart faltered, but it was a stubborn organ and could not be so easily weighed down. She smiled, feeling shy. "Good morning."

"Are you well?" he asked roughly.

"Aye," she answered, baffled. "Very well."

"Last night—" He took a deep breath, but still he did not turn to her. "I was too rough with you. I hurt you."

Embarrassment and relief made her light-headed. Anne felt her cheeks warm. He was worried about her, concerned that he had not been as gentle a lover as he should have been. Her knowledge was limited. She knew why their joining had caused her discomfort, but she had no knowledge of how to assure him there had been pleasure, too. Anne nibbled at her lower lip.

"You did not truly—"

"You cried out," he said flatly. "There was blood."

Her cheeks flamed. "Aye, well, 'tis normal for a woman—"

"We will be wed as soon as possible," Galen declared. He started to turn, but halted. "I'll not have it said I used you only to cast you aside when I was done."

Anne's heart frosted. "No one would ever suppose—"

Galen laughed a terrible laugh. He swung around, and Anne took a step back.

"You think not? 'Twas you who thought I meant to take you as my mistress."

"But that was—"

"I'll not take an innocent and leave her for others to call a whore." Anne flinched at his savage words. "I'll not have that on my soul as well."

He strode to the door and whipped it open. Turning, he impaled her with eyes as hard and glinting as an emerald. Anne started toward him, to touch him, to beg him to tell her why he was so abrupt. A horrible thought dawned upon her. Had she displeased him so much that he regretted sharing himself with her?

"Galen," she pleaded, distress creasing her brow, "what is wrong? Please, tell me. Have I—"

"I will have the children brought to you," Galen said.

Anne searched his face for the man she had known, but she could not find him. Framed within the doorway stood a stranger.

"In three days, lady," the stranger announced, "you will become my wife. You had best prepare."

And then he turned and was gone.

Chapter Ten

Coltrane gazed at what had once been a girl and curled his lip in disgust. She was pitiful.

The line between pleasure and pain was exquisitely thin, and blending the two was a fine art. He preferred his subjects to be equal to his skill. But this one—he nudged the body with his booted foot—had proved a disappointment.

Yet the hunger had been demanding, and the pitiful excuse of a girl had not sated it. Appetite only whetted, the hunger gnawed at him all the more.

But the carpenter's daughter? She would be different.

When he had Tarrant's little village whore in this one's place, the hunger could feed itself fully. And when Tarrant saw what she would become, what a true master could make of her? Coltrane shuddered with savage pleasure.

He touched the cooling cheek of the girl with whom he had made do. He was not finished with her. She had uses yet.

She had been given three days.

Anne walked the forest path and knew time was running out. Tomorrow she would wed the Lord of Rosethorn.

It should be the happiest day of her life. Was that not

what everyone said? A bride should look forward to her marriage with joy. Why then did dread coil around her heart? Why did it draw tighter and tighter with each passing hour?

Because tomorrow she wed the Lord of Rosethorn. Not Galen. Not the man who had asked for her hand, offered to share his life with her. Not the man of passion who had come to her in the night. Now she would not marry Galen, but the Lord of Rosethorn, a man of coldness and grim determination.

Anne furrowed her brow. What had gone wrong?

Discovering that his old foe stalked him again had shaken Galen. Of that, Anne had no doubt. But why had he turned from *her?*

Not for the first time in the last two days, frost spread through her veins. What if it was not only Coltrane that had made Galen draw away? What if it was her? It was almost too horrible to ponder, but Anne pondered it all the same. Could she have repulsed him? Given the time to consider what had happened between them, could Galen have been disgusted that she would give herself to him as she had?

Anne shook her head at her morbid fancies. These games of what-if would drive her mad.

Twigs snapped not far behind her, but Anne felt no fear. She knew others followed her. Never obtrusive, her guards were always there now. They followed her about the village, stood watch at the cottage. They were there at Galen's command, she knew, though she knew only because they bore his crest, not because he had seen fit to tell her. Certainly not because he had asked her if she wanted them.

The guards were there. Whether she liked it or not.

Sometimes, she thought she caught a glimpse of his tall figure dressed in somber garb, but in the past two days Anne had never actually seen Galen. It was as if, when he strode from her cottage, he had gone from her life as well. But for those fleeting glimpses, she might have sworn he had.

Somehow, a chasm had opened between them. And somehow, she had to find a way across it. Anne sighed. But how?

Once she had crossed the brook stone by stone just for

the pure joy of the challenge. Now she crossed it and hoped one of her guards would slip and soak his feet. Not a charitable thought, but these days Anne was not inclined toward charity.

Anselm and his wife were chatting in the doorway of the smithy. Anne's shoulders slumped when she saw how her appearance blighted their conversation. Both straightened like soldiers, and her heart sank when Anselm's wife dipped into an uncertain curtsy.

It was becoming typical. Though no crier had made the announcement, news of her betrothal had spread like wildfire through the village. No one knew quite how to behave. She bore no mark that set her apart. She was still the carpenter's daughter, but everyone knew she was changed. Those who did not bow before her in servility regarded her with open suspicion. There were those who did both, eyes narrowing and lips tightening as they made their reverence to their lord's intended. Anne was heartily sick of it, but nothing she said or did seemed to make any difference.

Though she had never felt less like smiling, Anne forced one to her lips. "Good day to you both."

"Good day to you . . . my lady," Anselm's wife replied awkwardly. Anselm just nodded in greeting.

"I realized I forgot something when last I visited." Anne felt her cheeks grow chilled, for the day she last visited had been the day her father was killed. She dug into the basket she carried. " 'Tis the sash for the gown I made."

Anselm's wife flushed. "Faith, lady, I had not even missed it. 'Tis good of you to bring it, especially when you've so much more . . . er, important matters to tend."

"Aye," Anselm agreed, and Anne did not like the way his eyes narrowed. Not him, too! "Marriage is a serious affair to prepare for. Especially to such a man."

Anne did not miss how his wife admonished him with a quick jab of her elbow, and she met his gaze without flinching. "Aye, 'tis a grave matter, indeed."

"Well, I thank you, lady." Anselm's wife stumbled through another curtsy, wringing the sash in her nervous hands. "You'll excuse me. I've supper to get ready . . . my lady."

Anne was sure her face would crumble if she smiled, so she just nodded instead. Misery enveloped her when the woman all but ran into the cottage. Anselm turned to his anvil and started to hammer away at an iron shaft grown too cool to be malleable. The message seemed clear. Leave. Now.

"Anselm." His hammering faltered, but he kept striking. "Anselm, please."

The hammer struck once more, then stilled. "Aye, lady?"

The dull tone of his voice kindled Anne's temper. "For heaven's sake, Anselm, you act as if I am diseased."

"Nay, lady."

"Do not call me that!"

His head bobbed obediently and made Anne want to scream. "What shall I call you, then?"

"Anne will do nicely."

One corner of his mouth twitched, but he did not quite smile. " 'Tis not right, a man like myself to address you so."

"A man like—" Anne reined in her temper and took a deep breath. "Do not be ridiculous."

" 'Tis the truth." He examined his hammer with undue care. "You are to wed a lord. You'll be his lady."

"I am myself first."

He darted her a look, then shook his head sadly.

"Anselm," she started, sorrow warring with temper inside her, "I am not changed. I am still Anne, and whatever marriage I make, I will remain Anne."

"Any marriage would change you, lady, but this one—" He shook his head again, more fiercely this time. "This marriage will change you more than most. You are foolish if you deny it."

Anne flushed, stung. "But inside, I am the same."

"Nay, lady, you are not the same." He faced her, then jerked his head toward the towers of Rosethorn. His expression darkened. "You are betrothed to yon lord. You think the village can forget that? You think we can forget that you would give yourself to such a man?"

Anne frowned. "Anselm, lord or not, Galen is a good man. Look at all he has done for the village."

"I know all he has done, lady." His hammer struck the anvil with a clang that echoed through the yard. Anne shivered at his expression, taut and hateful. "But all he has done, or will do, cannot blot out the darkness surrounding him."

Anne drew a steadying breath. This she understood. The villagers feared Galen. He made them uneasy, with his reclusive ways and mysterious absence for so many years. They did not know, and so they could not understand. But did *she* have the right to explain, to tell Galen's secrets? As Anselm said, she was Galen's betrothed. But considering the past days, what rights did that grant her?

"Anselm, there are reasons why Galen is how he is," she said carefully. "He has been used most foully. He—"

"And now he uses you."

"Nay!"

"Think, girl! There has been nothing but trouble since his return. He brings it with him like an evil cloud, hovering over all he touches. The village is torn apart all over again. Your own father has been murdered." Something of her shock must have shown upon her face, for Anselm's eyes narrowed. "You cannot have missed the connection."

Anne could not breathe for a moment. "What connection?"

"A lord returns. A lass is attacked in the wood, taken and kept within the lord's keep. In his very chamber, so they say. Not weeks later, her father is killed. After he had gone to speak to that same lord."

"Papa went . . ."

"You truly did not know?"

She shook her head, feeling as though the earth had slipped from beneath her feet. Neither Galen nor her father had ever mentioned such a meeting.

"Turned him away at the gates, his lordship did," Anselm told her. His mouth flattened. "Or rather, that seneschal of his did. The pair of them must have guessed what he wanted, and instead of meeting him like a man, Lord Galen sent him packing.''

Anne said nothing. Her thoughts tumbled in a blur. Turned her father away? Something did not feel right. She remembered Galen's words and his voice when he spoke of her father in the chapel, warm and sincere. Not ashamed. Not guilt-ridden. Before Anne could puzzle it out, Anselm touched her arm.

''Lass.'' She focused upon him once more and saw his features soften with concern. ''Consider well before you speak the words on the morrow. He cannot force you.''

''Force me?''

''Think on it, lass,'' he entreated. ''Ever since Lord Galen returned, there has been naught but grief for you and yours. And I fear he'll bring naught but more to you, if you dare give yourself to him. Remember, lass, you've a place here among us. If you seek protection with any in the village, we'll not give you up to him. We'll not let him destroy you as he did Daniel.''

Anne's belly roiled, and she felt every bit of blood drain from her face. Galen responsible for her father's death? For what possible reason? The idea was absurd! Surely Anselm knew that, deep within his heart. Surely all of Thornbury knew it. Didn't they?

Anselm heaved a sigh. ''Anne, do not let a title and wealth blind you.''

Anne flinched. It was even worse than she feared. This rift between Galen and his people was wider and deeper than she had thought. Bridging it would a difficult task. No matter. She firmed her lips and squared her shoulders. She had faced difficult tasks before.

She grasped his rough hand and smiled sadly. ''Do not fear, Anselm. I've not been blinded.''

He eased in obvious relief, and she stood on tiptoe to brush a kiss on his cheek.

''But you have,'' she went on, gazing deep into his eyes, ''if you believe Galen could take part in anything so vile. Very blind, indeed. And you'll see you are wrong.''

As she turned away and left the yard, Anne felt a strange

sense of elation wrap around her heart, as if a missing piece of a puzzle had suddenly been dropped into her hands.

May your wanderings lead you home.

She had said that to Galen weeks ago. And she had wondered since if he truly had returned home. Now she had her answer. He had not. The lord was in residence, but the man still wandered, searching for— For what? Peace? Acceptance?

Love?

Galen had not spoken of love to her. Nay, that word had never passed his lips. Want. Need. Those were the words he had used. Passion was a grand thing, and Anne's heart glowed that he felt it for her. But desire he could feel for any wench. Love was altogether different.

Did he feel only passion?

I'll not have it said I used you only to cast you aside when I was done.

Was it only grim determination to do right by her?

Anne smiled and knew she had found the bridge across the chasm between her and the man she loved. Her step quickened as she all but skipped down the lane. How foolish she had been!

No man could endure what Galen had endured and escape with his heart unscathed. As surely as he had posted guards to protect her from his foe, Anne knew he had posted guards at the gateway of his heart. And after so many years, was it any wonder he no longer knew how to reach out?

If Galen had never spoken of love, neither had she.

The realization floated around her like a warm embrace. Galen might be loath to step beyond his heart's gate into the unknown, but if he knew . . .

Perhaps knowing would make all the difference.

It made no difference.

Galen knelt before the simple altar of Saint Joseph, his hands clasped until his knuckles turned white, but he did not pray. What difference could prayers make? They could not answer the question that had haunted him for the last three days.

What had he done?

Nay, no prayer could answer that. Only he could.

And Galen knew the answer all too well.

He had taken Anne. Taken her. An accusation, the words reverberated through his head.

Until the day he died, Galen knew he would remember lying with Anne in his arms. He would never forget the feel of her lithe form nestled in the curve of his body, how her arms entwined about him, the way her lips curled in a half-smile. And he would never forget how he had met her bright morning smile with coldness and an ultimatum.

Three days he had given her to prepare.

The day had finally come.

Galen flinched. Anne had given him more pleasure than he had ever known, opened her arms and her heart to him. She gave him her innocence, her passion, and her comfort. He repaid her by taking her precious gift and turning it into a trap to ensnare her.

Because he needed her.

Because he could no longer conceive of life without her.

What a selfish bastard I am.

Had he thought of what Anne needed? Had he truly considered what joining her life with his would mean for her? He had stolen her innocence, abused her trust—all for himself. And for himself, he would continue to take from her, offering in return nothing but the shadows that were all his heart contained. Aye, bad as it was, it seemed that what he had done was nothing compared to what he would continue to do.

It was not too late. Even now, with the hour of their marriage drawing closer, he could stop it. He could let Anne go, free her to lead her life without the pall of his life hanging over her. She was a good woman, as strong as she was beautiful. There would be another, a man more worthy of her. He could release her to meet that unknown man, wed and bear that man's children. He could give her the chance to find real happiness.

He could stand in the shadows and watch it all.

Galen squeezed his eye shut, clenched his jaw until it

ached. Dear God, he would go mad if he did.

Perhaps if he left Rosethorn—

"Galen?"

He looked up and saw Bryan standing beside him, a wary look in his eyes. It was a look his seneschal had given him often of late, and Galen found no comfort in knowing he deserved it. His temper had grown as frayed as his conscience.

"She is coming," Bryan said simply.

A strange sensation crept through Galen, an urge to bolt, a desire to laugh with relief. Anne was coming. She meant to say the vows, join her life with his. He waited until his heart ceased its wild hammering before he rose to his feet.

"And the village?"

Bryan's lips quirked into a wry smile. "Is not missing a single moment. Every man, woman, and child is out lining the lane, watching every step she takes."

Galen snorted. "Can you blame them?"

"Nay." His seneschal narrowed his eyes. "It occurs to me that, for a man about to marry, you do not look very pleased with the prospect. Would you rather have heard me say Anne refused?"

"Nay!" Galen bit back the sharp words that sprang to the tip of his tongue and schooled his voice to a more even tone. "I just . . . I just hope all goes well."

Bryan nodded, but his gaze remained skeptical.

"Did—" Galen had to clear his throat. "Did Anne find the clothing pleasing?"

"I suppose." Bryan shrugged. "She did not say otherwise."

Galen surrendered to his restlessness and paced before the altar. "How did she seem to you?"

"Well. A bit pale, perhaps." Bryan tilted his head to one side. "Not as though she was preparing to march to her own funeral, if that is what you are trying to ask."

Galen shot him an angry look.

"She is on her way. She seems no more nervous than any bride might. What more do you want?"

An excellent question. Galen wished he had an answer.

Galen paced the length of the altar twice more before he came to a halt. From beyond the church's open door, voices rumbled low and indecipherable. The villagers were gathering, telling him Anne drew closer. His stomach clenched and fluttered. A chill skittered down his spine. Anticipation and fear warred within him, neither gaining the upper hand in the struggle.

He could stop this. He could stop it now.

But did he truly want to?

He wanted Anne, needed her in ways too deep within his soul to express in words. But was that reason enough? What of *her* needs? His gaze fixed upon the doorway, Galen balled his hands into fists and swallowed thickly.

"Am I doing the right thing, Bryan?"

His friend was curiously silent for a long moment; then he nodded with an odd smile lurking about the corners of his mouth. "Aye, you are."

Galen met Bryan's gaze, found it calm and assured, and he frowned. "You sound very certain."

"You asked," his seneschal replied. "I only answered what I see as the truth."

But was it the truth? Was it right to cling to Bryan's certainty when he had none of his own?

He could still stop this. It was not too late.

Father Elias emerged from the back of the church, and the men took their places before the altar. No one but Bryan would witness the ritual, though Galen knew the villagers would be just outside. Morbid curiosity drew them as surely as nectar drew bees. Galen smiled sharply. Aye, such a lovely lady binding herself to such a husband was an event not to be missed.

Lyssa was the first through the door, and at the sight of her, Galen's uncertainty redoubled. Dressed in a small gown of white under a sunny yellow bliaut, with her dark tresses gathered to fall in silky curls down her back, she was charming. If her elder sister made him think of wood elves, Lyssa made him think of fairies glittering through a night sky.

Halfway down the aisle, she looked up. Her step faltered, and her little mouth trembled when she met Galen's eye. For a horrible moment, he feared she would remember his face as the one that had made her scream. But she mastered herself swiftly. The way the little girl lifted her chin reminded Galen so much of Anne that he smiled as she took her place at the altar.

His gaze swung back to the door.

His breath locked in his chest.

In a white gown, her bliaut the exact match of her sapphire eyes, Anne enchanted him. The girdle slung daintily about her hips—its multitude of tiny bells chiming with her every step—had once belonged to his mother. Her hair was loosely gathered with silk ribbons of blue and white woven through the curls. Tendrils of honey-gold framed her face, making her creamy skin seem even richer and the rose-bloom in her cheeks look even fresher.

Lady Anne. His Anne. His wood elf.

Her gaze never left his as she walked down the aisle, but Galen's flickered to the boy at her side.

In her father's place, her hand firmly clasped within his smaller one, young Derek brought his sister to her husband. He wore his own new attire of hunter-green tunic, leggings, and cloak as if he had been born to such finery. His slender shoulders were squared, his back as straight as a lance. Galen caught his gaze and found it very solemn. Then the boy grinned, and those dark blue eyes sparkled roguishly. Galen held out his hand, and as the lad laid Anne's within it, he brushed a knuckle against the boyish cheek and lifted his brow in a mild warning to behave.

Good God. Galen regarded Anne, then Derek and Lyssa in turn. He was about to inherit a complete family. He would be responsible, not just for Anne as his wife, but for her brother and sister as well. Before he could absorb the full impact of that, though, the priest began to speak.

As the Latin words floated through his ears, Galen's mind raced. Not just Anne. The lives of Derek and Lyssa, too, were being bound to his.

He could stop this. All it took was a word.

And then he heard himself speaking, but the words he spoke were not those that severed the bond. They secured it. His voice held no doubt, was strong and sure.

Beside him, Derek fidgeted, and Bryan laid a calming hand on the boy's shoulder.

When her turn came, Anne lifted shy eyes to meet his gaze, then lowered them again. She smiled, and her fingers curled warmly in his grasp. The words she spoke were soft, almost a whisper, but they were calm and certain.

Lyssa twisted as though to twirl upon her toes, and Anne stayed her with a gentle palm stroking her hair.

Father Elias invoked the blessing of heaven.

The deed was done.

"Are you a lady, now, Anne?" Lyssa asked in wonder.

"She was always a lady," Galen answered instead.

Anne's gaze was locked upon his, and her eyes glimmered and filled with tears. As the first one escaped and left a crystal trail over her cheek, she gave a tiny laugh.

"I love you, Galen," she whispered.

With those simple words, Galen felt the earth drop from beneath his feet, and his heart fell into a deep, black void.

Chapter Eleven

Galen sat at the lord's table and brooded into the goblet of wine he held. Around him, Rosethorn's hall rang with music and laughter. Voices blended and swirled. Scents wafted by. After years of silence, the old hall throbbed with the life of a marriage feast. But the lord remained oblivious.

Love. The word lay within his mind like a lump of lead.

God have mercy. Anne loved him? He felt his cheek twitch beneath the mask he wore. It was not possible. Lovely fool that she was, Anne could not really love him.

And yet, Galen believed she did.

"Galen?"

The sound of his name from her lips drew his gaze to hers. She gave him a bewildered smile. He had barely spoken to her in the hours since they had wed, too consumed in making sense of the words she had blessed him with. Until she had said them, Galen had not known how he hungered to hear them from her. Did she know?

But Galen knew he could not speak those words in return. He could not love Anne. He could love no one. The scars upon his face went deeper than mere skin. They went all the way to his heart and deformed what lay within. He would not lie to Anne by promising love.

Anne laid her hand over his and her fingers burrowed into his palm. "What is—"

"Anne, Anne!" Lyssa danced at her sister's side. "See the juggler?"

Galen focused upon the child, who gazed with wonder at a man tossing painted balls in the air. Lyssa's cheeks were rosy and smudged with the remains of a sweet. She giggled when the juggler's partner snatched one of the balls from the air, shushed his audience, and then dropped the ball onto the juggler's head.

True, Lyssa was a beautiful child, but none of his blood flowed within her. How was it possible for him to ache at her smile?

"I could learn to juggle," Derek declared from his side. "I just bet I could."

Galen turned and saw the boy's expression daring Bryan to deny his claim. Like foes who had learned to be friends, the pair measured each other companionably. Like his sister, Derek was flushed with excitement, but his sense of manly decorum kept him from laughing. Until the juggler gave his partner a swift kick in the rear. Then Derek crumpled against Bryan in a fit of giggles.

Though he was dark, and Derek fair, Galen could see himself in the lad. But how could that be? The boy was not the fruit of his seed.

These children were not his. And yet, he felt very much as if they were connected.

Because of Anne. A bit of the tension within him eased. These were her brother and sister, blood of her blood, and Anne belonged to him now. His heart thumped heavily for a beat or two. Anne was his.

And Anne loved him.

She gazed at him, her eyes troubled. Galen drew her fingers more securely within his grasp, tightening his fingers on hers in reflex against the guilt lancing through him. It was wrong. He took from her but never gave in return. And God help him, he knew he would only keep on taking.

How could she love him?

"Bryan." His voice sounded odd to his ears, low and strained. He felt Bryan's gaze, but Galen kept his own upon Anne. "We are retiring for the evening."

"Aye, my lord," Bryan replied in a tone that assured Galen he understood his responsibilities.

Wine would flow freely on into the night, but no one would be permitted to take too much. There would be horseplay, but Bryan would ensure that it remained harmless fun. Any who disobeyed would be dealt with.

Anne blushed as Galen rose and pulled her to her feet. Lyssa tugged on her arm and pouted.

"Oh, Anne, do we have to go home now?"

"This is your home now, child," Galen told the little girl, and clenched his jaw when she flinched. Had she reacted to the roughness in his voice? Or from meeting his single eye? Not knowing made his tone sharper than he intended. "You and your brother belong here, at Rosethorn, from now on."

Both Derek and Lyssa looked stunned, but they had no chance to voice questions. All had seen Galen rise and, with good-natured smirks and ribald cheers, expressed their approval. The lord and his lady were retiring.

The wedding night awaited.

Galen led Anne from the hall before she could so much as murmur a good night to the children. As they started up the stairs, a brace of guards took their posts at the archway. Sober, few would dare Galen's wrath with the usual pranks reserved for newlyweds, but with wine and ale warming their bellies? Galen and Bryan had elected to make sure.

"Galen, the children—"

He steered Anne gently but firmly up the staircase. "Do not worry about the children. Freya will look after them and see them to their beds."

He opened the door of his chamber, ushered her within, and closed it again. Leaning against the door, Galen heaved a deep sigh. Thank God, it was quiet here.

"Where?" Anne whirled to face him.

He opened his eye and regarded her blankly. "Where, what?"

"Where are their beds?"

Galen shook his head wearily and straightened. "Freya will find them beds."

He went to the hearth, where a fire blazed and chased away the evening's chill. Hands braced upon the stone mantel, he stared at the flames until they blurred. Like the hours since Anne had spoken those three simple words were blurred.

"I want to thank you for all you've done," she said now in an uncertain tone. "The garments and the feast. 'Twas good of you to invite the village elders."

Galen would have laughed if he had not been so weary. Good of him? He did not believe for one moment that the villagers had come to celebrate. They had come to see how the beast lived in his lair. But if Anne believed otherwise, who was he to disillusion her? After all, the feast was for her.

" 'Twas nothing," he said.

She laughed shakily. " 'Twas not nothing. I imagine 'twas quite a feat, arranging everything in so short a time."

The reminder that he had given her naught but three days to prepare brought a bitter taste to Galen's tongue. Anne had deserved a long, sweet wooing with moonlight and roses and romance. But what had he given her instead? A flat ultimatum.

"The castle staff did the work," he replied, and wondered why his chest throbbed, why his throat ached.

Her skirts rustled as she came to him. "Galen, what is it? Please tell me. Have I done—"

"Did you mean it?" he asked starkly, without turning.

"Did I mean what?"

"In the church. Did you mean what you said?"

He could hear her smile in her words. "Of course I did."

"Not the vows." He knew she had meant every word of those. Anne was a woman who took such matters to heart. He had no doubt that, when she took a vow, nothing short of death could force her to break it. "What you said after? Did you mean it when you . . . said you loved me?"

He sought her gaze and found her eyes gleaming. Anne smiled shyly.

"Aye, I love you."

Galen turned away. "Anne, I . . ."

" 'Tis all right," she murmured, and stroked his back. Galen shuddered as though she had lashed a whip across his flesh. " 'Tis difficult for you to speak of such things. I understand 'tis because—"

"Nay!" He pushed away from the hearth and from her. "You cannot love me."

"Why?"

"Because I cannot love you." Galen rounded upon her in despair. She went deathly pale, and that struck him a blow as nothing else could. He started to reach for her, then dropped his hands to his sides. "Try to understand."

She hugged herself and, turning, walked away dazedly. A few steps took her to the bed.

"I will try to understand," she agreed dully, "if you will explain."

Galen swallowed thickly.

" 'Tis not you. If I could love, 'twould be you. But Anne, I cannot love any woman." A crease furrowed her brow, and he tried again. "I am not capable of it. There is no love within me."

"Because of Acre?"

"Who—Bryan told you?" She nodded, and Galen let out a breath. He hated her knowing anything so vile, but it was a relief, in a way. At least he did not have to recount the tale. Relive it for her. He did enough of that in his dreams, and every time he looked in a mirror. "Aye, because of Acre."

A chill worked down Anne's spine and spread into her limbs. She had hoped—oh, how she had hoped—that knowing she loved him would prove to Galen that he was safe in trusting her. But there was the mask. Always, there was the mask between them. Because of it, because of what it hid, Galen thought himself scarred beyond acceptance in both body and soul. He was wrong. But how could she convince him of that? What could she do or say to erase the conviction that had taken years to forge?

A warrior did not win a battle without taking a risk. Anne caught her lower lip between her teeth and took her own risk.

Lifting her chin, she met Galen's gaze without flinching. "The night you came to me," she said, her voice quavering, "you exacted a vow from me. You said I was never to touch, never to look at what lies beneath your mask. I said something to you, too. Do you remember?"

Galen's eye narrowed. "We said many things that night."

"I told you that nothing would come between us," Anne reminded him. "And now, I demand a vow of you."

Galen clenched his jaw, bracing himself. She had a right to her demand. After all he had demanded of her and would continue to demand, she more than had right.

"Name the vow."

Her fists balled at her sides.

"Never will you come to me as a husband comes to his wife. Not unless you remove your mask."

If she had struck him, he could not have been more stunned. Did she understand what she said? Galen stared at her long and hard. Aye, she knew.

His words came out in a savage whisper. "I will never remove the mask for you. Never."

"There will be no barrier between us." Her mouth trembled, but her chin thrust out. "Give me your vow."

"I am your husband."

"Swear to it."

"Anne—"

"Swear to it," she whispered.

So, it had begun already. Deep within his heart, Galen had known Anne would turn from him once she knew the full measure of the man she had wed. He had hoped— What did it matter what he had hoped? Perversely, Galen was tempted to whip the mask away, let her see his maimed face. His hand even went to the edge of the leather. But he could not do it. He could not bear seeing her horror at the sight.

Limbs numb and stiff, Galen bowed to her; then he

straightened and went to the door. He opened it before looking at her again. Anne had not moved.

"I hope, lady, you find your bed not too cold with your husband's absence," he said huskily. "You have my vow."

The door closed with a scrape, and Anne was left alone.

Now, in the coldest hour of night, he stalked.

Coltrane breathed deeply to still his racing heart, to cool the blood coursing hot through his veins. Like a lover's caress before completion, the stalking often proved sweeter than the kill. And he meant to relish every second.

It was dangerous, but he could not resist.

With the gates of Rosethorn opened to permit guests, it had proved a simple matter to gain entrance. A friendly hail, a wave of his hand, and the guards had stood aside. His garb, woolen tunic and leggings, let him blend with the others. No one suspected he might be other than the simple craftsman he portrayed. He could be just another of the many who had come and gone from the castle over the past days.

No one noticed how he slipped away from those milling about in the cobbled bailey and made for the kitchens, the only other entrance to Rosethorn's keep.

Even there, no one marked his passing. So great was the confusion as the staff scurried about their duties, he moved effortlessly toward the hall. Then it was but a moment until he found the archway that his loyal servant had told him led up the keep's tower. All the way to the lord's chamber.

"What business have you?"

Fury sizzled at the guard's interference at the base of the winding staircase. Coltrane glanced over his shoulder. His servant was not the only one who might recognize him. There were others. He must take care.

"I am on an errand to his lordship," he said.

The man slanted a look at his partner, then back to Coltrane. "We've heard of no such errand. Lord Galen's orders were to allow none to pass."

"Very well." Coltrane shrugged as though he cared not one way or the other. "But you'll have to answer to the seneschal, for 'tis he who sends me."

The pair exchanged another look, then one stood aside. "Go on, then, but be quick about it."

Coltrane bowed and slid past them, up the stairs.

Idiots. Fools. He sneered as he gained the second level. The dagger secreted within the sleeve of his tunic seemed to brand its form against his skin. Had they half a brain between them, they would have shown more caution. Could Tarrant have discounted the danger so swiftly?

He would learn the folly of that. And soon.

Coltrane stood before the door of the lord's chamber. His tongue licked lips dry with giddy anticipation. He drew the dagger and held it up in the flickering light from the torches. He would leave his mark here.

And then he had another task to complete before the night was done, a special gift he must leave in a special place.

Surely she had shed all the tears she could.

Anne lay in the center of Galen's massive bed. She stared into the dying flames in the hearth and faced the truth. She had taken her risk, and she had lost.

The first battle, at least.

Despite the ache in her heart, she smiled a little. The battle was lost, but the war was far from over. Her heart ached, but it would mend. She would live to fight another day.

Galen was right about one thing, though.

The bed was terribly cold without him.

This was her wedding night. Anne chuckled. Aye, she might as well take amusement where she could, even if it was a trifle grim. Some wedding night. She had never dreamed she would spend her bridal eve in such a fashion. But then she never dreamed she would wed a noble, either.

Were the children abed? Anne trusted Freya to look after them and see them nestled safe and sound. But she was lonely. Anne thought of rising, sneaking about the keep until she found them. It would be nice to cuddle together as they did sometimes on winter nights. It would be nice to be with someone. But knowing Derek and Lyssa were likely long since asleep kept her where she was.

Anne shivered. Aye, she was very lonely.

Where was Galen? This was his chamber. Anne scowled. She had demanded his vow, and meant to hold him to it, but it did not seem right to ban him from his own bed. The least she could do was seek her own. Remembering how empty Rosethorn had felt, all those weeks ago, she suspected there were many empty beds to be found. She decided to see about the matter in the morning. Wherever Galen was, she hoped he was warm and comfortable.

She had really set him back on his heels, and she was human enough to hope he realized he deserved it. The wretch. Not capable of love, indeed. Anne snorted and twitched the covers irately. What rot. As if a man's scars determined what rested in his heart.

A man's scars . . .

Anne was also human enough to be curious. What lay beneath the mask? What could be so horrible? Anne tried and tried, but she could think of nothing. Whatever had happened to him, he was still Galen. She nodded to herself. She would teach him to believe that before she was done.

And that she loved him.

She would teach the silly man to believe that, too.

Anne turned to her side and closed her eyes, determined to sleep. If she meant to pick up her battle where it had left off, she would need all the strength she could muster.

How long she slept, Anne did not know. Perhaps only minutes passed before she heard the scrape, the thunk against the door. Her heart leaped with hope, and she came fully awake.

"Galen?"

Nothing. Not a sound.

"Galen."

She called louder, but still only silence answered.

Brow furrowed, Anne rose, wrapping a brychan about her body to ward off the night's chill. Perhaps she had heard nothing at all. Perhaps only her wishful heart made her believe there had been footsteps beyond the door. Still, Anne went to the portal and opened it.

The corridor was empty.

Anne blew out a breath and rolled her eyes. She should

have known better. Galen was a proud man. And a stubborn one. It would take more than one encounter to find the key to the gate behind which he protected his heart. Turning, she made to close the door and froze with horror.

Candlelight sparkled ruby red through the stream of wine. Galen set the jug aside and picked up his goblet. Sipping, he made a face at the taste. Not that the brew was foul. Indeed, it came from a cask of the finest wine in Rosethorn's cellar. But Galen doubted even nectar from heaven would taste sweet to him this night. He started to sip again, paused, then set the goblet back on the table with a snort.

Getting drunk had seemed an excellent idea when he retreated to his study. He would drink himself into a stupor and forget everything—the past, the present and, especially, the future. But his heart was simply not in it.

Why was Anne doing this to him? To them both? What, in the name of God, had possessed her?

Galen lifted the mask from the table and gazed at it long and hard, as if it could impart some secret. The leather was soft and supple, sewn to mold itself to his face. It never chafed, and though it could be hot in summer, it weighed next to nothing. Most of the time, he scarcely noticed it.

He detested it.

And yet, he wore it because he knew he must. How many men had drawn back, their expressions twisted in disgust, at the sight of his face? How many women had gasped and looked away? How many children had fled?

And Anne expected him to remove the mask for her?

Galen flung it back to the table, sick. She was mad. Did she think he was made of iron? That he could bear seeing her horror when she beheld what her husband truly was?

He could never allow her to see beneath his mask.

But why? Why had she demanded such a thing?

To escape him on their wedding night? Galen frowned. That made no sense. Curiosity? His frown deepened into a scowl. Anne was human and no doubt as curious as any other, but he could not believe her capable of playing such a game. Perhaps his honesty had angered her, and this was her revenge. But even that explanation sat ill with him.

Galen stood in a rush, grabbed the mask, and secured it in place. He was damned if he would spend the night puzzling out her motives. He would go down to his chamber—*his* chamber, by God—and have it out with her, once and for all.

Out the door and down the stairs he trod.

And he was damned if he would live the life of a monk. Anne was his wife. To hell with guilt. She had known there were things he could never share with her. She had—

"Galen!"

He was halfway down the stairs when he heard Anne's horrified shout. Panic spurted through his veins. His feet flew over the steps. As he rounded the last spiral, he found her, her hand pressed between her breasts. Her lips trembled. Her skin as white as chalk, Anne stared at a dagger embedded in the wooden door. And at the square of vellum it held. Galen tore the scrap down and read the words inscribed upon it.

Acre will not be forgotten.

His stomach roiled, and his voice grated with fury. "Did you see who put this here?"

She shook her head. "I heard a sound. I thought it might be—But when I opened the door, I saw only this."

"Go back to bed," Galen said flatly.

"What does it say?"

"Go back to bed."

Anne lifted her chin, and despite her obvious fear, her eyes glinted. "Galen, do not treat me like a child."

He regarded her for a long moment and struggled against a smile. A carpenter's daughter she had been born, but Lady Anne still knew how to stand upon her dignity.

" 'Tis a message from Coltrane," he told her.

She betrayed no shock at that. "But how could he—"

"Leave it here?" he finished for her, and lifted a brow. " 'Tis what I mean to find out. Go back to bed."

Anne hesitated for a moment, but then she nodded and slipped back within the chamber. Galen closed the door and grasped the dagger, jerking it from the door.

"Bryan!"

His echoing bellow brought the guards at a trot.

"My lord?"

"Where is Bryan?" Galen snapped.

"Below in the hall, my lord," one of them replied.

"Fetch him. Tell him to come to my study. Now."

"Aye, my lord."

The two turned and started back down, but he stopped them. "And you two? You were standing watch all evening at the archway?" They exchanged uneasy looks and nodded. Galen narrowed his eye. "Get replacements, then return to your quarters, where you will remain until I call for you. Is that understood?"

Faces pale with dread, they nodded. "Aye, my lord."

Bryan paled as he read the missive.

"God above," he whispered. "How—"

"'Tis what I wish to know," Galen cut him off. He stalked around his friend like a wolf encircling his prey. "Two guards, Bryan. Two of them at the foot of the stairs, and still Coltrane manages to reach the very door of my chamber. You explain that, seneschal. You tell me how he did it."

Bryan drew a deep breath. Rarely had he seen Galen in such a rage. It behooved him to speak cautiously.

"I do not know."

"Then you find out," Galen snarled, and slammed the dagger's point into the surface of the table with a dull thud, "or by thunder, you'll wish you had."

"I'll not fail you," his friend replied evenly.

"Not twice, by God. Not in the same bloody night." Galen resumed his pacing. "And as for those idiots you chose for the guard, see that they are taught the value of obeying orders. When I say no one is allowed to pass, I mean *no one!*"

Standing ramrod straight, like a soldier in ranks, Bryan nodded and cleared his throat. "How did you find the note?"

"Anne found it," Galen snapped. "She heard a noise and rose to find it pinned to the door with this." He jerked the dagger free of the table and brandished it before Bryan's eyes. ''Do I need to tell you what could have happened if Coltrane had still been there, outside that door? Rather than pinning notes, he could have slit her throat.''

''But how did you—''

''I was here,'' Galen grated out, not thinking of what that revealed. ''She cried out when she found the damn thing.''

Bryan's brow creased with confusion. ''But why were you—''

''Or the children? Do you realize what could—'' Galen gasped at the thought and swung his gaze to an equally horrified Bryan. ''Good God, the children!''

''Are safe.''

Both men whirled to find Anne standing in the study doorway, wrapped in a robe of soft ruby-red wool that Galen recognized as his own. The garment was yards too large for her, and yet she wore it in a way that lent dignity to her small form. Her smile was unsteady, her eyes too bright, but her hands did not tremble as she stepped into the room.

''They are sleeping, sound as ever,'' she went on, but slanted Bryan a pointed look. ''Though they are abed just across from the lord's chamber, I daresay they heard nothing.''

''What are you doing up?'' Galen asked harshly. ''I told you to go—''

''I know what you told me to do.'' Anne perched on the edge of the large chair behind the table and regarded her husband from beneath her lashes. ''I thought, since you were discussing this latest event with Bryan, and no doubt charging him to investigate, that I would offer him what information I could.'' She smiled demurely. ''Before the memory cooled in my mind.''

And before he took his seneschal's head off in his rage and offered it back upon a platter. Galen flexed his jaw, then surrendered with a sigh. She did not fool him for a moment, and it was just as well. Tearing Bryan's head off was what he probably would have ended up doing.

''I have already told him your part,'' he said, making an

effort to match her calm. "There is no need for you to be here."

"Perhaps not," she allowed. "But I will remain."

"Anne—"

"I am now the lady of the castle, am I not? Do I not have an interest in what happens in my home?"

Bryan did his best to smother a snicker, and Galen ground his teeth, aware he had been neatly put in his place. "Very well, I will allow you to stay."

"Thank you, my lord." If Anne wanted to laugh, she hid it well. She turned her gaze upon Bryan. "Have you any idea how Coltrane could have gotten within the keep?"

"Aye, Bryan," Galen drawled, "do tell how you think that happened?"

Anne cast him a quelling look.

Bryan shook his head. "Only that he probably slipped in amid all the coming and going for the wedding. The gate has been open all day, and," he admitted with a flush, "I fear the watch might not have been able to determine the names of everyone."

"With so many, 'twould be difficult," she agreed.

"I'll question the guards posted at the archway and see what account they can give for themselves," he went on, and nodded to Galen. "You'll have my report in the morning."

Galen nodded back, stiffly. "See that I do."

"Good night to you both."

Alone with her husband once more, Anne shifted in her chair and looked about the chamber. It was austere, with only the table and a pair of chairs as furniture. Yet, for all its starkness, it did not feel cold. Not as the hall had felt, the first time she saw it. Galen had been here. The chamber had absorbed his presence and was warmed by it. The walls were adorned with shelves holding stack upon stack of books. Those volumes seemed to mock at her, for Anne had no way of knowing what words were inscribed upon their bindings. She averted her gaze and found Galen's upon her.

She cleared her throat. "Do you spend much time here?"

"On occasion."

His clipped reply made her shiver, but Anne forced herself to smile. " 'Tis a pleasant room."

Galen thought of how he had once dreamed of her here, in his study, in his home. Well, he had her in his home now, had bound her to him, had even heard her love professed from her own lips. Why then did his chest feel as though a band of iron were clamped around it?

"I am sorry for the fright you had tonight," he said.

She brushed his apology aside with a small laugh. " 'Tis no matter. I do not think either of us expected our wedding night to pass quite like . . ."

Just how their wedding night had started returned to mind, and Anne's words trailed into silence. She looked down at her fingers laced together in her lap.

"Why, Anne?" At his whisper, she looked up again and saw his brow furrow. "Why did you demand that vow of me?"

Anne drew a deep breath and rose. Crossing to him, she stood on tiptoe and brushed a kiss over his lips. His palm cupped her cheek, and he would have brought her more fully into his embrace if she had not stepped away.

"Why?" he asked, and Anne's heart throbbed at the pained confusion in his glimmering eye.

"Because, Galen," she replied evenly, "I love you."

Walking out of that chamber, leaving the man she loved to his loneliness, proved the hardest thing Anne had ever done.

Chapter Twelve

The next morning, Anne woke as she had fallen asleep.

Alone.

She sat up and swung her legs over the side of the bed. A sad smile curved her lips. At least she could not deny her wedding night had been eventful, though not precisely in the way wedding nights were supposed to be.

Galen had been furious, and he had every right to his anger. That horrid message was bad enough, but who knew what other malicious mischief Coltrane might have done? Even now she shivered when she thought of it. If she had opened that door even a second sooner—

Anne shook herself. Coltrane would be dealt with in good time. She had other matters to tend to. There was a day to prepare for, her first as the Lady of Rosethorn.

Anne made a wry face.

Somehow, that daunted her more than Coltrane ever could.

A knock sent a chill scurrying down Anne's spine. Would Galen come to her this morning? Would his pride allow him?

"Come in."

"Good morning to you, child," Freya chirped merrily.

Anne struggled to keep a smile in place, unsure if she felt relieved or disappointed. "And good morning to you. What is that you carry?"

"His lordship decreed you break your fast here," the maid explained as she set a tray on the bedside table.

" 'Twas not necessary."

"Well." Freya's hands fluttered a bit. "I suppose his lordship thought you would want privacy after . . . er, well . . ."

Anne flushed. Of course Rosethorn's household supposed their lord and new lady had passed the night as newlyweds were wont to do. She laced her fingers to keep them from trembling. How long could they remain deceived?

Not for the first time, Anne doubted the wisdom of her resolve. Had she gone too far? She meant to prove to Galen that he could trust her, even with what he believed his darkest secret. The vow was the only way she could think of to prod him to it.

But now, she found herself impaled on the horns of her own solution. Instead of prodding Galen closer, had she only succeeded in pushing him away? Could she recant the vow? Or would that do more harm than good?

Anne shoved her doubts aside. What was done was done. Right or wrong, she would see it through and hope for the best.

"His lordship will learn soon enough that I am no weakling to be coddled," she said, as much to herself as to Freya. Delicious scents wafted to her, and Anne's stomach growled. Since Freya had brought the tray, it seemed a pity to waste the food, "I should like to wander the castle this morning, get to know my way. Do you know where my husband took himself?"

Freya bustled about the chamber, neatening here and there, laying out Anne's comb and preparing the washing bowl for her. "I believe he has gone to the training field to work with his men. He keeps them jumping, right enough. Trains them every chance he gets."

Anne nodded to herself. That made sense. The land was settled, but it was an uneasy peace. King John had not the skills of managing his lords and barons that his brother,

Richard, had. Or his father, old King Henry. News seeped even into quiet Thornbury, and it always seemed to speak of some cloud looming on the horizon.

"Would you accompany me?"

"Oh, I would love to, child," the woman replied kindly, "but I've my work. Perhaps you can wait for his lordship."

Anne waved off the suggestion. She would not distract Galen from his duties as she learned her own. " 'Tis no matter. I will show myself around."

"Well, I am not sure that is such a—"

"Anne, Anne!"

Two young voices trilled with excitement, and Derek and Lyssa burst into the room. Scrambling onto the bed, they bounced and chattered and stole bits of her meal until Anne was forced to retaliate. She grabbed Derek and turned him head over heels to the center of the bed, then launched an attack of tickles on Lyssa.

"Scoot, now. Off with you." Freya herded them from the room when the horseplay slowed. "Let your sister dress."

"Come and see our rooms, Anne," Lyssa demanded from the doorway. "We've chambers all our own, grand chambers, and just across from you."

"Do you, now?" Anne affected an impressed air. "I'll come and see in a few minutes. And the two of you had best get ready as well. There is much to do, and I need your help for it."

The pair agreed happily and scampered off.

Freya regarded Anne curiously. "What have you to do, my lady?"

My lady. The title gave Anne a strange feeling. Not unpleasant. But not quite like herself, either. She supposed she had better get used to it.

"First of all," Anne explained, dressing in a simple gown and bliaut she had brought with her, "I must learn the household. 'Tis the work of more than a day, but I mean to begin. Then the children and I must return to the cottage. We've belongings to pack, as we are to live at Rosethorn now."

For an instant, her hands faltered in the act of combing

her hair. Such simple possessions in the riches of a lord's castle. That would be an oddity.

"'Tis not much," she went on, "but the children have playthings they'll be wanting, and their clothes. And I have some things I'll want as well." She made a teasing face. "I cannot go about in the same gown all the time."

Freya chuckled. "Oh, child, his lordship will—"

"I'll need help," Anne mused, too consumed in planning to heed the maid. "A cart, perhaps, and a strong back or two. Surely Bryan can help secure them."

"Aye, he will, but—"

"Come along, Freya," Anne commanded with a brightness she did not feel. In her plain garments, with her hair braided in its usual plain style, she pranced to the door and struck a pose. "The Lady of Rosethorn is ready to meet her day."

"Come for me!"

Galen snarled the command, and steel clashed against steel as his opponent attacked.

Scarcely noticing the weight of the sword he held, Galen deflected the blow and slashed with one of his own. The blade whistled through the air. Sweat beaded upon his brow, but he ignored it. Beneath the heavy hauberk, moisture dripped down his back, and he ignored that, too. His shoulders tightened and began a dull ache from exertion. Galen noted it only to acknowledge the flaw and resolve to work on it.

His opponent wore a helm. Galen did not. The mask impeded his sight badly enough. A helm would only restrict it more. Still, it made his head an excellent target. One his opponent had no qualms about aiming for.

Galen dodged in time to keep from being knocked senseless. Even then, he caught a glancing blow. He bared his teeth in a feral smile and blinked the stars from his sight.

"You've gotten faster," he growled.

His opponent swung to the attack again in reply.

The blades locked close to the pommels. Galen dug the balls of his feet into the loose dirt to keep his opponent from shoving him back. Grunting with effort, his grimace became a fierce grin.

But his opponent had yet a trick or two up his sleeve. The man broke off and slammed an elbow into Galen's belly. Winded, Galen went down from another elbow between his shoulder blades. He had only a second to roll to his back before his opponent straddled his waist.

"Death or surrender," came the choice.

Sword blade pressed to his throat, Galen gasped. "Oh, get off me, you lout."

Laughter rang from within the helm, and his opponent bounded to his feet. Sweeping the helm from his head, Bryan's hazel-green eyes mocked his prone lord. He thrust his sword point-first into the dirt and extended a hand. Galen took it and was pulled to his feet.

"What did I do wrong?" Galen asked the men watching them.

"You closed with him, my lord," one spoke up.

Galen nodded, admitting the error with a twinge of wounded pride. "Aye, we were too equal to risk wrestling. Remember, use your head in a fight, not your brawn."

"You'll find many foes who will be stronger," Bryan put in, slanting his lord a smug look. "Make sure you are smarter."

Galen snorted, accepting the good-natured laughter at his expense with a rueful smile. "That is all for today."

Bryan swiped his sweaty brow with the back of one hand as the men dispersed. Galen faced him with one brow lifted.

"Smarter, are you?"

Bryan chuckled. "This time, at least."

"Hmm. Next time, you'll not be so lucky."

"Luck?" Bryan laughed. " 'Twas naught but skill."

Aye, Galen admitted silently, Bryan's skill and his own distraction. Galen heaved a sigh as his squire removed the hauberk about his torso. Cool relief swept over him when the heavy garment was removed. Too bad his heated mind could not be relieved so easily.

"What preys upon you?" Bryan asked quietly, his own squire tending to him.

Galen waited until the boys, both in their teens, had scurried away to see to the cleaning and proper storage of the equipment before answering.

"What makes you think anything preys upon me?"

"Galen." Bryan drew his name out. "We've known each other a long time. I know you better than I know myself at times." When Galen did not reply, his friend guessed. "Is it Coltrane? We'll have him, Galen. Sooner or later, we'll have him."

"But when?" Galen growled, relieved that Bryan had guessed the one, instead of the other matter consuming his thoughts. Anne. He preferred to keep that problem to himself. "After he storms into Rosethorn again? And this time does more than pin notes to a door?"

Bryan flinched, and Galen regretted his outburst. It was not Bryan's fault. Or, if it was, he shared the blame for letting his guard down for even an instant. And that piqued his temper even more.

"I cannot believe *no one* saw him enter last night, no one recognized him." Galen turned and strode toward the keep, with Bryan following. "We've at least half a dozen men who were with us in the Holy Land, half a dozen who know Coltrane and have every reason to remember his damn face to their dying day. Someone *must* have seen him, seen something."

"There were near a hundred people about Rosethorn last night," Bryan replied reasonably, "both in and out of the hall. To most, what is one more face?"

"So," Galen grated out, "Coltrane is there, but he is not there. How, then, are we to stop him?"

"We've reinforced the patrols, stiffened the watch. Word is spreading through the village of his description, and beyond into the countryside. There is not much more we can do."

"That is not good enough!" Galen cursed savagely and halted, his teeth bared in frustration. "There must be something we've missed, some clue too small to notice right away."

Bryan heaved a deep sigh. "Well, if you think of it, kindly share it with me."

But Galen did not hear. His mind had come upon an idea.

"Small," he murmured, and his brow smoothed. "Bryan, that is it. The children." At his friend's confused frown, he went on, "The children might have seen him, the day of the fire."

"But that was days ago," Bryan countered doubtfully.

"They still might have seen something, heard something that can point us to the right path." Galen thrust a finger at Bryan's chest. "You seem to have struck a companionship with Derek. Talk to him. Do not say anything to alarm him, if you can help it, but see if he remembers anything useful."

Bryan shrugged in agreement. "What of Lyssa?"

"I will deal with Lyssa."

"She is not entirely sure about you, you know," his friend observed wryly.

"Aye, I know," Galen agreed, remembering how she had screamed at the sight of him. " 'Tis past time I remedied that."

"How?"

Galen thought of all he did not know about children in general and about little girls in particular. "I have no idea."

"I have run this keep long enough to know my business, and I should think I am quite capable of running it still."

Anne pursed her lips and considered her next move. When one did battle with a dragon, one did well to step lightly. Mayde had no scales, but she did breathe fire.

"Of course you are," Anne agreed soothingly. "Why, you've forgotten more about Rosethorn than I could hope to know."

She rolled her eyes at Freya's ill-stifled snicker.

" 'Tis a fact, missy." Mayde brandished a wooden spoon like a sword before stirring a pot with a vengeance. A scullery maid ventured too near and got a thwack across the knuckles. Anne winced and hid her own knuckles behind her back. Lady of Rosethorn or not, she knew Mayde would not stick at giving her a taste of the spoon if riled to it. Sour old dragon.

"I've sweated and worked my fingers to the bone to make

the hall and chambers fit to live in, slaved in this kitchen.'' Mayde advanced, and it was all Anne could do to stand her ground. The woman still held that spoon like a club. ''And what reward do I get? A little cat of a carpenter's daughter storming into *my* kitchen, telling *me* what to do.''

Anne heard Freya's gasp, and even the scullery maids froze with eyes wide. But Anne did not blink.

''Carpenter's daughter?'' she asked, and lifted her chin. ''Aye, so I was born. But now, Mayde, I am the lady of this castle. Like it or not.''

Mayde flushed an unbecoming shade of purple.

''You have served your lord well,'' Anne allowed, ''and I am sure you will continue to do so. But I am now your lady, and if I tell you I wish a thing done, that thing will be done.''

Mayde sputtered with rage, and Anne decided a withdrawal was in order. She did not want to press her advantage too hard just yet. Lay the rules before the old dragon, and then let time determine her next step.

Anne smiled. ''I trust we understand each other.''

For a second, Anne thought Mayde would strike her. Lord above knew, the woman must be tempted too. But if she did, Mayde would learn that a carpenter's daughter knew how to defend herself.

Mayde huffed and puffed a moment longer; then she subsided and nodded sharply. ''Aye, *lady,* that we do.''

''Excellent.'' Anne gave a delighted sigh. ''Well, I'll leave you to your work and see to my own. Good day to you.''

With that, Anne swept from the kitchen. It was not until she gained the hall that she let out the breath she was holding.

''My lady, that was astounding!'' Freya crowed. ''I have never seen Mayde so kerflummoxed!''

Anne laughed shakily. '' 'Twas rather a sight.''

''I must admit, I never knew you had it in you.'' Freya waggled her finger at Anne. ''Spirit I knew you possessed. But that— Why, child, if ever there could be a true Lady of Rosethorn, you just proved you are she.''

"I hope you are right, Freya." Anne fanned her flushed cheeks with her hands and prayed her belly would stop fluttering soon. "I hope you are right."

To find the children, Galen decided he must find Anne.

But Anne was not in their chamber.

She was not in the children's chambers.

She was not in the kitchen, though a ruffled Mayde was.

Nor was she in the hall or anywhere else Galen looked.

Anne was nowhere to be found.

And neither were Derek and Lyssa.

Stalking the forest path, Galen told himself he was being foolish. They were fine, all three of them. He had no reason for the burning knot in his belly. There was no reason to send Bryan and a troop of his men out to search. It was full daylight, and the village thummed with life. The woodland sounds were normal, and he smelled not a sniff of danger in the air.

Why then did he know—just know—something was wrong?

Twigs and leaves crackled behind him, and he turned to find Bryan in pursuit.

"Well?" Galen demanded. "Any sign of them?"

"You can relax," his seneschal replied. "I just spoke with Father Elias. He saw Anne and the children not minutes ago, heading toward the cottage. Anne told him they were going to fetch some things."

Galen drew a breath of relief. Then his temper flared.

"God above!" He batted a vine out of his way and continued down the path. "Does she not realize the danger in moving about unprotected?"

"The priest said she had two of our men-at-arms with her," Bryan explained, following him. "She is not alone."

"What the hell does she need from the cottage, anyway?" Galen raged on, oblivious to his friend. "If she wants or needs anything, I—"

A scream of pure terror ripped through the wood, followed by another. And another.

Galen and Bryan froze, then bolted down the path. Just

as they burst into the cottage clearing, Derek and Lyssa came pell-mell around the bend in the lane.

"Keep them out!" Galen commanded Bryan, who caught both children as they tried to dodge by.

His heart in his throat, Galen drew the dagger from his belt and charged into the cottage. One of his men stood in the doorway to Anne's tiny room. Galen flung him aside. His heart jerked back to life when Anne stumbled into his arms, her face ashen and her eyes huge. He clasped her to him and held her close. Thank God, she was unharmed. Then he realized she was sobbing.

"Oh, Galen . . . She—She—"

Galen looked over her head and felt the blood drain from his own face. She twisted to follow his gaze, but he caught her head and pressed her face to his chest.

"Do not look," he rasped, his stomach roiling.

And he averted his own gaze from the mangled remains of the girl sprawled upon the bed where first he had known Anne's love.

Again, Anne sat just beyond the cottage clearing, shielded by Galen's men. Lyssa and Derek cuddled close with fear in their faces. Anne closed her eyes.

Thank God, this time only her own fear had sparked theirs. Thank God, they had not seen.

Her tears had long since dried, but she could not still the patter of her heart. She pressed a hand to her belly when it heaved, as if to calm it. The worst of the spasms had passed, but every time she thought of that poor girl, she—

She would not think of it.

Bryan stumbled from within the cottage and leaned against the doorframe, his face gray and drawn. He collected himself and walked off in the direction of Saint Joseph's church. Aye, Anne thought dully, the priest would need to come and give what consolation he could to the spirit of that poor, wretched—

She gritted her teeth at the bile rising in her throat.

"Anne?" Lyssa asked timidly. "Anne, are you sick?"

She tried to smile but could not do it. "Nay, sweet."

"You look all pasty," Derek observed, his young brow puckered with concern.

"I will be fine," she assured him.

"What happened, Anne?" he asked. "Why did you scream like that? It scared us, Anne. We thought . . ."

His voice broke, and Anne stroked his cheek. "I am sorry I scared you."

"Should I go help?" Derek made to rise.

"Nay!" Anne seized his arm. "Do not go inside the cottage. Never, *never* will you go inside again, either of you. Do you understand?"

She was frightening them. She didn't mean to, but she could not bear the thought of them venturing where anything so horrid, so utterly vile . . .

"Promise me," she said more gently. They nodded slowly. She looked back to the doorway and saw Galen finally emerge. Anne came to her feet and told the children, "Stay here."

He just stood there, his brow against the doorframe, as she crossed to him. Not until she was within arm's reach did he seem to notice her. He shook his head, catching her by her upper arms in a punishing grip.

"Do not go inside," he rasped. "I'll not have you inside there ever again."

Anne nodded and laid her palms on his chest. "I will not."

Galen was ashen, even his lips. His one emerald eye flashed with fury, a cold fury that vowed retribution for this outrage. Anne finally felt warmth spread through her body, ignited by her own rage.

"My home has been defiled," she said tightly. "All my memories of it have been soiled by that—"

His arms went around her. His lips pressed to her brow. "'Twill not always be so. Time will let this fade." She shook her head, and he curved his palms around her cheeks, lifting her face to meet his gaze. For the first time in days, he looked at her with tenderness, touched her as the Galen she had first known did. "Aye, you will remember your parents living within, and your brother and sister coming into the world. The laughter you all shared."

Did his voice turn wistful? Or did she only imagine it? Anne wondered. Did Galen have no such memories of his own?

She sniffed and offered the best smile she could, clasping her hands over his. "And you. I will remember you."

"Did you know her, Anne?" he asked, still in the gentle tone she loved so. "Did you know that girl?"

"I am not sure," she replied. "She was so—I am not sure I recognized her. Perhaps if I saw her again."

"Nay," he refused flatly, "you'll not look on her ever again. I'll send out word, see if anyone is missing."

"Oh, Galen." Anne rested her brow above where his heart thudded strong and sure. "Who could do such things to another?"

" 'Twas no person," he answered, stark and cold, though his arms were warm and gentle around her. " 'Twas a beast that fed upon that wretched girl."

"A beast?"

"Aye." Galen spat the word. "A beast named Coltrane."

Within an hour's time, Galen had dispatched riders to every corner of the shire and beyond. Each carried a description of the murdered girl, or at least as much of one as could be put together from what remained of her. Each rider was charged to patrol his area, ask every person he met after the girl. Any stranger of note, any act open to question, was to be reported.

Galen took himself to the wood, leading his own detachment of men in search of something—anything—which might point him toward Coltrane's hiding place. For he knew, beyond a shadow of a doubt, that Coltrane had killed that girl. As another jeer.

Why else dump the body in Anne's cottage?

At least, Galen admitted grimly as he turned his men back toward Rosethorn, he could thank Coltrane for one thing. If there had ever been a doubt, Galen now knew just how important Anne and the children were to him, and nothing could be allowed to harm any of them.

But where was the bastard? Galen squinted into the deepening gloom of evening. Coltrane was close. He knew it as surely as he knew he breathed. But where?

He met Bryan in the bailey of Rosethorn, and his heart sank at his seneschal's slow shake of his head. Nothing. Not a damn sign of the bastard.

"You advised the villagers to be wary?" Galen asked as they started toward the hall.

Bryan nodded. "All have been warned."

"I want Anne and the children escorted anywhere they go outside the castle walls," Galen instructed in a low voice at the hall's door. "Even within, keep your eye upon them, as will I. He means to strike at me through them, and I'll not give him the satisfaction of it."

He and Bryan entered the hall, and Galen stumbled to a halt. There, in one of the massive chairs before the hearth, sat Lyssa. All alone. And with a very pensive expression on her young face.

Galen nearly let the opportunity pass. After the disruptive events of the day, he was not certain he could face the prospect of more upheaval. But if he wanted information from her, he might as well try now. He jerked his head at Bryan, and his seneschal took the hint. When they were alone, Galen peered at the child uneasily.

How did one go about interrogating a little girl?

"Where is your sister?" he asked quietly.

"Upstairs," came her subdued reply.

Galen waited, but she said no more. He stepped closer, trying to look as unthreatening as he could. "And what is she doing upstairs?"

"Scolding Derek." She gave him a wary look from beneath thick, dark lashes. "He was bad."

"What did he do?" Galen asked, not even trying to guess. From an energetic boy keen for mischief, anything was possible.

She flushed and muttered, "He said a dirty word. He

called Mayde a nasty old crone, and then he called her a bi—"

"I get the idea," he cut her off.

"Mayde does not like us."

"Well, I would not let that bother you," he advised, and stepped closer. "Mayde does not like anyone very much."

Her incredibly blue eyes looked away. "Do you like us?"

She played with her fingers, lacing and unlacing them, and Galen's heart melted. He crouched before her and tipped her little chin up with a finger.

"I like you very much."

Her gaze fastened on his chest, but a smile teased her lips. "Even if we are bad sometimes?"

"Even then." He tilted his head and tried to catch her gaze, to no avail. "Do you like me?"

That got her to look at him, but she did it as though he had sprouted an extra head.

"Anne likes you," she said at last.

"Lyssa," Galen began, then stopped. Strange how he was suddenly terrified of the answers this little girl might give him. He swallowed. "Does my face frighten you?"

"Anne said you wear a mask because a bad man hurt you." She darted him a look. "She said I was not to fear you."

"But do you?"

In answer, she reached out and touched the mask with her fingertip. Galen held very still as she traced the outline of it and watched her expression go from wary to curious. Then, she touched his other cheek, the corner of his mouth.

"You have a bump," she murmured, pausing at the bridge of his nose. "Derek has one, too. He fell. Did you fall?"

Galen's shoulders shook. "Something like that."

Lyssa leaned forward, rested her forehead against his, and asked seriously, "Are you sure you like us?"

"I am sure," he replied, equally serious.

She slid off the chair and into his arms, smacking a kiss on his cheek. "Then I like you, too."

Galen wrapped her in his arms and held her close for a long time. His throat ached, but it was a sweet ache. It was almost as if . . . as if Lyssa was his own child. He breathed the scent of her hair and growled as he nibbled at her soft neck. She giggled and jerked away, but her arms remained entwined around his shoulders.

"What am I to call you? You are not my papa." Her nose wrinkled. "And I do not want to call you *my lord* all the time."

"How about just Galen?" he suggested, and she nodded. "And now, sweetling, I need to talk to you about something very important." He stood and took her place in the chair, settling her in his lap. Lyssa nestled against him, and Galen could not resist stroking her smooth cheek. "Do you remember when the woodshed burned?"

Her mouth struggled against a quiver. "Papa got killed."

"I know, little one. You might be able to help me find the man who did the deed. Can you tell me what you remember? I know 'tis frightening to think about, but I need to know all you can recall."

"Papa saw them come," she began, burrowing her head into the crook of his shoulder. "He told us to hide in the shed loft. Papa argued with them, and they called him names. Derek went down to make them stop, but Papa told him to run. Then—" She swallowed. "Then there was a lot of yelling, and someone said they had to find me. But they said it so mean."

She shivered, and Galen tightened his embrace. " 'Twas scary, I know."

"A man climbed into the loft. He found me and tried to drag me out from behind the planks." Her eyes narrowed with relish. "I bit him."

"Hard?" Galen asked, curving his lips into a smile.

"Very hard," Lyssa confirmed, and he chuckled. "The man swore at me and threatened to run me through unless I came out. And then—" She worried her lower lip between her teeth. Galen waited. "The fire started. I do not know how, but one of them started swearing something awful. I cried for Papa, but he laid on the floor. There was blood."

When she remained silent too long, he tucked a lock of

her silky dark hair behind an ear. "Do you remember anything else?"

Lyssa pondered. "Then I saw the monster."

Monster . . . monster . . .

"Lyssa—"

"And then I saw you."

"*Then* you saw me?" Galen asked, trying to make sense of the order. "After you saw the monster?"

"Aye." She nodded, very sure. "After I saw the monster."

Galen narrowed his eyes. "Tell me about this monster."

Chapter Thirteen

"A griffin."

"A what?"

Anne turned at Galen's announcement and saw him descend the last stair leading to the great hall. He held up a leather-bound volume as thick as his palm.

Only she and Bryan remained at the hall's great trestle table after the evening meal, at which Galen had not appeared. Anne had not questioned Bryan about it, but Galen's absence left her with a hollow ache in the pit of her belly. Would he separate himself even from the family he had acquired? The prospect was not cheering.

But such was his air of satisfaction as he crossed to them that Anne brightened. Obviously, he had spent the time searching for a whatever-he-called-it in his collection of books.

"What is a griffin?" she asked, admiring the ornately worked cover of the book he set before her.

"A griffin," Galen explained, "is a beast from tales, half lion and half eagle. Depending upon the tale, it can represent good or evil, but to a little girl already frightened out of her wits, 'twould matter little."

He opened the book, and a slight musty odor tickled Anne's nose. Galen turned page after page with a delicate touch. Most of the sheets of parchment were plain with only black slashes and curves on them. Anne knew the shapes were letters, and that letters made words, but she could not decipher their meaning. Other pages were wonderfully colored in red, blue, green, and gold—all the shades of the rainbow. Little people and tiny beasts cavorted about or peeped shyly through huge, elaborate letters. The beauty of it charmed Anne. And intimidated her. The book held knowledge, and Galen had the skill to divine from it. At last, he came to the page he searched for.

"There." He tapped the page. "That is a griffin."

Anne's brow furrowed. It was a fearsome beast, indeed. Drawn in shades of brown and gold, a lion's body stood poised, muscles rippling for the killing lunge. One paw, claws razor-sharp, was lifted as if to swipe at the column of letters before it. The head was undoubtedly a bird of prey, its curved beak open in a silent scream. A great pair of wings extended from the back. Not poised for a lunge, Anne decided fancifully, but for a leap into flight.

"That is what Lyssa says she saw?" Bryan asked.

"Oh, Galen, you do not truly think she really saw this beast." Anne's disbelieving laugh was cut short. "Do you?"

"I do, indeed," he answered seriously.

"But you just said 'tis a beast of tales. Surely such an animal could not really exist. Could it?"

Did she imagine it? Or did his eye twinkle with a hint of mischief? "Nay, but I believe this is the monster Lyssa saw the day of the fire."

"I do not understand," Anne grumbled.

Galen's lips curved a bit, and he explained, "A griffin is sometimes used in crests, as a symbol of power. Lyssa told me the monster was as big as herself. The fire had started by then. The movement she saw, or thinks she saw, could either be the shadows of the flames or someone moving it about."

"A shield?" Bryan offered.

"Very possible." Galen nodded in agreement. "The size she reported is about right for a shield."

"So, you believe," Anne deduced, "that the griffin Lyssa saw could be part of someone's crest." Her smile spread. "That means, if we find the right crest, we'll find the one responsible for my father's death and the death of that poor girl."

"Well, at least a confederate," Galen hedged, and slanted a look at Bryan. "I remember no griffin as part of Coltrane's crest, do you?"

Bryan shook his head. "And he would be too canny to flash such a sign about the land, knowing it could identify him."

"Even if no one recognized the crest," Galen agreed, "the sight of a strange knight, bearing the symbol of a noble house, would cause comment. Aye, he would be too clever for that."

"But Coltrane had been stripped of his title," Anne said with a frown. "Without that, he would no longer be entitled to use the crest, anyway."

Both men smiled grimly, and Bryan replied, " 'Twould make no difference to him."

"But," Galen reminded them, "*someone* was foolish enough to carry such a mark, and they were foolish enough to allow another, who could possibly remember it, to escape."

"Oh, Galen." A chill crept down Anne's spine, and she grasped his forearm. "That means the children could still be in danger. If this someone begins to think one of them could point a finger at him—"

"No one knows that we know." Galen laid his hand over hers, and the warmth of it comforted Anne. "Everyone believes, when Lyssa screamed after escaping the shed, that the monster she screamed about was me."

"Aye, all say she saw your face," Bryan murmured.

It was not meant in offense, but Bryan said it with such detachment that Anne bristled.

"Do not be ridiculous," she snapped, and both men widened their eyes at her vehemence. "Galen's face could cause no one such distress."

Looking down at the fierce beast in the book, Anne missed Bryan's small smile and the odd expression that passed over the unmasked half of Galen's face.

"What do we do?" she asked Galen.

He sighed and shrugged. "There is not much we can do, for now. The riders I sent are already long gone, and there is no way to get word to them. But . . ." He drew the word out, and his lips curved. "In about a fortnight, there is the fair."

"The Michaelmas fair!" Anne crowed in delight. "You've decided to hold it?"

"I have," he stated simply. "I've already sent word throughout the land."

From time beyond memory, Rosethorn had marked the end of harvest and the beginning of winter with a three-day fair. It was held on the eve, the day, and the day after the feast of Saint Michael the Archangel.

Once, the fair had been an event of great note.

Not just the craftsmen of Thornbury, but merchants and tradesmen from miles around gathered in a vast meadow just outside the castle walls. Common wool and extraordinary silks, plain breads and exotic sweets, simple wood carvings and fantastic gold-set jewels—all these and more were offered for sale. Sellers often came from as far away as Scotland, Wales, and perhaps Ireland. Guided by the gleam of coin, some might even travel farther, from France, Spain, or Italy.

But those selling would waste their effort if buyers did not appear. For three days, the quiet fairground, usually an arena for romping children, would teem with folk. True, the villagers of Thornbury tended to confine themselves to the simpler goods, but gentry from neighboring shires would come, lured in scores by rich pickings not found any other time of year.

With no lord in residence, however, the Michaelmas fair had fallen into abeyance. Just one of the many sacrifices made in the hard times. The promise of it now gave one more sign that prosperity was returning to Thornbury. More than that, it showed peace and security had returned as well.

Anne's heart glowed with happiness. Oh, the villagers must be overjoyed!

"Why exhaust ourselves searching," Galen proposed, "when the griffin could very well come to roost of its own accord? If this villain was so foolish once, he may be again."

Aye, Anne agreed to herself, it was very possible that, among the throng, there could be someone from a house boasting a griffin on its crest. Or knew something of one that did.

"But for now," Galen cautioned, "keep this between ourselves. Anne is right. If Coltrane, or his associates, fear identification by Lyssa, the children could be in peril."

"My lord?"

A rustle of skirts and the quiet address made all three gathered at the table look up. Freya stood, flustered, in the entry leading to the kitchen. Mayde loomed at her shoulder.

"There is a . . . a problem at the—"

Mayde snorted. "The priest is at the gate, asking for you. Something about that girl what got herself slashed to ribbons."

The reminder of the day's horror chilled Anne, and Galen's expression hardened.

"I'll tend to him in a moment," he said evenly.

Bryan stood. "I'll go with you."

Anne waited, expecting Galen to say something to her. Perhaps that he would not be long. He would join her soon. Something. But he left the hall without saying a word.

The news spread, from one cottage to the next. Men scowled and narrowed their eyes. Women shook their heads sadly.

But not about the murdered girl.

Oh, that was a tragedy, no question. But the girl had not been one of their own. Nay, sad though it was, the murder of the girl did not occupy the tongues of Thornbury that night.

There had been no blood on the sheets.

No one seemed to remember who from Rosethorn first whispered it, but by nightfall, everyone had heard. No blood on the bridal sheets. And no one needed the meaning of it explained. People looked at each other knowingly. So, they had been right, after all.

The carpenter's daughter had been Lord Galen's lover.

Such a shame, they all agreed. And young Anne had always seemed such a wholesome girl, too. Who would have thought she would turn harlot?

At least she had found her reward for it. Aye, the villagers nodded to each other, she had her just reward, bound to such a fearsome man. Men turned speculative gazes toward the castle. Women shuddered delicately. They almost had pity for her.

And those poor children, trapped in that great edifice of stone with Lord Galen as their guardian. Who knew what torments they would suffer at his hands?

Well, Anne had made her choice, and they prayed she would not live to regret it. They of the village had made a choice of their own to protect themselves, and their own young, from the disgrace.

Anne sat for a long time, staring at the open book.

With her legs curled under her on the bed in the lord's chamber, she turned page after page and feasted her eyes upon the exquisite work. Anne knew the labor that went into creating such a volume could be the work of years, and she was awed.

After a while, her eyes had consumed all she could digest, and yet, Anne still hungered. The colorful drawings were all very good, but they only teased her. The meat of the dish dangled just out of her reach.

Her father had been illiterate, as was most everyone she knew. What use were letters, after all? Could they be eaten? Could they be worn or cooked or give shelter? Father Elias was educated, but he was a priest. Nay, common folk had no use for books.

And yet, Anne knew her father had longed to learn his letters. Often had he told her he wished he had been born a scholar. No one, not even Daniel, paused to consider that scholars were made, not born. Just as no one bothered to wonder if a carpenter's daughter was capable of learning. Or that she might even want to.

Anne traced the bold black symbols with a finger and wished with all her heart that she knew what they said.

So absorbed was she in her wistful thoughts, she never heard the chamber door open.

Galen stood in the doorway and stared at Anne, remembering the first time he had seen her. How could he ever have questioned her beauty? In only her plain white gown, her hair swirling about her shoulders in waves of honey gold, she was the loveliest woman he had ever beheld. Firelight from the hearth flickered upon her, tantalizing him with glimpses of her curves.

But after a moment or two, Galen realized there was something not right. Her brow was furrowed thoughtfully, and he sensed her thoughts were troubled.

There was a difference between ignorance and stupidity, and Galen had never made the mistake of confusing them. Stupidity was not thinking. Ignorance was not knowing. Anne was far from stupid. But it seemed she was ignorant.

"Anne."

She looked up, and the ache that pounded within Galen's chest nearly brought him to his knees. She knew she did not know. It was there, in her eyes. They gleamed with hunger and glittered with shame. Hastily, she closed the book.

"What did Father Elias want?" she asked quietly.

Galen shut the door. "Just concerns about the girl's—About her burial."

Her hands caressed the book's cover, and Galen could no longer bear the look in her eyes. Stupidity had no cure, but ignorance did.

"Was there something you wanted?" she asked.

He wanted many things, but he would deal with this first.

"I've been thinking," he said, cautioning himself to step with care. Pride could be a delicate thing, and he did not want Anne's injured. "Bryan is a capable seneschal, but there is too much for him to face alone. He could do with help, but his replacement must have an understanding of how to manage a household. I could, I suppose, give the task to Mayde, but then Bryan would likely kill her within the hour."

"Likely." Anne chuckled. "And then he would likely come after you in revenge."

"I was wondering if you would take the duty. For my sake." One corner of his mouth kicked up wryly. "I would hate to face Bryan over drawn swords."

Anne gave a laugh, then sobered. "I cannot."

"Why?"

She ducked her chin. "Because I would have to see to the accounts, and I would have to read and write to do that. I do not know how."

"Is that the only reason?"

" 'Tis reason enough."

"Nay, 'tis not," he countered, and her eyes flashed fire at him. "You could learn. I could teach you."

She actually trembled. Anne clutched the book to her chest and trembled. "Truly? You would do that?"

Strange, Galen thought, how giving the simplest of gifts could bring the greatest of pleasure. "Aye."

"When?" she demanded eagerly. "When could we begin?"

"Would tomorrow be too soon?"

She shook her head and gave him a bright smile. Laying the book on the bedside table, Anne all but flew across the chamber to him. Galen caught her in his arms just as she hurtled to him. On tiptoe, she smacked a kiss on his lips and hugged his waist, all laughter and brightness.

Galen told himself he should not. Even as he caught her cheeks between his palms and tilted her head to meet his, he told himself there was still the vow—that damned vow she had exacted from him.

Never will you come to me as a husband comes to his wife. Not unless you remove your mask.

But with Anne in his arms, so soft and warm, Galen's own resolve weakened.

I hope, lady, you find your bed not too cold from your husband's absence.

His lips moved upon hers, and a moan rumbled from his throat at the taste of her. The laughter faded from her eyes, replaced by something deeper, richer. Her palms flattened upon his back, her fingers digging into the muscle as he kissed her again. Holding her head in one hand, Galen splayed his other at the small of her back, bringing her closer. Close enough to feel the rigid length of his manhood pressed between them.

He needed her.

He needed to feel her arms around him, her naked breasts pressing into his chest, her slender thighs embracing his hips. Galen parted her lips with his tongue, then plundered within. He drank her startled gasp and offered her one of his own at the thought of burying himself deep within her body.

"Anne . . ."

"Galen, please, I—"

His mouth silenced hers. The bed was only a few feet away. And he needed her. Needed her to love him.

Before he realized what he did, Galen lifted Anne from her feet, strode to the bed and tumbled onto it with her. Never taking his lips from hers, not even when he grew light-headed and short of breath, he pressed her into the mattress with his body atop hers. Her fingers curled at his shoulders, plucked at his tunic. To help him shed it? Or to push him away?

Nay! His mind shrieked in denial. By God, she would not refuse him. She wanted him as much he wanted her. He knew it. He could feel it. She could not refuse. Not when he ached like this for her. Not when his body throbbed and strained for hers.

As if from a distance, he heard the ripping of fabric and realized his hands tore at her gown. His hands spread the ruined garment. His hands cupped the soft mounds of her breasts, made her whimper into his mouth. And yet, even as Galen realized he did all this, he only hungered for more.

Catching her wrists in his hands, he pinned them on either side of her head. Anne's cry, high and thin, reverberated in his ears as he took one taut nipple between his lips.

"Galen!"

He suckled upon her, nipped at her beaded crest tenderly.

"Galen . . ." Her voice sounded odd, as she sobbed his name. "Galen, please . . . not like this."

He rose to take her lips again, to silence her protest. But before he could, the haze of his passion cleared, and he saw tears marring her cheeks.

"Galen . . ." She drew a hitching breath. "Which one of us would you have forsworn?"

His skin prickled with shame, and he looked down at her: at the gown he had destroyed; at the flesh he had exposed; at his hips cradled where he had gathered her clothing. At the arms he held in a grip so tight, his knuckles showed white.

Bile rushed into Galen's throat.

Dear God, what had he done?

Galen stumbled to his feet and leaned against one of the bedposts, praying his legs would be steady enough to carry him from the room. To take him away from the girl who clutched the remains of her tattered garment to hide her nakedness.

Lyssa had been right, after all. He *was* a monster.

Anne scrambled to sit up and, incredibly, held out her hand. Galen stared at it, her fingers trembling as she reached for him. Her eyes were wide and glimmered with tears and . . . concern? How could that be possible?

"Galen?"

He jerked his head in denial.

"Galen."

How could she call to him so gently? After what he had done to her, she should be screaming.

"Sorry," he rasped, surprised he could speak around the ball of fire in his throat. "So sorry."

"Galen, wait! Stop!"

But Galen did not stop. Not until he had slammed the door behind him and run as far as his legs could carry him.

* * *

"He knows," came the hiss in the dark. "God above, he knows everything!"

"Nay," Coltrane countered, "he cannot know."

"But he does," his servant insisted. "The girl, Lyssa. She told him. She remembers everything, everything she heard, everything she saw. And she told him."

Coltrane's mind raced. This was ill news, but not unexpected. The chance had always existed.

"What did she tell him? Tell me all." Coltrane listened, and when the tale ended, he growled, " 'Tis your own fault."

"Mine?"

"Aye, for letting that damn crest be seen," Coltrane snarled. " 'Twas unnecessary."

"And what of you?" his servant accused in a harsh whisper. "How necessary was murdering that girl?"

"You dare question me?" Coltrane demanded.

Even worms turn eventually, and this one had done just that. "Aye, I dare. 'Twas unworthy. You have blackened our cause. I've half a mind to—"

The dagger hissed from the sheath, and his servant gave a strangled gasp when the tip pressed to his throat.

"You are a whimpering fool," Coltrane said icily. "That righteousness of yours is wearing upon my patience." He jabbed at his servant's throat and smiled at the thin sob. "Turn upon me now, and you will suffer even worse than that little bitch. You cannot hide from me. You cannot run far enough or fast enough. Betray me, and I will hunt you down and delight in destroying you."

"Please . . . Master . . ."

Coltrane needled his servant's chin with the tip of the dagger. "Swear your oath anew. And on your knees, beg me for mercy."

"Aye . . . aye, master." The sniveling fool slid to the ground, the dagger a mere hair from the final slice. Coltrane felt the hunger gnaw at him. He felt his body grow hot and swell in violent arousal as his servant obeyed. "I swear all unto you. Forgive me. Please . . . Have mercy."

"I will forgive you this once," Coltrane said huskily. "But not again. Remember that."

"What are we to do?"

"The problem must be dealt with."

"I cannot." His servant huddled at his feet. "The girl was perhaps nothing, but this child—"

"I will see to her." Coltrane smiled into the dark. "And you need not fret. 'Twill be swift and clean."

Anne greeted the next morning with bleary eyes from a sleepless night. How long it had taken her to find Bryan, and what in heaven's name she had said to him to explain? She could not quite remember. Somehow, she had convinced him of the urgency of finding Galen. That was the last she had heard from either of them.

Dawn had not even fully lit the sky when Anne could bear no more. Not giving Freya the time to assist her, she dressed and went to the great hall.

No one seemed to know where Bryan was.

And no one had seen Galen since late the night before.

Anne dismissed the servants to see to their duties and, hugging herself, sank down into one of the chairs before the hearth. She tried to ignore the looks they gave her, bewildered and pitying, as she watched them scurry about.

"Anne?"

She nearly leaped from her skin at Lyssa's call. Pressing a hand between her breasts, Anne drew a steadying breath. "Good heavens, you startled me. What is it?"

"Can Derek and I go the village this morning?"

Anne gave her best smile, which she knew was not very good, and nodded. "Aye, but do not be long. And do not forget to stay within sight of your guards."

They agreed, giving her the same doubtful look everyone did, and scampered off.

Somehow, the morning wore on.

Anne drummed her fingers on an arm of the chair. Her misgiving's twisted into a knot in her belly. Where had Galen gone? Was he all right? Posing the questions jerked the knot even tighter. He had looked so shattered when he had fled their chamber. Even desperate. Dear God, surely he would not—

Nay. Anne shook her head fiercely. Galen would not do such a thing. No harm had befallen him.

She should have followed him. She should have stopped him from even leaving the chamber, made him listen. Made him realize he was not to blame for what had happened between them. No one was to blame. Or if so, that she must take as great a share as he.

Anne banged her fist on the chair's arm. Galen had been wrong, but she had started it all with her damned vows. Pushing him. Prodding him. Why could she not just be content with what she had?

Because she loved him.

But was it love to spurn what trust he could offer? How could they heal what had been wounded the night before if someone did not bend?

Lost in her thoughts, Anne only became aware of the clanging of metal against metal by degrees. The noise was very faint. Her brow furrowed, and she stood. It sounded almost like swordplay.

Anne blinked in the sunlight as she entered the bailey and followed the sound to a patch of loose dirt in a far corner of the castle walls. She stumbled to a halt, seeing a ring of men surrounding two others. Her heart throbbed heavily as she recognized the dark hair and the set of the shoulders of one. She did not need to see the mask to know it was Galen.

A relieved smile spread over her face, and she would have gone closer had Bryan not caught her eye from where he stood in the circle of men. Their gazes locked, and he gave his head a quick shake. Anne did not understand why, but she understood that he was warning her off. She nodded, assuring him she would not interfere.

Not yet, anyway.

Just knowing Galen was safe gave her step a bounce as she turned back toward the keep. They had hurt each other, but with a little patience, perhaps they could heal each other.

For the first time that wretched morning, Anne felt hope glowing in her heart.

She rounded a corner and stopped dead in her tracks.

"Derek!"

Chapter Fourteen

Never had Anne beheld a more bedraggled little boy.

One eye blackened and swollen shut, Derek gave her a sullen look from his other eye. Blood from a cut on his lower lip had already dried to a dark crust. Scrapes on his chin and one cheek stood livid against the pallor of his skin. His golden hair was tangled, and both tunic and leggings were torn in several places. One shoe was missing.

"Derek." Anne shook her head in wonder. "What happened?"

He scuffed a toe on the cobbles of the bailey and lowered his gaze. "Nothing."

"Nothing?" she repeated, and tipped his chin up. "Your nothing looks very much like the result of a fight."

Derek just shrugged and winced at the movement.

"Who were you fighting?"

His young mouth flattened into a tight line.

"Derek," Anne said in her best sisterly tone, "tell me."

" 'Twas the miller's son," Lyssa volunteered from beside him. "He and Derek—Ow!"

"Shut up!" Derek punched her in the arm and glowered. "You didn't even see it!"

"I saw him running home!"

"Did not!"

"Did—"

"Enough!" Anne shouted them down and gave Derek a pointed look. "Now, young man, I want answers. Why were you—"

"Leave the boy alone."

Anne started at the gruff command and whirled about to find Galen striding toward them. Halting beside her, he took Derek's chin in his fingers, turning the lad's head this way and that to view the damage. The unmasked half of his face bore an odd expression, almost amused. Anne turned back to her brother.

"Derek, tell me—"

"I said to leave him alone," Galen cut her off evenly.

"I'll not!" Anne glared at her husband. "I mean to find out just what in blazes happened to him."

"Then I suggest," Galen countered with great patience, "that you leave him alone."

Anne's jaw dropped, but Galen ignored her. Derek certainly looked a sight. Having been through his own share of boyhood combats, Galen sympathized with the boy's unease. Poor lad, the last thing he needed was a hovering female, even if the female was his sister. Especially if the female was his sister.

Galen turned Derek around by his slender shoulders. "Come on, boy. Let us get you cleaned up."

"Galen!"

Anne sputtered as he steered the boy into the keep. He waved her off and marched young Derek to his chamber.

"Now, then." Galen plied a warm, wet cloth to Derek's split lip. "Tell me why you fought with the miller's son."

Alone in the chamber, safe from female intrusion, Derek sat on the edge of his bed with Galen kneeling before him. The boy winced as Galen cleaned the last of the dried blood from his lip, but he remained silent. Galen did not press. Yet. Instead, he set aside the cloth and examined the lad's blackened eye. Derek whimpered as Galen tenderly parted the lids.

"Easy," Galen crooned. "Let me check it. No real damage."

Flowing to his feet, he soaked another cloth in cold water and folded it into a pad. He knelt before Derek again and pressed it to the boy's eye.

"That should ease some of the swelling, but you'll have quite a black eye for a few days. Not to mention the devil's own headache for an hour or two." Taking Derek's hand, he put it to the pad to hold it in place. "Keep it there, and let us check the rest of you."

Working surely and swiftly, Galen stripped the boy of his tunic and whistled at the colorful array of bruises on his torso.

"That is quite a collection you have."

The darkness and sheer number of the splotches drew Galen's frown. This had been no common scuffle. Derek had been hit. Hard. Very hard and very often. Too often for the work of a single opponent. Galen kept both touch and tone crisp. Having been one, he understood the tender nature of a boy's pride.

"Who, besides the miller's lad, did you fight?"

"Just three others."

"Do they look as bad as you?"

Derek gave the first hint of a smile. "Worse."

Galen chuckled and tweaked his nose, making the smile become more than a hint. Derek flinched and fingered his cut lip.

"Careful, you do not want to reopen it." Galen rinsed the first cloth free of blood and wrung it out before scrubbing the boy's filthy body. "What were you fighting about?"

"Something they said," Derek mumbled.

"What did they say?"

The lad slanted him a wary look. "You'll be angry."

"Quite likely," Galen agreed, then stroked a finger over the boy's cheek. "But not at you."

Derek swallowed. "They called Anne a name, a bad one."

Galen narrowed his eye. "What name?"

"A *really* bad name." Derek's lower lip quivered. "I am not supposed to say such things."

He leaned forward and whispered into Galen's ear. Fury coursed through Galen's veins. His hold on the boy's arm tightened, and he made himself ease his grasp.

Damn them! Damn them all! Damn every last wagging tongue that spoke such filth before children and, in so doing, gave license to tease and torment a small boy.

" 'Tis not true," Derek insisted, attempting to battle the tears threatening to escape his control. "None of it. And I told them so. But they would not stop. And I had to do something to make them stop. So, I—"

"Hush, lad." Galen shushed the tumble of words with a finger across the boy's lips. "You did what you needed to do, what you thought you had to do. There is no wrong in that."

Derek lowered his gaze. "Would *you* have done it?"

"Aye, lordling, that I would. A lady's honor must be defended, as you defended your sister's."

The boy drew a deep, hitching breath. The adrenaline that had maintained his manly composure drained away, and Galen saw tears fill his open eye. He enfolded the lad's slender body in his embrace and let him lean upon a shoulder stronger than his own until the storm passed.

"Sorry," Derek muttered when he calmed, and sniffled.

"There is nothing to be sorry for."

"You'll not tell Anne?" His gaze beseeched Galen. "She must not know, not ever."

Galen's jaw worked for a second before he nodded. " 'Twill be between you and I alone."

Just between him, Derek, and whoever had started the vile gossip when he got his hands on the bastard. No one labeled Anne a harlot and escaped retribution.

But that was for later.

Now, Galen hoisted Derek into his arms with a growl, and then dropped him on the bed. Giggling, the boy rolled away from the attack of tickling fingers, then gave a jaw-popping yawn. He smiled dreamily at the man who drew the covers over him.

"I love you, Galen," Derek mumbled, and fell fast asleep.

Galen's heart thudded off beat. Swallowing with care, he stroked his hand over Derek's sun-bright hair and made sure the cool cloth covered the boy's injured eye. He did not even pause to think, but leaned over and pressed a kiss to Derek's brow.

"Sleep well, lordling."

Anne paced from one end of her chamber to the other. She could not help it. Every instinct she possessed insisted she storm into Derek's room and tend to her brother. Pacing seemed the only way she could keep herself from doing it.

Oh, she knew what Galen wanted.

Just as a girl's first heartache required a woman to understand, a boy's first serious battle needed a man. Her father would have seen to the task, but he no longer could. Instead, Galen had taken the duty. Anne could not decide which she wanted more, to throttle him for his high-handed manner or kiss him for taking her brother under his wing.

Imagine! Telling her to leave her brother alone!

"Anne?"

As she marched past, Anne glanced at her little sister perched upon the edge of the bed. "What is it, Lyssa?"

"Did Derek do a bad thing?"

"Fighting is never a good way to settle an argument," Anne replied, then hedged, "but sometimes, you must fight for what you believe is right."

Lyssa frowned. "So, was Derek good or bad?"

"I do not know," Anne admitted. Derek had never been quick with his fists, but why his silence? "I just do not know."

Lyssa plucked at the skirt of her gown. "If Derek was bad, what will Galen do?"

"Talk to him about it, I suppose."

"He would not—" Lyssa laced her fingers tightly together in her lap, and her voice became very small. "He would not . . . beat Derek. Would he?"

That brought Anne to a dead stop. She knelt before her sister, covering the small hands with her own.

"Lyssa, whatever put such a notion into your head?" she asked gently. "Galen would never beat Derek, or you."

"Are you sure?"

Anne did not think twice. "Very sure."

Lyssa gave a sigh. "I did not think so. And I told—"

Her large blue eyes grew even larger at her slip. Anne narrowed her own. "Who did you tell?"

"No one," came the reply a bit too instantly.

Anne let her lifted brow speak for her. It always worked.

Lyssa twisted her fingers into a knot. "*Someone* said Galen would have little patience with us, and that he would prove a hard master for us to obey. That he would likely rule with the whip. But I told them," she hastened to add, "that Galen was the best lord in the realm, and they were nothing but ninnies for thinking any different."

Anne listened in stony silence, certain that if she spoke before her temper could settle, she would speak nothing but the vilest profanity she could conjure up.

A pox on this someone! How dare they speak such blasphemy? And to a little girl!

Lyssa peered at her warily. "Are you angry?"

"Aye," Anne snarled, and surged to her feet, "I am angry. I am bloody furious!"

"I told them!" Lyssa vowed in tearful defense. "I *did!*"

Anne stamped her rage back under control, fell to her knees, and swept Lyssa into her arms. "Not at you, sweetling. You said just what you should have, no more than the truth."

"Galen is the best lord in the realm," Lyssa insisted, sobbing against Anne's shoulder. "He *is.*"

Anne crooned and rocked her little sister in her embrace until Lyssa quieted. Lyssa hiccuped and sniffed, and Anne stood her straight and wiped at her tears.

"Now, sweet," she said evenly, "will you tell me who told you these awful things?"

Lyssa nibbled her lower lip. "Must I?"

That stymied Anne for a moment. Why Lyssa would want to shield such a bald-faced liar escaped her comprehension, but she must have her reasons. Suppose the culprit was not an adult. Suppose it were a child, repeating what he or she had heard but not fully understood? Anne knew children could be cruel, far crueler than adults.

"Nay, Lyssa," she said at last, "you need not tell me. But remember, a friend who would tell such a terrible lie is no real friend. You think on that. If you decide to confide in me, all you need do is come to me."

Lyssa nodded, and Anne kissed her cheek.

"Now, you run along and wash up for the noon meal."

Her sister gave her a last hug and then scampered to the door. Just as she reached it, it swung open, and Lyssa collided with Galen's legs.

"Whoa!" He steadied her. "Where are you off to?"

"I must go wash up," she announced.

"Must you, now?" He stroked a finger over her tear-stained cheek and speared Anne with a knowing look. She shook her head slightly. Galen looked back to the little girl. "Well, you had best be about it, then."

Lyssa beamed and flitted by him. Then, pausing in the doorway, she turned and tilted her head to peer up at him. "Are we a family now, Galen?"

Anne's heart froze within her breast at the innocent question, and at the expression on Galen's face. Thunderstruck, he just stared at the child for a moment, and Anne saw him swallow with difficulty.

"I suppose we are," he finally said.

Lyssa nodded, satisfied. "I just wanted to make sure."

She flew off, and Galen turned a bemused look to Anne. "What was that all about?"

Anne gave him a small smile in reply. Galen did not understand, she realized. He really did not grasp the significance of his answer. But he would. Aye, Anne vowed, he would understand before she was done.

"Why had she been crying?" he pressed.

Anne faltered. "Someone made a remark that bothered her."

"What remark?" he asked darkly.

She should tell him. Anne knew she should, but Galen had enough to face without adding one more problem. She would deal with that hateful remark herself, and in her own way.

" 'Tis nothing I cannot work out with her," she hedged. His look said he was not satisfied, and Anne moved to forestall further discussion. "Is Derek all right? Did he tell you why he was fighting?"

"Aye, and aye."

Galen poured himself a goblet of wine. Crossing the chamber, he sank down into a chair before the hearth and waited for the questions. He did not wait long.

"Well?"

"I can tell you no more." She glared at him, and Galen smiled grimly. "I gave Derek my word, and contrary to recent evidence, I generally keep it."

"Oh, Galen." Anne knelt beside him and laid her hand on his thigh. He kept his gaze fixed upon the depths of his goblet. If he looked at her now, he would touch her. And if he touched her? He did not look at her. "Last night—"

"Last night was an abomination," he growled. "I cannot excuse it or offer apology good enough for it."

"Nay, you—"

"Dammit, woman!" he snapped, and felt her flinch in the jerk of her hand on his thigh. "I nearly raped you!"

She paled and withdrew her touch. Galen leaned his head back against the chair and closed his eye.

"If you had any sense," he said wearily, "you would gather the children and flee Rosethorn as though the hounds of hell nipped at your heels."

"Which is precisely what you expect me to do."

Galen swung a bewildered gaze to her.

"I am sorry to disappoint you, Galen," Anne went on serenely, "but I have no such intention. And you cannot drive me away, so stop wasting your time trying."

He lowered his brow. "You sound very certain."

"Oh, I am."

"Why?"

The question popped from his lips before Galen realized it, and he felt disquieted. He had not wanted to ask, afraid of the answer he might get, and yet he had to know. After all he had done, all he had demanded of her, how could she remain with him? How could she want to?

Anne rose and brushed a kiss upon his lips, answering his question with one of her own.

"*Are* we a family, Galen?"

Anselm nearly leaped from his own skin when he turned around. Framed in the doorway of his smithy, a tall form stood silhouetted against the afternoon sun. He blinked and squinted, and a chill worked its frosty fingers into his belly.

The Lord of Rosethorn.

That half-masked face gave nothing away. The one eye glittered in the reflected flames from the forge. The lean cheek and arch of a dark eyebrow looked almost demonic in the flickering shadows. Anselm's grip tightened upon the hammer he held.

"My lord," he said roughly, nodding his head in greeting.

One corner of Lord Galen's mouth twitched, though Anselm did not think it exactly a smile. "Good day."

The silence stretched until Anselm found himself having to swallow to ease the strange constriction in his throat.

"What . . . ah, what can I do for you, my lord?"

Lord Galen stepped into the smithy, and it was all Anselm could do to keep from taking a step back. The slight shuffle of his feet did not escape his lordship, and the man's expression turned rueful. "You need have no fear of me, Anselm."

"Fear of you, my lord?" Anselm asked, overly hearty.

"I know what is said of me." He lifted one brow. "But you need not worry. I am not here to ravish your daughter or cast some sorcerer's spell upon your house." His smile turned sharp. "Perhaps some other time."

From Lord Galen's lips, the tales sounded every bit as ridiculous as they were. Anselm felt his face flame from more than the heat of the forge.

"Nay, I am here on a different errand," Lord Galen went on. "You are a man of influence in the village, and I felt you should be the first to know I have decided to hold the Michaelmas fair this year."

The words were so unlike what he expected that Anselm's jaw dropped. "The fair? But the fair has not been held for years, not since . . . er, well . . ."

"Not since my father's death, I know," Lord Galen murmured.

"There is so little time. How—"

"I sent out couriers with the news weeks ago. If the response they reported is even half true, we should have quite a gathering."

"I do not know what to say, my lord." Anselm felt a smile spread slowly upon his face. " 'Twill mean much to the village."

"Aye, you are grateful now," Lord Galen said wryly, "but I doubt we'll escape the usual dispute between the village and castle over stall rents and tolls."

Anselm chuckled. "Even so, my lord, 'tis good of you to see it begun again."

"Goodness has nothing to do with it." Lord Galen shrugged. " 'Tis plain sense. The castle needs the village, and the village needs the coin. You'll spread the word?"

Anselm nodded and grinned. "With pleasure, my lord."

"Excellent. My seneschal will contact you to settle the arrangements." Lord Galen half-turned, then stopped in the doorway. "Oh, and Anselm, you would not know anything about a fight between young Derek and a group of other lads, would you?"

"I heard the lad got into a scuffle this morning." The smith's smile tilted wryly. " 'Twas no doubt just a row over naught. Boys can have the devil's own temper."

"There was naught common about this one." Anselm frowned, and Lord Galen explained, "Derek was beaten by four boys, goaded into it by some comments concerning my wife."

Anselm felt the blood drain from his face. Truly, he had heard nothing about any comments made, but considering the latest whispers, he could make a fair guess what had been said. Lord Galen's mouth compressed into a hard line.

"Understand this, Anselm, and understand it well," Lord Galen said softly. "No one—man, woman, or child—calls my wife a whore and escapes my rage. Derek dealt with the boys this morning, and I am content to leave that as it stands. But you see that lie killed, and killed completely."

"Aye, my lord," Anselm mumbled through numb lips.

"I'll not allow a member of my—" His lordship stopped, and a strange expression passed over the revealed side of his face. Then, the half-bemused and half-delighted look dissolved into utter determination. "I'll not allow a member of my family to be hurt by such filth. Do we understand each other?"

Anselm narrowed his eyes thoughtfully. There was something different about Lord Galen. The man seemed easier, as though the key to some vexing riddle had just been handed to him.

But Anselm only replied, "Aye, my lord."

"Good." Lord Galen's smile held none of the bitterness that had sharpened it before. "I know I can depend upon you."

Galen rode slowly back to Rosethorn.

Are we a family, Galen?

I suppose we are.

Galen thought of his wedding and of the moment he had looked at Anne and her brother and sister in turn. He remembered thinking he had inherited a complete family. Was he now part of it?

He had little experience with family. His mother had died when he was young. He could barely even call her face to mind now. All he knew of her were the tales he had heard over the years, stories from servants, a few comments from his father. Galen could not recall exactly missing her, more just being aware that she was not there.

And his father? Galen curled his lips into a thin smile. Lord Geoffery had been a difficult man, both the idol and bane of his childhood. Respecting him had been as natural as breathing. Loving him had proved harder. A wall, as solid as the walls of Rosethorn itself, had always existed between them.

A wall of pride.

Entering the castle gates, Galen dismounted and handed the reins to a stablehand, but his gaze remained fixed inward. Pride. Had he never succeeded in scaling the wall between himself and his father because of his pride? And had his father never been able to reach him for the same reason? Had they wasted all those years because of nothing but their own pride?

And when you return, when you find out what sort of man you are, you'll come to me on your knees. On your knees, you hear!

His father's bellow reverberated through Galen's mind even now. He had vowed never to do it. He would rather have died before he gave the old man that satisfaction. But Lord Geoffery had died first, with all the miles, all the silence, still separating them. Who was to blame for that? Himself? His father?

Both of them?

With slow tread, Galen walked across the bailey, paused before the keep, then turned aside and walked on.

In a forgotten corner of Rosethorn, he halted before a door, barred with a thick wooden plank. He had commanded every room, every nook and cranny of the old castle cleaned and made fit for habitation. Every place but this one. This small structure, fashioned of stone and seeming to grow from the thick wall behind it, he had ordered not to be entered.

He placed the heels of his hands upon the bar and shoved at it. When it did not budge, Galen gritted his teeth and pushed at it as hard as he could. Finally, the plank gave a scrape and shifted. Again he pushed it, not stopping until it clattered onto the cobbled ground. He grasped the old iron handle and pulled with all his might. He heard a creak, and then a great sigh. Musty air rushed to his nose.

The sun cast feeble rays through the open door, barely penetrating the shadows within. Galen's footsteps sounded harsh upon the stone floor as he stepped inside and looked around. Though covered in a thick coat of dust and grime, the room was just as he remembered. Nothing had been disturbed.

He stood before the altar of Rosethorn's chapel and stared

at it for a long time. Then he went to where an iron gate stood behind it. The gate screeched as he forced it open. Galen hesitated for a moment, then went down the short flight of stairs beyond.

The air was cool there, damp and dank. Galen fumbled his hand along a ledge at the foot of the stairs and found the means to light the torch left in the bracket. Ghostly shapes greeted him as he thrust the torch into the gloom. He could not seem to draw breath deeply enough as he gazed at the final resting place of the lords of Rosethorn.

One by one, Galen read the inscriptions marking his forebears' remains, from the first one titled just after the Conquest to—to his father. He ran his fingers over the lettering, and something rose into his throat. It throbbed there until Galen was no longer sure if he breathed at all.

"Papa." His whisper was nearly soundless.

"Galen?"

He whirled at the soft call of his name. Anne stood, hesitating over the last stair. Timidly, she crossed to him. Galen turned back to the crypt.

"Is that your father's?" she asked.

"Aye, Lord Geoffery Tarrant of Rosethorn." Galen fell silent for a time. Then, in a soft tone, he said, "When I left, he told me to return to him on my knees. I told him both he and Rosethorn could rot in hell for all I cared."

Anne shivered. "You did not mean it."

"How do you know?" he replied roughly.

"Because you came back."

"I stayed away for over eleven years."

"Why?" She laid her hand on his arm, and Galen felt a tremor run through him at her touch. "Because of your face?"

" 'Twould be easy to say aye." He shook his head slowly. "Perhaps 'twas part of it, but mostly because I could not bear the thought that he would expect me to do as he commanded—return on my knees."

Anne leaned against him and slipped an arm around his waist. "Do you think he would have?"

"Nay." Strange, how he was so very certain all of a sudden. Even stranger, he felt one corner of his mouth lift into a smile. "I think he would have grumbled and groaned, and complained bitterly, but he would not have expected that of me."

When had his own arm wrapped around her? Holding the torch aloft with one hand, Galen brought Anne closer with the other and buried his face in her hair.

"I am sorry, Anne," he whispered. "Sorry for what I did to you last night, for what I've done to you from the start."

"That is odd," she replied, and leaned back to smile up at him. "I am not sorry at all."

He scowled. "But—"

"We've made mistakes," Anne went on, "but mistakes can be forgiven."

Galen swallowed thickly. "Can they?"

Her chuckle brought a shaft of brightness into the gloomy chamber. " 'Tis what *families* do best."

"And the vow?" He stroked her cheek. "What of it?"

"Another mistake." Anne lowered her gaze. "I know that now. Nothing that causes so much anguish could be right."

He understood what she told him, that she had released him from the vow. A mistake, she called it. Perhaps it was. And perhaps she had demanded no more than her due.

"I wish I could give you what you want," Galen murmured. "I wish I could—"

"Nay, say no more." She pressed a finger to his lips, and her voice shook. "I love you, Galen. You did not force me to love you. 'Twas a choice I made as I came to know you. You gave me that choice. I can do no less for you."

"I'll not remove the mask for you, Anne," he warned.

"I know." Did regret flicker over her expression? Or only shadows cast by the blazing torch? "Perhaps one day."

"Never." Galen shook his head and narrowed his eye. "I would rather slit my own throat than watch your eyes round with horror at the sight of my face."

"Are you so sure I would, then?"

"Oh, you would." He gave a travesty of a laugh. "You would take one look, and you would never be able to look upon me again. You would know, then. You would know exactly what kind of man I am."

She laid her hand upon his chest. "But I already know—"

"Nay!" Galen stepped away from her. "You know nothing. You've conjured some idea of me in your mind, and you've let that blind you to the truth. I should show you. I should prove just wrong you are, but God help me, I cannot. So I should let you go, set you free, but I cannot do that either."

"You cannot allow me close, and you cannot send me away," Anne said, and Galen's flesh crawled at the hollow ache in her voice. "Where does that leave us, Galen?"

"Right back where we started," he replied huskily. "I need you, want you, but if I take you, 'twould be the same as lying to you. I'll not use you like that. You may have released me from the vow, but I cannot release myself."

Anne closed her eyes, and Galen watched her take a long breath. When she opened her eyes again, they shimmered with sorrow.

"Very well," she said softly, and turned toward the stairway. Then she stopped and turned back. "But know this, Galen. I love you, and that is no trick of my mind. I do know who you are, what you are, and that is no trick, either. Perhaps one day, you'll know, too."

Chapter Fifteen

Somehow, time slipped by.

Anne filled her days with learning the workings of the keep, and her nights with waiting. Every night, Galen retired to their chamber with her. He spoke of small things, issues of the household or plans for the village. True to his word, he introduced her to letters and the mysteries of language. He proved a gentle and patient teacher, and Anne treasured the moments they spent together.

But then, as the castle settled for the night, Galen would rise, press his lips to her brow, and leave. Every night, she struggled to think of some way to thwart him, and every night, she failed. By the beginning of the second week, Anne had to admit she was no closer to convincing Galen to stay. The conviction of unworthiness, ground into him for so many years, proved stronger than she was.

Still, Anne refused to admit defeat.

Before she knew it, the Michaelmas fair was upon them.

The fair opened with all the excitement that could be desired. After missing the event for so long, everyone seemed determined to enjoy it to the fullest. Merchants had come from far and wide. Performers of all kinds arrived to delight and amaze with their skill. People flocked to Rosethorn to view and buy.

At first, Anne had feared the village would prove aloof, but she soon discovered she need not worry. Thornbury came with their own wares to sell and did their own share of buying, too. If a villager or two looked askance at their lord, most decided to bury their misgivings, at least during the fair.

Master Anselm seemed to lead the way. He greeted Galen with respect the first morning, and more than one villager lifted a brow when they saw Galen clap Anselm on the back and clasp hands amicably with him.

Her own dealings with her neighbors were strained at first. Several would not meet her gaze, but as the fair wore on, that seemed to ease as well. Soon, folk she had known all her life spoke and laughed just as they always had, and Anne began to hope the chasm between village and castle could be bridged at long last.

Between them, Galen and his men seemed to be everywhere at once—greeting guests, directing merchants to their stalls and collecting the rents, levying the tolls for the goods passing over the lord's roads. They settled disputes and exercised justice when a pickpocket was nabbed in the act.

Anne watched Galen grow haggard, saw shadows deepen beneath his eye, but such was his air of satisfaction, she had not the heart to scold. A holiday spirit had infected him, and she was loath to disturb it.

Only one note sounded in discord.

Though she, Galen, and his soldiers kept their eyes peeled, no one had yet seen a crest bearing a griffin or heard tell of one. The riders Galen had dispatched returned in ones and twos and reported little. The only news was grim. The murdered girl had been identified as belonging to a neighboring holding. A stablemaster's daughter, she was. Folk recalled her speaking of a handsome suitor, but no one remembered having seen the man.

The third and final day of the fair dawned just like the others. Autumn put on her summer memories and promised sunshine, though a certain tang in the air said chilly days were coming. Mindful of that, Anne decided to seek out the cloth and wool merchants first thing that morning. The children needed clothing for the winter, and she could do with a few things herself.

"Here." Galen handed her a pouch filled with coin and offered a wry smile. "I had thought of the matter before, but—"

"There has not been time," Anne said in unison with him, and giggled. "How much may I spend?"

He gave her an odd look. "Spend as much you need. Spend it all, if you want."

"But Galen, this pouch holds at least—"

"Anne." He took her hands and kissed her lightly. "I am a wealthy man, and I can think of no greater use for my wealth than outfitting my wife. Buy what you need, what you want, for both you and the children."

His generosity brought an ache to her throat, but Anne wanted nothing to disturb the lighthearted twinkle in his eye. So, instead of saying what her heart longed to, she lowered her lashes coyly.

" 'Tis a dangerous thing, my lord, giving a woman free rein with your purse."

Her teasing remark only made his expression sober. Galen stroked the back of his fingers over her cheek. "Nay, lady, 'tis not mine. 'Tis *ours.*"

He pressed another kiss to her lips and was gone before she could respond.

Ours.

Anne found herself smiling. She liked the word. She liked the way Galen used it even more. Perhaps she would not win his trust in one grand moment. Perhaps it would happen bit by bit, day by day. Today, he spoke of his purse. Tomorrow? Her smile became a grin, and Anne tossed the soft leather pouch and caught it again. Tomorrow, perhaps he would speak of deeper things.

Her morning proved productive. Anne found excellent wools at one stall, threads in a rainbow of colors at another, and allowed herself to be tempted into purchasing a beautiful bolt of silk at a third. All was paid for and would be delivered to the keep that evening. By midday, she was well satisfied, but her eye caught sight of a length of cloth that lured her to it. She did not need it for herself or the children, but she could not help but think how precise a match it was to Galen's emerald gaze, how handsome he would look in a tunic fashioned from it. Delighted, she began to dicker with the merchant, determined to have that cloth.

Her bargaining received a rude interruption when she was jostled from behind. Anne gasped and teetered off balance.

"Your pardon, my lady," said the man, who caught her about the waist. He smiled most attractively. "I am so sorry, but the crowd is rather thick."

"No matter," she replied with a smile of her own. "I am quite unharmed."

Anne considered the incident at an end and returned to her haggling. After a few sharp exchanges, the merchant flung up his hands and declared her far too shrewd. Anne chuckled as he complained she would beggar him with her quick wit and paid the agreed coin. She collected her purchase and turned to find the stranger still there. He bowed before her.

"Please, my lady," he entreated, "allow me to carry it."

What could she say? He seemed pleasant enough, a gentleman of means judging from his garb. He was very handsome, with his golden hair glinting in the sun and twinkling blue eyes, and he looked to be fairly young—about Galen's age. But there was something about him that made the back of her neck prickle. His smile meant to charm, but it looked a shade too sharp. His manly form felt just a little too close for comfort, even though he did not actually crowd her at all.

It was almost as if his presence threatened her.

Nonsense. Anne shook herself. She was just tired. She was imagining things. But even so . . .

"Thank you, but nay," she refused politely.

"You are visiting the fair?" he asked, remaining beside her as she walked away from the stall. Again, he kept himself at a respectful distance and made no move to alarm her.

Anne was alarmed anyway. "Nay."

He came a sudden halt and grasped her arm, his expression one of wonder. "Do not tell me *you* are the lady I've heard so much about. You cannot be the Lady of Rosethorn."

"I am, indeed." Anne tugged from his grip. Exactly why, she could not decipher, but the sooner she got away from this man, the easier she would feel. "Excuse me, but I must find my brother and sister. I fear they have wandered too far."

He caught her hand and bowed over it. Anne flinched when his lips caressed her fingertips. "May I say, lady, you are even lovelier than I had heard? I should like very much to make acquaintance with you better."

"I fear my husband, Lord Galen Tarrant, might have something to say about that," Anne snapped, and jerked her hand from his. Her instincts were at full alarm. Thank heaven Galen still insisted that a pair of his men follow her wherever she went. She saw them closing in. "Good day to you, sir."

Anne tried not to panic as she darted through the crowd. What was there to panic over, after all? One over-zealous admirer? It was ridiculous, and yet she could not rid herself of the sensation of being stalked. She caught sight of Galen and all but ran to him. He smiled when he saw her, but his smile faded as she came closer.

"What is it, sweet?" He caught her close, his brow furrowed. "You look as though you've seen a ghost."

"Galen, that man—" Anne turned to point him out and frowned instead. "He is gone!" She searched all around and saw her guards doing the same. "But he was just there, not two seconds ago."

"What man?" Galen demanded. "Who was there?"

"A man, about your size and age." Anne continued to search, but it was as though he had melted into thin air. "Gold hair, blue eyes."

"Anne." Galen caught her chin and forced her to look up at him. She did not like the urgency she saw in him. "Was there a scar? About here, just above the left brow?"

"Aye." She thought and nodded, her answer becoming

firmer. "Now that you mention it, there was. 'Twas very small."

"Coltrane."

Anne felt the blood drain from her face. "And I spoke with him. Lord, I looked him right in the eye and told him—" Her heart squeezed tight. "Oh, Galen, I told him I had to find the children. Where are they?"

"Calm down," he commanded gently. "They cannot be far, and wherever they are, they are guarded, remember?" Anne remembered and felt dizzy with relief. "I'll find them. Go back to the keep. Have the door barred and stay there until I come. Let no one else within. No one."

She nodded, and he kissed her brow as he made to go.

"Galen." Anne called to him, and he turned. "Be careful."

"I will."

And then he, too, melted into the crowd.

Anne headed toward the keep. Galen would find Derek and Lyssa, and he would bring them to her safe and sound. She was sure of that. What would happen next, Anne did not ponder too deeply. No doubt he and Bryan would take off in search of Coltrane, and she suddenly was not sure she wanted them to find him. Hearing about the man, being told he was near, was one thing. Experiencing his closeness proved quite another.

Oh, she knew there was a reason she had disliked him!

As she neared the castle gate, Anne heard laughter, childish and carefree. She turned toward it and, to her intense relief, saw Derek and Lyssa racing pell-mell from the forest. Their smiles assured her that no cloud had overcast their adventures thus far, but where was their guard? There should be at least two men, but Anne saw no one. All at once, she knew.

Those two imps had shaken their guards somewhere in their rambling. She gritted her teeth. Just wait until she got a hold on them. Fun was fun, but there were limits!

"Come here, both of you, now." She called. They faltered at the tone they recognized. "Come on, I mean it."

Young faces drawn into lines of complaint, both of them

continued across the field. Anne could already hear their excuses and youthful scorn for adult caution. And then she heard something else.

She heard the heavy thud of hooves. She heard cries of alarm and stalls overturning. Distracted, she swung her gaze around. A rider upon a great steed exploded from within the crowd, thundering toward her.

Anne moved on instinct, diving and rolling clear. The horse came so close that she could feel the ground tremble. She heard a curse, a snarl of rage, and whipped her head up. The rider had gone on. Toward the wood. Toward the children.

"Nay!"

Anne screamed and leaped to her feet at the same time. She was running before she even realized it, but she was no match for the horse and rider. Still, she kept running, kept watching in helpless horror.

Derek and Lyssa stumbled to a halt. The sun glinted off a drawn blade. Derek grabbed Lyssa and flung her aside. He turned and faced the rider.

And then it was over.

"Nay!"

Galen whirled about at the scream. Anne's scream. A great surge of people made toward the castle walls, and a terrible rumble of voices floated by. Pushing and shoving others aside, Galen heard only that scream.

"Derek!"

At long last, Galen cleared the throng and saw Bryan racing from the castle gates. His gaze followed his friend's direction, and his heart froze in his chest. There was Anne, huddled upon the ground.

"Oh, God . . ."

Galen ran as he had never run before, beating everyone to her side. Anne looked up at him, eyes glittering. On the ground where she knelt, Derek's small body lay like a doll dropped carelessly in the grass. A large, ugly blot of red soaked his tunic's torn front. Galen fell to his knees and pressed his hand to the wound to stanch the blood. By the time Bryan reached them, Galen had found the boy's pulse, thin and rapid. But there.

"He is alive," he told Bryan breathlessly, "but he bleeds far too much."

" 'Tis more in his shoulder, praise God." The seneschal dropped beside him.

"Aye, but we will still lose him if we cannot stop the bleeding." Galen lifted the lad and cradled him close. "Run ahead and have his bed prepared."

Bryan took off, and Galen rose to his feet. Anne hovered, smoothing back a lock of the boy's hair, arranging his arms so they did not dangle. Neither she nor Lyssa cried, but both were the color of chalk.

"We must get him to the keep," Galen muttered.

Anne took Lyssa's hand and walked at his side. "Galen, he is so still. He cannot—"

"He will not." Galen pressed his lips to boy's brow. "Nay, I'll not let him die."

Not until the lad had been laid upon his bed did Derek show signs of life. He moaned, and his eyelids fluttered. Galen looked down into blue eyes glazed with pain. After a moment, recognition flickered in them, and Derek's ashen lips moved.

"Galen . . ."

"Quiet, lordling." Galen stroked Derek's brow, his clammy cheeks. He took the boy's hand in his own. "Be quiet, now."

"Tr-tried . . . save Lyssa." Incredibly, one corner of Derek's mouth twitched upward. "Was . . . hero?"

"Aye." Galen choked on the word. "That you are."

His eyes closed. "L-like you."

Derek tightened his fingers upon Galen's for an instant before they went slack once more. Galen could not breathe for the throbbing in his throat, the burning in his chest.

God have mercy, the boy thought Galen was a hero?

"Move aside." Galen twisted at the command. Mayde stood like a grim statue behind him. "Well? Do you want me to see to the boy or not?"

Galen released his hold on the lad's hand and rose. Mayde took his place, cutting away Derek's tunic with a sharp knife and inspecting the wound.

"'Tis bad enough, but I've seen worse." Mayde snorted. "The fool boy is lucky."

Oddly, the dispassionate words comforted Anne more than any show of sympathy could. The housekeeper worked briskly, but for all her apparent lack of caring, Anne noticed that she handled Derek with a gentle touch. Finally, Mayde straightened and glared.

"Out, all of you," she commanded everyone. Then she looked Anne over. "Except you, girl. You look like you've a strong stomach and quick hands." The housekeeper smiled grimly. "I've a stomach like iron, but time has slowed my hands some. This boy will not withstand fumbling."

"Perhaps Freya—" Anne started to suggest.

"That weak-willed ninny?" Mayde barked a laugh. "I'll not have her in here. Like as not, she would swoon and land right atop the boy. Your help will have to do."

As Mayde snapped out orders for hot water, linens, and such, Anne went to Galen. He stood with face pale and as hard as stone, staring at the bed. When Anne laid her hand upon his arm, it was as if she touched stone, too.

"Galen?"

He blinked and focused upon Mayde. "He'll not die."

"Did I say he would?" the housekeeper countered. "He has a far way to go before I'll claim he's safe, but any boy who causes as much trouble as this one will not die easily."

"See that he does not," he growled.

Mayde narrowed her eyes at him. "Aye, my lord."

His gaze went back to the little boy, and the corner of his mouth jerked. Anne stroked his arm and tried to tuck her fingers within his grasp, but it was as though she had ceased to exist to him. Galen did not even look at her as he turned and left the chamber.

"Galen?" she called after him.

"Let him go," Mayde advised flatly. Anne lingered, staring after her husband until the housekeeper snapped, "Now, girl! You'll not do this boy any good by mooning over his lordship. He has his work to do. We have ours. Turn to it."

Galen strode down the winding stairs and into the hall. Bryan whirled at the sound of his footsteps, took in his lord's fierce expression and shook his head slowly.

"Derek has not—"

"Not yet," Galen replied, voice rock-hard. He never slowed his step. "We have work to do. Saddle horses and call out every man from among our own, the village, and any who wish to join us. Everyone."

Galen flung open the doors and kept right on going. Bryan scrambled to follow.

"We will beat every tree in the forest to splinters," Galen vowed in a cold rage, "tear every cottage to the ground, if we must. I will have Coltrane, and I'll have the bastard on his knees before I kill him for this."

Anne sat in a chair by Derek's bed and clasped her fingers together to keep them from shaking. Her stomach was upset, and she drew a calming breath to settle it.

They were finished.

It was in God's hands now.

"You work well, girl," Mayde observed briskly. She rolled spare strips of linen and laid them in a neat pile on the bedside table. "You've clean, quick hands, and you do not flinch enough to notice, though I see you've paled a bit."

Oh, Mayde could be utterly unbearable at times. Anne snorted. "I'm all right."

"Of course you are. Here." Anne started a little when Mayde thrust a goblet before her nose. "Drink that. 'Twill put some color back in your cheeks."

Anne took the drink and sipped, finding the wine had an unusual bite to it. "What is—"

"A bit of crushed herb. Go on, drink it. Every last drop." Mayde smirked. "I'll not poison you, girl, if that is what concerns you."

Anne obeyed. The taste was unpleasant, but she began to feel better. Calmer. Silence reigned for a while.

"You know, there will likely be fever," Mayde commented.

Anne's lips trembled before she could steady them. "Aye."

"He'll not die of the wound itself, though. If he does die, 'twill be from fever. He will need someone to sit by him, keep him cool, hold him down when he thrashes in his sleep. He'll tear his stitches and I'll not have my work mangled."

"You need not fear that. I will sit with him."

"Aye, you will," Mayde agreed, and Anne clenched her jaw to keep from shrieking at the woman. "But you'll show sense and share the duty."

Duty. Anne closed her eyes and felt a wave of despair dash over her heart. She had not done her duty by Derek. She had not kept him safe. She blinked back tears.

"I will ask Freya."

"Hah! She'll not be much use to you. You would do better to leave her in charge of the lass."

Anne balled her hand into a fist. "Who do you suggest?"

"I will do it."

"You?" Astonishment swept Anne's mind blank for a moment, and she twisted to stare at Mayde. "You cannot abide Derek, or me. Why would you want to help?"

"Did I say I wanted to?" Anne frowned, for something suspiciously close to a twinkle lit Mayde's eyes. It was so fleet, Anne decided that she had imagined it. "You must see to it first, though. His lordship will have every man for miles around leaping for hours, and all will be tired and hungry when he finally lets them go. I must see they'll have food and drink ready."

At mention of Galen, Anne worried her lower lip. He had been so distant, looked so shattered. Concern for Derek? No doubt. But there was something else, something horrid tormenting him, and Anne could not quite put a finger on it.

"You are worried about him," Mayde said, surprisingly gently. Somehow, Anne knew they thought of the same person, and she nodded a little. "Aye, well, I suppose you've cause."

Anne angled her a look. "Why do you say that?"

"Because, girl, his lordship is out hunting the villain who dared harm that boy. And he means to find and punish him, or die in the attempt."

Anne hated to admit it, but Mayde proved right.

Freya was disconsolate over Derek, so much so that Anne finally had to find another maid to keep watch over Lyssa. Freya's constant weeping had frightened the little girl more than witnessing her brother's wounding had.

"Poor, poor little lamb," Freya whimpered, shaking her head at Derek lying pale and still on the bed. "So young to be taken from us."

"But Freya," Anne tried to reason with her, "Derek is not dead, nor is he likely to die of his wound, according to Mayde."

"And you believe the word of that old crone?" Freya scoffed through her tears. "She would snort at the Crucifixion, that one would."

Once, Anne might have agreed without hesitation, but now she was not so sure. Not after the past day or so. "Mayde has done everything she can for Derek and done it well."

"I'll not deny she knows her way with healing, but that woman has a heart of stone. She despises that blessed boy." Her kindly face crumpled with fresh tears. "That poor, blessed little child . . ."

For the first time since she had met her, Anne gave up on Freya. The woman meant well, but she was no help at all. Surprising, really, Anne reflected. Freya had always been such a support to her, but now the poor maid crept like a wraith about the castle. Anne felt terribly disloyal, but Freya was beginning to get on her nerves.

Mayde was completely different. The housekeeper did what needed to be done and did not shrink from it. For a reason Anne had not the energy to determine, she preferred Mayde's company at Derek's sickbed, comforted by her biting remarks and no-nonsense presence. Often, they were the only things that kept Anne herself from sinking into despair.

For Derek was a very sick little boy. True to Mayde's

word, the wound looked as though it would heal, but his fever soared. The two women took turns with him, bathing him to keep him cool, soothing him when fever dreams seized him. For three days, he tossed in delirium, and Anne was very worried. Suppose he did not wake? Suppose the fever carried him off? He was so weak, so wan.

Between tending Derek and soothing Lyssa, Anne had little time to spare for thought, but those few times haunted her. She would lie in bed, seeking snatches of sleep, but her mind kept her awake with all sorts of horrible images. Often, in such dark moments, she would hear footsteps pass outside the door and lay in an agony of hope that Galen would come to her, soothe her with his warm, sure presence.

He never did.

Anne sat beside her brother and bathed his hot brow, but her thoughts were upon Galen. She was almost more concerned about him than about Derek. In the past three days, she had barely laid eyes on him. He left at first light, and she did not hear his footsteps again until far into the night. When she did see him, he lingered only long enough to eat and change his soiled clothing and exhausted mount, before setting out again. The few times she had managed to make him look at her, Anne shivered at what she saw.

He means to find and punish him, or die in the attempt.

Anne told herself it was foolish to let those words prey upon her so. Mayde was a grim biddy, even under the best of circumstances. Yet Anne could not deny that the words frightened her, for truth lurked within them.

Galen was like a man possessed, driven to find Coltrane. Anne feared he would drive himself into the ground instead.

Or worse, he would drive himself to madness.

It had to end. But unless they were rid of Coltrane once and for all, Anne knew it would continue. When she peered into that future, she became truly afraid—for Rosethorn, the village, the children, herself. And especially for Galen.

Consumed by her thoughts, Anne did not notice Derek's sudden restlessness at first.

The little boy gasped and panted for breath until she knew his slender chest would burst with the effort. Piteous moans seeped from his lips. Another fever dream? Anne stroked him with a wet, cool cloth and crooned to him, but nothing eased the child. The moans deepened into choking sobs.

"Mayde!"

Anne rose, keeping one eye on her brother writhing helplessly upon the bed, and stepped backward to the door. Dear Lord, what was happening to him? She flung open the door.

"Mayde! Mayde, come quickly! Derek is dying!"

Chapter Sixteen

Bryan had gone beyond exhaustion. He leaned against the hall door. His stomach growled, reminding him that he had not eaten since—Bryan blinked. He could not remember. Sometime that morning. Or was it the night before?

He blew out a breath. Who cared? All he wanted now was sleep, just a few hours until he rejoined Galen.

Bryan shoved himself from the door and stumbled a step or two before he caught his balance again. His back ached from hours in the saddle, and he grimaced as he straightened.

Galen. Bryan shook his head wearily. The man was a fool, pure and simple. He would kill himself before he ever came close to killing Coltrane. For three days, from before the first rays of dawn until far into the night, Galen had led the hunt for that bastard. They had scoured the shire from one end to the other, but always Coltrane proved as elusive as mist.

If failure had discouraged Galen, he did not show it. Every dead end and cold trail only seemed to drive him harder, but it was the drive of hatred. How long before that hate finally exploded into madness? Galen could not keep going like this. And Bryan had told him so.

He rubbed his shoulder, wincing. Old age. Time was when

he could dodge a blow as quick as a wink, but he had not been quite fast enough when Galen had swung at him for daring to challenge him.

"Derek is dying!"

The shout froze Bryan. Exhaustion drowned under a wave of terror the likes of which he had never known. Not even in his darkest hours, when he had lain in chains and listened helplessly to Galen's screams, had he felt this. He shot across the hall and up the stairs.

Just as he reached the third level, Anne stumbled from the boy's chamber and sagged against the door frame. Tears streamed down her face, and she slid to the floor. He had not seen her cry since the moment the child was struck down, and seeing her tears now horrified him. Bryan knelt before her, seized her hands, and shook his head.

"Nay! 'Tis not—"

"He is hungry," she told him, sobbing.

Lack of sleep could cause a man to see things, but Bryan had never known it could make him hear things. "What?"

"Derek is hungry." She laughed and cried at the same time. "He woke, and he told me he is hungry."

As soon as Galen entered the hall, he knew what had happened. His shoulders slumped with relief, and for a brief moment, his heart lightened. All the to-do upstairs could mean only one thing.

Derek's life no longer swung in the balance.

Then, just as swiftly, the burden lowered upon him again. Derek would not have faced such danger at all, if Galen had kept him safe. He climbed the stairs to the boy's chamber.

First he saw Bryan, standing in the doorway, grinning from ear to ear. Stepping into the chamber, he saw Anne, her eyes bright with tears, sitting by her brother. She twisted as he drew near and beamed up at him. He looked over her shoulder, and his throat constricted.

Derek was yet very pale, and his eyelids drooped, but his lips curved when he saw Galen. Galen felt his own mouth shape into the first smile that had touched it in three days. He reached around Anne and tweaked the boy's nose.

"You are still with us, I see," he murmured, "and look as though you intend to remain so."

Derek made an attempt at a giggle. "Aye, my lord."

"His first words," Anne said, "informed us he was hungry."

Galen laid a hand on her shoulder. "When a boy is hungry, there cannot be much wrong with him." He pressed his fingertips to the lad's cheek. "You must grow strong again, lordling."

Derek hovered on the threshold of sleep, but he roused himself enough to nod and smile again before slipping into a deep slumber. Satisfied, grateful, Galen straightened and left the chamber.

"Galen?"

Anne's voice followed him, but he kept walking down the stairs. He heard a murmur of voices and a rustle of skirts, but still he kept going.

"Galen." She spoke from just behind him, but he did not turn. "Galen, where are you going?"

"Out."

He entered the hall. Why, Galen was not sure. He had meant to take to his bed, to find sleep for a few hours as Bryan had caustically suggested. Just before Galen had swung a fist at him. Galen's jaw hardened. His seneschal had not deserved to be the victim of his foul temper for only speaking sense.

"Galen," Anne called more sharply. "You've barely rested in three days." Her tone softened. "Please, come to bed. You look so tired."

Aye, Galen agreed, *I am tired.* His hand grasped the door handle but did not pull on it. He was tired all the way to his soul, but this tiredness could not be cured by sleep. He knew not what could ease it, but he meant to find out, if he had to ride the night through.

Hero. Like you.

Galen shuddered.

"Please, come to bed," Anne repeated, very close to him. Her hand rested in the center of his back, stroking gently.

She peeped at him from around his shoulder. Her lips curled. "Please."

The past days had extracted their toll from her, too. Despite her smile, her face was pale and strained. Dark smudges shadowed her eyes. Her hair, usually confined in a neat braid, strayed in wisps around her cheeks and brow. And yet, Anne was as lovely as ever he had seen her, with her eyes twinkling at him and her hands so warm upon him. Galen released the door handle, and her smile deepened when his fingers traced the line of her jaw. He pressed a kiss to her brow.

"Nay, sweet," he murmured, and stepped away. "There is yet much to do."

The opening of the hall door grated loudly in the silence, and Galen took care not to let his gaze linger upon her bewildered expression.

"What must be done?" she demanded. "Galen, you are exhausted. You look as if a strong wind could blow you over. What is so vital that you cannot rest for even a few hours?"

He paused in the doorway.

Hero. Like you.

"I must find Coltrane."

Anselm had gone out to ensure that his small domain was secure before retiring when he heard the slow thud of hooves upon the lane. He turned and peered into the evening gloom. The sound grew closer, and he saw the Lord of Rosethorn ride by.

The sight had become all too familiar over the past days. Anselm shook his head. His lordship would kill himself if this hunt did not end soon.

Anselm knew of Lord Galen's search. The whole village knew how he sought the man who had dared harm young Derek. The tale of how he rode for hours on end had flashed through Thornbury like wildfire. Those who had seen the attack told how their lord had cradled the lad in his arms, held him close, and kissed his brow. Word had even seeped from Rosethorn of how his lordship had wept over the boy's sickbed.

Strange, Anselm pondered wryly, how suddenly a monster could become a man.

Aye, they had all known from the start what sort of man Lord Galen truly was. None of them had ever believed those wild tales. They nodded to each other and agreed.

Had he not eased their rents after the hard seasons they had suffered? Had he not brought grain to the shire, at his own expense, to tide them through the winter until planting could begin in earnest next spring? Had he not cleaned the shire of outlaws and brought order again?

And if his marriage had been a bit odd, well, what of it? The carpenter's daughter was one of their own, and a finer lass could not be found in all the realm. Some even whispered the match might not be so odd, after all. They spoke of Lord Galen's gentleness with Anne. Over the course of the fair, many had seen how his smile came more readily when she was near.

Then there were the children. Could there be a more patient man with them? Could a man listen more intently to a little girl pouring out her excitement over the sights of the fair? Or hold a lad more tenderly when he had been struck down?

Anselm lowered his gaze. All of Thornbury had judged his lordship harshly and falsely. The evidence of it rode by them every day as they watched Lord Galen about his search; it stared them in the face every time they beheld his single eye and the bleakness glinting within it.

The smith firmed his jaw and stared down the lane after Lord Galen. Let the past be buried. Let there be no more doubt of who was loyal to whom, of who would stand by whom. Anselm nodded to himself and strode to the gate of his yard. Never mind how late it was. He would call on the other elders. Right now. This very minute.

By God, Lord Galen was their lord. They were his people. It was about time they proved it.

* * *

They held a festival in Derek's chamber the next day, or at least it felt like a festival. Weak as he was, Derek could not remain awake for long, and since he could not yet go to the castle, the castle had come to him.

Freya had taken over much of his nursing, and Anne foresaw a very spoiled little boy if he was bed-bound for much longer. Mayde puzzled her still. The woman hovered like a grim guardian spirit, never staying in the chamber long, rarely speaking more than a few words. But she was there, just the same. Maybe the old dragon was finally softening. Bryan found excuses, as transparent as they were frequent, to stop by Derek's chamber.

Even Galen appeared early that morning. He sat by Derek, ruffled his hair with a gentle hand, and—mimicking the boy's embarrassment at the act—made Derek giggle. When the lad became overexcited and paled, Galen cuddled him close.

"I am tired of hurting," Derek whimpered.

"I know, lordling," Galen murmured, stroking the boy's back, "but 'twill not last forever. Only a few days, and then you will be out running around like a little devil once more."

Derek looked up, and Anne smiled at the glimmer in her brother's eyes. The lad liked Bryan, but Galen was the one he adored. She wondered if Galen realized her brother and sister all but worshiped him. With a boy's hunger, Derek watched every move Galen made. And no one's word of praise or censure weighed as heavily with Lyssa than his.

"He was a bad man, Galen," Derek said solemnly. "He was going to hurt Lyssa. I saw him. He looked right at her, and then he smiled."

"He is a bad man," Galen agreed. Then his gaze narrowed. "He looked at Lyssa, you say? Not at you?"

"Right at her. He would have hurt her, if I had not pushed her from his way. I know it."

Galen nodded and kissed the boy's cheek. "You need to rest, lordling. I will come and see you again later today."

"Are you going to hunt him down?" Derek asked as Galen settled him upon the pillows heaped at his back. He grinned eagerly. "Can I help?"

Anne swore Galen flinched, but his face cleared so swiftly, she decided it had been a trick of the light.

"Not yet," Galen replied. At Derek's disgruntled expression, he scowled back at him. "I need you to stay here and keep an eye on your sisters. Make sure they behave themselves."

"Aye, my lord," the boy agreed with a brisk nod. When Galen reached the doorway, Derek stopped him. "You'll not be too angry with Marcus and Farrell? 'Twas not their fault Lyssa and I gave them the slip." He had the grace to look sheepish. " 'Twas just for fun, but I suppose we should not have done it."

Galen arched his brow. " 'Tis a fact, but I will deal leniently with them, I promise." He jerked his thumb at Anne. "Remember, see that she behaves."

Anne stuck out her tongue at Derek, who stuck out his own in return, before she followed her husband. He was already halfway down the stairs before she caught up with him.

"You were not too hard on the men, were you?" Anne smiled ruefully. "Fighting a legion must be easier than following those two scamps. Derek and Lyssa know every crack and crevice good for hiding within the wood."

"I said I was not," he replied dully.

Anne felt she had been chastised, though she had not the slightest notion why. "You must have come in very late last night. I did not hear you."

Galen halted just within the hall and swung his head to her. "Do my movements require your approval?"

"Of course not. I am just concerned for you. You've not been resting well, or eating well." Anne felt the full force of his emerald gaze bore into her, but she dared approach him and laid a hand upon his chest. "You will sicken, if you do not soon take ease."

"I am well enough," he said gruffly, and reached to open the hall door. "Your worry should be for—"

Galen froze in both word and step, and the strangest expression crept over his face. Anne's brow furrowed as he stepped cautiously into the sunlight. Following him, she stopped at his side, and delight speared through her heart.

It was not an impressive gathering, at least in numbers, for Thornbury was a small village. But the spirit of it was dazzling. Bryan stood at the foot of the steps leading to the hall, arms crossed over his chest and a small smile curving his lips. Anne felt Galen take her hand, and she entwined her fingers tightly with his as Master Anselm stepped from the knot of men. The smith bowed his head.

"My lord," he said in a calm voice that carried to every corner of the bailey, "Thornbury has been remiss, and we are here, every man of us, to right the wrong. If you've a use for us in hunting down that monster who harmed young Derek, you have but to say the word. We are at your service." He settled his gaze upon Anne and nodded. "Aye, to you and your family."

The men behind him nodded and rumbled their agreement.

Galen was silent for a long moment, his gaze sweeping over the villagers before him. Finally, he cleared his throat and cast Bryan a look.

"Well?"

The seneschal's smile became a grin. "Oh, I believe we can make good use of them."

Galen nodded and left Anne standing alone at the top of the stairs as he met the smith at the foot. The two men clasped hands, and Galen nodded again, firmer this time.

"Then let us be about it."

If Anne had hoped the villagers' aid would enable Galen to finally take ease—that Derek beginning to heal and become more himself would make Galen become more himself as well—her hopes were soon dashed.

If anything, Galen's cold determination grew, and her worry mounted.

He rode ceaselessly, sending his men here and there in search of clues to Coltrane's whereabouts. The fair had sapped his energy, and now this endless hunt added even more to his weariness. Galen had become short-tempered, snapping at small matters he would have shrugged off before. Bryan ventured one evening that there was no need for him to continue as he had, now that their ranks had swelled to include the village. Anne thought Galen would flatten his seneschal with his mere glare at the suggestion. With her, though he never raised his voice, he proved more distant with every passing day.

Only the children escaped his mood, but even they could not help but notice the change.

"What is wrong with Galen?" Lyssa asked. "He seems sad."

Sad. Anne stroked her sister's hair and nodded. That was precisely the word. Beneath the short temper, and the exhaustion that caused it, Galen was sad. More than sad. Something tormented him, and Anne was at her wit's end to decipher what.

"I do not know, sweetling. We must be patient."

Lyssa sighed but accepted the advice. Anne, however, could not. When a full week had passed since Derek first woke from fever, her cup of worry and exasperation finally ran over.

"By thunder," she snapped early one morning, and slapped her palms upon the kitchen's table hard enough to make bowls rattle, "I have had bloody well enough. Where has he gone?"

Freya fluttered her hands. "His lordship did not say. Only that he meant to continue the search."

"Well, this is going to end," Anne vowed through clenched teeth, "and 'tis going to end, now. Aye, Coltrane must be found and stopped, but not at the cost of my husband's sanity. Or mine."

Mayde cackled softly as she seasoned a stew, and Anne narrowed her eyes. The old dragon probably loved all this. Anne turned an oversweet smile upon Freya.

"When is his lordship expected to return?" The good woman could only shrug. Anne just sweetened her smile more. "Well, when he returns, no matter what the hour, kindly have him informed that her ladyship wishes to see him. She has words for him. Many words for him."

Mayde's cackle became a little louder. Anne arched her brow and tilted her chin at the woman in challenge.

"You find aught amusing?"

"Nay, my lady." For the first time, the title slipped easily from Mayde's thin lips. "I find nothing amusing, but I find much that is interesting." She brazenly took stock of the slim girl quivering with indignation, and this time, Anne knew she saw a twinkle in those eyes. "Aye, very interesting."

Feeling she had made a fool of herself, Anne knew not what to reply and made to leave with as much dignity as remained to her. Mayde's voice halted her before she had taken two steps.

"Give no quarter, girl." The housekeeper did not even look up. "Take no prisoners."

Anne flushed, but suddenly she felt an odd kinship with the sour old dragon.

"Aye," she agreed briskly. "That I will not."

"My lord?"

Galen turned at the address and found Anselm regarding him with hesitant eyes.

"Aye?"

The man tilted his head inquiringly. "I hear you are looking for a certain crest, one with a beast upon it. I might know a bit to help you."

Galen had ridden most of the day around Rosethorn's boundaries and, again, found nothing to point him toward Coltrane's whereabouts. Finally, discouraged, he had returned to Thornbury late in the evening to see if anything had turned up there.

Every village household had turned itself inside-out twice over. After the first search through stable and shed, hayloft and cottage—any likely place a man might hide—Galen knew the second search had been done more because the villagers longed to do *something* rather than admit defeat. But defeat was all they had to offer thus far.

Now, however, discouragement vanished under a wave of alarm. None but three should know of the griffin crest, and Anselm was not among them. Galen kept his tone even.

"What crest? Where did you hear of such a thing?"

"Just today from a fellow at Rosethorn," Anselm answered. "I cannot recall his name, but I could point him out, if 'twould help."

Galen pondered, and he did not like his ponderings one bit. It was a great temptation to take up Anselm's offer of pointing out his informer, but Galen knew his enemy too well. Somehow, word had gotten to Coltrane that Lyssa remembered the crest, and if Anselm exposed the villain and not his master, Galen was sure the blacksmith's life would be forfeit.

"Nay, 'tis not necessary. Not yet." He closed the distance between them with a step. "Tell me what you know of this crest you hear that I seek."

"It bears just the sort of beast I heard tell of," Anselm said, and he told what he knew. At the end of his tale, he peered at Galen, ill at ease with his lord's grim silence. "Does it offer help to you?"

"It might." Galen turned the information over in his mind. Then he clapped the blacksmith on the back and gave him a grateful nod. "It just might at that."

Give no quarter. Take no prisoners.

Like any commander preparing for battle, Anne laid out her strategy carefully.

Galen had not appeared for the evening meal, but she had not expected him to. He likely would not return to Rosethorn until late. Usually, if he came to the chamber at all, he found her already asleep. Tonight, he would be in for a surprise. Anne smiled grimly. A sneak attack he would never suspect.

She sat curled up on the bed, watching the fire lick lazily at the logs in the chamber's hearth, and primed her patience.

Torchlight flickered along the walls of Rosethorn. Here and there, a brazier warmed those who kept watch. The autumn air was chill, heavy with the scent of coming rain.

Breath fogging from between his lips, Coltrane lurked just within the forest. It was dangerous to venture this close, but he wanted to see, just catch a glimpse of his quarry. A chuckle worked up from his throat.

Poor Tarrant. He had beaten the bushes ceaselessly, and still he'd come up with empty hands. He must be mad with frustration by now. Coltrane shivered with delight. Dared he hope Tarrant might also be frightened at having his foe slip so completely through his fingers?

It had been inconvenient to withdraw from the shire for the last several days, but necessary. After all his planning, all his work, Coltrane could not jeopardize the goal now, and upon reflection, he saw other advantages in it.

An enemy who could seemingly appear and vanish at will was an enemy who was supremely dangerous. Tarrant would have no idea where he might strike next. How it must be eating at him, clawing at him. Coltrane's breathing deepened, and the hunger gnawed deep within him.

Just one look. That was all he wanted right now.

A rider approached the gates from the lane, and Coltrane saw him dismount as another man came out. Recognition ignited a flash fire of yearning in Coltrane's gut. Tarrant had come.

Tarrant stood, talking to the one who met him. Coltrane gasped in frustration. He was not close enough. He could not see Tarrant's face. Or what remained of it. A smile trembled upon Coltrane's lips.

The other man nodded and led Tarrant's horse into the gates. Tarrant paused, and Coltrane snarled silently at the proud straightness of his foe's back. Then Tarrant's head bowed, and his shoulders slumped as he went within himself.

Coltrane was satisfied. It was enough, for now.

He had another meeting to attend. One that would begin the end of Tarrant at last.

After hours of silence, the opening door grated harshly in Anne's ears. Galen stood framed in the doorway, and for a moment, she feared he might withdraw. Indeed, he hesitated at the threshold; then he stepped inside and closed the door again.

"'Tis late," he observed tiredly. "You should be asleep."

"Aye," Anne agreed as she stood, "but then, so should you."

He gave her a sharp look, then returned to removing his sword and dagger from about his waist. Laying them aside, he ran a hand through his hair. Anne saw his fingers tremble, and her heart squeezed tight. He was worn to the bone. For an instant, she considered against her plan. After all, he was home at a decent hour, and he apparently meant to remain. Perhaps she should leave well enough alone for tonight.

"I hear you wish to have words with me, lady." He folded his arms over his chest, and his lips formed a thin smile. "As it happens, I have something to discuss with you as well."

"I yield the floor to you, then," Anne granted quietly. Better to let him have his say. Then she would have her own.

"A crest bearing a griffin has been sighted."

Anne smiled with delight. "Oh, Galen, that is wonderful. Where did you see it? Do you know who it belongs to?"

" 'Twould be wonderful, but for one matter." His brow lifted. "And you placed your finger right on it. The family name is not known, but a possible district has been pointed out. A day or two will yield what I need to know."

"What is the cause of concern, then?"

"I did not see the crest myself. Nor did Bryan, that I am aware of." He leveled her a stony look. "No one who resides within Rosethorn saw it. In fact, I was told by one who should have known nothing about it."

"Who—"

"I'll not name the man." His gaze narrowed. "Nay, I'll not be one to endanger another like that."

"I do not understand." Anne sat on the edge of the bed. "You said most plainly that none but—Oh, Galen." Anne rose to her feet again. "You think *I* spoke of it to another?"

"I make no judgments, and I ask you to make none either. But I must know, Anne." He stepped closer and took her chin in his fingers to keep her gaze upon him. "Did you speak of the crest to anyone? Perhaps inquire too freely after it?"

"How could you think such a thing of me?" she whispered, hurt to core at this evidence of his distrust. The gentle fingers upon her chin tightened just a bit, and Anne clenched her jaw. "I would never betray you so."

Anne did not know whether to feel relief or not. He accepted her word instantly, but the sudden fall of his limp hand back to his side alarmed her.

" 'Tis as I feared, then," he whispered almost too low to hear. He turned away and stared at the blazing hearth.

"What, Galen? What did you fear?" She went to him and laid a hand on his arm. He shook his head, and Anne growled. "Galen, I am your wife. Your cares are my own, so share them with me, dammit!"

His head snapped around, and Galen lifted his brow. This little cat had claws when she willed to use them. But he had always known that. All sweetness and softness Anne might appear, but she possessed a spirit as fierce as any warrior's. He felt one corner of his mouth twist up as he cupped her flushed cheek in his palm.

"This," he murmured, "I cannot share. Not yet."

"Fine, just fine." She batted his hand away. " 'Tis just as well. You've denied me everything else. Why not this, too?"

Guilt stabbed at him. She had every right to her anger, but he was so weary.

"Anne, please." Galen heaved a sigh. "Leave me be."

"Leave you be," she echoed, far too calmly as she prowled the chamber. "Aye, Galen, I'll leave you be. I'll leave you to rot in your misery alone, and I will rot alone in mine. We'll not speak of it." Anne whirled and faced him with hands on her hips, eyes flashing blue fire. "We'll not talk of how you are killing yourself, or how you are worrying near everyone to death along with you. I'll not say that if you cannot spare me one wee spot in your heart, the least you could do is spare the children."

"The children?"

Galen scowled. He must be more exhausted than he thought, for she made no sense at all. Had she gone mad? Or had he?

"Aye, Galen, the children," she replied blandly. "Remember them? The two small people who adore you? Lyssa thinks the sun cannot rise or fall but by your command, and Derek believes you are the greatest hero he has ever—"

"Nay!"

Galen roared the denial, and he lifted a hand as if to ward off a blow. But it was too late. That word, the word that had haunted him since it first passed Derek's lips, slipped beneath his guard and slashed at him like a dagger.

Hero. Like you.

"He cannot think that of me. His hero!" Galen gave a raw laugh that twisted into a sound of anguish. He pressed his hands to his face, felt his flesh under one and the smoothness of leather under the other. "I am not—can *never* be—that little boy's hero!"

"Why?" Her voice softened, and he felt her draw close. She touched his arm. "Galen, what is so terrible about Derek thinking of you as—"

Galen rounded upon her. Her eyes, huge with alarm, bored into him. Into his very soul, as if she could see everything laid bare before her. But, he thought, she could not truly see everything. Perhaps, to convince her once and for all, it was time she did.

"What is so terrible?" he demanded savagely.

Galen curled his fingers at his jaw, at the edge of the mask. He peeled it away with flick of his wrist and snarled.

"Is this the face of a hero?"

Chapter Seventeen

Anne gasped and pressed her fingers to her lips as she beheld the full face of her husband.

"Galen." Her lips shaped his name.

"Take a good look," he commanded brutally. "Take a very good look."

Anne remembered thinking that Galen had once been a very handsome man. And he had. She could see the proof in what remained. Galen had once possessed a near flawless countenance, well-formed and masculine.

But all was well-formed no longer.

From his right brow to his jaw, a jagged scar marred his face. It bisected his eyebrow and twisted his cheek. The terrible ridge pulled the corner of his mouth slightly askew. And his eye—Anne made a small sound of protest. Where the mate to his beautiful, emerald-green eye had once been, the scar expanded into a fine web that sealed the lid forever shut.

Bryan's tale flashed through her mind. This was Coltrane's work, and it was horrible. But was he a horror?

"Are you satisfied now? Do you understand now?" Galen snarled. "This face can be no boy's hero, or any woman's love. This face is as horrible and twisted as the heart it reflects."

"Nay!" Anne spat. "I'll not hear such blasphemy!"

"'Tis the truth, woman! Face it!" He flashed a feral smile. "Aye, face the scarred beast you—"

Whap! Her palm struck his left cheek, snapping his head to one side. Anne did not know who was more shocked, her or Galen. He grasped her wrist in a punishing grip as he turned to gaze into her eyes once more. Emerald fire leaped in fury to his eye. Nay, Anne corrected—in agony. Every muscle in his body bunched taut, and she thrust her chin up at him.

"Go ahead," she challenged. "Strike me. If you are the monster you claim, you'll do it." They stared at each other in silence for a long moment. "If your heart is twisted, you've wrung it yourself. If 'tis naught but an empty shell, your own bitterness has bled it dry. Blame yourself, Galen. Not your scars."

She jerked free of his grasp. Tears stung her eyes, but she blinked them back.

"I love you." Her breath hitched before she could control it. "But 'tis *you* I love, not your face. I cannot believe your heart is empty, but you've kept its gate locked as securely as you've masked your face. Open it, Galen. Open the gate."

Anne felt the tears trailing over her cheeks, and she saw the one slip over Galen's, leaving a glistening trail. The fingers of her one hand touched his flawless cheek, while those of her other touched the savage scar on his right.

"I've touched your face, love," she whispered. "Let me touch your heart."

His lips worked, but no sound emerged. Then Galen swallowed and uttered in a thick voice, "You have already."

Anne slid her arms around his neck and rose on tiptoe to brush her lips over his. Galen took her into his embrace and burrowed his face into the hollow below her ear. His shoulders quaked, and his chest gave a great heave. Anne felt his tears moisten her skin.

"Lady Anne," he whispered. "I want to love you. Show me how. Tell me how."

She threaded her fingers into his hair. "Just say it."

He kissed the curve of her jaw, her cheek, and lingered a long time at her lips. Galen could almost hear the gate of his heart give a great creak, and then it swung light and free. Instead of the swelling ache he had braced himself for, Galen felt only a deep warmth fill his chest before it overflowed and coursed through his whole being. He pressed his lips to Anne's once more.

"I love you."

"You see?" She leaned back, and a smile spread upon her tearstained cheeks. "Your tongue did not fall out, after all."

Galen laughed and lifted her from her feet, swinging her around. He set her down beside the bed, his lips never leaving hers. Anne plucked at the laces of his tunic as he gathered her gown and lifted it, but they were both too preoccupied with their kiss to go further. Galen felt the bed at the back of his legs. He brought Anne so close, he could no longer tell where he ended and she began.

"Galen," Anne murmured, and he made a rough sound of acknowledgment. "We are falling."

Galen let himself fall and took her down with him to bounce onto the bed. He drank her laughter as he pulled her to sprawl atop him. Then he rolled until she lay beneath him.

"Ah, sweet love," he murmured into her ear, "you've turned me inside out and upside down. From the moment I met you, you've taken my soul and shaken it until nothing I thought I knew remained. How can I ever thank you?"

"Just love me, Galen."

"I do." He kissed her hungrily. As his lips trailed to her cheek, hers traveled to his. Galen held very still as she kissed the jagged scar, and when her kiss settled upon his damaged eye, he shuddered. "I am sorry, love, so sorry. I should have known. You tried to tell me. All the wasted time, all the hurt, could have been avoided if only I had listened."

"What should you have known?"

"I should have known I could trust you in all things." He stroked his thumbs over her cheeks, drying the last remains of her tears. "I should have admitted that I loved you."

" 'Tis a fact," she replied tartly, and he chuckled.

"Oh, Anne." He rested his brow against hers. "What would I have done if you had never come into my life?"

"You would have become a mean, crotchety old man."

Galen wanted to laugh, but the silkiness of her throat proved too tempting. He nuzzled her there, and, delighted with her quivering response, he did it again. What was it about this woman that aroused him so? No other had the power to heat his blood as Anne did. Already his body throbbed and pulsed, his every heartbeat echoing within the swelling flesh of his loins.

She was beautiful. With her soft skin and enticing curves, Anne stole his breath. She responded in a way no man could resist, writhing and uttering those small sounds that drove him wild to hear more. But there was more to Anne.

There was her honesty, her generous offering of herself in both body and soul. There was the way she looked at him, seeing the man he was rather than the title he bore or the wealth he possessed. Or the scars that marked him. Galen smiled against the hollow of her throat. Anne was unique, and she was his.

"Lady Anne," he whispered, and she moaned in reply. "I think I am going to rip your gown again."

Her answer was to arch toward him and smile as the sound of tearing fabric filling the air. But then she gasped and shivered in the cool air of the chamber.

"Galen, the bed drapes—"

"Nay." He kissed the valley between her breasts. "I'll not confine us to darkness again. You are much too lovely."

Anne flushed and enchanted him. She tugged at his tunic, but the caution of so many years was not easily subdued. Galen caught her wrists in his hands. Her brow furrowed.

"Anne, there are other scars, ones I have never allowed you to see or touch."

Her smile warmed his soul. "I've not run screaming yet, have I?"

He rose, shed his clothing, and then returned to her arms.

On reflex, Galen took her hands and held them to his chest where marks were few. Anne's gaze never faltered as she slid her hands from his grasp. He shivered when her palms skimmed over his back, and he arched into her caress like a great cat.

"Oh, Galen." Anne's throat tightened. Beneath her fingers, the thin slashes and ridged gouges of the lash told more of what he had suffered at Coltrane's hands. Her eyes stung with fresh tears. "Why did he hurt you like this?"

" 'Twas long ago." He stroked her cheek, and a small smile curved his lips. "There is no more hurt now."

Anne sighed as Galen began kissing her again, shivered when he laved his tongue over the peak of one breast, and cried out at the slow, strong suckling of his mouth. Her hands traveled over him, his back and chest, his sides and belly. She no longer felt the scars, only Galen.

"Anne . . . touch me."

The taut roughness of his voice made her smile. Their moans mingled when her fingers found his male flesh hot and full, and finding him so sent heat and fullness coursing through her own body. Anne stroked his length and smiled at his groan. She lifted the cradle of her hips to him and shuddered with him. She pressed him to the moistened petals of her body, and they both writhed.

"Galen, please." She pleaded with him, begging him to fill the aching emptiness deep inside her. "Please . . . now."

"Aye, love." He lifted from her and took her hips in his hands. "Now."

Trepidation fluttered within Anne. The only time Galen had lain with her before had been in darkness. She knew his shape and power by feel, but feeling, Anne discovered, was very different from seeing. His manhood rose from his loins, fierce and potent, poised to join with her. And despite the pleasure Anne knew awaited her, she felt terribly vulnerable of a sudden.

Then he slid within her as gently as he did completely, and Anne felt only pleasure rippling from her into him, from him into her.

* * *

Anne admired the play of firelight upon Galen's skin. With her fingertip, she traced the flickering shadows across his chest, following the rough silk of dark hair as it thinned to a line that ran down his belly. His muscles jerked under her touch, and she smiled as she pressed her lips to the small nub of his nipple.

"Lord above, woman," he complained in a deep rumble, "you'll see me dead this night yet."

Anne giggled and nipped at him.

Galen groaned and rolled atop her, scowling. " 'Twas you who shrieked at me for not sleeping enough."

"Perhaps I was mistaken," she drawled, and wiggled under him suggestively. "You do not seem so tired, after all."

He kissed her, hard and quick. "A man can only withstand so much, wood elf."

"You've not called me that for a long time," she said, caressing his scarred cheek with gentle fingers. "I've missed hearing it."

"Have you?" She nodded, and he kissed her again, slower this time. "Then I must remember to say it more often. 'Twas my first thought of you, you know. Sitting outside your cottage, combing your hair by firelight, you looked like a dainty little wood elf. You enchanted me."

Anne chuckled. "And you scared me half to death."

He grinned wickedly. "You should have seen your face when I stepped from the wood."

Galen widened his eye and mimicked her expression of that night weeks ago. In revenge, Anne reached around and pinched his bottom. He winced and started, nudging his flesh more intimately against hers. Both wrapped themselves around the other, limbs tangling, lips melding, sighs mingling.

Anne felt her world spin and she found herself atop Galen. Her thighs parted over his, and a wave of shyness overcame her at how exposed the position felt. Her cheeks warmed, and she tried to scurry off him, but Galen would have none of it. He held her in place and, taking her hand in his, guided it to where their bodies caressed each other. Anne felt him, sleek with the moisture from her own arousal. She quivered with delight.

"Galen?"

"Join us, wood elf." He ground his head back into the pillow as she grasped him. "Join us."

Never had Galen felt anything as perfect as Anne sheathing him. Slowly, she lowered herself upon him, and he groaned. She rose, and he felt her tremor as she joined with him completely once more.

"Anne." Her name came out low and harsh from the effort of his control. "Anne, you are beautiful."

And she was. Anne was no longer a wood elf, shy and elusive, but a goddess. She straightened and took him within her, deeper than ever before. Tossing her hair over her shoulders to flow down her back, she let him view every detail of her form. Her hands urged his away from her hips, up the taper of her waist, and then shaped them over her breasts. A sensual smile curled at the corners of her lips as he stroked her beaded crests with his thumbs. And never did she take her gaze from his.

Then, just as he teetered on the brink, she slipped off him.

"Anne?"

Galen heard the desperation in his voice, and he felt it throb mercilessly within his body.

"Anne!"

He fisted the linens beneath him at the bolder, even hotter caress she gave him. With her lips and hands, Anne tormented him, but it was the sweetest torture he could imagine. Inch by inch, she claimed him as her own, until at last Galen was willing to do anything—*anything*—she commanded.

"Anne . . . Anne, I cannot bear—"

She was in his arms again. She rolled with him, took his enflamed flesh within her. Galen felt her ripple around him, clasp him tight. He heard her cries as she lost herself in her release. Then he stiffened as he lost himself in his own.

It was a long time before Galen could even think, much less move. He lay in Anne's embrace, his head nestled above where her heart still pounded. He smiled at how her hands stroked his hair and turned his head to kiss the silky curve of one breast.

"They will miss us come morning and search us out," he told her in a voice still rough from cries of fulfilled passion, "and they'll find us expired in a knot of limbs beneath the bedclothes." She shook with a giggle. "You find it amusing, now, but imagine Father Elias when he is told how we took our leave from this world. The poor man will faint."

Anne only laughed harder as Galen slid from atop her and gathered her into the curve of his body. He sighed as she snuggled close and draped one leg over his.

"Galen," she said after a while, "you spoke of the crest earlier and of a fear you had. Will you tell me?"

"Nay." He shushed her with a finger over her lips when she started to protest. "Not because I do not trust you, but because I cannot until I am sure."

But Anne was nothing if not quick. Galen admitted he would have to be on his toes if he wished anything to slip by her.

"If I did not speak of the crest, and you did not, then who did?" He did not reply, for he knew she already had the answer. "Galen, the only other one who knew of it was Bryan."

"Aye."

"And if Bryan spoke of the crest to another," she went on in a small voice, "he could also be responsible for other things. How could Coltrane learn where to be and where not to be to elude your search? How did he gain entry to the keep and escape notice? *Did* he even gain entry, or was it another who acted for him? Then there is my father's death, that murdered girl, and the arrow fired at us."

Galen flinched. "I've asked myself the same questions, and I've found only one answer. We've a spy in our midst."

Anne rose on one elbow to look down at him. "But why would Bryan betray you? Coltrane betrayed him, the same as you. Held him captive, the same as you. Bryan has every reason to despise the man as much as you do."

"I know, love, and I wish I had the answer." He pulled her back down into his embrace. "Remember, we do not know that our traitor is Bryan. There is no proof."

But Galen knew as well as she that hate and bitterness could seethe for years, drive a man mad though hidden behind a mask of sanity. Even the smallest of causes could plant them, and they could grow and fester far beyond their beginnings. Coltrane was proof of that. Galen's brow furrowed. But could Bryan be, as well? The notion was all but unthinkable.

Anne gave a despairing sigh. "I pray 'tis not so, for I like Bryan very much."

"Aye," Galen murmured around the tightness in his throat. "He is my closest friend. He stood by me when all others fled at the very sight of me. I have trusted him as I have trusted no other." He smiled and kissed her brow. "Until you."

"Will you tell me of the years before you returned to Rosethorn?" she asked softly. "Of your life after Acre?"

"One day," he promised. "After this is over."

And Galen knew he would.

"What will we do, now?"

"We'll wait," he replied.

He brought her fingers to his lips, then pressed them to his scarred cheek. Contentment warmed his heart at how she caressed the unsightly mark. He had not realized how much he longed for just such a touch until Anne gave it to him.

"Aye, we wait," he repeated.

"And the crest?"

"I will look after that."

"And Bryan?"

That was the most difficult to answer. "I do not know."

Silence enfolded them, and after a while, Galen knew Anne slept. Sleep, however tempting, proved harder for him.

It was an ugly thought, that Bryan might have betrayed him. His flesh crawled at the notion. Not Bryan. Not the man closer to him than any brother. Never Bryan.

Yet, too much hung upon facing all the possibilities, and Galen forced himself to face this one. Solid proof or not, it was the only explanation he had. Still, something did not feel right about it.

Anselm had heard of the crest from a fellow at Rosethorn. He did not know the man's name, though he could point him out. Bryan was too well known for his face to go unrecognized, especially by one of the village leaders. Could he have started a rumor, left it to others to unknowingly spread? That did not feel right, either. Again, it would be too easy to link Bryan with the deed. All it required was a bit of questioning.

Derek had said Coltrane looked right at Lyssa as he made to ride them down. Not at the boy. At Lyssa. So Coltrane knew Lyssa remembered something. How? From Bryan? When? From the time they'd first discussed the crest until Coltrane's attack, Bryan had been as busy as himself. They had been almost constantly in each other's company as they prepared and oversaw the fair, and even when apart, there were too many people who could mark both their actions.

And the things Anne had mentioned. Each one pointed to a traitor within Rosethorn, no doubt of that. Yet Galen felt in his heart that the traitor was not Bryan.

Wishful thinking?

He hoped not.

For he was about to gamble everything he held dear upon it.

Deep within the shadows of a chamber somewhere in Rosethorn, a figure rocked slowly, to and fro, in a chair. A vial was clutched in one hand.

I cannot do it.

But I must.

'Twill not harm her. She will only sleep.

I can put it in her goblet. She will never know.

Then I will take her to Master.

Bait is all he needs her for. Bait for the beast.

The beast who defiled her, shamed her.

The filthy beast who abandoned my darling.

She will thank me when 'tis done.

She will know 'twas only justice.

The beast must suffer. Master promised he would.

Soon, Master promised. 'Twill all be over soon.

* * *

Wood scraped softly against wood, and Galen growled in protest. He burrowed his head into a pillow and willed the world away a little longer. He curled on his right side with a contented sigh.

"Galen?" A boy's voice intruded into his peace. Then, a girl's singsong lilt joined in. "Galen?"

The little imps dared to wake him, did they? He snorted loudly and pulled the covers over his head. Childish giggles made him chuckle, and he felt one of them climb onto the bed. A small hand carefully pulled back the sheet just enough to uncover one eye peering up at them. There was another burst of giggles, and the sheet floated back over his head.

"Who disturbs me?" Galen demanded in a deep voice.

Derek lifted the sheet again. "We do."

"Wake up, Galen, wake up," Lyssa commanded, pulling and shoving on his shoulder. " 'Tis time to wake up."

Derek took up the cry, and they soon had a merry chorus between them. Galen grunted when Lyssa climbed atop him and bounced. He rolled onto his belly. Galen felt the sheet slip down his back just as their chorus gasped to a halt. Too late, he remembered the scars.

Silence stretched.

"Did the bad man do this to you?" Lyssa asked in a small voice, her fingers tracing the marks crisscrossing his back.

Galen swallowed. "Aye."

"Did it hurt?" Derek wanted to know, and touched a slash high on Galen's shoulder.

"Once. Not any longer," he replied. And strange to say, it was true. With every stroke of their palms over his marred skin, Galen felt the painful memories slip further and further away. "Nay, not any longer."

Derek pressed his fingertip to the corner of Galen's mouth, and Galen growled, snapping at it. The boy laughed, then sobered again. Tilting his head, he peered straight into Galen's eye. And Galen remembered something else. Though the right side of his face was still hidden against the pillow, the mask was obviously not there.

With a child's frankness, Derek asked, "Can we see?"

Galen hesitated, and then he raised himself up on his elbow, lifting his head from the pillow's protection.

Both children stared at him. Lyssa's fingers feathered over his scarred cheek, and her brow furrowed at his damaged eye. Derek followed the scar from end to end with a light touch. His expression was utterly calm, wholly accepting. Soft lips pressed against the scar, and Galen looked to find Lyssa regarding him with a gaze just as serene.

"Must you still wear your mask?" Lyssa asked.

Galen kissed her nose. "Aye, most times."

She scowled at him, but she said nothing. Derek, meanwhile, had made another interesting discovery by peering further under the covers.

"You got no clothes on."

Lyssa crawled around to look as well, and Galen grabbed the bedclothes from Derek's grasp, securing them about his nakedness. Like little wolves scenting their prey's weakness, the pair attacked him with snarling kisses. Derek poked him in the ribs, and Galen started with a gasp.

"He's ticklish!" Lyssa shrieked in delight.

Anne had followed the sound of giggles. Standing in the doorway, she had to admire her siblings' cunning. Derek was in the best position, able to swoop his fingers in for a quick dig at Galen's ribs before retreating to safety. Lyssa took advantage of the bed's width, scooting in for the attack, and then slipping just beyond Galen's reach. Trapped as he was by keeping himself covered, her husband was routed.

"Anne! Do not just stand there!" Galen commanded as Lyssa jabbed at him again. "Do something!"

Ever the dutiful wife, Anne dived into the fray. Together with her brother and sister, she tickled Galen to within an inch of his life. It was a breathless knot they made, when the battle finally ended. From her position atop the pile, Lyssa peered down at their victim.

"Galen, are you ready to wake up now?"

He blew out a breath. "Do I have a choice?"

"Nay," she replied brightly.

"Scoot now, the both of you," Anne ordered, laughing. "Let Galen get dressed."

Flushed with victory, the children obeyed. Anne made to rise as well, but Galen drew her back into his embrace. She discovered there was something very sensual about lying fully clothed so close to a naked man. Especially when he kissed her as if the night before had not been enough to sate him.

"Never think, my lady," he said in a rumble, "that I'll forget who joined whose side just now."

Anne chuckled. "And will I pay for it, my lord?"

"That you will." He kissed her again. Finally, he rolled onto his back and stretched. "What hour is it?"

"Just a bit before mid-day," she answered. "The Sext bell has not yet rung."

His eye rounded. "Good Lord, I slept the morning away?"

He did not seem truly bothered by his late rising. Instead, Galen sat up and stretched again; then he sighed as she settled behind him and stroked his back. Sleek muscle bunched and shifted under her fingers, and Anne admired his body. Damaged it might be, but Galen still possessed as manly a figure as a woman could hope for. Her hands slid around his waist and her palms flattened upon his chest.

"Anne," he murmured, "I must leave you for a day or two."

She hugged him tight. "The crest?"

He nodded.

"I will miss you terribly." She rubbed her cheek against his shoulder. "Be careful, Galen. Be very careful and return to us safe."

He took her hand and kissed her fingers. "I will take Bryan and a trio of men with me."

"Bryan?"

"Aye." When she started to speak again, he squeezed her hand. "Trust me, love. I know what I am about."

"Galen," she said anyway, "what if Bryan is the one?"

"Then he will be within my sight."

"And Coltrane?" She moved to face him.

His expression was grim. "Coltrane wants me. If I leave Rosethorn, 'tis likely he will follow."

''So you believe he is still near,'' Anne concluded, ''even though we've seen no sign of him since the fair.''

''Oh, he is near.'' Galen smiled thinly. ''I know him. He'll never give up. Never. And so I cannot give up either, not until I have him.''

Anne trembled, looking into her husband's determined face. She slid her arms around his neck and clung to him. He was right. She knew it, but she could not forget Mayde's prophecy. It haunted her, never more strongly than now.

He means to find and punish him, or die in the attempt.

Chapter Eighteen

Galen left the next day with Bryan and a trio of others.

Anne watched from the castle entrance until they vanished from sight and still smiled from their send-off. Galen had looked quite overwhelmed by the fracas Derek and Lyssa had made, cautioning him to be careful and wheedling promises of reward for good behavior when he returned—all in the same breath.

Derek flitted off as soon as the men were gone, and Anne wisely let him go. Though still not quite recovered, her brother was growing fretful with confinement. Rambling in the fresh air would do him good, but she took the precaution of drawing one of Galen's men aside. Marcus nodded at her request and vowed to keep an eye on the boy, as much to guard him from overexertion as from danger, and to keep him within the castle walls. Anne's smile deepened at the image they made, the burly warrior tagging after the slender lad. It was difficult to say who was more delighted with the other.

Lyssa, though, remained at her side, scowling as she gazed at the now vacant castle gate and the lane beyond. Anne regarded her sister curiously.

"Whatever is the matter, sweetling?"

If anything, the child's scowl grew fiercer. "Galen still wears his mask."

"Well," Anne murmured, with a little frown of her own, "I think he prefers to keep his scars hidden. Some people might stare or say unkind things."

"What unkind things?"

Anne resisted the urge to chuckle at the outrage in Lyssa's eyes.

"Some people believe such marks mean a man is evil," Anne answered slowly. It was not easy to explain to a child what made little sense even to an adult. "Some people might even be afraid of Galen because of them."

Lyssa greeted the notion with scorn. "That is silly. Galen is the best lord in the realm. Anyone knows that."

"That he is." Anne did not hide her laughter this time and hugged her sister. Tapping the little girl's nose, she grinned. "But some people are not as smart as you are."

Lyssa glowed, but something remained very much on her mind. She cast another scowl after the riders.

"It cannot be very comfortable," she remarked, "to wear a mask like that all the time."

"I am sure 'tis not," Anne granted. Even as supple and finely crafted as it was, the mask must be stifling at times. How he must long to shed it.

"Anne." Lyssa's face lit with sudden eagerness. "Can I make Galen a present?"

"If you wish," Anne replied. "What sort of present did you have in mind?"

Lyssa just arched a brow. " 'Tis a secret."

With that, the little girl ran back inside the keep, leaving Anne bewildered.

And lonely. She shivered. Mere minutes had passed, and already she missed Galen dreadfully. Anne rubbed her arms, but she knew her chill would not be warmed again until he returned. It was something she must grow accustomed to, she supposed. Anne turned and wandered back into the keep. Galen must part from her at times, seeing to affairs among his other holdings or answering any summons to court. She could perhaps travel with him on occasion, but with Derek and Lyssa to look after, those occasions would be rare. And if she became—

Anne felt light-headed of a sudden. She stumbled to the hall's great hearth and sank into one of the chairs before it. A bemused laugh burst from her lips. It was ridiculous, but she had not considered the matter even once. Had Galen?

"Is aught amiss, lady?" Anne blinked and saw Mayde gazing at her with guarded concern. "You look like you've had shock."

Anne gasped. "I could be with child."

"You need not sound so surprised." Mayde snorted. " 'Tis a common enough happening, once you are wed."

"But I never thought . . ." Anne shook her head slowly and pressed a hand to her belly, laughing again. She looked up at the housekeeper. "What are the signs? How would I know?"

Mayde pursed her lips. "Your mother never spoke of such things with you?"

"Nay," Anne admitted, flushing. "I was quite young when she died, and Papa . . . well, we never truly discussed it."

"When was your last cycle?"

Anne thought. "Before Papa died."

" 'Twould make it over a month since." The housekeeper tallied the weeks on her fingers. " 'Tis possible. And you've not had one since? Not even a small one?"

Anne shook her head.

"Well, 'tis too early to say for certain, but you well could be." Mayde snorted again. "I thought his lordship would set you to breeding in quick order."

Oh, why had she not asked Freya instead? Anne heaved a sigh. Mayde had a way of turning everything disagreeable. Sour old dragon.

"Thank you," she said wryly, and rose.

But the housekeeper was not done with her.

"Until we are certain, we must assume you carry." Her gaze flickered over Anne and made her feel very much like a brood mare up for purchase. Anne's cheeks scorched.

"You are a bit slim through the hips, but you'll do. You must guard your health, lady. Eat well, rest often. No climbing upon chairs or stools. No lifting aught heavier than a pillow. And for heaven's sake, do not let anyone feed you any herbal concoction without consulting me. Some can cause the babe distress or even kill it."

Anne splayed her fingers over her belly and shivered.

"This child, if it exists yet, must be protected at all costs," Mayde concluded with grim determination. Anne lifted her brow. "With that vile creature his lordship is after still gallivanting about the land, you cannot be too careful. He has already struck too often and too close. Why he hates Lord Galen so, I know not, but 'tis plain he does."

"Aye," Anne murmured. "So you've heard no whispers concerning Coltrane?"

"There are always whispers inside a keep, lady. You'd have to be deaf not to hear them, but I've caught wind of nothing beyond what is already known."

"I see." Anne nibbled her lower lip thoughtfully. "If you should hear anything that might prove useful, I expect you to tell me immediately."

Mayde drew herself up haughtily. "I'll do my duty by his lordship, on that you may rely."

"Thank you," Anne replied, every bit as haughty. She made to leave. "Have Freya come to my chamber, will you? There is some mending I need her help with."

"Humph. Much good may she do you, as she has proved no use to me these last days. That one was always addlepated, but now she has grown as flighty as a feather. And that muttering to herself wears on my patience. Why I took her on, I'll never know."

Anne paused in the archway. "Freya wasn't one of Galen's original servants?"

"Nay," Mayde growled. "Showed up here about a fortnight after we returned, she did, looking for a position. She seemed biddable enough, for all her ladylike ways, so I took her on."

"Where did you all come from?" Anne asked curiously.

"Oh, here and there." Mayde pursed her lips, thinking.

''Most of us were already in service at his lordship's other holdings. Some had gone to one or the other of them after old Lord Geoffery passed on, times here having got so hard. Rosethorn is a mite out of the way, you see, and the other Tarrant holdings were closer to court. More protected that way.''

''Hmm.'' Anne pondered and murmured to herself, ''Everyone thought Galen would never return.''

''But he did.'' Did she imagine it? Or was there a grim note of satisfaction in the housekeeper's voice. ''I always figured he would.''

Anne lifted a brow. ''Did you, now?''

''His lordship only had to get the wandering out of his blood first.'' Mayde sniffed. ''Just like a man. Not a one of them can seem to settle down until they've taken on the world. All too often, the world takes them on, instead, and usually wins. His lordship proved luckier than most.''

With an air of innocence, Anne came closer and asked, ''So you've served the Tarrant family for a long time?''

''All my life. Born at Stagmount Manor, I was, one of Lord Geoffery's smaller holdings. I entered his service there as a young lass, about your age, lady.''

''Why did you come to Rosethorn? Why not stay there?'' Anne gave a small smile. ''It must have been very hard, leaving the only home you've ever known and coming to a strange place.''

''Let us just say I thought I'd find a better . . . opportunity for myself here.'' Did Mayde actually flinch? ''There was nothing for me at Stagmount. Not anymore.''

How odd. The housekeeper sounded almost . . . sad. Had she suffered a loss? Something that had driven her to seek a new beginning in a place where bitter memories did not exist? Anne started to probe further, then stopped. Mayde's memories were none of her affair.

''Well, you are here now,'' Anne said brightly, though her mind was troubled for some reason she could not divine. ''I hope you've found happiness.''

Mayde just snorted and drew her face into scornful lines as she swept from the hall.

Watching her go, Anne rolled her eyes and started up the stairs again. Some people, she decided, could not be happy no matter what.

Galen rode south. About dusk, he called a halt and ordered camp made for the night. He was pleased. They had made good time and, with luck, would find the keep he sought before the noon hour the next day. None but he had more than a vague notion of their purpose.

Not even Bryan.

Galen was taking a great risk, and he knew it. Was it a mark of loyalty, that Bryan had not questioned him? Or a sign of a traitor's patience? If his heart had counseled him falsely, it would not be the first mistake in his life, but it could well prove the last.

Galen had dropped hints along the way. A word here. A phrase there. Always careful not to reveal too much. An innocent man would glean little from them. But a guilty one? A guilty man could piece the puzzle together, if he were clever.

And Bryan was very clever.

Clever enough to understand. Clever enough to know he must act, and tonight, to keep from being exposed.

If there was anything at this holding to expose him.

Galen sat on the ground, leaning back against a tree, and cursed into the silence of his mind. That was just the trouble. He knew not if this holding, Briarhaven, would yield aught useful or not. The traitor, if he was truly among his companions, knew more than Galen did.

Galen chafed at not being able to confide in Bryan. It felt wrong, left a bitter taste upon his tongue. Always had they been in each other's confidence. Always, from the moment he had stumbled into Bryan's cell, bleeding and half-mad with pain, had they been friends.

Grateful as they were, the handful of others he had managed to free the night he escaped had shrunk back at the sight of him. But not the last man he had found. Galen could not remember exactly how he had succeeded in his escape, but never could he forget Bryan.

Bryan had caught him as he sank into the stinking straw of that cell. Bryan had cleaned the blood and filth from the ravaged remains of his face. Bryan had supported him, sometimes all but carried him, as they crept from within the prison. Bryan nursed him at the monastery they'd found refuge at. Bryan had drawn the bandages away and held the mirror that first terrible time. Bryan had held him while he sobbed in utter despair. And Bryan had stayed by his side during all the years after. Always loyal. Always steadfast. Always a friend.

Nay, Galen thought, not merely a friend. He and Bryan had been comrades before Acre. Brothers after.

Galen's throat tightened, and he closed his eye. It would tear his heart out if he was forced to destroy the man he owed his life to.

"You look exhausted," came an amused observation from close by. Galen looked over and found Bryan seated at his side. His friend smirked amicably. "You must be getting old, for such a paltry ride to tire you so."

"Old?" Galen snorted. "At times, I feel ancient."

"Aye," Bryan agreed with a sigh, "there are times I, too, feel as though I've lived forever."

Galen chuckled. "Then along comes a comely lass sauntering by you, and I notice you perk up well enough."

"Well," his friend replied wryly, "even an old man is still a man. And you seem to have grown lively yourself, since your own comely lass sauntered by."

Galen thought of Anne and smiled. Only a day from her side, and already he ached with missing her.

"She has seen beneath the mask," he murmured.

Bryan looked at him sharply. Then a grin crept slowly over his face. "Has she?"

Galen slanted him a look. "And if you say *I told you so,* I'll beat you to a pulp."

"I'd not dream of it." Bryan snickered. "But I did tell you so."

His snicker became a laugh as Galen punched his shoulder.

Bryan sobered after a moment. He picked up a small

stone, rolled it between his fingertips thoughtfully, then sent it skipping into the undergrowth with a flick of his wrist.

At length, he said quietly, "I've not asked where we are headed. Nor will I. But I will ask why you've not told me."

"You may ask," Galen replied, just as quiet, "but I'll not answer. Not yet."

"Very well." Bryan's tone was stony, and Galen flinched. His friend rose stiffly and stared at the fire kindled not far from them. " 'Tis an early day tomorrow."

Without another word, Bryan went to the others gathered at the fire, and they settled for the night. Galen sat alone, lost in his thoughts, until the fire burned low. But for the sounds of the woodland night, all became silent and still.

In the morning, Galen prayed, he would give Bryan the apology he owed him. And the answers.

In the chill of pre-dawn, Bryan snarled drowsily.

"Farrell, if you kick me once more, I'll rip your foot off and stuff the bloody thing down your throat. I swear I will."

Standing between them, Galen cast a rueful glance at Farrell, snoozing in an innocent sprawl not an arm's width away.

" 'Tis not Farrell," he said in a low voice, and shoved Bryan with the toe of his boot once more.

"Galen." Bryan rolled within the cocoon of brychans upon the ground and sat up in a rush, blinking in sleepy alarm. "Is aught amiss?"

"Nay, my friend." Galen crouched by him and signaled for quiet. "Come, before the others stir. I must talk with you."

Bewildered, and frowning to show it, Bryan obeyed.

"I should beat you senseless, you know that?" Bryan hissed between clenched teeth. "Bad enough suspecting me, but to make yourself such a target! God above, Galen, are you mad?"

"Keep quiet." Galen shushed him when his voice rose above a murmur and shot a glance at his other men, breaking camp not far away. He turned a regretful eye back upon his friend. "I apologize."

"Apologize?" Bryan kicked at a clump of weed. His jaw worked, grinding over the outrage Galen granted was justly felt. "And what changed your mind about me?"

"My mind was never changed, Bryan. Only confirmed."

"You could still be wrong," his friend snarled softly. "I could be biding my time, waiting for a better chance to slit your throat. Or I could be waiting to return to Rosethorn, take Anne and the children with you in same swipe. You could still be dead wrong, Galen."

Galen met Bryan's gaze without flinching. "Am I?"

His seneschal glared at him.

"No, damn your hide." Bryan's voice thickened, and he turned his back. "I cannot believe you thought I . . ."

If he had slashed Bryan with a dagger, Galen knew he could not have struck his friend's heart more surely. He laid a hand on Bryan's shoulder and winced when he jerked away.

"I had to face the possibility." Galen drew a deep breath to keep his own voice from faltering. "Dammit, I had to—"

"I swore fealty to you once." Bryan whirled back to face him, pain and fury etched in his face. "Shall I go down upon my knee and do it again? Would that satisfy you?"

"Bryan—"

Bryan grasped Galen by his tunic and shoved him hard against a tree. Galen grunted at the force of it but made no move to dodge whatever blow Bryan dealt him.

"Never, never doubt my loyalty again," the seneschal rasped. "You hear, Galen? *Never.*"

"Aye," his lord vowed solemnly. "Never."

Bryan eased his grip and released Galen. The two men stared long and hard at each other. At last, Bryan nodded, and when Galen extended his hand, he grasped his lord's forearm in a clasp that renewed the bond between them.

"Why did you not hit me?" Galen asked.

Bryan snorted. "Why should I bruise my knuckles on the

likes of you?'' Galen laughed which Bryan echoed a second later. ''What do we do now?''

''We keep going. We should reach Briarhaven by midday at least, and then . . .'' Galen shrugged. ''Then, perhaps we find some answers.''

''And perhaps lay hand on Coltrane?''

''Perhaps, but I doubt it.'' Galen shook his head. ''I doubt he'll make it so easy for us, though I wager he'll not be far. I am his prey, Bryan. A hunter follows his prey.''

''So you think he has followed us. 'Tis just as well, I suppose.'' Bryan angled Galen a sly look. ''I had wondered why you insisted I join you on this journey, and leave Anne and the children at Rosethorn alone.''

They started back toward camp.

''I liked the notion no more than you do,'' Galen admitted with an uneasy frown, ''but 'twas a risk I had to take. Marcus has his orders. The staff will keep watch over them, and Anne is no fool. She'll not take unnecessary chances.''

Bryan stumbled to a halt and caught Galen's arm. ''But if I am not your spy, who is?''

A cold fist clenched Galen's belly. ''I do not know.''

Lyssa sat before the hall's hearth and scowled in concentration. The scrap she labored over was very supple, almost like cloth, but it was difficult to draw a needle through. Her fingers were raw with the evidence of just how difficult the task was. When she stabbed her thumb yet again, she huffed.

''What vexes you so, little one?''

Lyssa looked up and made a face at Freya. ''I cannot do it right. The stitches keep pulling.''

''Perhaps I can help.''

Freya leaned closer, and Lyssa snatched her work close to her chest. ''Nay, 'tis a secret.''

''A secret?'' An odd expression passed over Freya's face; then she smiled. ''Secrets must be kept.''

''There you are, Freya,'' Anne called from the archway. She crossed the hall and peered down at her sister's work. ''What in heaven's name are you doing, Lyssa?''

'' 'Tis a *secret,*'' the little girl declared irately. She balled the scraps in her fist, sticking her hand again with the needle. Growling, she leaped to her feet. "I am going to my chamber. And *no one* had better follow me, either."

Anne snapped to attention. "Aye, my lady."

She had the grace to contain her giggle until Lyssa was out of earshot. Galen's present, no doubt. Her sister had guarded it zealously since the day before. Anne still chuckled when she turned back to Freya. The maid's lips were compressed in controlling a laugh of her own.

"I've learned that Thomas, the shepherd, and his wife have a new babe," Anne told her. "I would like to visit them, and I wondered if you'd join me, help me carry a few gifts to them."

"Certainly, lady."

The cottage they entered a while later was small for a family of six. Seven, Anne corrected with a grin. But it bore evidence of once being trim and neat. Without Thomas's good wife, Adela, to see to matters, though, the cottage had fallen into quite a clutter.

"Oh, lady," the new mother protested with a blush from her narrow bed, " 'tis not right that you do such work. My man can see to it well enough until I am about again."

While Freya prepared a meal, Anne was scrubbing the table.

She laughed. "Adela, Thomas is a dear man, but for a housekeeper, he makes a far better shepherd."

" 'Tis true," Adela agreed, giggling.

The visit passed pleasantly, especially when Adela forgot her shyness with the Lady of Rosethorn and fell to gossiping with her friend, Anne. As she strolled back toward Rosethorn with Freya by her side, Anne felt relieved. The shepherd's family was poor, and children born to poor homes often suffered, in spite of all their parents did to prevent it. Adela was only a few years older than she was, but already she had borne several children. Her first babe had died at birth, and the one before this newest arrival was lost soon afterward. This wee lad, though, seemed healthy. Certainly, she reflected, his chest was strong enough. Her ears still rang from his squalling when his nursing had not come swiftly enough to suit him.

"Such a sweet little babe," Freya murmured.

"Aye," Anne agreed, and frowned. "But I must speak to Galen about that cottage. 'Tis much too small. Thomas is loyal and has given good service. He deserves better for his family."

"You are a kind lady," Freya said. "Not all would take such care with her people. I pray fate keeps you for them."

" 'Tis an odd thing to say," Anne remarked.

"Nay, lady." Freya shook her head sadly. "You never know what lies around the next bend in this life. Good ladies before you have been torn from their people by tragedy."

"Well, I foresee no such threat," Anne countered, smiling. Then the image of Coltrane came to mind, and a chill crept down her spine. Without realizing it, Anne quickened her step. "Is that what happened in your home shire? Did tragedy take the lord and lady from it?"

"Aye, lady," came the subdued answer.

"And so you came to Rosethorn."

"Aye." Freya's usually placid face creased into anguish. "I had heard of Rosethorn, and that its lord had returned. I came to seek . . . peace at last."

"I understand." Anne grasped the other woman's hand. "You've been a dear friend to me, loyal and true, and you'll always have a place here."

"Oh, lady." The maid sniffled and clung to Anne's hand tightly. "God protect you."

"What desolation."

Galen looked around in horrified awe.

"Aye," Bryan agreed, shoving a charred hulk that was once a table with his boot. " 'Tis a disgrace."

The ruins of Briarhaven loomed high upon a hill like a decrepit old man on the verge of collapse. While the other men scouted around the outside, Galen and Bryan had gone within the gaping hole that once had been a grand entrance. They stood now and viewed the damage.

"Fire caused most of it," Galen stated. "See how the

walls are blackened, and the timbers of the upper levels were eaten away."

"This was once quite a keep." Bryan rubbed at a soot-encrusted plate warped by heat. His effort revealed a gleam of silver. He tossed it aside and looked around.

Galen lifted a corner of his mouth ruefully. "Well, there is certainly not much left."

"I would not be too sure of that, if I were you."

Galen turned and found his friend kneeling at a heap of rubble. He picked his way through the mess and crouched beside Bryan. His seneschal held up a round wooden object partially gnawed by flames. He brushed some of the filth from the carving upon it.

"Damn," Galen breathed, and wiped at it more.

"A griffin," Bryan declared. " 'Tis half burned, but you can see the head and wings."

"And it matches what Lyssa saw perfectly."

"I wonder—"

"Here, you!" Both men straightened and whirled, hands going to their swords. They eased. A portly, unkempt man stepped within the entrance. "What do you think you are doing, eh?"

Galen narrowed his eye. "Who are you?"

"I'll be doing the asking," the fellow stated, and peered into the gloom at them. "You do the answering."

Galen stepped carefully toward the irascible man. There were times, he granted wryly, when wearing a mask like his proved handy. He walked into a ray of weak sunlight and let it slash over his face. The man paled. His eyes widened, and he stumbled back.

"God have mercy," he whispered. "What the devil are you?"

Galen smiled grimly. "The Lord of Rosethorn."

"Rosethorn, eh?" The fellow squinted and shifted uneasily. "I've heard tell of you."

"Do you belong to this holding?" Bryan asked, coming to stand by Galen's side.

The man scoffed. "No holding, now. Naught but ruins."

"*Did* you belong once, then?" Galen probed coolly.

"Aye. Once."

The man shuffled a bit, morbidly curious about that fearsome half-mask and the creature wearing it. Galen suffered the look without comment. Indeed, he went out of his way to increase the effect he caused by stepping even closer.

"And you are?"

The fleshy jowls quivered. "Newlin . . . my lord."

Behind him, Galen heard Bryan do his best to stifle a snicker. If their new friend's eyes widened any more, Galen feared they might pop from his head.

"Well, Newlin." Galen said the name silkily. "Suppose you tell us about Briarhaven." He gestured to the crest Bryan still held. "And about this crest here."

"Wh-why should I?"

"Because, Newlin," Galen replied with a thin smile, "if you do not, I will be very displeased."

Chapter Nineteen

Newlin was a cowherd, a fact Bryan discovered soon after entering the gate guarding the man's cottage. He slipped and made a strangled sound as he scraped his boot on the ground.

"Watch your step," Galen advised blandly.

"Amusing. Very amusing."

Not that the man's cattle were worth herding, Galen noted. The four beasts were unpenned, but he doubted there was much risk of their escaping. They stood with heads hung low and eyes sunken, every bit as haggard as Newlin. Sunlight had revealed a portly form, true, but it also showed creases at his eyes and mouth, and a pallor not caused entirely by fear. His shoulders, perhaps once brawny and proud, slumped with weariness. Like his beasts, Newlin was long past caring.

Yet, care had once been taken. Galen could see the signs in the sturdy cottage. Even the cattle bore marks of healthy bloodstock. Like the once-great Briarhaven, though, the cottage was now a place of desolation. Galen scowled. It was a disgrace, and though Newlin appeared a man not overly concerned with neatness, Galen knew all the blame was not his. Poverty had done its filthy work here.

"Where are the others?" Bryan asked, looking around.

Galen wondered with him. It was quiet about what remained of the village. Too quiet.

"Not many others hereabouts," Newlin answered. "Most folk from the village left years ago. Others died. A few, like me, stay because we've nowhere else to go."

It was not an appeal for pity. Newlin simply stated fact. And perhaps, Galen pondered, his first thought of the man was wrong. For as Newlin held the door to his cottage open, Galen saw those tired eyes flicker with shame. Oh, Newlin cared very much, but like a rabbit caught in a snare, he was trapped and saw no way out.

Bryan wrinkled his nose as they entered the cottage, but he had the grace to hold his tongue. Fury seethed in Galen's belly as he took it all in. Not even the poorest of Thornbury's poor suffered such bleakness.

"Ale?" Newlin offered. Both men declined. "Suit yourself."

He poured himself a cupful, and Galen watched him gulp down a good portion before he poured another draught. Drink no doubt smoothed some of the rough edges from the man's life, but that, too, would exact a price of its own in the end.

"Now, Newlin," he said after the man's first thirst was quenched, "tell me about Briarhaven."

"Not much to tell, my lord," Newlin replied. Though he had eased some, Galen noticed the man took care to stay as far from him as possible. "Long about ten, twelve years ago, the Lord of Briarhaven took off to the Holy Land. Took his son with him. The pair of them never returned, and good riddance, I say."

"Oh?"

"Never liked them." Newlin's face twisted with distaste. "The son was the worst. Always prancing about with his nose in the air. But it came down quick enough when a comely village lass crossed his path, I tell you. More than one girl came to grief because of his rutting ways."

"What happened after the lord left?" Bryan asked.

Newlin shrugged and sat at his rickety table. Galen sat

across from him, never taking his gaze from the man. Newlin met his eye, hesitated, and then answered.

"Things went on for the village more or less like always for a while." He shook his head and sipped his ale. "But her ladyship was left alone. Poor woman, 'twas the end for her. She'd never been what you'd call strong in the head, if you get my meaning." Galen nodded. "She'd take a fit, like. Gave the maids the shivers with her wailing and crying. She would sit and rock and rock, muttering to herself. Right as rain, most times, though. Sweet lady, she was, in her right mind. Had a kindly face and manner about her."

It was an old story, all too common during the years of crusade. An absent lord and a weak lady made a disastrous combination for the people who depended upon them. At least, Galen thought tiredly, Thornbury had not been vulnerable for too long, for his father had stayed and had lived many years after his son followed King Richard.

"What happened to the lady?" he asked.

"Year or two after her lord and son left, a messenger came. Her son, the rakehell, had gotten himself killed at someplace called . . . er, Acher, I think."

A chill went down Galen's spine. "Acre."

"Aye, my lord. 'Tis the place. You know of it?"

"Once." Galen's reply was soft. "Long ago. How was the son killed?"

"I never heard. Nor any word about his lordship, either. Her ladyship took it hard." Newlin narrowed his eyes. "Doubt she really cared much for her husband, and I cannot blame her, but her boy . . . aye, the lad was the light of her life, though she must have been blind to dote on him so. Heard tell she screamed and wailed something awful. Shrieked how she was going to find the murderous bastard what killed her sweet boy. A maid told me later they had quite a scuffle trying to calm her, and somehow a fire got started. Some who escaped the flames said her ladyship set the torch herself. Burned the keep to the husk you see today. The people left quick enough after that."

"And the lady was killed in the fire?" Bryan asked.

Newlin shrugged. "Suppose so."

"You suppose?" Galen lifted a brow.

"Never found no body. But then, not much escaped them flames. 'Twas hell's own fire, I tell you. Likely burned the poor woman to cinders, leaving naught to find."

Galen templed his fingers against his lips, pondering. "What was the family name?"

"Renton."

Galen turned the name over in his mind, but it tugged on no memories. Bryan's small shake of his head said it brought nothing from the past to him, either.

"What of the lord's name, and those of his family?"

"Lord's name was Gaylord, Gaylord Renton." Bryan shook his head again, and Galen shrugged. "The boy's name was . . . ah, Darryl. Aye, Darryl."

Now that name rang a bell, but Galen could not swear a Darryl Renton numbered among those he knew from Acre. A headache pinched behind his eyes. There had been so many men there. He could not say if such a man was among those in the siege and battle, or among those betrayed with him on the march toward home. Perhaps once they had a chance to think on it, he or Bryan might be able to place the name.

"What of the lady's?" Bryan asked.

"Pretty-sounding name, she had, real soft and gentle." Newlin thought hard and finally shook his head. "Sorry, my lord, I cannot seem to think of it."

"No matter." Galen heaved a deep sigh. "Have you seen anyone besides ourselves around the castle of late? Perhaps a man of my years, close to my height and build, golden hair?"

"Not a soul has been about that keep for years."

Galen rose and unlaced a pouch tied to his belt. The bag landed with a clink on the table before Newlin. The man's eyes lit with wonder as he opened it and sent a small spill of silver across the table. He looked up at Galen, eyes just as round as they had been before, but there was no fear in them now.

"My lord . . ."

"You said you've nowhere else to go," Galen said quietly, and nodded toward the coin. "That should help you find somewhere, and if you cannot find a place, the village of Thornbury is but a day's ride or so north, three on foot, if you step lively. Perhaps we could find use for a cowherd."

Newlin's hands shook. "Thank you, my lord."

Galen jerked his head toward Bryan. "Ask for this man, Bryan of Rosethorn. He is my seneschal."

He and Bryan left the cottage. Bryan looked as discouraged as Galen felt. Even the sky appeared disheartened, with clouds hanging heavy and dark. They had traveled, so it seemed, for precious little—a holding called Briarhaven, a half-burned crest bearing a griffin, and a destroyed family.

"What a waste," he muttered.

A low rumble from above echoed his words, and Galen gave a pained chuckle as the first drop struck him. Bryan grinned.

"Rain," the seneschal observed, and leaned an elbow on the gatepost. " 'Tis perfect."

"Come on," Galen said wearily. "We cannot hope to get far before nightfall, but we can at least find somewhere sheltered to wait the storm out."

Bryan had just closed the gate, and they had turned, when Newlin burst from the cottage. He scurried toward them as fast as his girth allowed.

"My lord!"

Galen and Bryan turned back, and Newlin gave them a wide, pleased smile.

"Wait, my lord! I remembered her ladyship's name!"

Briarhaven!

Coltrane bared his teeth in a silent snarl at the news his servant had delivered. In the deepening gloom of evening, he paced back and forth along the forest path and tried to ignore how his palms grew moist.

Bloody hell, what had led Tarrant to Briarhaven?

No matter. He drew a deep breath to still his racing heart, cool his burning gut. Tarrant could learn nothing of use there, naught but a sad tale of a ruined family. But names—

Coltrane's heart stumbled to a halt, then hammered back

to life. Tarrant might come to hear names, if anyone thought to speak up. And that would lead to his servant, and then to him.

He brushed the concern aside. What harm could that do? Even if Tarrant heard a name he recognized, another would suffer for it. And small loss that would be. His eyes narrowed on the spot where his servant had stood not moments ago. He needed that one for only a single task more.

Just one task more.

Coltrane's snarl eased into a sharp smile. And then the hunger could feed itself full at long last. Already, he could feel the pleasure, the power swelling his flesh. When the hunger was sated, it would reward him with power, invincible power.

Tarrant would be helpless before the master.

Coltrane nodded to himself. He was the master, and the master could not be defeated. Tarrant would be punished for defying him. And the girl. She would be punished as well, for daring to look upon the master's work and not tremble with awe. They would suffer.

All of them.

He knew the place. He had decided upon the methods, the tools he would use. He stood at the threshold of culminating all his work. It must be perfect.

The hunger would settle for nothing less.

The more Anne pondered, the less easy she felt. Bracing an elbow upon the hall's trestle table, she cupped her chin in her hand and blew out a deep breath. The problem with being uneasy was that she could not be sure about what she felt uneasy about. She did not even know there was cause in the first place. A frown creased her brows.

Just an odd prickle at the back of her neck.

Muck like she had felt that last day of the fair, when she had unknowingly encountered Coltrane.

Just thinking of that villain sent a shiver through Anne. Galen thought Coltrane would follow him, like a hunter stalking his prey. Anne did not know if she wished for that or not. Heaven knew, the idea of Galen running afoul of the worm frightened her near witless, especially since she could not be certain those with him were loyal. But neither did she relish the thought of encountering Coltrane herself. After all, how loyal were those around her?

Who could she turn to? Freya? The woman was a dear but near useless in a crisis. Marcus? Galen had great faith in the burly warrior. Anne nodded to herself. She could depend upon Marcus, but capable warrior that he was, Marcus was not a leader. And it was a leader she needed. Mayde? A fresh tingle of uneasiness shimmied down her spine. What of Mayde?

Perhaps she would never truly like the housekeeper, but Anne had to admit she now respected the woman. If they felt no fondness for each other, Anne granted that they had at least learned to work together.

But she could not deny that an odd feeling came back every time Mayde's name crossed her mind.

This would drive her mad. Anne slapped the table with her palms. If only she could put a name to what plagued her. If only Galen were here.

"Anne."

Anne shrieked and twisted, then laid a hand over her pounding heart and laughed unsteadily. "Oh, Lyssa, you scared me witless, sneaking up like that."

Her little sister stood by her chair with a morose expression. In her hands, she held a mass of dark scraps and tangled thread. Anne looked at it curiously.

"What is that you have?"

"Oh, Anne." Lyssa shoved the mess at her. "I've tried and tried, and I cannot do it right."

Anne took the little bundle and laid it flat upon the table. It was leather, black and very supple. As she pressed it out, its shape began to make sense, and she smiled softly.

"This is the present you make for Galen?" Lyssa nodded in disgust, and Anne's throat ached sweetly. "I think you've done very well."

"But 'tis all scrunched up and looks funny," Lyssa said, her voice quivering. "I cannot make the stitches straight, and the thread keeps snarling."

Anne examined the mess ruefully. It was all true, but the gift was still the loveliest thing she had ever seen. Unfortunately, she doubted Lyssa would understand that Galen would appreciate her present just the way it was, for every snip and stitch had been made with love, if not with skill. Anne plucked at a thread, turned the scraps this way and that, and finally, she grinned.

"I think we can fix it," she said, and stood. "Come on, I'll show you how."

Lyssa nodded eagerly and followed Anne up the stairs.

From the shadows of a doorway leading from the hall, another watched, and her heart ached within her breast.

Such a lovely girl, her ladyship was, gentle and wise far beyond her years. And the child would be just as beautiful, given the fullness of time. Even the boy, mischief-maker that he was, could not be called anything but straight and handsome.

Had she been wrong? Had bitterness so warped her spirit?

She knew it had. Her crimes were great and were against those who had done her nothing but good. Her flesh crawled with shame. She thought she had suffered, but others had suffered more, far more than she. The seneschal had endured torments he never deserved. And his lordship . . . Oh, what *he* had borne! And still, despite it all, both were as fine and noble as ever men could be.

Was it too late? Could she make amends?

Her pride bristled at the thought, but she stamped it down again. Pride would not stand in her way this time. She would do what she could and pray she could do enough.

Before it was too late.

Galen raced through the night as though the hounds of hell nipped at his heels. Bryan kept pace right alongside, but with their superior mounts, they had lost the others. Galen had not noticed at first and did not care now. They knew the danger and would follow as fast as they could. Only one thing mattered.

He had to reach Rosethorn. And Anne.

Perhaps he was leaping to conclusions. All he had was the name of a woman thought long dead. But his heart insisted otherwise, and Galen could not ignore its urgings.

The rain had been short but heavy enough to turn the road into a quagmire. His mount was still game but lathered from the brutal pace he had demanded of it. Galen did not care. He had to make it. By heaven, he would make it, before dawn or soon after, even if he had to ride the poor horse into the mud to do it.

Betrayed! And by one right under his nose! One he would never have suspected! If he was right—and Galen knew in his heart that he was—their traitor had motive and means. And now there was opportunity and time.

The moon hung low on the horizon, peeping from behind a cloak of clouds, but it climbed ever higher into the night sky. Galen urged his mount on.

The traitor had already had too damn much time.

Anne dreaded the approach of this night as much as she had the one before. Nay, she dreaded it more. The evening before, she had lain awake, tossing and turning, until the wee hours. Again and again, she had reached for Galen only to find him absent. Exhaustion finally carried her into sleep.

But this night, more than loneliness plagued her. Anne stood before the hearth, but her hands were chilled beyond the fire's ability to warm them. The idea of lying in that large bed with only her uneasy thoughts to keep her company made Anne recoil. She eyed the goblet upon the bedside table, a treat of the type Freya often brought as she helped Anne prepare for bed. The mulled brew of the night before had offered little ease, and Anne had even less hope for tonight.

"'Tis a gloomy eve," Freya remarked, looking out the unshuttered window. "We'll likely see more rain tomorrow."

"'Tis chilly, too." Anne shivered and drew her shawl closer around her shoulders. "I hope Galen has found someplace warm and dry. 'Tis a bad night to camp on the open road."

''I am sure he'll do well enough,'' the maid replied distantly. ''His lordship can see to himself.''

''I know.'' Anne left the hearth and curled her legs under herself upon the bed. She laughed ruefully. ''But I worry about him all the same.''

''And well you should, lady,'' Freya said, closing the shutters. ''After all, he is your husband, and you care for him very much, do you not?''

''Very much,'' Anne murmured. She hugged herself through another shiver. ''I wish he was here.''

''He will return tomorrow, most likely.'' The maid's brow creased with a thoughtful frown as she moved slowly from the window. ''Aye, the Lord of Rosethorn will return.''

Something in those softly spoken words spread frost into Anne's heart, but she shrugged the feeling off a second later. Without Galen, Rosethorn felt large and forbidding, and with Coltrane's threat still hanging over them, every shadow seem tinged with menace. No doubt Freya felt the same eerie emptiness she did.

''I do not know how I'll ever sleep tonight,'' she remarked, and rubbed her arms as she surveyed the massive bed. ''The bed feels like a cavern when I am alone.''

Freya gave her a look, and Anne shifted, frowning a little at the oddness of it. It was swiftly gone, though, replaced by the maid's usual kindly smile.

''Well, then, lady,'' Freya said brightly, and lifted the goblet from the bedside table to offer it to Anne, ''perhaps a warm brew inside you will make it feel cozy again. Mayde prepared this for you.''

''Did she, indeed?''

''Especially for you,'' Freya told her. She neatened the garments Anne had shed, tucked in a stray fold of the bedclothes. ''She said to drink it all. Muttered something about it doing naught but good.''

Anne lifted her brows. Would wonders never cease when it came to Mayde? No doubt about it, the old dragon really was softening. The goblet was warm to the touch, and Anne sniffed at the contents. It was pleasant, with just a hint of spice that teased her nose.

"'Tis unlike anything I know of." She sniffed again. "I wonder what it contains."

Anne hesitated in bringing the goblet to her lips. Mayde herself had cautioned against drinking any concoction until they knew if she carried Galen's child. Then Anne scoffed at herself. She was being ridiculous, sniffing at the brew like a timid rabbit. Whatever else the woman might think of her, Mayde had certainly been adamant about safeguarding her lord's possible offspring.

This child must be protected at all costs.

"Oh, Mayde knows many tricks with herbs," Freya replied. "Likely, 'tis only some sort of mulled cider."

Anne took a cautious sip. The brew tasted very much like a mulled cider, though a bit sweeter than usual. It was not bad, actually. The tang of cinnamon lingered upon her tongue, and the warmth of the liquid spread rather agreeably through her veins. She took another sip.

"Drink it down, lady." Freya came to stand by the bed and waited patiently until Anne drank every drop. When Anne passed her the goblet, she peered into it and nodded in satisfaction. "I am sure you'll sleep through the night now."

"I am sure I will." Anne scooted under the covers and smiled ruefully, hoping she spoke true. "You'll check on the children?"

Freya paused at the door but did not turn. "Of course, lady." She stood for a long moment, then twisted around slowly, a worried look upon her face. "My lady, I . . ."

"What is it, Freya?" Anne asked gently when the woman said no more.

"'Tis nothing, lady." The maid's lips curved a little, and she cradled the goblet between her palms. "Sleep well."

"And you, Freya."

When the door closed, Anne snuggled down in the bed and watched the fire burn. Sleep well? She snorted and rolled her eyes. Not likely. She could already feel that pesky uneasiness creep around her heart again. She would probably pass this night as she had the one before, tossing and turning with her thoughts whirling about her mind.

But Anne did not lie awake and think. Her eyelids felt heavier and heavier. Soon Anne did sleep.

She slept deeply, indeed.

Galen smiled tiredly.

At long last, the towers of Rosethorn had come within view. The band drawn about his heart eased the slightest bit, but Galen kept his mount charging as hard as the poor animal could manage. Never before had he used a steed so harshly. Guilt stabbed at him, and he patted the horse's neck. Soon, he promised the beast silently. The terrible ride would end soon.

He just prayed it would end in time.

He and Bryan thundered up to the gates and reined in sharply. The drawbridge was up. Though he had left orders to lift it every night until he returned, Galen chafed at the delay it caused. Every second felt like a precious eternity until he beheld Anne and the children, safe and sound, with his own gaze.

"Drop the bridge!" Bryan's bellow rang out into the coming dawn. " 'Tis his lordship, Lord Galen, and his seneschal! Drop the bloody bridge!"

From within the barbican, a harsh grate signaled compliance. Exhausted though they were, the horses danced nervously at the thud of the heavy timbers striking the ground. Galen and Bryan sent their horses stumbling into the bailey. His own horse groaned as he dismounted, and Galen saw Bryan's hang its head wearily. Grooms scurried forth, half-asleep but wide-eyed at this breech in custom.

"See them well groomed," Galen instructed tightly, and showed his mount his gratitude with another stroke along its neck. "They've more than earned their rest."

That task seen to, he and Bryan sprinted toward the keep. The hall's door banged open, and they rushed inside. Not a soul stirred, which was expected. It was barely dawn, after all. Galen took the stairs two at a time, breathless and heart pounding with more than mere exertion.

"Check on the children," he snapped.

Bryan nodded, but Galen did not pause to hear his friend's

reply. He jerked on the handle of his own chamber door and flung it wide. Only the fire dying in the hearth gave light, but his sight quickly became accustomed to the dimness. Galen stalked to the bed and flung back the drapery.

His heart stopped, then thundered back to life again.

"Derek and Lyssa are safe." Bryan's voice reported from the doorway, but not a sound passed Galen's lips in acknowledgment. Not a muscle did he move. "Galen?"

Galen stumbled to one side, the world spinning around and around in his head. Leaning against the bedpost, he forced air into his chest and swallowed against the bitterness of bile rising into his throat. He looked at Bryan and slowly straightened, strength flooding back within his body as suddenly as weakness had sapped it a moment ago. His words erupted in a roar.

"Where the hell is Anne?"

Chapter Twenty

"Ohhh . . ."

Anne struggled through the sticky tangle of her mind. She swallowed, and her tongue felt thick in her mouth.

Useless. It was useless.

She could not grasp awareness, but something within her urged her on. Slowly, very slowly, she forced her eyelids open.

"Lady?"

A voice called to her, soft and concerned.

Anne turned her head and stared. Eventually, the dull shapes she saw sharpened and took form.

"Freya . . ." Anne took a deep breath. "Freya?"

"Aye, lady," the maid acknowledged. " 'Tis Freya."

Anne blinked and squinted into the gloom. "Where . . ."

"Here, lady."

Anne stared very hard and finally saw the woman clearly. Freya sat in a chair across from her, back straight, arms oddly stiffened at her sides. *If only my head would stop spinning.* Anne heaved a sigh that ended with a whimper. Her own arms tingled with numbness. She tried to move them, to ease the bothersome ache, but they would not obey. Anne tried again, and shock rippled through her.

Bound. Her wrists and ankles were bound. She felt the roughness of the cord when she twisted her hands. Another small sound seeped from her lips as she tugged, but her arms were stretched over her head to their fullest. Her legs were drawn straight. Panic pierced her lingering stupor, and she twisted her wrists, frantically trying to free herself.

"Freya?" she called out, weak and afraid. "What—"

"Do not struggle so, lady," the maid counseled. "You'll shred your flesh to ribbons."

The advice made sense. Already, she could feel the cord cutting into her skin. Anne stilled. Instead of struggling against what she could not fight, it made more sense to take full stock of her plight. But the languor plagued her so, muddled her senses. Blinking and shaking her head hard, Anne tried to keep firm hold on awareness.

Flat. She lay on something flat and hard. Anne thought furiously. A table of some type? It felt cold. She shivered from the chill dampness that seeped into her flesh. Stone. She lay upon a slab of stone? She looked around but could discern little. Ghostly shadows danced from a flickering light. A torch or brazier somewhere close made an island of brightness in the dark. And beyond it? Just more dark. Not a glimmer of light existed beyond this place.

Gradually, as her eyes adjusted, Anne saw the outline of other stone slabs. About waist-height. Rather longer than wide. Some were plain. Others were adorned with figures and lettering. And from everywhere, the musty scent of mildew wafted to her nose. Anne trembled. A chamber? Where? She looked over at Freya again, brows furrowed.

The maid had not moved. She still sat as straight as a rod with her arms stiff at her sides.

"Are you tied, too?" Anne asked, her words mumbled through lips that still did not work very well. Tired. She was so tired. "Freya? Are you bound?"

The woman's face softened with a smile. Fear quivered through Anne at that smile. So gentle. So kind. So empty.

As if pulled by strings, that empty curve never faltering upon her lips, Freya rose to her feet.

"Nay, lady. Master would never do such a thing."

Nay! Oh, dear Lord, nay!

Anne's breath hitched with a gasp that turned into a sob. Freya drew close and peered down at her. Her fingers, light as a breath, stroked Anne's cheek and patted it. Gray edged into Anne's mind once more and began to darken into black. Freya's voice floated through her mind like a frosty mist.

". . . Not to me, his devoted servant."

Galen swung about to face Bryan as he came from searching the castle. His belly knotted, and when his seneschal shook his head, the knot iced over.

"She is nowhere," Bryan reported dismally. "I've searched the keep, the grounds, from the cellar to the far tower. No one has seen her since she retired last night. One of the maids said Freya escorted her to bed."

It was like taking a blow to the chest. Dear Lord, Anne was gone. His sweet Lady Anne. His wood elf had been taken. Galen shuddered and braced his palms upon the table to keep from crumpling to the floor when his knees buckled. Bryan was there in an instant, lending support with an arm about his shoulders.

"Nay," Galen uttered with a gasp. He waved Bryan off. "I'll not go down."

There could be no doubt. Anne had been taken. Just as there was no doubt who had taken her. And why. For a long moment, Galen saw nothing—not Bryan close at his side, not his men and staff gathered around him, not Derek or Lyssa standing wide-eyed with terror before him. Galen felt nothing. He knew nothing but one simple fact.

He had failed.

He had failed to protect Anne.

And he could well pay the price by losing her forever.

" 'Tis incredible." Bryan shrugged helplessly, rubbing the back of his neck. "I cannot believe she would do such vile things. Not Freya."

"She is mad," Galen growled. "You remember Newlin's

tale. Freya is sick with her grief and her revenge. Has she been seen at all?'' Bryan shook his head again. ''And Mayde?''

''Not a sign of her, either.''

''Damn and blast!''

Feeling returned in a scorching wave of rage. Galen pounded his fist on the table hard enough to make the echo resound through the hall. He pinched the bridge of his nose.

He had to take hold of himself. Nothing could be served by flying into a fury. He must be calm. Galen drew a deep breath that caught in his chest.

But dear God, how could he be calm when Anne was—

''How?'' he breathed. If he could understand that, perhaps it would light his way to his next move. ''The bridge was raised since nightfall. Marcus has attested to that. No one has gone in or out since then.''

''They've got to be somewhere within the walls.'' Bryan's shoulders slumped in defeat. ''I must have missed something.''

''Nay.'' Galen shook his head slowly, a new thought dawning. ''Perhaps not. The bridge was lowered when we arrived.''

''But with so many about—''

''Aye, in confusion because of our sudden arrival.''

''You think they could have smuggled her out then?'' Bryan's eyes widened as he followed along. ''Anne must have been silenced somehow, bound to prevent escape. Who would notice one, or maybe two, moving through the shadows with her?'' Galen nodded, and Bryan gave a half-laugh. ''Then they cannot be gone long or far.''

''They would not take Anne far, anyway,'' Galen replied. ''I am the prey, remember? Coltrane means to draw me out. He would not lay the bait in his trap beyond reach.'' He struggled to keep up with his whirling thoughts. ''Bryan, think of a place, a deserted place where no one ever goes. A place they could hold Anne until they wish to be discovered.''

Bryan nodded, and Galen could all but see the gears of his friend's mind turn the matter over and over. He, too, thought of all the places in or around Thornbury that could be used thus. It was difficult work. They had scoured the countryside more than once and found no hiding place that could be useful. But perhaps they had missed something.

"Galen?"

A young voice scattered Galen's thoughts like dead leaves upon the wind. Brow furrowed in exasperation with the interruption, he looked down and saw the children looking up at him. He bit back the sharp words poised upon the tip of his tongue at the fear glimmering in their eyes.

"What is it, Derek?"

"I can help find Anne," the little boy offered, his voice quivering. "I can."

"I know you want to help, lordling . . ." Galen crouched before the lad and tried to keep his impatience reined in. He took Derek's hand and squeezed it gently. "And I appreciate your offer, but the best way you and Lyssa can help us is to stay here, out of harm's way."

The boy's face twisted with youthful indignation. "But—"

"Derek, please," Galen pleaded, frustration seeping into his tone. He looked at a maid lingering close at hand and gestured to the little ones. "Take them to their chambers. Stay with them until I or Bryan come."

"Aye, my lord," she murmured, and curtsied.

The girl scooted forth and took each child by the hand, but Derek pulled free.

"I *can* help, Galen."

"Galen?" Lyssa clung to his sleeve. "You'll find Anne? You'll not let the bad man hurt her?"

"Nay, sweetling," he assured her, and prayed he uttered truth. Kissing her soft cheek, he made an effort to smile. "I'll let no harm come to her. Go, now. Bryan or I will come for you soon."

"But, *Galen*—"

Derek was still whining when the maid caught his hand fast in her own and guided him and Lyssa from the hall. Galen watched them go, and his chest throbbed. They were not of his blood, but they were the children of his heart. He had failed Anne. But he would not fail to protect these children.

"Remember," he called after the maid, "allow none but Bryan or myself to come within arm's reach of either of them."

"Never fear, my lord." She stood in the archway and nodded with determination. "I'll keep them safe, if I have to bar the chamber door and wield a sword myself to do it."

Galen gave a wan smile. "Bar the chamber door, anyway."

When they were gone, silence stretched taut within the hall. Galen bowed his head, slumping his shoulders beneath the near-crushing weight settled upon them. Then he straightened, and his jaw hardened until it ached.

"Search every inch of ground," he grated. "Look in every cottage, every shed, under every rock and behind every blade of grass." He swept his gaze through the men. "You've all heard Coltrane's description, and you know the woman, Freya. I want them. I want them alive and before me to answer for their crimes." His control faltered for an instant before he shored it up again. "But most of all, before aught else you do, find the Lady Anne. Make sure she is safe. No harm—*none*—must befall her."

Every man nodded and went to his duty. When the last of them had filed out of the hall, Galen swallowed thickly. Bryan laid a hand on his shoulder and squeezed.

"We must find her," Galen whispered. He thrust his chin out fiercely. "By God, we *will* find her."

With Bryan at his side, he stalked from the hall.

Anne sputtered and coughed as the liquid trickled too quickly down her throat.

"Slowly, lady," Freya intoned, holding a cup of water to her prisoner's lips. "You'll choke if you do not take care."

Anne glared at the maid. She had fought the cup, fearing it contained another dose of sleeping elixir, but Freya was determined. With unnatural calm, she had seized Anne's jaw in a surprisingly strong grip and forced her mouth open.

Even then, Anne did not swallow until she was certain only water lay upon her tongue.

When Freya finally took the cup away and blotted at the spilled water on Anne's face, Anne bared her teeth and snapped at the woman's hand. The bite missed by only a hair's width. Anne braced herself as Freya raised her hand as if to strike her. Then, the maid's fingers curled into her palm, and she lowered her hand. The grimace of outrage etched upon Freya's face softened once more into kindliness—a terrible, blank kindliness.

"Now, lady," she crooned, "I only thought you might be thirsty. You've no reason to take on so."

"No reason?" Anne gave a thin laugh and jerked against the cords binding her to the stone slab. "You fed me God only knows what evil brew, stole me from my very bed, and trussed me tighter than a fatted pig. And I have no reason to take on?"

"No harm will befall you," Freya assured her. "Master has promised."

Anne snorted. "Your master is evil incarnate."

Freya looked injured. "Oh, lady, nay. He is a wise lord, much wronged. He seeks only justice."

"And I will have it," said a voice, deeply male and triumphant. "I'll have justice at last."

Freya turned and stepped away from the table, giving her prisoner full view of the man framed in a stone archway. He was naught but an outline in the dark. Then he stepped into the light cast by the brazier close by Anne, and she trembled.

Coltrane.

Anne's flesh crawled at the sight of him. Handsome he was, all golden hair and shocking blue eyes. Just as she remembered from the fair, and just as she remembered, all sharp-edged smiles and vile smoothness. Anne realized then she had not truly been afraid before. But she was now.

She narrowed her eyes. This miserable creature fed on fear. She would be damned before she gave him the satisfaction.

"Bastard," she hissed between her clenched teeth.

Coltrane chuckled as he looked down at her, his eyes gleaming with victory. Anne's belly roiled.

"Such spirit," he murmured approvingly. "I knew you would prove an excellent selection."

"Let me go, you miserable worm," Anne demanded.

"Now, my lady," he replied reasonably, "you know I am very unlikely to do that. I told you, that day at the fair, I wanted to become better acquainted with you. And I will. We will come to know each other very well."

Anne could not keep a quiver from running through her, but she kept her tone biting. "And how will we become *acquainted,* Coltrane?"

His smile deepened. "I prefer for the anticipation to linger for a while yet."

He feathered his fingertips over the hollow of her throat, tracing a line back and forth. Anne squeezed her eyes shut and held her breath as his touch trailed to outline the loose opening of her sleeping gown. He glided his fingers to her breast, skimming them around the crest. Around and around, before he stroked it tenderly. Bitterness seared Anne's throat. Bile swelled within it as her flesh prickled with horrible chills. Coltrane grasped her jaw, forced her face to turn, and waited until her eyes finally met his.

"Anticipation must be relished, lady," he said softly. "It heightens the senses, makes every sensation so much keener. So much sharper."

Anne thought she would be sick. In fact, she hoped desperately she would be. All over him. But that would give him a sort of satisfaction, too, would it not? A sign of her terror, her weakness?

"The only sensation I wish to savor," she ground out, "is watching you cower like the miserable cur you are."

"Cower before your husband? Before Tarrant? Not bloody likely." Coltrane laughed in delight. Then he leaned close and whispered, "The Lord of Rosethorn will cower before *me*. He will plead with me as I made him plead once before. Have you heard the tale? How I once made him scream for mercy?"

Galen's beloved face, desecrated by that terrible scar,

floated into her mind. Anne drew a breath that came out as a whimper.

"I see you have," he murmured. "The punishment he suffered then was nothing to what he will endure now."

"Nay . . ." The word seeped from her lips weakly.

"Have you seen his face?" Coltrane's smile could have sliced granite. "Has he permitted you to look beneath that mask? See what I did to him? 'Tis a bit crude, I admit, but my work has improved with time. I can make him suffer so much more now. Make him watch what I do to you. Make him witness how I will extract from you every shriek your sweet body possesses. Make him feel all the pleasure of your agony."

"You are mad," Anne whispered in horror.

"I think not."

He chuckled and tapped her cheek lightly. Anne jerked her head as far away as she could manage. Coltrane leaned even closer and brushed his lips at her temple, then nibbled upon the spot just below her ear. Anne sobbed.

"I am looking forward to using you," he told her. "I am looking forward to it so much."

He straightened and looked to his faithful servant.

"See that she remains bound," he instructed. "We cannot risk losing so precious a prize."

"Aye, master." Hovering by the chair, Freya gazed at him with pleading eyes. "Will it be long now?"

"Nay," Coltrane replied. For a second, Anne saw his eyes narrow, and a feral glint appeared. " 'Twill not be long before you receive your reward."

With a last satisfied look at Anne, he left, disappearing into the darkness. Freya sat in her chair once more.

Anne blinked furiously and swallowed her tears. She had to think. Her plight loomed all around her like the damp smell of stone, filling her senses. Like a cavern, it was. Deep and dark. Anne closed her eyes and breathed deeply to ease the constriction tightening her throat.

Galen. Had he returned? She had no idea of time here. Was he, even now, searching for her? Was his foot hovering over whatever trap Coltrane set for him?

There had to be a way out of this. She must find it.
And soon.

Galen reined his mount to a halt with his troop, meeting Bryan and his own men coming from the opposite direction. They had ridden in a wide circle around Rosethorn and its lands, spiraling inward until they reached the castle again. The task had taken time, precious hours he did not have the luxury of wasting.

But a waste it had been.

Bryan shook his head, and Galen's heart sank.

From close by, the sound of thrashing and footsteps came to them. Galen looked toward it. The villagers were out in force, sweeping through the wood and fields. They searched their homes, high and low. They were scouring every inch of Rosethorn land.

''We must change the horses,'' Galen said dully, and led the others within the castle gates.

As he dismounted, Galen stumbled. Bryan caught his arm, and Galen nodded his thanks. After riding the night through and searching all morning, he was exhausted. He looked at Bryan and saw the same lines bracketing his friend's mouth that he knew lined his own, the same shadows beneath his eyes. And yet, Galen knew they could not rest, could find no ease until Anne was found. Safe. Alive.

But what if Coltrane had already—

Galen jerked his mind back from the edge of that thought. He would find her. She would be safe. Coltrane would not harm her, would not defile a single hair upon her lovely head. He simply had to *believe*. Else he would go mad.

''Come,'' Bryan said on a deep sigh. ''Let us drink and eat, or we'll be sprawling in the dust before long.''

It was the voice of sense, but Galen's belly rebelled at the mere thought of food. Still, he walked with his friend to the keep.

The hall was so quiet when they entered that the closing door sounded like a clap of thunder. Alerted, servants rushed in with hopeful faces, only to have them fall at their lord's expression. They brought meat and bread and wine at

Bryan's bidding, and the two men sat at the table. Bryan managed to chew a morsel or two, but Galen pushed his own trencher away. His friend said nothing, letting his frown speak for him.

"Has anyone seen Mayde?" Bryan asked a girl pouring wine.

She shook her head. "Nay, my lord, not hide nor hair of her since the wee hours this morning."

" 'Tis strange," Bryan mulled to himself.

Galen rose. "I must check on Derek and Lyssa."

There was really no need. Galen knew that, but he did feel the need to see them, to hear their young voices. Perhaps, he thought with a small smile, to feel their hugs. His step slowed by more than just weariness, he climbed the stairs to their chambers. Derek's door stood open, and the chamber was vacant. Lyssa's was shut tight. Galen heard the murmur of voices within and knocked. The murmur hushed.

"Who goes?" the maid's voice called, thin and hesitant.

" 'Tis I, Lord Galen."

There was a scrape of wood against wood. The door opened just a crack, then swung wide. Galen saw the children, sitting on the edge of the bed. They looked up, their eyes alight with hope, but their expressions, too, fell at the sight of his. He entered and sat by them.

Warmth stabbed at his heart when Derek leaned against him. Galen encircled the lad's slender shoulders, and a lump lodged in his throat when Lyssa scooted around to his other side and cuddled under his arm. He buried his lips in her silky hair and just held them both in silence for a long time.

" 'Twill be all right, Galen," Lyssa murmured, and patted his chest. "Anne will be safe. You'll find her."

Galen's shoulders quaked, half with a laugh and half with a sob. He had to breathe very deeply before he could speak. "Thank you, sweetling."

He looked over at Derek and took in the lad's glum face. Galen tweaked his nose.

"Take heart, lordling."

Derek pulled such a face that Galen's brow lifted.

"What is it, Derek?"

The boy cast him a sullen look. "I can help find Anne, but you will not let me."

Galen sighed. "Derek—"

"But I know where she could be," the lad insisted hotly. "A deserted place, you said, a place no one ever goes."

"You know of such a place?" Galen asked, brow furrowed. Derek nodded vehemently. "Where?"

Where, indeed? They had searched every nook and cranny.

"The chapel," Derek blurted out. "Here, inside Rosethorn. Anne said we must never go there. That you did not like anyone to go inside."

Galen stared at the boy. Rosethorn's chapel? But that was ridiculous! It was right under their noses! Still—Had Freya not been right under their noses the whole time, too?

"Oh, my God . . ."

Galen breathed the words and rose to his feet.

"Galen?" Derek caught his hand. "Galen, did I help?"

Galen caught the boy under his arms and swung him up into a fierce embrace. Smacking a kiss on the lad's cheek, he dropped him back onto the bed. Derek bounced and giggled.

"Aye, lordling," he crowed, and ruffled the boy's hair, "that you did. 'Tis sorry I am that I did not listen to you when you tried to tell me before." He turned to the maid as he strode from the room. "Bar the door after me."

Feeling light-headed of a sudden, Galen leaned against the closed door and heard the bar fall back into place. At long last, he had a hope. It was a slim one, true, and could so easily come to naught.

A laugh rumbled from his throat, and Galen pushed away from the door and raced down the stairs.

It mattered not. Hope was hope.

"Why, Freya?"

Anne's question floated softly through darkness. The silence stretched a long time, and Anne turned her head to the woman. Freya sat, still as straight as a lance. Then she began rocking slowly back and forth. Her face was a blank mask, and her eyes stared at nothing.

"Freya?"

The maid rested her eyes upon her prisoner, and Anne shivered. Nothing. There was nothing in those eyes. But she persisted. Her only hope was to somehow reach Freya, to convince her to help. Surely the woman had not slipped so far into madness that she could not remember where, and with whom, her loyalty should lie.

No sound trickled to her from outside. No bells tolled to mark the hours. But Anne knew time sped by. How long would Coltrane wait before springing his trap? Soon, her heart answered. Very soon.

"Why, Freya?" Gently, Anne reminded herself. Step carefully. "Will you tell me why you've done this?"

Freya blinked. "Because of my darling, my sweet one."

"Sweet one?" Anne frowned. "Your husband?"

"Gaylord?" Freya scoffed. "Nay, I'd not waste justice on him." She leaned forward, as though imparting some secret. "He was an evil man, lady, a brute. A lustful, rutting brute. I did not want to wed him, but I had to. You understand. My parents said I had to, to unite the lands."

"Your husband was titled?"

"Aye," Freya agreed brightly. "A proper lady I was. The Lady of Briarhaven." Her brow puckered in bewilderment. "A lady should be wed to a proper lord, and Gaylord was not proper, for all he bore was a title. He was too rough, demanded his . . . his rights too often. Rutting beast." Her expression lightened. "But even the worst of trials can yield reward in the end. From Gaylord's rutting, I got my sweet darling."

A child, Anne realized. Her mind whirled over this new piece of information, tried to find a use for it.

"Darryl was such a beautiful lad." With a mother's joy, Freya sighed. "So handsome and straight. People did not understand him." She frowned sadly. "They said such unkind things about him."

"What happened to Darryl?" Anne asked gently.

Freya's eyes were stark with anguish. "He went away.

His father tricked him into going away. He lied to him, lady.'' Freya shook her head, and her voice grew shrill. ''He *lied!*''

''Did they go to the Holy Land, on crusade?'' Freya nodded. ''And they did not return?''

''My darling lad did not return.'' Freya stood and wrung her hands. Her face became a stricken mask. ''He was at Acre. You know about Acre.''

Anne nodded.

'' 'Twas terrible, terrible for the infidels to do such a thing. They took my sweet boy, put him in prison.'' Freya sobbed quietly. ''Heaven only knows what happened to him there, how he was tortured.''

Tortured. In prison. Anne's eyes widened. Freya's son was with Galen? Was it possible?

''Lord Galen was there, too,'' Freya went on, calm again. Unnaturally calm. ''He was with my Darryl. He could have helped him.'' Her lips drew back to bare her teeth. ''But he did not. That worthless seneschal he saved, but my lamb . . . my son he left to die.''

She suddenly loomed over her prisoner, and Anne trembled. '' 'Twas not right. My Darryl was worth all the rest put together, and *that filthy, scarred beast left him there!*''

Anne flinched at Freya's shriek.

''I swore,'' Freya told her in a snarl, ''I would see him punished for leaving my son. I swore I would have justice for it. The beast has to pay for his crimes.''

''Freya . . . Freya, listen to me,'' Anne pleaded softly. ''Galen was not to blame. He was betrayed the same as your Darryl—suffered torment, too. You cannot blame him.''

That seemed to baffle the maid for a moment; then she shook her head sadly. ''You do not understand, lady. He left my sweet boy to die.''

''Galen did what he could,'' Anne insisted. Freya shook her head again, and Anne growled in frustration. ''You've lived so long with your bitterness, you've become blind to the truth. Galen is not to blame!''

''Master said he was,'' Freya claimed. ''Master suffered, too, because of that scarred monster. He would not lie.''

"Your master is the one who betrayed them! Freya, Coltrane is the one who betrayed them, betrayed your son!"

Anne was relentless. It was her only hope. Somehow, she had to convince Freya that Coltrane was their common foe.

"Coltrane is the one who led the Moslems in that battle." Freya shook her head wildly, and Anne sobbed a little. "Coltrane is the one who cast them into prison, the one who tortured and tormented them all!"

"Nay." Freya took a step back, then another and another, all the while shaking her head. "The beast has poisoned your mind. Master would never—"

Anne blinked at the metallic thunk that suddenly echoed through the darkness. Freya's face went strangely blank. Then she crumpled into a heap upon the floor.

Chapter Twenty-one

Eyes wide, Anne saw Mayde step into the light, a triumphant smile upon her lips and a spade clutched in both hands.

"I knew there was a reason I distrusted that woman," the housekeeper declared.

The spade landed with a clatter on the floor, and Mayde rushed to where Anne lay limp with shock. The woman's competent hands dealt with the cords swiftly, untying the knots. Anne's arms screeched in protest when she tried to lower them, and she whimpered.

"Careful, lady," Mayde advised, and rubbed her lady's arms to ease the stinging flow of blood within them. "Move slowly at first, or you'll end with Satan's own cramp in the muscles."

Anne laughed with a blend of relief and pain. "Oh, Mayde, I take back every foul thought I ever had about you."

" 'Tis well you should." The housekeeper's eyes twinkled down at her. She braced an arm under Anne's shoulders. "Up with you, now. We've no time for dawdling."

Anne sat up carefully, her head spinning a little, and swung her legs over the side of the slab. Mayde crouched by Freya's crumpled form and shoved the maid onto her back.

"Not dead, more's the pity," Mayde growled.

Anne slid her feet to the floor, and her legs promptly buckled beneath her weight. Mayde was by her side in an instant, sliding her arms about Anne's waist and holding her upright.

"All right, girl," Mayde snapped. "Let us get you out of here. Step lively, now."

Anne gave another laugh as they shuffled as fast as her wobbly legs could carry her. Wonderful old dragon.

Galen, Bryan, and a troop of men gathered just outside the chapel door. The bar lay on the ground. Galen cast Bryan a wry look.

"I'll ask about how that escaped someone's notice later," he said in a low voice.

Bryan just cleared his throat.

Galen drew his sword and held it at the ready. Carefully, he eased the door open, flinching when it creaked. It took only a step to enter, and he did it swiftly.

Nothing. Not a sound. Not a single movement.

Bryan was right behind him, and they looked around.

"Galen." At Bryan's near soundless whisper, Galen looked at his friend, then followed the nod of his head. "There. The gate to the crypt."

The iron gate guarding the Tarrant family crypt stood ajar. Galen stepped to it and extended his hand for the torch one of his men held. He handed his sword to Bryan. Holding the blazing torch in one hand, the fingers of the other wrapped around one of the bars. He flung the gate open with so quick a jerk that only the barest hint of a creak escaped the old hinges. Bryan caught it, keeping it from banging against the wall.

Still nothing. No sign of life.

Galen drew a deep breath.

"I am going down."

"Nay!" Bryan caught his arm and whispered furiously. "Are you mad? Coltrane could be down there. Anywhere down there, just waiting for you."

"The thought had crossed my mind." Galen felt a thin smile curve his lips. He shook his friend's grasp off. "Anne could also be down there, Bryan. I must find her."

They were between a rock and a hard place, and both men knew it. To find Anne, they had to go down into the crypt. But to go within the crypt could very well mean stepping right into Coltrane's trap.

"I'll go first," Bryan insisted.

Galen shook his head. "Nay. I need you to cover my back."

Bryan blew out a breath, then nodded.

Torch held high, Galen descended into the pitch black of Rosethorn's crypt.

Anne paused by Freya's body and worried her lower lip between her teeth.

"You did not kill her?"

"Nay, lady."

In spite of everything, Anne eased in relief. Freya had betrayed them all, sold them to Coltrane in the name of her mad revenge. Yet Anne also remembered the kindness that had supported her through waking that first time in Rosethorn, her father's death, and the early days as lady of the keep.

How could it happen? How could so warm and gentle a woman harbor such malignancy within her soul?

"She has not stirred," Anne murmured.

"Do not deceive yourself, lady," Mayde replied stonily. "There is nothing left of the Freya you think you knew. You see a woman snared in naught but madness now."

Anne sighed. "I know."

" 'Tis a harsh judgment, I know, child," the housekeeper said, uncommonly gentle. "But the kindest thing fate can do for her is to let her slip away in her sleep. You know, do you not, that your husband will be merciless with those who have betrayed him?" Anne nodded slowly. Mayde patted her shoulder. "Granting this one mercy, lady, would be granting her naught but torment instead."

Mayde was right. Galen's justice would be swift and fair,

but he would not flinch from judging Freya the same way as any other traitor. Yet Anne still could not bear the thought of what his punishment would likely be. Not for Freya. Anne rested her head on Mayde's supportive shoulder. In spite of it all, the end should not come like that.

"Come, lady," the housekeeper urged. "We must quit this accursed place. Your husband is no doubt frantic for you by now."

Anne allowed Mayde to usher her from the chamber. For a chamber it proved to be. They moved from one into another. Then another. By the light of Mayde's torch, Anne saw that the rooms were made of roughly hewn stone and lined with long objects that looked very like—

"What is this place?" Anne asked in a small voice, though she thought she already knew.

"The crypt beneath Rosethorn's chapel."

Anne shivered. So, those objects were vaults holding the remains of Tarrants long dead. "I was here once before, with Galen. I did not realize it had more than the one chamber."

"Not many do." Mayde led her along a narrow corridor that emptied into another chamber. "The crypt is in two sections, you see. The one you saw is where the lords and their ladies are laid to rest. Other family members are here, in the deeper reaches. And others."

"Others?"

"Rosethorn was not always in the hands of the Tarrants," Mayde told her. "Long ago, before William the Bastard conquered the land, 'twas held by Saxon lords. Many of their bones rest here as well. The chapel, you see, was built atop the old Saxon crypt. 'Twas all that was left after the Norman hordes razed the first fortress to the ground."

Anne gasped at a high, squeaking sound from some dark, dark corner and lifted the hem of her gown from about her feet. It was so damp, the stone floor felt covered with slime under her bare feet.

"How . . . How do you know so much of it?" she asked, not really wanting to know but needing the sound of her companion's voice to cling to.

"Oh, I know much about the Tarrants, lady," Mayde answered. Her voice saddened. "I was once one of them, in a way."

Anne stopped dead in her tracks. "What?"

Mayde turned to her, and her smile was filled with sorrow. " 'Twas long ago. I once belonged to Lord Geoffery's brother." She smiled sadly at Anne's thunderstruck expression. "That took the wind from you, did it not?"

"Then that makes you Galen's—"

"Nay, child, I am not his aunt." At Anne's confused frown, she explained, "I was Richard's mistress. His whore. Lord Galen does not know. He knows only that I served at Stagmount. He believes I served as housekeeper there, for so I did, after Richard went and got himself killed in the Holy Land."

She took Anne's hand and led her along.

"Was he at Acre, too?"

Mayde shook her head. "Nay, Richard died of fever long before Acre. He was not like his brother. Lord Geoffery was a stubborn man, set in his ways and with a quick temper, but he was a good man. The only thing the brothers shared was the temper. Where his brother's ire was quickly repented, Richard only turned more brutal."

"How did you . . . I mean, how did he . . ."

"How did I end up in his bed?" Mayde chuckled dryly. "I was female, and I yet breathed. Richard took a fancy to me. You might not think so to look at me now, but I was once quite attractive. He bought me from my father and kept me at Stagmount, the manor he had inherited and held for Lord Geoffery as his vassal. I was there for twenty years, exchanging my body for food and shelter. I hated him, hated all the Tarrants, for a long time."

"Why?" Anne breathed.

Mayde shrugged. "Hate kept me strong."

"But you speak so well of old Lord—"

"Aye," she agreed wryly. "Remember, lady, hate gives strength, but it does not give sense."

"So when Galen returned and offered the position here at Rosethorn, you took it to escape the memories."

" 'Tis just so." Mayde heaved a sigh. "Problem was, hate

had gotten to be a habit with me. I knew I should be grateful to Lord Galen. He'd given me a chance, you see, to leave the past behind, but I could not seem to stop hating."

"Have you, now?" Anne asked softly. "Stopped hating?"

The housekeeper did not reply. They entered yet another chamber, having wound their way through the labyrinth of the crypt. Mayde hesitated.

"What is it?" Anne asked, shivering.

"I do not know what to do now, lady."

"We get out of here," Anne declared.

"Aye, but I know not where the man is," the housekeeper explained. "I saw him leave and followed him a ways. He headed back toward the entry, and we are close to there now."

"Coltrane could be lying in wait for Galen at the entry," Anne reasoned, and Mayde nodded. "We cannot risk stumbling upon him, but we can hardly stay here."

"Lady . . ."

Mayde's thin whisper, and the way she grasped Anne tighter about the waist, sent a chill down Anne's spine. She followed the woman's gaze and saw a shadow, a tall and broad-shouldered shadow, move just beyond the archway on the far side of the chamber. Torchlight gleamed faintly beyond burial vaults, ornately carved with crucifixes and spires decorating their covers. The women took one step back, then two.

"I have you," a voice growled in Anne's ear.

Anne gasped and tried to struggle free of the arm that wrapped tightly around her. Mayde was torn from her side, shoved away by a rough hand. When the cold edge of a blade scraped at her throat, Anne went utterly still.

"Lady!"

"Coltrane."

Mayde's cry and the harsh rumble of Galen's voice blended into one. Anne dared do no more than breathe, but her eyes fluttered closed when the form of her beloved husband stood in the archway.

"Let her go, Coltrane," Galen commanded evenly.

Coltrane only tightened his arm around her and pressed the dagger's blade to her throat. Anne could hear his smile.

"I knew you would come."

"Let her go." Galen entered cautiously, torch held aloft in one hand, his sword in the other. He felt Bryan close at his back. "You want me, and here I am. She has nothing to do with what lies between us."

"On the contrary, Tarrant," Coltrane refuted, "your sweet lady has everything to do with what I want from you." The blade pressed against Anne's throat, and Galen heard her gasp. "I've dreamed of this."

Bryan was visible in the archway, now, and Coltrane jerked Anne harder to his body. The villain leaned against the nearest burial vault, his sword hand resting next to one of the casket's wicked-looking ornamental spires.

"Tell your man to draw off," he warned, "or by thunder, I'll slit her throat right here before you."

Galen froze as the dagger scraped at Anne's throat. It would take only a flick of his wrist and Coltrane would lay open her skin, pierce the delicate vein beneath, and spill her life's blood.

"Draw off, Bryan."

"Galen—"

"Draw off!" Galen snapped.

Galen felt Bryan slip his sword into its scabbard; then the seneschal edged back. Galen focused all his being upon Coltrane once more. And upon Anne. In the harsh glare of the torchlight, her eyes were huge and dark. Her expression was a stony mask, but he knew she must be terrified. Galen's heart tightened within his chest. Then, incredibly, a small smile curved her lips, and Galen nearly chuckled.

Spirited wood elf.

"Release her."

"Nay. I prefer her precisely where she is. Soft. So soft." Coltrane hugged her close and moved his lips in her hair. Galen's belly clenched with disgust. Never taking his eyes from his foe, Coltrane inched his hand over his captive until he cupped her breast and squeezed it. Anne gave an instinctive gasp, and fury fired Galen's blood. "I like touching her. I like having you watch me touch her."

"I wager you do," Galen returned smoothly. "A faithless mongrel you are, rutting after anything that moves. And a coward, using a woman for your shield."

Coltrane narrowed his eyes and hissed, "I am the master."

"You are a coward, Coltrane." Galen stepped closer. "You slither in the shadows, striking down harmless villagers and innocent children. Oh, you are very brave with children. You can even handle full-grown men, once they are chained and helpless." He smiled coldly. "And after you cut and slice them to ribbons so they cannot fight you."

Galen peeled the half-mask away and revealed his face. Coltrane gasped at the sight of the scar, and his eyes glittered with delight.

"You like looking at me?" Galen closed the distance between them, step by step. "You like looking at what you did to me? I remember every instant, Coltrane, every moment of hanging by the chains in that filthy cell. I'll never forget."

"As well you should not," Coltrane rasped. The hunger exploded in a violent longing, and his body trembled as its voracious teeth gnawed upon him. "I am your master. I created you."

Galen shook his head. "You are the master of nothing. You are a coward, a sick and pathetic coward."

"You will not speak to the master so!" The hunger roared its outrage, and Coltrane's voice grew shrill. "You will respect the master!"

"Oh, I respect you, Coltrane," Galen hissed. "Just like I respect a rabid dog, and I'll deal with you the same way."

Coltrane bellowed his rage and flung Anne away. She sprawled upon the stone floor and lay stunned for a second before she lifted her head. Coltrane had his own sword drawn and lunged at Galen.

"Nay!"

Galen tossed the torch aside and caught the wild slash of Coltrane's sword with his own to deflect it. The light flickered and nearly died. Then it flared to life once more. Anne had scurried to retrieve the torch and held it up. Coltrane growled and hacked at Galen again and again. Each time, Galen parried the blow. Steel clashed against steel as the two men fought, Coltrane lashing out, Galen defending. Both grunted with the force of each impact. Galen's arm tired under the onslaught, but in his madness, Coltrane showed no sign of backing off.

"Bryan!" Anne sobbed the name. She would have flown into the fray herself had Mayde not caught her close. "Do something!"

But Bryan was helpless. The chamber was narrow, and Galen's back was before him. He would have to overcome the obstacles of the vaults to reach a position of advantage. Even then, he had no way of ensuring that he struck Coltrane instead of Galen, so furious was the battle. He could only watch as Coltrane forced Galen back. Inch by inch. Blow by hacking blow. He motioned for their men to draw off, to give Galen room to maneuver as he stepped back through the archway into the crypt's main chamber. He held his own torch high to provide light.

"I'll kill you," Coltrane snarled. "I'll kill you this time, and then I'll cut open that village bitch of yours and watch her insides spill out onto the floor."

"I'll see you in hell first," Galen vowed. "Aye, I'll—"

Galen cried out. His sword arm went numb. Pain burned through his arm, his shoulder. Coltrane drew his blade back. It gleamed wet and dark. Galen saw the next blow coming, tried to lift his blade to deflect it. But his arm would not obey. His sword clattered to the stone floor, struck from his useless hand.

"Galen! *Nay!*"

Galen heard Anne's scream. He staggered back against the wall. His hand clutched his shoulder and felt the warm stickiness of his own blood.

And he smiled.

He was beaten. But he had still won. Coltrane would cut him down. Then he would pay the price for it on Bryan's sword.

The only thing he regretted was that Anne must watch him die.

It all seemed to happen so slowly. Mere moments took an eternity to pass. Coltrane's blade lifted one last time. It glinted in the torchlight. Crazed laughter rang in Galen's ears. A shriek of fury. A scream of victory.

"Darryl! My sweet Darryl, I will avenge you!"

A form hurtled from the shadows. Blazing light revealed Freya's face twisted into a mask of hysteria. Coltrane turned. Her wailing was abruptly strangled into silence. Coltrane's red-smeared blade jutted through the small of Freya's back. She pitched forward onto her master.

"Nay!"

Coltrane howled with rage. Freya's dead weight crashed into him and took him down with her.

In the eerie silence, all Galen heard was his own rasping breath. He slid down the wall and sank to the floor.

And stared at Coltrane's body impaled upon a stone spike that adorned a vault, his deadened eyes glaring up into the darkness.

It was over. Galen closed his own eyes.

It was truly over.

"Galen?"

Anne's voice, high and frightened, called to him. Galen opened his eye and saw her, kneeling at his side, her hands tearing his own away from the wound in his shoulder. He flinched.

"You . . . you are hurt," she whimpered.

He shook his head and swallowed. " 'Tis not bad. I—"

"Move aside, girl."

Mayde, all crisp manner and sour expression, pushed Anne from her way. She tore the rip in Galen's tunic wider and poked at the wounded flesh beneath. Galen jerked and gasped. She covered the wound again and nodded grimly.

" 'Tis naught," she announced.

Galen glared at her. "It hurts."

"Oh, 'tis naught but a scratch." Mayde huffed and stood. "Just like a man. Tough and brave with his woman. Whining like a child with his nurse."

"Will you two stop your bickering?" Anne settled at his other side and buried her face in his good shoulder. Then she lifted her head and laughed through her tears. "Galen, can you stand?"

"Aye," he admitted in a growl.

Bryan, his own shoulders shaking with relieved laughter, grinned as he took his lord's outstretched hand and helped him to his feet. Galen's head spun a bit, and he leaned on Anne. Together, they looked down at the pair sprawled in a thickening pool of their own blood. Anne shivered, and he held her closer.

" 'Tis over," she whispered.

"Aye." Galen kissed her hair. " 'Tis finally over."

She looked up at him, concern furrowing her brow. "We must get you back to the keep, see to your shoulder."

He nodded and started to turn away with her. Then he stopped, and his eyes narrowed upon the vault Coltrane and Freya had fallen. Galen smiled slowly.

"What is it?"

"The vault," he murmured.

"What about it?" Bryan asked, peering at it with them.

A small, breathless laugh seeped from Galen's lips. " 'Tis my father's."

Was it a sign? Galen wondered. After all the years that had passed, had Lord Geoffery—the man who had never seemed capable of reaching out to his son—reached out at last to save his son's life? Could fate move in such ways?

Perhaps.

Anne's arms tightened around his waist, reminding Galen of all he had longed for, all he had spent eleven years searching for. All he had found. He turned with her, and together they left the crypt.

In the lord's chamber, Mayde ignored Galen's growling as she bound the linen strips about his wound. She nodded with satisfaction at her work.

" 'Twill heal well," she predicted, "though you'll likely bear a scar from it."

Galen had to chuckle. " 'Tis not my first."

Mayde snorted and started to move away from the bed. Sitting on its edge, Galen reached out and caught her hand before she could get far. Squeezing it gently, he brushed his lips over her fingertips.

"You saved my lady's life," he murmured. "I owe you more than I can repay."

"Stuff and nonsense." The housekeeper flushed, and Galen grinned. "As if I would let that she-wolf make off with Lady Anne from beneath my very nose and not lift a finger."

"How did you know where Freya had taken me?" Anne asked from beside Galen.

" 'Twas simple to deduce," Mayde proclaimed. "No one ever goes within the chapel, and 'twas impossible for those two villains to take you beyond the gates. Knowing his lordship here was away, and that you were a mite uneasy without him, I'd come to check on you, lady, after I looked in on the little ones. When I saw you were gone, the chapel and the crypt beneath were the first places I thought of."

Galen made a sheepish face. "They were the last places I thought of, and I would not even have considered them had Derek not spoken up."

"Aye, well," the housekeeper granted gruffly. "You were likely not thinking too clear." She shrugged. "I went down into the crypt. Took me a while to find you, amid all the twists and turns in that cursed place. I could not take a torch with me. Too much light would give me away, so the dark slowed me some, too. Freya I knew I could deal with, but I had to wait for that creature, Coltrane, to make off. Or at least, I thought he had."

Anne giggled. "Whacked Freya over the head with a spade, she did. Never have I been so shocked as I was then."

"You did look a mite pop-eyed, girl," Mayde agreed sourly. "Her ladyship and I made our way toward the entry. Heavens, but my heart gave a thump when that bastard appeared from nowhere. The rest you know, my lord."

Galen nodded, well satisfied. He squeezed Mayde's hand again. "Thank you. For everything."

"Aye, my lord, you are . . . You are welcome." She curtsied and made to leave. At the door, though, she halted and turned slowly. "Lady, I . . ."

"What is it, Mayde?"

"I . . ." The housekeeper twisted her hands together. "I have been . . . unfair toward you."

Remembering many of her own less than kind thoughts, Anne felt her cheeks warm. "I think perhaps we've been unfair toward each other."

"Perhaps," Mayde allowed reluctantly. Her face softened as close to a true smile of happiness as Anne had ever seen the housekeeper give. "Perhaps we will . . . reconsider our opinions, once we come to know one another better."

"I think we will." Anne smiled, and Mayde's tale returned to mind. "I think perhaps we already have."

The other woman's eyes gleamed suspiciously moist, and Mayde nodded. "Aye, lady, I believe we have."

The housekeeper left the chamber, closing the door as she went. Alone with her husband, Anne met Galen's bemused look with a bright look of her own. She caressed his flawless cheek, then the mask again covering the other side. Sliding her arms about his waist, she brushed her lips at the corner his mouth. He rumbled deep in his throat and sought to capture her in another kiss.

"Anne, wood elf . . ."

His lips had barely touched hers when the chamber door burst open, and two children hurtled in. Derek and Lyssa shrieked in delight and climbed up on the bed. Anne saw Galen wince and caught Derek in her arms to calm his exuberant bouncing. Lyssa snuggled close between Galen and her sister.

"Anne!" both cried at full volume. "We knew Galen would find you! We just knew it!"

Both listened, wide-eyed, as the tale was retold in answer to their questions. Lyssa peered up at Galen anxiously, stroking his injured shoulder.

"And that horrible man will never come back?" she asked.

He kissed the tip of her nose. "Never."

"But what about Freya?" Derek wanted to know. "Freya was not bad, not *really* bad."

Anne cast Galen a look of entreaty. They had decided to keep this to themselves for a while, but in the way of children, the pair had refused to allow it to remain unspoken. Galen cleared his throat carefully.

"Freya was . . . unwell, Derek." When the boy frowned, Galen tried to explain. "Sometimes, when someone dwells too much upon something bad in their life, it makes their mind turn away from what is true. That is what happened to Freya. She lost someone very special to her, and it haunted her."

Anne stroked her brother's hair, then Lyssa's soft cheek. "Freya cared for you both very much. Never forget that. She never wished any ill to befall either of you."

"She is at peace, now," Galen added.

He prayed, for the sake of the tormented woman's soul, that he spoke the truth. Freya had betrayed them, but like Anne, he found it difficult to condemn her entirely.

"I'll miss her." Lyssa's little mouth trembled, and Derek nodded in agreement. "She was nice."

"I know you will." Galen smiled as she cuddled closer. "You must remember Freya as she was at her best with us."

Suddenly, Derek grinned up at Galen. "You saved Anne. You really are a hero."

The word shimmered through Galen's soul, but this time it brought only a rush of warmth and an odd humility with it. He dragged the boy onto his lap and hugged him.

"I try, lordling," he murmured gruffly. "I try."

"Oh! I almost forgot!"

Lyssa scrambled off the bed and dashed from the chamber. Galen watched her go, then turned bemused eyes to Anne. His lady only returned his look with a rather smug gaze of her own. The little girl returned in a flash, bearing a small parcel carefully wrapped in a square of bright cloth. Suddenly shy, she flushed and thrust it at him.

"What is this?"

"Open it," she instructed in a small voice.

Galen plucked at the silk ribbon binding the parcel together and peeled away the cloth. A small scrap of leather, black and supple, lay in his palm. Galen held it up. Recognition came with a suddenness that rendered him breathless, and he had to swallow to ease the ache swelling in his throat.

It was a patch of leather, the size of his fist, with two slim bands sewn with utmost care on either side.

"I—" Lyssa shifted from foot to foot at his silence. "I thought you might be tired of wearing your mask all the time, but I did not want people to stare and say unkind things." She gave him a pleading look. "Anne helped me because I could not do the sewing right, but 'tis still not very good. She could make you a better one."

Galen handed the gift back to her and lowered his head to her reach.

"I like this one," he said roughly. "Put it on me."

Lower lip caught between her teeth, Lyssa plucked at the mask and peeled it from his face. Then she placed the patch over his damaged eye and tied the slim bands around his head. Adjusting it just so, she stood back and regarded the result.

"I like your face, Galen." She stroked her fingertips over the scar and smiled shyly. " 'Tis not right to cover it up all the time. 'Tis handsome."

"Aye," Anne agreed with a smile, " 'tis very handsome."

Galen gathered the little girl in his arms and caressed her hair with his marred cheek. Not in more years than he cared to remember had anyone called him handsome. He met Anne's misty gaze with his own blurred look.

Not until Anne and these children had stormed into his life and changed it forever.

He chuckled as Derek flung his arms about his neck and smacked a kiss on his cheek. Not to be denied, Anne scooted close and joined her brother and sister in the embrace. Her lips nibbled at his lips.

"I love you," she whispered.

"And I love you," he whispered back.

Derek groaned with boyish disgust at the kiss, and Lyssa

giggled. Galen fell back onto the bed and only flinched a little as they all tumbled over him.

Family. His family. He hugged the three of them close and murmured with contentment. Dark times might come again one day, but with his Lady Anne and the family she had brought to him, his heart need never endure them alone.

"Aye," Galen said, "I love all of you."

Epilogue

As it had for centuries before, and would for centuries to come, spring returned to Rosethorn and its lands.

In the village of Thornbury, cattle and sheep were turned out to graze after being penned within sheltering stables through the frosty winter. Craftsmen opened the shutters of their workshops. Others set about preparing the fields and sowing seed for summer crops. Neighbors had kept mostly to themselves while the winds and snows had raged outside their cottages, but now they emerged to pass the news among themselves.

Life stirred anew.

But if life stirred in the village, it took care to include Rosethorn in its celebration as well. One fine morn in mid-June, the castle walls seemed to glow resplendently, warmed by the sun's kiss from without and by joy from within.

Anne lay back against the pillows in the massive lord's bed and smiled, weary but triumphant. Galen had sat with her through the long hours of labor, held her and encouraged her through the final wrenching moments. Now he gazed awestruck at the delicate bundle cradled in his arms.

His long sinewy fingers smoothed dark, silky curls and

traced the line of tiny, arched brows. Rosebud lips flattened, then puckered again, as he stroked his fingertip over the downy cheek. Anne saw Galen's lips curve as small fingers curled around his larger one.

"Are you pleased?" she asked quietly.

"Pleased?" He gave her such an incredulous look that Anne had to chuckle. His gaze turned once more to the small being he held, and his expression softened back into reverence. "I've never known anything so perfect."

Anne plucked at the bedclothes. "Some men might prefer—"

"Some men are fools," he murmured.

Galen pressed a kiss to the tiny fingers. Laying the bundle in Anne's arms, he tipped her chin up until she met his gaze and kissed her, lingering over her lips for a long while.

"You've given me so much," he whispered. "You've brought light and laughter into my life when I thought there was naught but darkness and despair. You found the key to my heart when I was certain it no longer existed, and you gave me the strength to say the words I thought could never pass my lips. And now, sweet wood elf . . ." He kissed her smile. "Now you've given me a gift more precious than any I could imagine. How could you believe I would not treasure it as I treasure you?"

Anne flushed, and her love for him swelled within her heart until she thought it would burst. "Have you thought of a name?"

"Aye," he replied, and peered down at the babe.

His marred cheek creased with a smile, and Anne almost wept with her joy. Galen never wore the half-mask anymore, had cast it aside in favor of Lyssa's present from the moment the little girl had put it on him. Some still faltered at the sight of the scar, but if Galen noticed, he gave no sign of it. So paltry a thing could not dent his contentment.

"What name have you decided upon?" she asked.

"Danielle."

Anne's heart thudded to a halt, then throbbed back to life again. His smile softened at the tears gathering in her eyes and stroked her cheek.

"I was never able to know your father very well," he said. "But what little I learned of him taught me that he was a very wise man. I would be honored for our first-born, our daughter, to bear his name."

"Danielle." Anne savored the name upon her tongue. "Aye, Papa would be very pleased. Thank you."

"Nay, wood elf," Galen countered, "if thanks are due, 'tis to Daniel that I owe them. He bequeathed his family to me and let me claim them, all three of them, as my own."

Little Danielle stirred between them, a tiny murmur seeping from her rose-pink lips, and reminded both Anne and Galen that their family had grown. And would continue to grow and thrive with the love they shared.